A LABYRINTH OF FANGS AND THORNS

A LABYRINTH OF FANGS AND THORNS

A FAE GUARDIANS NOVEL

LANA PECHERCZYK

A Labyrinth of Fangs and Thorns
ASIN: B09DP7BJ1K
ISBN: 978-1-922989-09-3

Text copyright © Lana Pecherczyk 2021
Cover design © Lana Pecherczyk 2021
Structural Editor: Ann Harth

www.lanapecherczyk.com

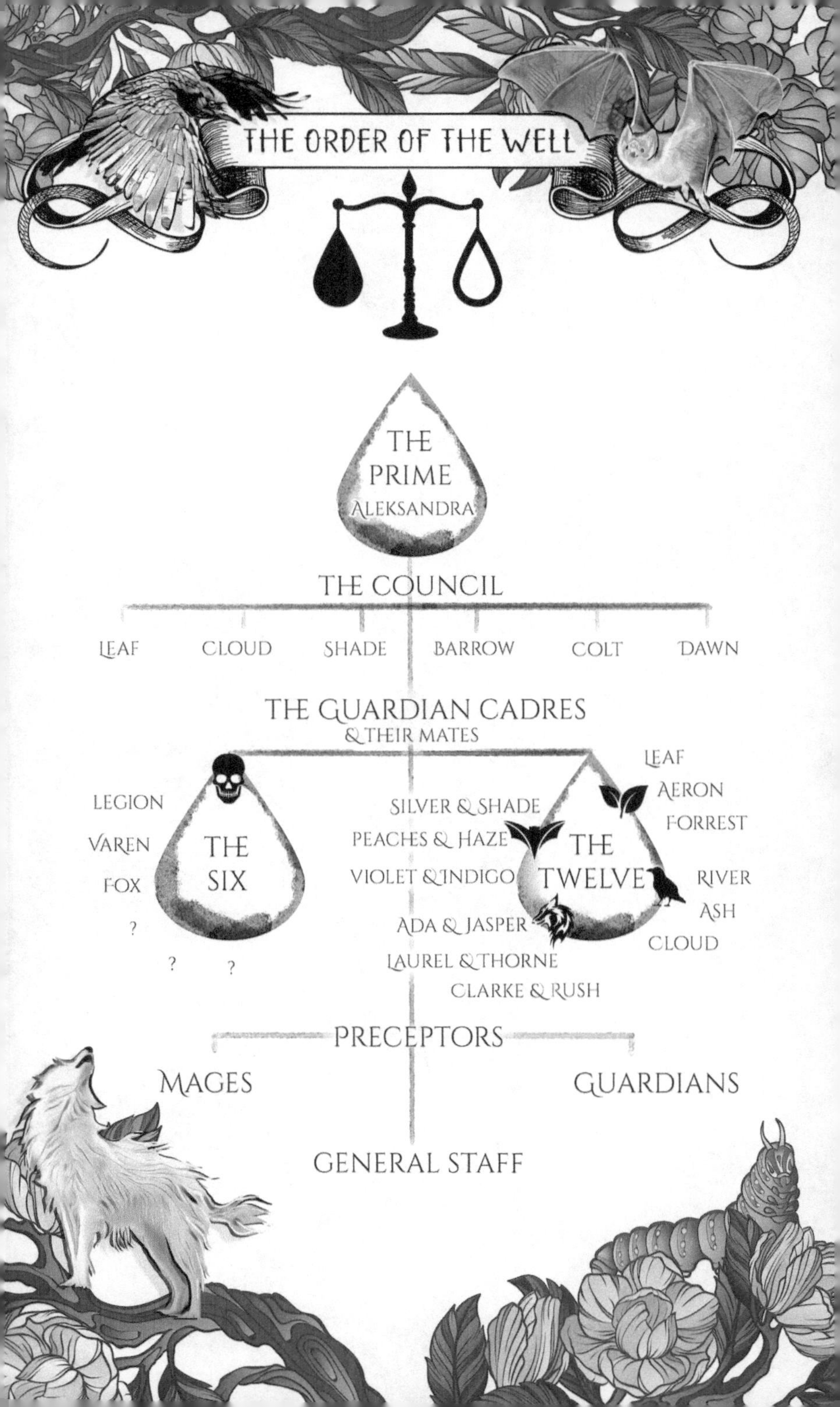

THE ORDER OF THE WELL

THE PRIME
ALEKSANDRA

THE COUNCIL

LEAF   CLOUD   SHADE   BARROW   COLT   DAWN

THE GUARDIAN CADRES
& THEIR MATES

LEGION
VAREN
FOX
?
?   ?

THE SIX

SILVER & SHADE
PEACHES & HAZE
VIOLET & INDIGO
ADA & JASPER
LAUREL & THORNE
CLARKE & RUSH

THE TWELVE

LEAF
AERON
FORREST
RIVER
ASH
CLOUD

PRECEPTORS

MAGES   GUARDIANS

GENERAL STAFF

EL
WINTER COURT
ACONITE CITY
ACONITE SEA
ICE WITCH
THE ICE FOREST
HUMAN TERRITORY
UNSEELIE KINGDOM
SEELIE KINGDOM
CRYSTAL CITY
RUSH'S CABIN
MEANDERING WOODS
WHISPERING WOODS
CRESCENT HOLLOW

NE
OBSIDIAN MINE
OBSCENDIA
CLAW BASIN
ORDER OUTPOST
AUTUMN COURT
RUBRUM CITY
CORNUCOPIA
TRADE CITY
FENRYSFIELD
THE CEREMONIAL LAKE
THE ORDER OF THE WELL
DELPHINIUM CITY
SPRING COURT
HELIANTHUS CITY
SUMMER COURT

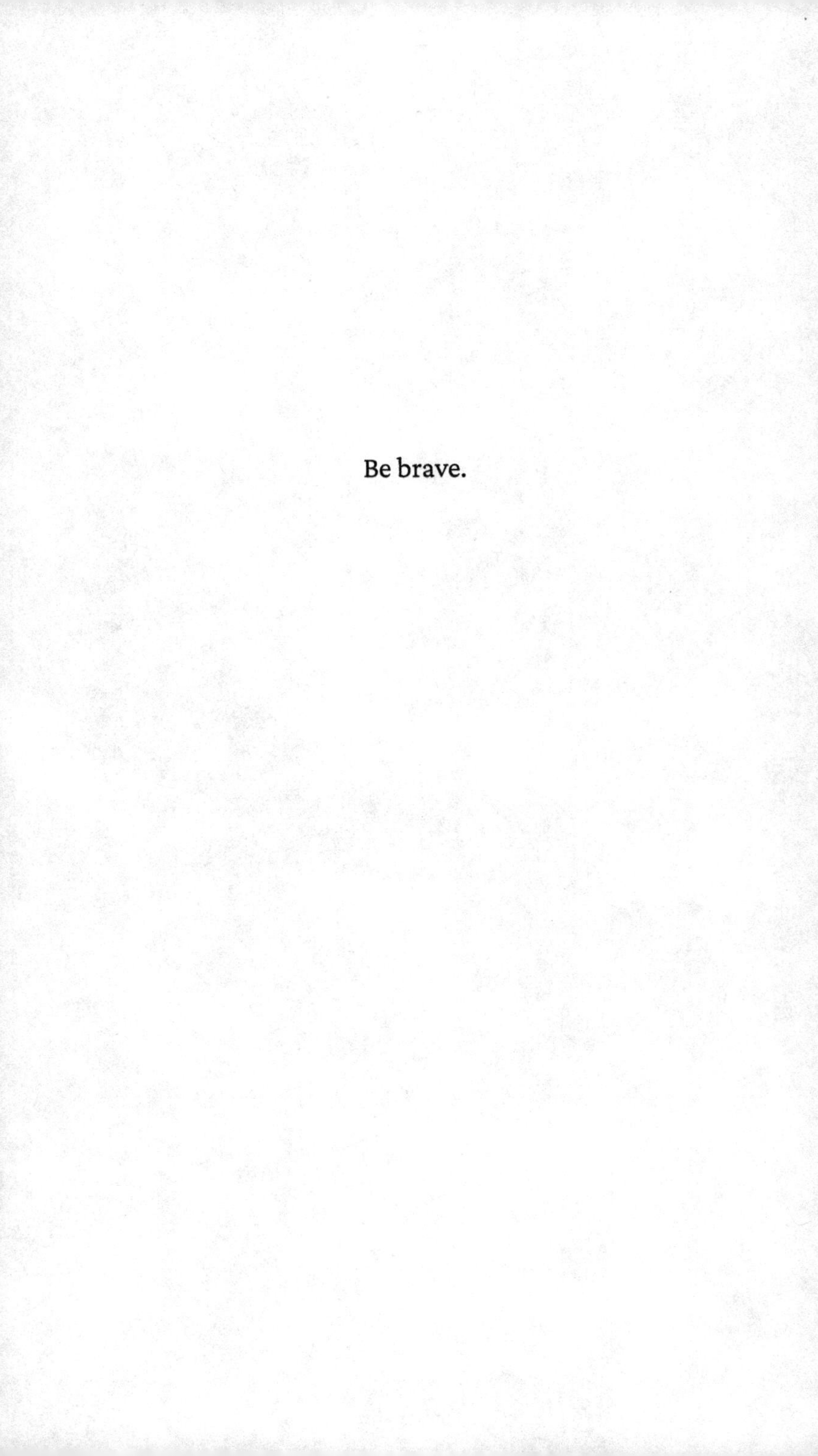

Be brave.

Haze dragged a sniveling satyr by the collar through the gray, snow-sodden streets of a local village. Under the light of the moon, they passed cobblestone houses with flickering manabee lanterns. A gust of arctic wind slapped him in the face. He ducked, braced himself and trudged onward, ignoring the less than stellar reception from Unseelie residents.

A crow squawked, warning fae of Haze's arrival. Doors slammed. Window shutters closed. Anyone daring to get in his way would face the wrath of the biggest Guardian in the Cadre of Twelve. With his height and muscle, dragging the satyr felt like dragging a child. If only he could put him in the corner with a timeout.

Now, there's an idea.

"It was an accident," the satyr whined, his cloven hooves making tracks in the old snow.

Haze's battle-scarred vampiric wings flared out in vexation. He glared at the satyr. Haze's shadow, a heartbeat delayed, also looked down.

"So it was an accident forbidden metal found its way to a cord around your neck?" The deep rumble of his voice rivaled thunder and rolled through the streets like a stone.

Haze's shadow peeked over his shoulder, curious. Anyone else would see a smokey silhouette the same shape and height as Haze, but Haze saw an extension of himself. A gift he'd received from the Well after being submerged in the ceremonial lake and judged, coming out worthy of the teardrop mark beneath his left eye. As a Guardian, he was also given a bigger personal reservoir to hold mana and could hold forbidden materials without cutting his connection to the Well.

The satyr's desperate eyes landed on Haze's black reinforced leather armor, his intentions clear. Probably wondering if curved horns could pierce the thick hide.

They could not.

What could the satyr hope to achieve against a vampire three times his size? Haze could drink the fae dry, smother him in shadow, or crush his skull with a titanic fist.

Maybe Haze should drink from him. That would shut him up. Or maybe he should accidentally let go of the floater—and watch him run—watch him get to that point at the edge of the street, where he believed he'd escaped justice from the Order of the Well. Then squash that hope like a milli-bug.

"Um..." The satyr tried to push Haze away, but he barely made an impression. Haze was a mountain to his mole hill. "Come on... it was only a tiny piece of metal."

"Don't care."

"But—"

"Shut it."

"I only thought it looked cool!" He gave a nervous laugh. "Like a fashion piece. The females dig ancient things."

Haze's eyes narrowed. "There's only one reason fae keep something like this on their person. It's to avoid the scrying eyes of Seers. Who are you hiding from?"

Haze dipped into the tight pocket of his leather breeches and pulled out the tiny, rusted metal disc of contention. It had little bumps around the rim. Perhaps the ancient humans used it to cap a bottle. Corks were much easier, in Haze's opinion. Humans were so odd. They found obscene ways to use metal and plastic when there had already been a simple solution in place. They even used to put plastic in clothing. Ridiculous.

"You do realize," he drawled, "that this 'tiny piece of metal' has blocked the magic of the Well. And the Well does not take kindly to being denied. Why would it gift you with mana if you blatantly break the only rule it's ever set? If fae like you can't see through their selfishness, then the Well will forsake the fae, and Elphyne will become as barren as the human wasteland. Is that what you want?"

"But I'm lesser fae. I don't even have mana."

"That's what all you lessers think until it's cut off. Something as small as this won't cut you off in an obvious way, but it still happens." Haze rubbed his chin. "Perhaps I need to educate you in terms you understand."

The satyr clamped his lips shut, his complexion paling. In the grand scheme of things, a tiny scrap of tin wasn't a huge deal. But if Haze allowed this coward to break the rules, then others would follow. And the wasteland would grow.

"You disgust me," he growled, and then shoved the contraband in his pocket before continuing to drag the floater through the street. This time, the satyr stayed silent and limp, resigned to his fate.

Being a Guardian was a shitty job, but someone had to do it.

As Haze walked, mud spattered the abandoned wooden carts. Curtains twitched in windows as Unseelie residents stayed hidden, afraid of capturing the attention of a Guardian on the war path. Only children were brave, or naïve enough to play in the streets.

A pebble hit Haze on the shoulder. Giggles, light footsteps, and fluttering wings chased him in the night shadows. Vampire pups. He could smell the fresh blood on their breaths. He ignored them and focused on getting to the town square fifty paces ahead. By now, gossip should have traveled to the town magistrate. Haze expected him to be waiting. If he wasn't, there would be consequences.

A sting at Haze's temple made him whirl around.

Another rock. He snarled at the tiny vampires hiding behind a stone column, their wings a dead giveaway. Haze's physical body stayed rooted to the spot while his shadow detached and slithered over to the column. Through his shadow's eyes, Haze saw the soot-covered children. Two males and a smaller female clutching a rag doll made of tumbleweed and straw. Harmless.

His shadow retreated, but then paused as a male pushed the female. She stumbled and dropped her doll. Tiny fangs gleamed as her bottom lip pushed out in a snarl-pout. Haze's heart squeezed. With her long dark hair and chubby face, she was exactly the kind of child he'd imagined his own would have grown into... had she survived infancy.

"Throw another one, Macy," ordered the first male—a pup with stubby wings not fully grown. He might be a half-breed.

"I don't wanna," she whined.

"But it's a coin-grubbing Guardian bastard. That's what my da' calls 'em."

"Do it," said the second male, his foot hovering over the doll. "Or I kill Thirsty."

Little shits. Haze's eyes narrowed.

He called his shadow back and stomped obviously toward the column, still dragging the squirming satyr. Wide eyes and youthful gasps of terror greeted him. When the boys tried to run, he pointed at them. Haze's shadow melted into the darkness and popped up behind them, blocking their escape with a monstrous mimed roar. The boys screamed and covered their eyes, as though it would hide them from the shadow monster. The stench of their urine caused Haze to snort out a breath. Perhaps he'd been a bit overzealous with the scare tactic.

He collected Thirsty, dusted it on his pants, and handed it to the girl. Big eyes blinked up at him. Trembling fists stayed at her sides.

A flash of guilt hit Haze. He seemed to have that effect on females, whether young or old.

"I won't hurt you," he said, but that deep gravel of his voice only made the girl blanch. "I promise."

"But yaw'a Guardian." Her little tinkling voice melted his insides. "Monsters are scared of you."

"That's right." He smiled gently. "But you don't have to be."

With a bashful glance from beneath long lashes, she nabbed the toy and then stomped on Haze's foot before running away. *Well-damn it.* He bit his lip. The kid had strength. But he couldn't be angry at her. She was Unseelie. This was their way.

Don't owe nobody, but everybody owes me.

The satyr chuckled at Haze's misfortune.

Haze growled. He switched his hold to the satyr's curved horns and resumed dragging. The weather decided to rub salt in his wounds by sending sleet, taking his mood to an all-time low. He tossed the offender beneath the swinging wooden cage at the center of town.

"I swear to the Well if that magistrate is one more second—"

"I'm here. I'm here." A dark shadow rushed out from beneath the eaves of the council building.

Tiny ice pellets bounced off Haze's shaved head and shoulders. The magistrate, a fat satyr, cowered until it seemed his black embroidered robe swallowed him whole.

"Third offender this week, Endor." Haze showed the metal cap. "Perhaps the previous punishments weren't harsh enough."

While Guardians were responsible for policing the use of metal and plastic in Elphyne, it wasn't their only task. They also had to protect the integrity of the Well, which meant neutralizing threats from within and without Elphyne. Often they left the sentencing of petty offenders for local authorities. Clearly, the deterrent wasn't working, and the fae were becoming complacent. Time for that to stop.

"One week in the cage," Haze decreed.

Both Endor and the criminal gasped, eyes wide.

"Holding metal isn't on par with actually being cut off completely from the Well. One week will possibly age him. He might not survive."

Haze scoffed. "Of course he'll survive. But he'll suffer, won't you, floater? And I'm sure the females will love a few wrinkles around the eyes. Maybe without access to your mana, you'll finally understand what life without the Well will be like. What life living with contraband will give us." To prove his point, Haze tossed the coin through his watching shadow. The smokey substance dissipated and avoided the coin like it was poison. Haze might be able to hold metal and use his mana, but his shadow couldn't. Haze picked the coin up. "You see, small things can have big consequences. It's time you learned those."

He tossed the satyr into the cage and bade the magistrate to lock it. Even lesser fae, who held no mana inside their bodies with which to manipulate, could feel the emptiness of being cut from the Well. It was as though all color drained from the world, all sound, all energy. And yet, it was life as usual. Just a dulled, fucked up, mana-weed hangover version of it.

Haze assumed it was what being human felt like.

The offender whimpered and begged like a child, yet eighty years of being a Guardian had made Haze deaf to the stupidity of fae like this. Someone had to protect the Well, and Haze had the best incarceration record, even among the Cadre of Twelve. He hoisted the cage into the air by a length of rope connected to a hangman's frame twenty feet high. The satyr whimpered the moment the cage left the ground. It took two feet of air for him to moan and roll dramatically in discomfort. Five feet and he was squirming in agony and loss.

Vampires and other winged fae needed a lot more height to lose their connection to the Well—a fact Haze had learned from tragedy, just as he knew that first hit of disconnection was the worst. There was a reason vampires didn't fly too high.

Haze tied off the length and dusted his hands.

"If I may suggest," Endor said, his hands clasped at the front. "Perhaps a week is a little excessive."

Haze bared his fangs. "Three crimes in one week is excessive."

A crowd had started to gather around the square. Vampires and crow shifters perched on roofs, some in bat and bird form, others in angel form. They were black silhouettes against a moonlit sky striped with falling snow. While Unseelie usually kept to themselves and disliked strangers in town, they loved a good display of punishment and suffering.

Haze rolled his shoulders. Wet leather was beginning to chafe, as was his patience. He snapped his wings wide to rid them of snow and took pleasure as the crowd flinched in fear. Time was running out. If he didn't take to the air soon, flying would become worrisome. He'd have to use a portal stone, and he'd rather not waste the expensive commodity.

"I'll be back in a week," Haze said, his knees bending, ready for take off.

The criminal groaned, "Father... help me."

Father?

Endor's face paled. "How much?"

"What?"

"How much coin will it take to make all this go away?"

"Are you trying to bribe me?" Elven runes glowed blue as he withdrew Justice, his war hammer, from the belt at his hips. Power-enhancing tattoos riddled over Haze's body flared, casting a prismatic glow beneath his leather battle armor. "There are rules for a reason, magistrate. Be very careful what you say next."

"Um. It's only that. Um. I meant how much compensation for the crime? The Order has a coin or time-served policy, correct? We're willing to pay for his crime." He slid his gaze to his son in warning. "This time."

Haze rubbed the bone studs piercing his ear and considered the proposal. He was Cadre. He had zero time to waste for returning in a week.

"I'm not sure, magistrate," he pondered. "How much is the Well worth to you?"

Haze could almost see Endor calculating, which was worth more: leaving his offspring suffering or paying Haze enough coin to satisfy him.

"A black coin," Endor offered, as though the words were wrenched from his soul.

Haze allowed his disappointment to show. Black coin in the land of the Unseelie Queen was, indeed, the highest you could get, but it cost twice that amount to have a new portal stone made. Not many had the knowledge of such alchemy, and those that did closely guarded their secrets. The Order had a mana stone alchemist, but he was in high demand. Extracting manabeeze from fae had many moral caveats. Funding the Order of the Well was expensive. And every time one of these ingrates acted like contraband didn't matter, they raised the cost.

"Fine." He opened his palm. He needed to get back to the outpost, anyway. And the sleet was coming down. The temperature was dropping.

Endor dropped a smooth obsidian coin into Haze's palm. Haze checked to ensure it was sealed with High Queen Maebh's emblem—a crown with thorns, roses and antlers. Then he pocketed it and took to the sky.

TWO

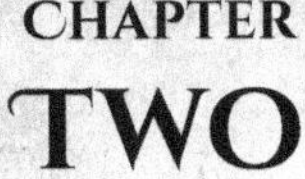

Within the hour of leaving Endor and his criminal son, Haze was back at the Order outpost on a small island east of Aconite City and the Winter Court.

Haze's boots landed on the ground near the largest wood and stone building. A Guardian on a watchtower gave a genial nod. Despite being in Unseelie territory, the island belonged to the Order. Intruders were killed on sight.

Haze shook off snow and made his way to the second outpost building, the smaller log cabin toward the back reserved for the Cadre of Twelve.

Shade leaned casually against the front door frame, dark eyes tracking Haze as he walked up. As well as being one of the elite Guardians in the Twelve, Shade was also one of the six council members next in the chain of command beneath the Prime herself.

Haze was stronger than Shade, in both mana capacity and bodily strength, but Shade's wit, charisma, and seductive looks were his weapon. Haze preferred to crush first and ask questions later.

"You're late," Shade observed.

Haze tossed the obsidian coin. Shade snatched it out of the air and turned it over, taking in what Haze had been doing. Patrolling random villages and completing spot raids was not in the job description for any member of the Twelve. That lovely menial task was reserved for the recruits or regular Guardians. It lowered the tone, Leaf— the Twelve's Elven team leader—had always said. Haze couldn't give a floater's fuck. In his opinion, cadre should make themselves known randomly around Elphyne. It kept the fear alive.

"You already have a job," Shade reminded him.

"Indi isn't here yet."

"That's beside the point."

Haze shouldered past Shade, which was a feat without shifting his wings away. The big, leathery hindrances barely fit through the door. But it was pointless wasting precious mana to shift them away when he'd be out again before sunrise and with no time to refill from a source of power. His stomach rumbled. He needed to feed. Refilling had to wait.

Their outpost cabin had four bedrooms, a small

kitchen, and a living room with a crackling fire in a stone fireplace. Without house brownies to keep the place stocked and cleaned, it was up to visiting Guardians to do the job. Haze didn't expect a supply of blood in the cupboards, but checked anyway. The room had a small amount of food but no blood. He grimaced. Shade waited for him by the door.

Haze's mood darkened.

It wasn't as though he had blood donors lining up around the corner as Shade did. Haze cowed females with his size. He frightened children. That little girl today had seemed fierce as she'd stomped on him, but he'd smelled the tang of urine on all of them. Haze thumbed his bone stud piercings and wished he'd ignored the pups and carried on down the street. It was more than the unintended intimidation. It was the tease of what his daughter might have been.

On the flight over, that girl's trembling hands had plucked a memory deep from his soul. His baby also had trembling fingers as she'd once wrapped them around Haze's thumb. So tiny at the end. So weak.

"I'll call one of the Mages from the main outpost," Shade offered.

The instinct to see to the feeding needs of their roost was inbuilt in all vampires. If one was lacking, the others helped source sustenance. Sometimes, out in the unlawful towns and cities, this could result in gang activity. Here, it was a sign of their brotherhood.

"I can feed myself, Shade," he grumbled.

The vampire clicked a disapproving tongue. "Between you and Indigo, I sometimes doubt that."

"He's suffering from a completely different affliction."

A few turns of the moon back, Indigo had fed from Ada, the Seelie High King's Well-blessed mate and queen. Human blood was already particularly tasty, but as a Well-blessed human who'd been frozen for thousands of years, Ada's blood was so nutrient dense that it sustained Indigo for weeks instead of a single day. It also gifted Indigo with a pleasant drugging sensation, not unlike mana-weed mixed with divilixir, a potent aphrodisiac distilled by the elves. Unfortunately for Indigo, it meant any other blood tasted like cardboard.

"So you have an affliction, now?" Shade arched his eyebrow.

Haze grunted, annoyed. He would feed in Obscendia. "When did you say Indi was due back?"

"In a few hours."

Fuck. "I'm leaving. He can catch up."

Reproach swam in Shade's eyes, but Haze ignored it because he knew what the vampire would say. He would believe Haze's haste was an avoidance to connect with a Mage—or with any fae, for that matter—on an intimate level. Feeding was a tactile and often sensual act, something Shade took advantage of almost every time he fed.

But Haze wasn't the type to share his bed or his heart. Any lustful urges were met in the arms of a Rosebud Courtesan or with a quick jerk of his fist. He had no desire, nor the inclination to waste valuable time when there were wrongs to right.

"You can't save the entire world, Haze," Shade said quietly. "It won't bring them back."

Icy thorns wrapped around Haze's heart. He shrugged and was airborne and flying north through the thickening snow before Shade could stop him.

The night was looking like a bust, much to Haze's annoyance.

He'd been standing for hours on the porch of Indigo's parents' house in Obscendia, glowering at nocturnal fae walking or flying past. A tavern across the road ensured the street remained busy. Some were even brave enough to glare back at Haze. Most took one look at his Guardian battle gear, or Justice hanging from his hip, and made haste in the opposite direction.

He waited for Indigo's brother, Demeter, to turn up and spill the details about the queen's latest escapades. The vampire was almost identical to Indigo in looks, but the opposite in temperament. Where Indigo was jovial and adventurous, Demeter was mean and preferred his routine. Being a member of the Unseelie High Queen's Guard suited him.

Demeter's failure to turn up meant one of two things.

Maebh had caught wind of his betrayal and now he was in hiding or a prisoner. Alternatively, Demeter had decided to fuck off the Order and was now completely loyal to Maebh.

Haze drained the last drop of market-purchased blood from a waxed paper cup and placed it on the doorstep with a small coin left inside. Indigo's mother had offered the blood earlier. She'd not asked for payment, but Haze would rather give a coin than find out he owed a favor. He didn't want ties to anyone.

Not long ago, Indigo had arrived. He'd come to observe Demeter's behavior as he'd not seen his brother in decades. Indigo didn't trust Demeter's offer to share sovereign secrets. But Indigo's mission was different to Haze's. Where Haze's mission was to find the source of these mana-warped corpses cropping up around Elphyne, Indigo had been tasked with tracking down Well-blessed humans from the old world.

At first glance, these humans were indistinguishable from today's humans. They had no glittering teardrop tattoo beneath their left eye like the Guardians, nor did they have it on their bottom lip like the Mages. But they held a capacity to hold mana within that was second to none. Almost unending. Thus, it was imperative the Order bring all such powered humans into their fold. In the wrong hands, unending power would be perverted. Just look at the queen. She'd always been strong, but after making half of Elphyne her queendom, she'd received a tithe from the Well in return for respecting its laws. Maebh's power had grown.

One would imagine a ruler of all of Elphyne would receive the biggest tithe of all. Their mana capacity might truly be infinite. Something not even a Well-blessed human could compete with. And as long as they respected the laws of the Well, they would hold this power.

Indigo had only been here for moments when, like a bloodhound, he'd caught the scent of a Well-blessed human. He'd given chase through Redvein Forest. He wouldn't be back.

And with sunrise not far away, it looked like Demeter was a no-show. *Fuck it.* Haze spat in distaste. He hated waiting. The longer he waited, the more he felt the pinch of loneliness, the prick of icy thorns, and the need to do something. Anything.

Preferably teaching ingrates lessons.

"Well-dammit," Haze grumbled and squinted at the snow thickening. If Demeter wasn't coming here, then Haze would go to him and find out exactly what had held him back. Maybe Haze would use his time to conduct his own internal investigation at the palace. No doubt Demeter had scurried home there, if he'd even left. Haze had long suspected the queen's thirst for power was the cause behind the mana-warped bodies. She'd already created the Sluagh. Now that she'd lost a few to the Order, and she was discovering her most feared weapons were defecting, she wanted to birth something new.

All he needed to do was prove it.

HAZE DESCENDED into Aconite City on the currents of icy air. During the brisk flight across from Obscendia, he'd considered his options. He could claim he had Guardian business with Demeter and locate him that way, but that would bring unwanted attention and effectively destroy their informant relationship. Haze wasn't sure if he was ready to burn that bridge. So that left subterfuge. As long as Haze's mana wasn't depleted, his shadow could be pulled over him like a cloaking spell, hiding his identity.

But shadow wasn't infallible. If someone already knew he was there, it would be harder to hide. And then there were the Sluagh to contend with. Those roaming inside the palace might sense Haze through the heartache that never left his soul, or through using their ability to reach into minds.

An extended intelligence mission took careful planning. Standing around waiting for something to happen was worse. It left him alone with his memories.

An uninvited Guardian inside the palace gates would be seen as a hostile act by Maebh. She was already on the Order's shit list for dubious acts involving contraband, but she'd hidden the evidence upon investigation. It was only a matter of time before she slipped up. No one, not even kings and queens were above the Order of the Well when it came to policing the Well's laws.

A few turns of the moon back, D'arn Jasper had defeated one of Maebh's scariest weapons, a Sluagh. It was probably the reason Maebh was trying to make something scarier. This defeat had been in her own throne room. The Unseelie people were questioning if Maebh was fit to rule. No contenders had made a play for the throne, but anything was possible. Haze had heard a rumor the Autumn Court—D'arn Forrest's old family—had been lurking. Watching.

That was how fickle and ruthless the Unseelie were. At the first sign of weakness, another would swoop in, cut off a head or eat a soul, and take control. Queen Maebh's sanity was up for debate, but she'd protected all fae-kind years ago in the Great War against the humans of Crystal City. She'd earned her station.

Since Jasper had taken over Mithras's rule in the Seelie kingdom, reports out of the Obsidian Palace were Maebh was sometimes a recluse, other times a sadistic hedonist who seemed a little unhinged. Something was going on. Haze felt it like ripples on the surface of the Well.

Gathering darkness around him, he circled over the enormous palace cut into the side of a mountain. It was made of black stone and writhing vines, spires and towers, courtyards and labyrinths. Aconite City extended into subterranean tunnels under the mountain, and through randomly placed snow-capped buildings on top. Haze spiraled down to a dark corner of the barracks yard near the palace battlement walls.

With his shadow rendering him invisible, Haze coasted until he hit the soggy ground with a grace that belied his size. Once certain he'd not been seen, he crept silently past the sleeping quarters and stinking stables until he stopped outside a bone smithy bursting with noise. Male voices filtered out of the smithy hut, drawing him closer. Smoke billowed from the chimney. With so many nocturnal fae in the Unseelie kingdom, the palace was abuzz with activity. The smell of some kind of acrid chemical hit Haze. He held in a sneeze. As he approached, the voices became clearer, and he slowed to listen.

"I mean, it's like her blood is going to waste. So unfair," came a nasally male voice.

"I hear ya, brother. I know she belongs to the queen"—the smithy lowered his voice—"but there's plenty to go around."

"Would she even notice if we took a tiny sip?"

"One sip is all we need."

"She heals fast. I heard."

"How do you know that?"

"Dolten shoved her and she cut herself. He panicked because the queen might have thought he'd drunk from her personal blood slave, so he went to see her the next day and—mark my words, brother—he found the wound almost gone. I jest you not."

Silence. Haze's ears pricked up. He eased his head

around the hut doorway to look inside. Two vampires stood over a stonework desk, filing down bone swords. A tall, skinny male and a portly one. Neither had their wings shifted out, and both were covered in bone dust and a foul attitude. Pointed and arched ears twitched as they worked.

Haze should find Demeter, but their conversation intrigued him. The queen had an exclusive blood slave that tasted different? Maebh was a vampire, but over the millennia she'd been alive, she'd evolved into something else no one really understood. Even Shade, who'd lived in this palace for decades, said he never believed he truly understood her motivations. Haze supposed it wasn't uncommon for the queen to not share her blood source, but there was something in the tone of these vampires' voices that gave him pause.

The tall vamp paused sanding a sword. "You know Bain? Well, he fell face first into her and nicked her with his fangs."

The portly vamp stilled. "Bain?"

A nod. "He said he tasted a drop—accidentally—and it felt like he'd taken a hit of mana-weed. Or an Elven pleasure elixir. One drop, Marit. One drop! Can you imagine the coin we'd make if we could—"

"Don't even start," warned Marit. "We get caught tapping the queen's personal source. She'll tan our hides and throw us to the tachi. Or worse, a wyrm."

Both vampires shuddered.

Haze eased back from the doorway and stared at the

empty training yard. Dawn approached and most vampires felt the drag of the sun like a physical thing. Nocturnal creatures would soon head to bed. As a trained Guardian, Haze had learned to function during the day, despite this ingrained lethargy. Now was one of those times. He had to keep going.

There was only one type of blood that intoxicated the feeder: a Well-blessed human's. The existence of these rare and special humans was relatively new. The knowledge wasn't widely known, but it sounded like the queen was using one as a blood slave.

That meant Demeter was no longer priority. This human was.

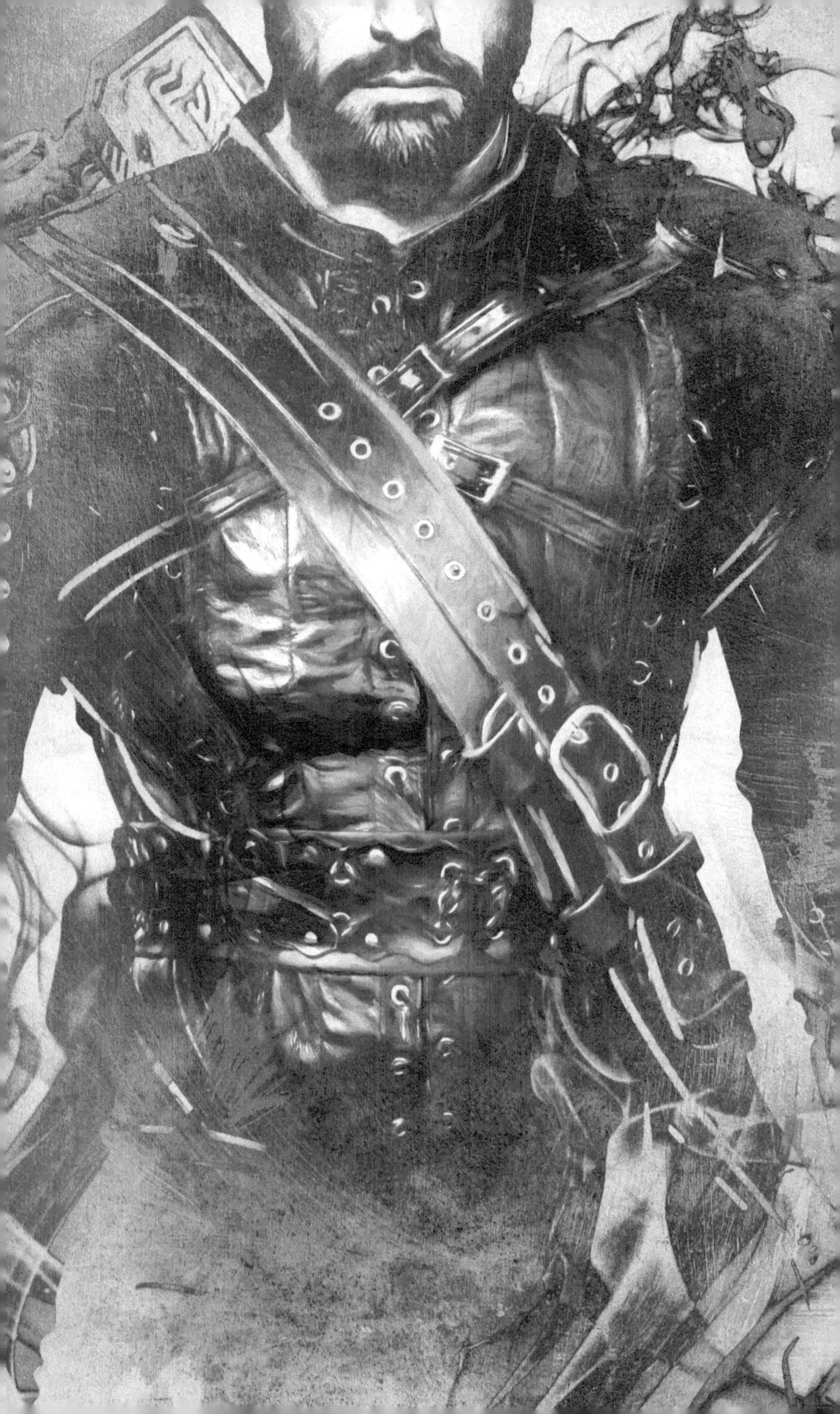

Deep in the bowels of the Obsidian Palace, Peaches flattened herself against a narrow hallway wall as one of the Sluagh walked toward her, his tattered robe swishing. Clutching her food tray, she tried to become invisible. She wished the glamor cast over her appearance actually made her fae instead of look it. Her human teeth looked pixie-pointed, as did her ears. Her hair was peach-colored instead of dull brown. Trembling legs reminded her the Sluagh would see through it all if they entered her mind.

The fae with the hauntingly beautiful face glided past, ignoring her.

She exhaled and relaxed. It had been six years since she'd awoken in this time, two thousand years from her own and, yet, she still wasn't used to the otherworldliness of the creatures she lived with. Peaches gingerly touched the black velvet ribbon at her throat—if she could call what she did living.

The ribbon symbolized her blood slave status, in particular the queen's. The choker matched the velvet clinging to her petite curves. The skirt flared out at the waist like some kind of medieval princess' dark wedding dress. Her slippers were made of leather and lace. With ribbon around her long peach hair and waist, and ugly bows at the back, she felt like a wrapped gift.

Peaches had been in this palace for two years now. She supposed it wasn't so bad. No other vampires were allowed to feed from the queen's personal source. In the grand scheme of things, she'd been in worse situations. The queen's bite only hurt for a few minutes. Peaches found if she counted down the seconds, it helped pass the time. The feedings were only a few seconds in the trillions of her future life. At least she was fed, had a roof over her head, and the freedom to roam the palace and grounds when she wasn't wanted by the queen.

Peaches balanced the tray on her hip so she could place a palm over her fluttering heart. She focused on her breathing until her pulse calmed. Shouts and curses of soldiers running somewhere down a distant hall ruined her efforts. She glanced the way the Sluagh had come. A fluffy rabbit with antlers and chicken wings half-hopped, half-flew toward her with fear in its eyes.

If the soldiers caught it inside the palace, it would be dead, so she hiked up her big skirt and motioned the terrified animal beneath. With only seconds to spare, she dropped her skirt, completely hiding the fluffball.

Two guards wearing black velvet long coats stopped to peer down her hallway.

"Did you see a wolpertinger come this way?" one of them barked.

She shook her head and tried not to giggle as fur and feathers tickled her legs. For a moment, she thought the guards wouldn't believe her, but then one continued in another direction. The remaining guard cast a wary eye down the hall at her.

"I just saw a Sluagh go this way," she said and pointed down the hall. "Maybe it's gone there."

The whites of the guard's eyes showed, and then he followed his fellow soldier. After a few more beats of silence, Peaches nabbed a carrot from the stew on her tray. Balos won't miss it. She hitched her skirt and nudged the wolpertinger out.

"Here," she said, crouching to feed it. "Now, you best hurry out of this palace before you become part of the next stew."

As she continued down the hall, a moment of weakness had her glancing over her shoulder. The wolpertinger's big dark eyes glistened. *It will be fine.* She faced the front and forced her legs to move until she went down a staircase to the basement levels.

To get to Balos' workshop, she had to pass the dungeons and other strange nefarious laboratories she didn't like to think about. The stench of piss, shit, vomit and blood assaulted her nose, along with some kind of chemical that made her gag. She held her breath because her destination was just beyond the torture chambers, laboratories, apothecaries and mana stonemasons. Someone screamed. She flinched but stared straight ahead, lengthening her rapid strides, counting each step until she arrived at a closed door with a ceramic knocker.

Balancing the tray on her hip, she rapped three times. "Balos, it's me."

"Go away." The stony male voice pierced the heavy door.

She smiled affectionately at the familiar grump. "It's Peaches. I need a favor."

A pause. Then the door opened to reveal a goblin who reminded her of a garden gnome. When he straightened his red beret, his white long beard shuddered all the way down to his feet. Great leathery bat-like ears stuck out at the side. She'd bet he could pick up radio frequencies with those things—if radios still existed.

Balos judged her from beneath wood-rimmed glasses balanced on his long gnarled nose. Even at a foot shorter than Peaches' five, the goblin could intimidate an army with his cantankerous demeanor.

He was also the first and only unlikely friend Peaches had made since she'd been at the Winter Court.

Redcaps were among the most feared yet revered members of the Unseelie army. They dipped their hats in the blood of their enemies and lived for murder. The more coats of blood, the more murderous. Balos' cap was heavy, oily, and thick with cloying globs. She hated looking at it and assumed it had been preserved magically to remain so vibrant. It was disgusting, but he wasn't. He was different from the other goblins. He'd locked himself in this room to create apothecary tinctures, Elven elixirs, and all sorts of magical weaponry and torture devices. He also created portal stones. Something he kept locked away tightly in a little warded chest beneath the ground.

"Another favor?" His words held an undertone of derision, but his eyes lit up at the pot of stew and steaming stein of mead on her tray. "I don't want it."

"I know you don't want it," she replied kindly. "But I have it and I need to unload it. Like I said, you'd be doing me a favor if you take it."

He harrumphed, but took the tray from her and waddled back to his work desk. "One day I might boil you in a pot as payment. Or feed you to the wyrm god."

Peaches grinned. This was the same song and dance every time. She'd learned the grumpy redcap underfed himself because he avoided court life. Something had happened in his past that Peaches couldn't glean, but it was enough to make him hide. Much in this palace made her skin crawl. From the pornographic and elixir-hazed balls, to the public humiliation of captured humans as entertainment, to the dark deeds done in the basement dungeons. It was all bad, in her opinion, so she'd given up guessing the cause of his withdrawal from society.

Besides... he never asked her about her situation. She appreciated that.

He was a bad-tempered old bastard, but when she'd brought him food and interesting rocks from her subterranean wanders, he'd started teaching her things.

She shut the door, then followed him to his workbench cluttered with tools, stones, and jars of manabeeze.

Manabeeze were little buzzing balls of white light—the very essence of the Well itself, and the purest form of mana. They exited fae at the moment of death. Peaches sometimes wondered if it was the physical embodiment of a soul because each manabee held a memory. Contact was to be avoided at all cost. The last thing anyone wanted was to experience a bad memory along with the intoxicating energy hit. It was like a bad LSD trip. But the same little balls could power many things, like portal stones.

She sighed and sat on a stool at his workbench, then plopped her head in her hand and picked through the latest projects. If only she held mana within her own body, she might be able to create magical stones herself. But after six years of being awake in this time, there was nothing. Barely a spark.

Balos shoveled stew into his mouth and slapped her

hand as she went for a smooth, palm sized stone inscribed with an Elven rune.

"Ow," she whined.

"That's not finished," he said. "What do I always tell you?"

"Unfinished stones bite sharper than fangs."

As she withdrew her hand, Balos jerked his chin at the stone. "You remember that rune?"

Peaches bit her lip and tried to recall all the times he'd explained Elven runes. It had been difficult to grasp at times when it seemed like a non-linear language. But she'd learned the runes were a mixture of Japanese kanji, Korean hangul and something completely new, which had excited her. Her grandparents had immigrated to America from Korea, and had always tried to share their culture, but the grandkids' urge to learn wasn't so great. Peaches' life had been all about Instagram, the next Marvel movie, and her job as a geologist.

She sniffed and wiped her nose with the back of her hand. Seeing the runes made her feel a little closer to the family she'd lost. It made them feel more real and less like a dream. And working with rocks gave her a sense of familiarity. Of comfort.

"Ooh. I forgot... I found this in one of the tunnels." She fished into her deep dress pocket and pulled out two rocks. The first was a roughhewn chunk of quartz, but the second was something rarer—a raw fire opal. "Have you seen this before?"

Balos' spoon lowered as he stared at the flecked fiery rock. From the way his eyes widened, she knew she had found something valuable. Each type of rock had different qualities and alchemic reactions when infused with mana. She wondered what reaction the opal would give when infused. Gnarled and wrinkly fingers reached out. Peaches snatched the rocks back.

"You want them," she said, "then you need to bargain for them."

Bushy brows lowered and disappeared beneath wood-rimmed spectacles.

"You nasty pix. Of all the..." He smacked his lips dramatically. "Perhaps I'll claim one of my debts from you. Hm?"

Peaches tried to hide her smile. "How many debts? All of them?"

While they'd never truly kept track, she was sure every time she brought him a meal and every time he taught her something was a transaction. She just hated not knowing exactly who owed who.

He thought about it. She wiggled the rock teasingly.

"All of them. Deal." He snatched the rock and turned it over in his hands. Then he shoved rocks, tools, and jars out of the way on his bench to pull out a magnifying glass on a lever. He studied the opal beneath it. "By the balls of a banshee. I've not seen one of these in years. Where did you find it?"

Peaches shrugged. "I can't remember. Somewhere in the tunnels."

Balos gave her an unconvinced side-eye, but knew not to push further. The fae were strange people. Not only from their mixed human and animal DNA, but their behavior. Everything had a transaction. From words out of a mouth, to the actions of a body, and sometimes even a look. She'd learned to be quiet and vague whenever she could.

"This is good," Balos mumbled, studying the rock.

"What does it do when infused with mana?"

"A number of things. It is quite conducive to mana and doesn't get burned out from one use. Treated in a bath of acid and salt before infusion makes it store an exorbitant amount of energy. When the energy releases, it causes lightning in one's veins."

"Like a battery," she blurted before she realized her mistake.

Balos' eyes slid to her. She shrunk in her chair. As far as everyone knew, she was a pixie without wings, not a human. A battery was something only a human would know about. The queen had kept Peaches' secret, and even replenished her glamor, probably because it was to her benefit that no one knew she had an old-world human in her midst with special, tasty and intoxicating blood. But Peaches had long suspected Balos knew she was human. She was constantly slipping up. She was so crap at blending in. It was the reason Peaches was a captive, and her friends Violet and Silver probably weren't. But she hadn't seen either of them for six years, since they'd all awoken from their time and decided to go separate ways. They'd all learned that, together, their knowledge could build another nuclear bomb. After a short time together, it was better to separate. She missed them all the same.

They were her people.

"You know," Balos said to the rock, as if it was no big deal. "If you ever want to make that hair color permanent, I have just the tincture for it. For a cost, of course."

"I don't know what you're talking about," she grumbled and pulled out a third, bigger rock from her pocket. "So if the first fire opal was enough to wipe all my debts, how much is this one worth?"

Balos made a choking sound. His jaw dropped. She could see the fibers of meat in his teeth. He smacked his lips closed and glared at her.

"You did that on purpose," he snapped. "You deliberately baited and tricked me with the first opal."

"I have a good teacher."

He grunted, somewhat placated but not appeased. Beady eyes kept tracking to the larger raw opal in her hands. It had weighed her pocket down as she'd walked. She was surprised he hadn't noticed it. Must be off today.

"So do you want it or not?" she asked.

Trepidation and need warred across his expression. Peaches could almost taste his longing in the air. If there was one thing she knew for sure, it was when a goblin set its sights on a treasure, be it a trinket or rock, nothing would stand in its way to possess it.

She put it back in her pocket. "I'll find another buyer."

"You filthy thieving pix. You rotten scum of the Well. You stole that from the queen's land. It's hers first, and thereby it's mine. Give it to me."

"Maybe I'll just give it to her then."

"No!" He bit his thin lower lip. "Fine. Have it your way."

He turned and hunched. For a moment, Peaches thought she'd taken it too far and almost caved, her heart softening, but then she caught the small smile he tried to hide with his position. It wasn't vicious, or murderous. It was... pride? His expression deadpanned as he faced her. "I will give you my cap."

She gasped. "But that's the most valuable thing you own. I can't take it."

The red cap was a status symbol amongst the goblin community. Anyone wearing it was treated like royalty. No questions asked. But she wasn't his kind, so what would she do with a greasy, bloody cap anyway?

"You might need it one day, Peaches." There was something foreboding in his words that stayed her next rebuttal. Perhaps it was that he'd used her name instead of calling her a filthy pix. Or perhaps it was the ominous tone that had bled into the words. Then again, he could be playing her.

"Suit yourself." Balos turned his back and went back to

studying the smaller opal. "Take your tray on the way out. I told you I didn't want it."

His sudden dismissal made her deflate. Her eyes watered and she swallowed the lump in her throat. If only he knew she didn't give a rat's ass about the rock, or his damned red cap. She only wanted to keep their relationship profitable and, therefore, alive. She needed this contact like she needed love.

From the moment she'd awoken in this time, she'd had nothing but horror, loneliness and never-ending servitude. Only the few small days she'd had with Violet and Silver had broken through the darkness surrounding her heart. Without Balos' grumpy tuition, she had nothing but a cold, empty room and a hard bed.

"It's a deal," she said. "The cap for the opal."

Balos ripped the cap off. It had stuck to his hair in patches and subsequently pulled chunks out when he handed it to her. The ripping sound grated her teeth. She smothered her distaste so he wouldn't see and demurely exchanged the opal for the cap. Then she folded it as though it were the queen's napkin and stuffed it in her deep pocket—all the way down. Thank god the velvet skirt was thick and voluminous. It hid the nasty thing perfectly.

"Now go away." Balos turned his back and studied his new treasures.

Peaches scooped up the tray and left, stopping outside the hall to catch her breath and to ease the ache in her chest. Why did it hurt so much? Why did she need the love of anyone so much that she put up with the insults and the dismissal of an onerous old goblin?

After a few moments of calm breathing, she glanced down at the tray. A small leather pouch sat inside the empty stew bowl. She almost knocked on the door to give it back, but knew Balos never made a mistake. He would have put that pouch there for her to find. A thrill skipped down her spine and ended in her twitching fingertips. It took all her resolve to stop inspecting the contents for fear that he'd open the door, see her accept the gift, and claim a debt. Then they'd have to start their morbid dance all over again.

But she couldn't help the hopeful feeling that this was a gift without strings. An act of kindness from a cruel, murderous creature. Maybe it was a sign of what she'd suspected all along—that the goblin had a heart, and that was why he'd cloistered himself away down here. He didn't fit in with his kind. That was the fantasy she'd told herself at night when she tried to justify her visits.

After dropping the tray back at the kitchen, Peaches went through the maze of halls and floors down toward her room in the basement. Grateful that she lived far away from the respected palace staff and court, she was able to open the small leather pouch without being watched. Inside was a silt-like sky blue powder. She sniffed it and recognized a familiar chalky scent. Balos had made this sleeping powder a few weeks ago.

She pinched out a small amount and searched the dirty

basement hallway for a mouse. No mouse, but a cockroach —an even better test subject, as they were renowned for their resilience. She blew on her powder. A cloud bloomed over the bug, shimmering momentarily with trapped mana, and then dissipating. Seconds later, the cockroach teetered to the side and didn't get back up.

Peaches smiled. If she kept it on herself, tucked into a pocket, she could use it against the next vampire who decided to trip and accidentally land with his fangs in her arm. That guard had been lucky it was all he'd done. If the queen had found out, she would suck his mana out of him. Permanently.

As it was, Peaches was terrified to be the one to tell the queen why she had an unsanctioned wound on her body. Hopefully, Peaches wasn't called to feed upon for a while— long enough for her body to heal, and then she wouldn't have to explain anything.

With a stifled yawn, she took a turn at the end of the hallway, then another, and finally found herself before two canvas tapestries hanging over the dirty walls. A single red door existed between. This was her hovel, her sleeping chamber. Like most other servants, she was relegated to the levels below the grand Obsidian Palace. She was lucky to get anything at all, but since the queen ingested Peaches' blood, she owed Peaches some form of payment.

Peaches scoffed inwardly. As if a debt would matter to a fae like Maebh.

With a vague wish that a blood slave didn't have to be

nocturnal like a vampire, she opened the door and entered her windowless room. The moment the door closed, the hairs on the back of her neck lifted. *Someone is here.* A rustling beneath her bed warned her moments before a little fluffy and feathered rabbit skidded out, a pair of Peaches' underwear stuck in its antlers. The guilty look on the wolpertinger's face sent Peaches into fits of giggles.

"How on earth did you get in here, little guy?"

She crouched and held out her knuckles so it could sniff her. It bounded up to her, flapped its chicken wings, and made a sound between a bok and a squawk. Then its little nose twitched, and he sniffed her fingers. She'd always heard to be cautious around these creatures. Rumor had it they were attracted to unmated females... but rumor also said they kidnapped said females and took them home to breed with. Apparently, they shifted into something human sized to do it, but she'd never seen one in any other form than the flying rabbit.

The wolpertinger jumped into her lap and sniffed about before it wiggled in and stared at her, almost daring her to tell him to get off. But this little warm fluffball was the only friendly contact she'd had with any warm blooded being lately. His antler tine was broken. He'd been hurt. She pulled left over bread from her pocket.

"I'm keeping you," she decided as it nibbled straight from her fingers. "And just so you know, I belong to the queen. So... you can't kidnap me and take me home."

It stopped nibbling, looked at her, but then continued to eat. Hmm. Maybe the rumors were true.

"Well, if you accept, I'm giving you a name," she declared.

More nibbling, this time a little more voraciously. Peaches had to be nimble to keep her fingers from being pierced by the wolpertinger's fangs. She told herself this was the only reason she didn't notice the vampire in her room.

It hadn't taken Haze long to track down the Well-blessed human. It made sense her scent clung to the subterranean hallways and dirt tunnels beneath the palace. This was where most of the lower-level palace servants were quartered. Upon finding the red door with a hint of lingering feminine sweetness, he'd entered.

Inside was a bed covered in velvet and pillows. A poorly fueled and flickering manabee lamp buzzed on the wall beside old threadbare tapestries depicting colorful pixies dancing in the twilight. Scattered on the bedside table, rickety wooden chair, and sideboard were pixie trinkets and knickknacks. A jar of wing polish—unused. A black glass mirror. And pots of pixie face paints and jewelry.

This was all a lie.

All of it too obvious to be honest... except the collection of rocks on the sideboard. He picked up a few and looked beneath. He sniffed them. No mana inside. No magical properties. Just rocks. In a drawer beside her bed he found a lock of silver hair, and a scrap of purple fabric. He picked up each one and scented them, but they were old. Any sign of the fae or person they belonged to was long gone.

Haze's shadow tapped him on the shoulder. When he turned, he found it pointing at the closed door, warning him. *Footsteps.* Quickly, Haze gathered his shadow around him and sank back to stand in the corner of the room where it was darkest. He waited, his breath held and his mana brimming beneath the surface of his control, ready to be deployed at a thought's notice.

The door opened.

And in walked the prettiest, most delicate female Haze had ever laid eyes on. Strips of leather and ribbon wove through her peach-colored wavy hair—dark at the roots, light at the ends as though each strand had been dipped into an artist's paint pot. Big brown eyes searched the room, drawing him in like a magnet, making him wonder what had put the sadness there. Her features were doll-like, yet a proud, unyielding jaw made Haze think she had a spine made of steel. Fragile yet strong. Like a poppy flower.

Boning on her black velvet dress hugged her waist and pushed up her modest breasts. A thin vein meandered deep into the V of her bodice, showing him exactly where to bury his face and feed. Haze's mouth watered and he shook his head in self-reproach. He shouldn't be thinking about feeding from her, no matter how enticing she smelled. And he most certainly should not be this attracted to her.

She was his mission, and in need of rescue, not another predator.

He lifted his nose and inhaled, drawing in her sweet scent. Definitely not pix. Human pretending to be fae.

She bent down as a little fluffy thing came out from beneath her bed. It hopped onto her lap and nibbled from her fingers. Then he realized what sort of creature it was. A wolpertinger. He jolted, arm flying out to warn her, but then snatched it back and held his breath. She giggled and talked to it. She was either naïve to a wolpertinger's true purpose. Or mated.

Unease prickled him. The thought of this female mated didn't sit well with him.

She froze and stared at his dark corner.

She can't see me.

Impossible.

But, perhaps she sensed him because she dipped fingers into a leathery pouch at her waist, mumbled some-thing to the wolpertinger, and blew shimmering blue dust in Haze's direction. A bloom of cloud filled the room. Haze sneezed, giving away his position. *For Crimson's sake.*

"Show yourself," she demanded, and shoved the fluffy antlered menace beneath her bed.

He allowed the shadows to peel away. The moment he emerged, her eyes widened. She looked up, and up, to his face. Her complexion turned bone white.

"Guardian," she gasped, horrified.

He winced, hating that she had the same first reaction most others did. He showed his palms, hoping she would see him as non-threatening. But with his enormous stature, power-enhancing tattoos, blood-encrusted uniform, and scars, somehow he wasn't sure if that was possible.

"I'm not here to hurt you." He cringed at the sound of his deep, rough voice dragging her sweetness through the mud.

She backed into the door. "That's what they all say."

"I promise. I'm here to... to..." His words slurred. His head felt heavy and dipped. What was... the powder. *What was it?*

Unable to stop his eyes from closing, Haze fell with an almighty floor-shuddering thud. Rocks fell on his head from the dresser, his face smooshed into the compacted dirt floor, but he was powerless to care. As darkness closed in, Haze's shadow tried to rouse him by slapping him in the face. It was no use. Haze was succumbing to the effects of a sleeping spell. His last sane thought was to instruct his shadow not to retaliate. But to protect her.

FIVE

Peaches placed a palm over her hammering heart as the big vampire dropped to the floor and began to softly snore. Even with his great leathery wings shifted away, he took up all the free space between her bed and the wall. Muscles in repose still pushed indecently against the seams of his leather uniform.

Every cell in her body buzzed with adrenaline. Thank god Balos had given her the sleeping powder. She shuddered to think what would have happened if the Guardian—

Her thoughts stuttered.

Why *was* a Guardian in her room?

She'd only ever encountered one from a distance. Most of the time fae avoided them like the plague. Guardians were ruthless, monster-hunting warriors. They cared little for the plight or politics of the everyday fae and only stepped in to help when the dispute involved the integrity of the Well. Which could mean anything they deemed fit. And if one had their sights set on you, it was said you could be dead by morning... or taxed a lot of coin. Same thing in many opinions.

But Peaches hadn't done anything wrong, especially not when it came to the Well. She had zero mana. Was he here because she was pretending to be fae? A few hundred years ago, the conflict between the humans and fae had blown out into a devastating war. Despite being the reason most of the world was uninhabitable, humans weren't happy with their small patch of barren wasteland. They wanted the abundant resources inside Elphyne. But they didn't want to observe the rules the Well had set—no metal, no plastic—and so they'd fought.

It made Peaches ashamed to be human, and a little glad they'd lost the war.

But humans hadn't given up. When Peaches, Silver, and Violet had first met, they'd discovered they were being hunted by two separate factions. The Unseelie Queen and the banished humans of today. Everyone wanted the nuclear bomb rebuilt so they could use the threat of power to take back the land. Violet was a nuclear physicist. Silver, a metal worker. And Peaches... with the right equipment, she could locate uranium.

A nuclear bomb was definitely a threat to the Well. What if this Guardian knew what Peaches could do? What if he'd decided she was better off dead? At least the queen had given up asking Peaches about uranium months ago. Whether that was because she was drunk on Peaches' blood, or because they didn't have the right scientific equipment, or the queen was obsessed with something new, Peaches wasn't sure. And she certainly wasn't going to ask.

As long as Violet and Silver stayed hidden, they were all relatively safe.

Peaches crouched to get closer to the sleeping giant. Such a powerful body. She'd never come across a fae so big. He could crush her skull with one hand and a sneeze. But, strangely, in sleep he looked vulnerable and... soft. Which was weird to think considering he was carved from stone. Handsome, too, she supposed. In a barbaric sort of way. Sexy scruff on his square jaw offset his buzzed head. He had those brackets beside his mouth that were made from smiling... or stress. The teardrop beneath his eye glowed with inner light. Drawn to it like a magnet, she trailed her finger over the light. It represented the Well's approval. No others in Elphyne had this endorsement. Like all Guardians, he had been chosen to protect.

A vampire. The same species that had tried to drain her dry and continued to use and abuse her for what pumped through her veins.

She touched the tiny bone studs piercing his earlobes. His pointed ear twitched. She snatched her hand back, held her breath, and then exhaled when his lip curled and he scratched his nose before sighing in an adorable kind of way.

The wolpertinger ventured slowly from beneath the bed, sniffing about the area before snarling at the Guardian, its fluffy hackles raising and its broken antlers down and ready to stab.

"Yeah," Peaches said. "I agree. He's no cuddly teddy bear."

The glimpse of sharp fangs reminded her the Guardian was a predator, and like the rest of them, he would somehow find a way to own her and use her. Maybe even kill her.

A feed should be as simple as a small prick from fangs and then lapping at the oozing blood with a tongue, but sometimes a vampire was greedy. Sometimes they sucked and bit and gnawed. She'd been hurt one too many times. There was a reason Peaches had taken the pixie disguise. Every fae knew pixies were delicate, if a little vicious. Even the males of their kind protected their females in groups— three or more males in a harem to one female queen.

Peaches wanted to survive, but she wasn't emotionally or physically strong like Silver or Violet. She had to come up with her own defensive measures. She'd hoped taking on the persona of a pixie would make her feel more like something worthy of being treasured... but so far that fantasy had fallen flat. No prince had saved her. They'd only bled her.

An ache in her chest made her realize that she was

different to all fae-kind. She would always be different. She would never fit in anywhere. And her position with the queen was the best she'd had in years. The sooner Peaches accepted the devil she knew, the easier her life would be.

That was why she called for the palace guards at the top of her lungs. She wouldn't be taken for a fool a second time around. When no one came, she bade the wolpertinger to keep watch and then rushed out the door and down the halls until she found guards posted at the dungeons.

Nik was a well-known vampire, pale and lanky with a hook nose. The second guard was a dark-skinned elf with pointed ears and long black hair. Peaches hadn't met him. Standing before another prison cell, staring morosely through the rune-enforced wooden bars was the Sluagh she'd passed earlier. Just watching... waiting until the prisoner was near death so he could sup on his soul.

Peaches had heard the rumors about the Sluagh stealing souls of any kind, but she noticed they mainly ate from those near death, or those who were sad and broken hearted. When the queen called the Wild Hunt—their hoard of swallowed and damned souls—all bets were off. The Sluagh were free to consume any soul in their path—woman, child, elderly, sick, innocent.

The queen had a way of making people do things they didn't want to do. Were the Sluagh truly evil, or just made that way? Was this Wild Hunt some kind of frenzy state they couldn't control?

She was probably rationalizing to make herself less afraid. As long as Peaches kept to herself and tried to remain somewhat optimistic about her situation, the Sluagh left her alone.

Both guards were talking amongst themselves, unruffled by the screams coming from within the cells further down.

"Yes, pix?" Nik drawled as she walked up. "Come to entertain us?"

For a moment, she lost her nerve. The Sluagh also angled his head her way.

"Is she mute?" asked the second guard.

She cleared her throat and pointed back toward her rooms. "Guardian."

A moment of doubt flickered between them. Peaches thought they disbelieved, but when Nik spoke, she realized his apprehension was for another reason.

"Roka, *you* go see what it's all about." Nik made an imperious face, as though he weren't to be trifled with, but she caught the doubt flickering in his eyes.

Roka raised his brows incredulously. "As if a Guardian is in here. Nope."

Nik turned back to the cells, ignoring Peaches. "We didn't hear anything."

Peaches frowned. "The queen will have your heads if you let a Guardian infiltrate her castle."

The elf gnashed his teeth at Peaches. "Be careful of your station, little pix. I know all about you."

Her hands fisted at her sides, fingernails digging into her palms, but she didn't budge. He was bluffing. The only fae in this palace that knew her secret was the queen herself, and she'd taken steps to hide it. Roka must be talking about something else. She forced her trembling legs to still, but the elf crowded her and pushed her backward until her back hit the grimy wall.

"There is a Guardian on the floor in my room," she repeated as steady as she could.

"Fine." Nik rolled his eyes. "I'll check it out."

Roka shoved her, causing her to stumble. "Say thank you, pix."

She touched her fingers to her lips and pushed her hand down and out in the fae hand sign of gratitude. As if she'd actually say thank you and become indebted to him.

Roka begrudgingly went back to his post while Nik gestured for Peaches to lead the way. When they arrived at her room, she found the wolpertinger had gone. Nik swore profusely under his breath and backed out of the room.

"Not just any Guardian," Nik said in the hallway, gesturing back in. "He's one of *The Twelve*. Haze. Brutal motherfucker. He doesn't care about anything but Order law. Shit. Shit. *Shit.*" Wild eyes darted from Peaches to the fallen Guardian. "How in the Well's name did you best him?"

She shrugged. "I have my ways."

"Get Roka. No, get the Captain of the Queens' Guard.

Shit. *Shit.* Get one of the Sluagh. Well-damn it. Get all of them."

"They're not going to listen to me. You barely did."

They both stared back at the fallen Guardian. The surrounding darkness seemed to magnify, to pulse and move with life. Nik stumbled back, almost tripping. "You're right. I'll go. You... you keep an eye on him."

She gulped. "What do I do if he wakes?"

"You said you had ways. Use them."

The sound of Nik's boots thudding away on the stone brought shivers to Peaches' spine. She hugged herself and turned back to the Guardian. His shadow was closer. She stepped back, alert. The shadow was... lifting and taking the form of the Guardian. *Oh god, oh god.* Sleeping powder wouldn't work on something that didn't breathe.

She backed into the hall and hit the other side, frozen in terror, but the shadow slithered out and passed her to where it stood sentry a few feet away in the hallway. It folded its arms.

Peaches couldn't tell if the shadow was facing out, looking down the hall, or facing her. Frowning, she summoned every last scrap of bravery, stepped closer, and swiped her fingers through it. There was a cool substance, like dark mist. Black ribbons of shadow trailed her finger swipe and curled in the air, just like ink in water. But the shadow didn't feel threatening. It felt strangely comforting, as though it was keeping an eye on her.

A groan from her room. The Guardian was awake.

That was fast.

Panicking, she dug into her pocket to find the sleeping powder, but her fingers scraped the grimy red cap and her body revolted. She flinched, dragging her fingers out. *Other pocket.*

"Hold her," the Guardian grumbled, slowly sitting and glaring at her from the bedroom.

Who was he talking to? Her head whipped to the side, searching for another Guardian, perhaps, but it was the shadow that responded. The dark silhouette slid between her and the wall and then reached around her body to grasp her wrists, the curls of darkness becoming manacles of substance pinning her in place.

Haze shook from top to toe like a dog and then pushed to his feet. Dark eyes locked onto her, his intent clear. Awake, he had even more presence than asleep. And she'd done something very, very bad.

CHAPTER

SIX

Sleep still clouded Haze's mind as he stalked toward the timid, beautiful female and joined her in the narrow hallway. She'd taken him by surprise. But Guardians train to fight the lethargy from the drugging sun. A sleeping spell was no different. He forced his arms and legs to move through the drag and gave himself an invigorating shake.

She blinked up at him and tried to shrink into herself.

"Do you know what I am?" he asked.

She gave a short, quick nod.

"Then you know what I represent. You're coming with me."

"I've done nothing wrong."

Her voice was like whiskey, warming his insides. "I know."

"What?"

A smile twitched at the corner of his lips.

She straightened. "So… why?"

"You know what you are."

She hesitated and glanced down at the dark restraints. He gestured at his shadow. The incorporeal silhouette oozed back to where it belonged, next to him and pooled on the floor.

She rubbed her wrists and eyed him warily.

"What's your name?" he asked.

"Peaches."

No hesitation. Interesting. He scratched his scruff and studied her. She was either obedient or simply afraid. His gaze went to her hair, then to the piranha teeth glimpsed in her mouth. He doubted any of it was real, but he wouldn't shatter her glamor in case it was a security blanket she'd wrapped around herself.

"I'm D'arn Haze." Giving his official name was an attempt to alleviate her fears. He wasn't the nurturing kind. Or soft at heart. He waited for her to say something, to look less terrified, but when she didn't he retrieved the portal stone from his pocket. "This will take us to the Order. There are more of your kind there who will want to speak with you. We just need to get out in the open or the portal will rip a hole through the walls."

And he'd rather not have to explain to the queen why the Order was destroying her property.

"My kind?" Peaches asked, suspicion lacing her tone. "You mean pixies?"

He shot her a dubious look. "Sure. Let's go with that."

He held out his hand, but the small human still hesitated to take it.

"I—" She clamped her lips shut and glanced at her room with longing.

Here? Why would she want to remain in this palace of debauchery and torture? It was filthy and cold. He glanced down his front and tried to see what she saw. A big, scary vampire. Who hadn't given her any reason to trust him. He scrubbed his hand over his buzzed head and sighed.

"Peaches, you know fae can't lie, so believe me when I say I'm not going to hurt you. The new Seelie High Queen is like you, and she's mated to one like me—a Guardian."

Peaches' wary gaze snapped to him. "I thought... I thought that was just a rumor."

He nodded. "She's also from your—" He stopped himself and had to reframe his words. The walls could be listening. "She was born the same time as you."

"What?"

"Come." He held up the portal stone. "I can explain at the Order."

"*Halt!*"

Haze stilled. On both sides of the hallway, Unseelie soldiers converged. Each was a different kind of Unseelie fae race. Shifters, elves, vampires, goblins, a green-skinned orc with meaty arms. Their weapons ranged from knives to spears to serrated bone swords with glowing Elven runes, red light glancing menacingly off the dark walls and beneath faces.

Haze stifled a yawn and locked eyes with Peaches.

The five feet between them felt like a mountain. He could take her hand and activate the portal stone, be damned with the destruction it caused indoors. But there were rules of engagement that needed to be honored between the Order and the high born fae, the royals in particular. He'd already broken rules when he entered the palace without permission. If he continued on this path, the queen would have legitimate grounds to reprimand him. Possibly the Prime, too. And there was no guarantee Peaches wouldn't be caught in the crossfire.

Haze's hesitation cost him.

Using some kind of tacky wind, an Elven guard wrenched the stone from Haze's possession. It flew toward the elf who pocketed it with a smug smile.

No, he fucking didn't.

Haze snarled, his fangs glinting and dripping histamines—ready to bite. His shadow oozed out from beneath him, preparing for battle.

"Get back in your room and don't come out until I say so," he said to Peaches, and then cracked his knuckles, eyeing each of the guards. Fuck the rules of engagement. They stole his portal stone.

Which one first?

He assessed the soldiers, working out the priority threat. The goblin wore no red cap, meaning his position within the goblin military ranks was low. None of the guards had rank patches on their epaulettes. *Small fry.* And the captain and the lieutenant weren't there. This would be over in minutes.

Peaches didn't move.

"Get in your room," he ordered.

"She's not yours to instruct," the elf spat, eying Haze curiously. This guard had an intricate braid that trailed down his back like a rat's tail. An aura of power lifted around him, thickening the air. He would be the first Haze needed to take out.

"In fact, she's not yours at all," the elf continued. "She belongs to the queen. And you, Guardian, *you* should not be here."

Two sets of Unseelie hands emerged from the darkness to grab Peaches by the shoulders. She stumbled backward into the shadows of the hallway until she was almost taken from sight. Only the vague peach of her hair revealed she was still there, captive.

Every protective instinct in Haze's body bristled. Power crackled at his fists. "Unhand her."

The elf scoffed. "You're in no position to make demands."

A vampire stepped forward, sweat dappling his brow. Probably because his shift had ended when the sun came up an hour ago. He'd be struggling to stay awake. When the vampire spoke, his voice came out shaky. "Why are you here, Guardian?"

"None of your fucking business."

The vampire lifted his chin. "There is a Sluagh on the way and I have called the lieutenant of the Queen's Guard. Surrender now, or they will bring suffering to your eternal soul."

No, they wouldn't. Haze was above fae law. He only answered to the Well, and by extension, the Prime of the Order of the Well. He calmly rolled his shoulders. So a Sluagh was on his way. That meant Haze had a few minutes. *That's all I need.*

He summoned a strong hit of mana and let it build beneath his skin. The power enhancing tattoos across half his body burned and itched as they activated, ready to amplify any mana sent from his body. He released his war hammer from his belt. Static crackled as he moved. The glint of Justice caught everyone's attention.

Metal.

Contraband for everyone else but Guardians. It could pulverize more readily than bone. It could cut through a spell. It stopped mana in its tracks. It was anathema to fae. *Crimson*, it could even kill Haze if it pierced his flesh. But, unlike others, Haze's mana wasn't cut off if he held it. To them, he was a god.

He clenched the handle and eyed the guards warily, daring them to step forward, to make the first move.

The goblin leaped like a frog, its spindly four-foot body flailing in the air. Haze swung. A wave of power rushed outward from Justice as it connected with the goblin. Bone cracked. The walls rattled. The ground shook.

Haze grinned.

Peaches had wondered how Haze received the brackets around his mouth, what had made him smile so much, and now she knew. It was the love of battle. Being a Guardian.

He grinned, wicked eyes shifting to her in delight before jumping back into the fray. Watching Haze move was like watching a nature documentary. He was a predator in his element. *This* was what those bulging muscles were made for—destruction.

The guards holding Peaches let go and joined the fight. She flattened against the wall, trying to avoid becoming collateral damage. Haze's shadow stood before her, deflecting anyone getting close, protecting her. Boots pounding behind her signaled backup arriving. Shouts and grunts filled her ears as guards took on damage. Haze didn't even break a sweat.

He also didn't kill anyone, she realized.

He was toying with them, using the confined space to throw them against each other like bowling pins. Peaches' heart leaped into her throat and she jerked back, just as a goblin went flying past her face.

Maybe she should have gone with him. He was fae. He couldn't lie. Not like her. Maybe there *were* humans from her time at the Order. Maybe one of them was Silver or Violet. She clutched her chest, adrenaline coursing through her body, numbing her to sense and logic. She couldn't think of what to do. The part of her that had accepted life here didn't want to leave. It was afraid of the unknown, of misdirection and mistakes. But part of her wanted to trust him.

He was strong. Powerful. He could protect her.

Or he could end her, just like he did with the guards— with a wicked grin on his face.

Coldness entered the hallway. A shiver down her spine. Goosebumps along her flesh. A whisper in the darkness.

The Sluagh was here.

Terrified, she clutched the sleeping powder bag; her knuckles whitening. Moving into her room seemed like a good idea, but it was too late. Worried, she glanced at the Guardian. He moved like liquid fire, burning anything in his path, but he wouldn't see the Sluagh coming.

She should warn him.

Her mouth failed.

And then the Sluagh was there... moving like a flicker in

the darkness. This particular monster was Haze's height, haggard, and hungry. His gothic face reminded Peaches of Dorian Gray, eternally beautiful but doomed. Sadness etched in his eyes. Hollows in his cheeks. Dressed in a ripped charcoal suit, the Sluagh's wings draped like a mantle made of glorious black leather that rustled with every step.

Coming to a stop before Peaches, the creature peered through matted, long locks and pointed at the battle. Electricity crackled. Peaches' hair lifted on end. For a chilling moment, the outline of his skull illuminated his pretty face, and then it was gone. Air whooshed past Peaches, gusting her body. No, not air... the wraith part of the Sluagh. The unseen spirit that walked. It was going for Haze, and he wouldn't stand a chance.

One thought permeated Peaches's fear. *I don't want him to die.*

She tossed the contents of the pouch into the battle. Blue dust clouded everywhere, raining down. Fae sneezed. Fae dropped, asleep. Haze's dark eyes slid to Peaches, betrayal on his face before he slumped to the ground.

Air whooshed again as the Sluagh's spirit returned to his body. His skull flickered beneath his skin. He slowly craned his head to look at her with dark, soulless eyes.

You stole my meal from me, human. His words slid into her mind like oil on water.

"He's a Guardian," she said. "You can't kill him."

Maybe I will take you instead. The Sluagh bent toward

her, eyes piercing her soul. The smell of rotting flesh wafted into her nose. Yeah, this one definitely wasn't healthy. She'd noticed more of the Host—the Sluagh that lived in the palace—had become decrepit like this one as the years went on.

She closed her eyes and tilted her face away as the stench grew stronger. If only she had more of Balos' sleeping powder. It might work on the Sluagh.

It won't work on me.

"What has happened here?" a commanding voice clipped.

Peaches' face cooled, and she opened her eyes. The Sluagh straightened his spine. Despite exhaustion roughening his features, he was still formidable and perhaps slightly insane.

He slid his gaze to the owner of the voice—the lieutenant in the Queen's Guard, Demeter. A striking vampire with eyelids drooping from the heat of the day. His slick, black uniform was embroidered with extra roses, thorns and stag antlers on the high collar accentuating a sharp, stubbled jaw. Hard eyes darted between Peaches and the Sluagh, then to the sleeping pile of bodies, both bloody and clean.

Some kind of mental exchange occurred between Demeter and his monster. One moment the Sluagh stood before Peaches, the next he was five feet down the hall. His position skipped, flickering like this until he disappeared altogether.

Demeter came to Peaches. He nodded to approaching guards and then pointed at the pile of bodies.

"Take the Guardian into custody. Strip him and remove his weapon. Put him in a warded cell." Then he stared at Peaches. "The Sluagh said you are to blame for the sleeping powder."

"He was going to sup on the Guardian's soul. I couldn't let that happen."

Demeter's eyes narrowed. "You're not a guard, pix. You have no right to make decisions regarding the security of the palace. You will be punished for overstepping your station."

Yeah, she suspected as much. No matter what she did in this place, there was punishment. "What are you going to do with him?"

Hard eyes snapped to her in warning. Right. Not her station.

"I'll just..." She pointed at her room. "I'll go back to my room."

"You do that."

Trying to avoid eye contact, or stepping on bodies, Peaches tiptoed past the mess and slipped into her room, shutting the door firmly. She flopped onto her bed and covered her head with a pillow. But try as she might, she couldn't hide from the heavy feeling that she'd made a mistake.

She should have taken the Guardian's hand while she'd had the chance. But she was too afraid to leave the comfort of this room. Contrary to belief, freedom wasn't a straight walk. It was a labyrinth of fangs and thorns with no map. She was too scared to put one foot in front of the other because, left to her own devices, she inevitably messed up and got hurt. It was better this way.

At least the Guardian's soul was intact. At least she could be thankful for that.

As the pull of exhaustion dragged her into oblivion, the sounds of torture filtered down from the dungeons. Maybe it was Haze. She covered her head with a second pillow.

Better him than me.

The lie coated her tongue with bitterness.

A BOOK
MYTH

EIGHT

Maebh stalked into her private reading parlor. Bookcases lined the walls. Ancient tomes preserved with mana were strewn around, their pages opened and ink-stained from her fingers rubbing along curious lines. Filled with old world mythology and war strategy, the books had done nothing but provide her a fantastical distraction. She snarled and slid her hand across a side table, swiping the books to the floor.

She whirled to face Demeter as he entered the chamber. "Why is the Guardian here? And *where* is Gastnor?"

It had been the lieutenant of her guard, not the captain who'd cleaned up the mess in the basement dungeons. Her good-for-nothing captain was becoming less reliable as the years went on. Soon she would have to make a hard decision, despite his years of loyalty.

To his credit, Demeter remained poised under her wrath and closed the door quietly, bravely cloistering the two of them together. Perhaps there was worth in him, after all. How she hated a groveling male. She'd had too many of them in her long life, the latest of which was nowhere in sight. Maebh rubbed her tired eyes and attempted to remember the last time she'd seen her greatest disappointment.

"He's disposing of waste from your... improvements," Demeter reminded her.

She looked at him blankly.

"The mana-warped bodies, my queen," he elaborated. "But of course you knew that."

Maebh resisted rubbing her eyes again. Her fingers were black-stained. The residue was either from the books or her experiments. Either one was worth it. Those books had given her ideas. Those experiments had birthed the Sluagh centuries ago. For a time, she and her Sluagh had been invincible. They'd crushed the human resistance together. But then six of them defected to the Order. That break had done something to the Sluagh left behind. The Host had shattered without six of their hive. What was left was not the same.

So she had to make something new. Better.

She was tired of waiting around for her foretold humans with their old world weapon building knowledge. She'd recovered but one of the three required to build the bomb, and she was out of patience. Even if Peaches couldn't light a spark with her mana, her blood confirmed she had untapped power running through her veins. There were other uses for her.

Six years ago, Maebh had all three humans needed to build this mythical weapon in her grasp, and Gastnor had messed up. It was their blood, he'd said. It was addictive like a drug. It had turned a military squadron of her best fighters into drooling messes. They'd all perished but Gastnor.

Her Seers confirmed Peaches' tale was true—she knew nothing about the current whereabouts of the companions she woke with in this time. Maebh had her Seers scry for the whereabouts of these women, but nothing. The only one flickering in and out of the Seers' visions was Peaches, and even that was unreliable. Peaches had been out there in the wild for *four years* before Maebh took her from the Autumn Court. There was nothing they could do but wait for news of the remaining two humans.

Maebh did not become queen by waiting.

Acid rose in her gullet, coating her tongue with bitterness. She did not become queen through a human weapon. She created her own weapons, something she'd forgotten until she'd procured Peaches. Somehow, being faced with failure yet again, she realized she needed a Plan B.

Her new experiments weren't exactly in line with the laws set by The Order. She touched the forbidden inky side of the Well to harness her creatures with chaos and death.

And now a Guardian—their biggest—had infiltrated her palace.

"My queen?" Demeter stepped forward. He calmly picked up strewn books, shut them and stacked them on a table. "Do you want the guards to continue torturing him until he gives us answers? Or send one of the Sluagh to rape his mind?"

"No," she clipped. The air felt thick in her throat. She threw a hand toward her stained-glass windows, using mana to open the shutters and let the icy air blast in. She inhaled deeply, then spoke. "You've fucked up by torturing him. Now we must tread carefully. He has done naught but turn up uninvited and defended himself." She couldn't decide if that meant he knew what Maebh was making down in her basement cells. "He probably warded his mind against the Sluagh, in any case."

"Haze was found near your blood-slave's room. Perhaps she has something to do with his arrival."

"That timid thing?" Maebh scoffed and shook her head.

"Not so timid. She faced a Sluagh and neutralized the battle by using some kind of powdered sleeping agent."

Maebh's brow rose at Demeter. If anyone else spoke to her like that, she would cut them down. But she always liked a male with confidence. And arrogance. She was curious to see if those traits extended to her bedroom. None of her harem seemed to satisfy her enough these days.

"Probably got the powder from Balos," she mumbled, a sneer on her lips. "That withered old goblin has a Seelie heart. Peaches has been known to visit him. If he wasn't so useful in creating weaponry, I'd have fed him to the pit years ago."

"So why else would he be here if not for knowledge of your secret?"

"You're the one feeding the Guardian misleading information. You tell me."

Since they'd learned Guardians were sniffing around Aconite City, asking about the mana-warped corpses improperly disposed of, she knew she had to get ahead of the gossip. Demeter's relationship to D'arn Indigo was perfect to exploit. It ensured she created the conversation and tested Demeter's loyalty at the same time. So far, her lieutenant had proven himself at the expense of his family. He was a worthy contender to replace the captain.

Demeter's face darkened. "Haze has taken every piece of information I've offered without faltering. They trust me because Indi is my brother, despite having not spoken to him for years. I was due to meet them both at my parents' home, but there were more pressing matters here. The raiding human parties from Crystal City are increasing in fervor and frequency. They're desperate to pillage the resources we have—everything from metal scraps to livestock to heated mana stones."

Cold hard fury flashed through Maebh's veins. "How many did you catch?"

"Over fifty."

Maebh's brows went up. "And how many did we lose?"

Demeter's lips curved. "Five."

"Good. I want every single human you've captured put into a cell until I decide what to do with them. Their punishment must be public." She would have to concoct something exceedingly humiliating. "And we will allow one to escape to return with the tale."

"Yes, my queen." Demeter bowed. He tried to leave, but she made a hissing sound with her teeth. She wasn't done with him and he knew it. He lifted his gaze brazenly to hers, knowing exactly why she'd stopped him.

"I never expected Haze would actually try to approach me here." Demeter's frown was as good as an apology. "But I guess the Order doesn't care about my reputation."

"Of course they don't. They were going to chew you up and spit you out. But they don't know what we know." She traced long black nails down his stubbled jaw, seeing the truth. The Order most likely knew nothing about her experiments, and that was why Haze risked coming here. If he hadn't given Demeter up—the easy scapegoat—during his torture session, then the chances were Haze still tried to protect Demeter's turncoat role. Demeter had played his part perfectly. "Have you spoken with the Guardian?"

"No, my queen. I wanted to wait until we spoke."

"You have done well, my lamb."

"I will do anything you need."

He wanted to be her captain. He wanted more. He

pressed his jaw into her hand, his eyes meeting hers before lowering demurely. She went to the windowsill. Ice moved on the waves as the Aconite Sea swelled. This icy landscape had been her home for centuries. It calmed her just to look at it. No matter how wretched her life had become, no matter the suffering or the loss, the sea reminded her there was always worse. The changing tide embodied the mercurial nature of every living thing. No one was to be trusted, especially those closest to her. She'd learned that lesson the day her most trusted and beloved *amado*—one of her harem—betrayed her by submerging in the ceremonial lake and coming out a Guardian, severing his ties to her.

She'd wanted to elevate him to consort. She'd wanted to rule Elphyne with him. Until that moment, she'd thought he'd wanted the same thing.

Maebh glanced over her shoulder at Demeter. Contrary to his belief, she didn't trust him. Anyone could turn on her, even those proclaiming to love her. Demeter had been with her for six years, since Gastnor had come back empty handed with a scratch ruining his handsome face.

Maebh's lip curled. As punishment, she'd permanently taken half of Gastnor's mana until he'd aged like a human and wrinkled. Now he disgusted her. That's why she'd sent him into the tachi infested Redvein Forest with a half deranged human pet and a redcap. She'd wanted him to prove himself, but he'd failed, yet again.

The sun glinting over the water tired her. She hadn't felt the dragging effects of day for years. Millenia old, she'd outgrown the nocturnal shackles of her original life. Years on and filled with so much mana from her queendom, she'd become something else, something beyond vampire. Yet now, after sacrificing mana to her experiments, she felt weak. Exactly like that young, naïve girl she used to be. Before King Mithras. Before the war with humans. Before her daughter had been—*Enough. Stop wallowing.*

She went to rub her tired eyes and then curled her fingers.

"The Guardian is a problem," Demeter reminded her, stifling his own yawn. "What will you have me do?"

"The last time I attempted to humiliate a Guardian, *he* humiliated me. Now he is the Seelie High King and mated to a Well-blessed human." Irritation bubbled in her bones. That prick of a wolf shifter—that scum-of-the-Well *Mithras* descendant—came into *her* home, into *her* palace, and proved her most fearful weapon was not infallible. It was only a matter of time before others learned the fact, too.

But he'd also revealed something she hadn't known yet. The Well-blessed humans waking from the old world were full of untapped power—if her Untouched human pet was to be believed. Bones, his name was. He was from Crystal City and the trusted advisor to the human leader intent on taking over Elphyne. The Guardians had captured Bones, yet she'd managed to weasel him away through a loophole they were yet to discover. She'd promised to interrogate, but in doing so, she'd stopped Bones' heart.

She'd told the Order she'd killed Bones—a truth—but didn't tell them she'd brought him back to life. Now he was Maebh's source of human information. That was how she'd learned the old world weapon could mean the end of the world, and she didn't want that. But she wasn't ready to dismiss it. She had to keep her options open. Just in case her own experiments failed.

At the very least, she had to stop this weapon from getting into human hands.

Maebh wanted to rule, to dominate, but she was done sharing Elphyne. She wanted it all. Even Crystal City.

"So what do we do?" Demeter asked.

"We need more time."

"Shall we lock him up? Throw him in the pit?"

"We only have a few days before the Order notices him missing. Even if he did enter my palace without permission, it is not grounds for holding him captive. Certainly not the torture your guards exacted without my consent." She clicked her teeth with disparagement, inwardly seething at the ineptitude of her staff sometimes.

"What about the labyrinth? We could say he lost himself in there after we found him. It would be true, to a point."

Maebh thought about it. The Obsidian Palace was a vast structure half dug into a mountain side. A pretty labyrinth made of hedges and walls sat at the center. At first glance, to any visiting person, it was simply a garden maze to feast your eyes upon at a party. Something for dignitaries and nobles to play in or have secret trysts and dangerous liaisons. But what the eye could see was only the tip of the iceberg. What lied beneath was something not even she liked to enter.

Haze being trapped down there would give Maebh time to finalize her new weapons without prying eyes or word getting back to the Order. But he might die. And then there would be consequences.

"No," she said, a shiver running down her spine. "Not the labyrinth yet."

"What about the pit?"

"Another last resort." The pit would hold the Guardian, like the rest of her abandoned prisoners, but there would be no denying it if the Order asked. She truly needed her new weapon complete before taking extreme measures. She tapped her lips, thinking about how thirsty she was, and how she had to keep denying herself the blood of the human. For a queen to become beholden to anything, especially when there was only one available source, was foolhardy.

Peaches' true identity was a mystery to everyone but Maebh and Gastnor. And since one more mistake meant Gastnor was out of her service, he'd studiously kept this secret, and his fangs, to himself. Even after he knew her blood would appease his cravings.

Haze, however, did not need to remain abstinent. He

was a vampire, as thirsty and vulnerable as the rest of them. If Maebh could entice him to drink from Peaches, then he might reveal his true intentions for being at the palace. For all she knew, Haze knew nothing about her weapon, and then all she needed to do was send him back to the vultures at the Order with naught but a spanking. Crisis averted. A smile stretched her dark stained lips as a plan began to form.

"He should never have been tortured," she said. "Your soldiers were out of line to do that without my consent. We must make reparations."

"My queen?" Poor lamb. He looked confused.

She stroked his cheek before sliding her fingers along his pointed ear and gripping tight, squeezing until he winced in pain. "Do you not trust your queen?"

"Of course. I trust you completely."

"Then have a luxury guest suite prepared, and ensure only my blood-slave attends to the Guardian's injuries. She is to be his only source of offered sustenance. Do you understand?"

Demeter nodded, winced again at the pain from her grip, his fangs peeking out and cutting his bottom lip. Blood welled there.

"And what if he refuses?" Demeter asked.

"He can only refuse for so long before he starves."

Her eyes were stuck on Demeter's bottom lip. She licked the wound, delighting in his moan of need. She scraped her nails along his neck and toyed with his collar.

It was time to see if her lamb was strong enough to be her captain. To test his loyalty one last time.

"My blood slave is precious because she is a Well-blessed human," she confessed.

"She is?" Demeter's eyes were already glazing over as Maebh's fingers trailed down his torso and circled the growing bulge between his legs.

"And, as Gastnor has discovered, a Well-blessed human has unique blood. Not only does it taste better than anything you've experienced, but one feeding can sustain for weeks."

Demeter's eyes widened at the thought.

"But that's not the best part," she crooned in his ear and squeezed his erection. "The blood is almost as intoxicating as a hit of divilixir. And more addictive."

Demeter grunted in pleasure as she continued to rub.

"But not you, my queen," he panted. "You're not addicted."

"Of course not." She squeezed. "I am beyond addiction."

"My queen is so clever," he breathed, a smile stretching his lips, making his cruel features something she almost enjoyed looking at. He would never be as handsome as her most favored bed partner, but that particular vampire was no longer available. Demeter would never desert her for the Order. And her last bed partner outside her harem— Gastnor—had also failed heinously. At the memory of all the betrayal in her love life, she yanked hard on Demeter's genitals until he cried out, his pupils dilating from plea-sure-pain.

"I'm trusting you with this knowledge, my lamb. The last person who couldn't contain himself around this human now looks like a wrinkled prune. Do you understand?"

He nodded vehemently, comprehension dawning in his eyes. No one knew Gastnor had sampled the humans he'd been sent to retrieve. She might have forgiven him if he'd returned with at least with one of them, but Gastnor had been a slave to his cravings. As most males were.

So disappointing.

"Do not tell anyone about her true identity. She is more important than you know."

She let go of Demeter. He exhaled, but kept his lust-filled eyes on her. Wanting more pain? Perhaps he was a worthy bed partner after all. It had been a long time since someone kept up with her wild urges.

Demeter licked his lips, a question in his eyes. "Perhaps if the human fails to entice him, we can loosen his tongue at one of your parties."

Her brow arched dubiously. "He is a Guardian, Deme-ter. He will not participate in our frivolities."

"He does if you say he does."

"True." She smiled wickedly. She could always spell him to do her bidding.

"We just need to ply him with elixir or your human's blood. I will pretend to be his informant one last time."

"You are right," she said, again impressed at his cleverness. "Even a fae with his honor won't see it coming. Very well. We will host a pleasure party—as a means of reparation. Where torture has failed, diplomacy and seduction will prevail. By the end of the night we will learn his reasons for being here, or we will send him to the labyrinth. Bring the human to me. It's high time we had a little chat."

MAEBH SAT IN HER PARLOR, her books scattered around her as she sipped on the blood of a regular human prisoner. The naked woman looked thoroughly debased and dirty, yet she still had the gumption to try to wriggle out of Maebh's control. Maebh let the human think that she could. She even let her crawl to the edge of the rug. It gave Maebh the opportunity to admire the tapestry she'd had replicated from an old world book found during her youth. For a moment, she remembered how different her life had been millennia ago. How she used to hunt down ruins to play in. How she used to dream about sharing this joy of adventure with her daughter.

How she'd wanted to grow Elphyne.

One of those dreams was dead.

Maebh picked up the book by her side and flipped through the pages of mythology. From cyclops to centaurs to Cerberus. Beasts of all kinds no longer lived in the imagination of the past, but here in the real world. And she enjoyed bringing them to life.

The woman dragged blood across the rug, defiling it with her stench.

Maebh snapped her fingers, sending her mana into the human, forcing the weak limbs to do her bidding. Maebh twisted her fingers, and the human twisted too, horror evident in her eyes. She should have thought twice about stealing from the fae. Maebh crooked her finger. The human jerked and crawled back to place her head in Maebh's lap, exposing her neck.

"That's a good little Untouched whore," Maebh crooned.

She located the juicy jugular vein, pulsing with lifeblood just as the door to her chambers opened, and the petite peach-haired human pretending to be a pixie shuffled in. Maebh waited until Peaches stood at the foot of the rug, and then sank her fangs into the neck on her lap. A burst of warm liquid entered Maebh's mouth. It should have been delicious, but instead it was dirt. Maebh forced herself to drink, letting Peaches see that she was not beholden to cravings like the rest of them.

When she'd had her fill, she wrapped her fingers around the human's neck and crushed it like one of her little birds. Then she dabbed the corners of her mouth with a red napkin and turned to the latest thorn in her side.

"You have displeased me," Maebh clipped.

Peaches bowed. Good. At least she had humility.

"You continue to refuse to locate your human friends with science knowledge, and now you create a mess of gargantuan proportions between my court and the Order. I'm beginning to wonder if there is any use to keeping you here at all." She pushed the dead human from her lap. "Clearly, I don't *need* to feed from you. Yes, you taste better. And, yes, your blood will sustain for longer than normal, but in case you haven't noticed, I'm not like the other vampires. I rarely need to feed. I am so old that the Well itself sustains me." She stood, her dress rustling like crawling spiders. "Do you understand what that means, human?"

Peaches fidgeted, her flowing locks dangled in front of her face.

"Look at me," Maebh demanded.

Peaches looked up, eyes glistening.

"Your tears will not help you here. Answer my question. Do you understand what that means?"

"No, my queen."

Must she remind everyone? "It means that I am so interwoven with the Well, we are like one. No one, not even the Order, can take that from me. I am law. Not them."

"Yes, my queen."

Sniveling little lesser. She may not be fae, but she *was* touched by the magic of the Well. That was clear in the taste of her blood and how she healed. Only, she wasn't as powerful as the others who had arisen from the old world.

Such a disappointment she was the one they'd found. Maebh shook her head, disgusted.

"I've allowed you almost two years here, and in return, I've had your blood. This arrangement tires me. Unless you can offer more, like the names and locations of your friends, then I'll have to find other uses for you." She motioned for the captain of her guard to come forward. Gastnor had come in hours ago, exhausted and secretive. The redcap she'd sent with him revealed another Guardian had caught them dumping bodies. He'd also told Maebh this Guardian was Demeter's brother, and a human had been with him. The only reason the trio had escaped unscathed from Redvein Forest was because D'arn Indigo had been preoccupied with protecting this woman. Maebh was willing to bet she was one of the humans who'd escaped six years ago.

The same one who'd scarred Gastnor's ugly, wrinkled face.

"Gastnor," she said, and indicated to Peaches. "This human is to be D'arn Haze's personal slave while he is a guest of the Winter Court. She will feed him, dress him, and fuck him if he so wishes. If she performs to your satisfaction, then she may remain in our good graces for a little longer. If he utters a complaint about her..." Maebh glared at Peaches. "Then I want to know about it."

"Yes, my queen." Gastnor bowed, his salacious eyes sliding to Peaches.

"You mess this up, Gastnor, you lose control of your cravings again, and I am finished with you."

His eyes snapped to her. "I won't. You have my word."

She didn't believe him. He was as weak as any male when it came to blood and sex. She should have asked Demeter.

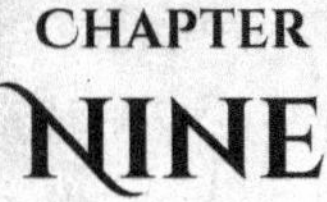

CHAPTER NINE

Through a cloud of pain, Haze floated in a memory.

"Let me in," he shouted, his fist pounding on the big wooden doors of the Obscendia colony. "I want to see Holly."

His heart thudded in his chest. His lungs heaved. Holly wasn't right. He should be in there, looking after both mother and child.

"I said, let me in," he bellowed, knocking again.

The enormous doors cracked open and a female vampire peered out. Avalon was an elder by the years she'd lived and the color of her dress, not by the wrinkles on her face. She was as youthful as any high fae. "It is no use complaining, young male. This is female business. Go and let us do our job."

"I should be in there helping."

Avalon laughed. "What could one male such as yourself possibly do that an entire colony of females can't?"

"She's not well." Holly was a party girl. A wild one. It was what had attracted Haze to her in the first place, but now her quest for freedom was consuming her.

"She was well enough to open her legs to you."

His chest hurt. It was as though Holly's sadness had spread to him like a banshee's wail, engulfing his heart. All Holly wanted to do was fly away, to go back to a life where she had nothing to worry about but the next party. She hated the vampiric traditions forced on her as a female, including taking on the responsibilities of motherhood. Everything ached in Haze and the only cure was to see their daughter. To know she was safe. "But... she's my child."

"And you did your job. You beget a child. Now it's our turn. Go. You cannot protect her from everything, especially not from motherhood."

The door slammed in his face, displacing air, gushing wind into his stinging eyes.

The sound of a door whooshing closed roused Haze from sleep. Footsteps amplified in his head, making each decibel pound with pain. In his arms, his legs, his face. He ached everywhere. What had happened?

He grunted and tried to sit, but his muscles declined. Opening his eyes, he found shallow lacerations over his naked torso and arms. He was propped against pillows in a bed, a black sheet covering his legs and hips.

He'd been whipped. It all came back to him. The damned sleeping powder. The subsequent capture and torture for information in the dungeons. The sneering

Unseelie guards... the... he pressed his forehead, straining to remember... the lieutenant—Indigo's brother, Demeter—came in and put a halt to his torture, but didn't stay to talk. Then the Unseelie High Queen herself entered. Her strange regret for the hasty behavior of her soldiers toward a representative of the Order, and her pledge to make it up to him with a celebration in his honor. An indulgent party befitting the Unseelie Court. If Maebh thought he'd stick around for that, she was truly as mad as they said.

And he had doubts about all of it.

Demeter's behavior seemed a little off. While Haze could understand Demeter evading conversation with Haze to avoid suspicion, Demeter had groveled to his queen. A little too sycophantic for someone who claimed to spy for the Order. Any time Haze had spoken to him in the past, Demeter had come across as aloof or abrupt, but always confident and... just different to how he was now. It was almost as though Demeter was acting to hide his true loyalties—but to which faction he was loyal, Haze wasn't sure. His intuition was going haywire. Fae were never good liars, not like humans.

The sooner he got out of there, the better.

Water sloshing to his left stole his attention. He swung his head with a warning snarl. His hand snapped out, ready to release a defensive spell. *Peaches*. He flinched and withdrew his hand upon seeing her walk toward him from across an opulently decorated room. She struggled to carry a heavy bowl of steaming water. Each step spilled more over the edges, making her brow pucker and her lips purse.

She'd used the sleeping powder, but he didn't think she was a risk to him. He searched the room, assessing. Beyond his four-poster bed with black embroidered drapes, was a large, noble guest chamber. From the view outside the stained-glass window, they were perhaps on the fifth floor. The last rays of sun painted the sky in purples as it dipped beyond the horizon. Flames crackled in the fireplace. A family of fire sprites jumped from log to log, stoking the heat from fresh kindling.

So... going by the sunset, he'd been out for a while, but going by the new fire, he hadn't been here for long. Perhaps an hour, no more.

He surveyed the rest of the room. Black damask wall-paper matched the curtains. Every part of the decor was dark. In fact, the only light came from the fire, or manabee lanterns secured in sconces at regular intervals.

They were alone.

He closed his eyes briefly and sent his awareness within—testing his personal mana reserve. He'd spent most of his natural stores in the battle against the guards. The only reason they'd been able to torture him all day had been because he was out of mana, otherwise, he would have retaliated in a heartbeat. It could take him days to replenish naturally... unless he found a natural source of power—a hot spring. He could take a chance and use the palace's source without the queen's permission or wait until he had enough to shift his wings out and fly back to the Outpost. Neither was ideal.

He glanced down his naked torso. The welts were all over his abdomen, all the way down to where the sheet covered his groin and legs. *Crimson.* His back hurt. Probably as sliced up as his front. He winced and tried to move, but Peaches' voice stopped him.

"I'm glad you're awake."

She brought a gust of sweet perfume as she placed the bowl down on a side table next to his bed. Kohl-lined eyes stared at him. Her hesitant smile sat perfectly within a heart-shaped face. Tiny jewels glistened like tear drops in her lashes. Gloss sparkled on her dainty lips. The rosy blush on her cheeks almost matched the colored tips of her long, wavy hair.

He let his gaze roam down her body, silently appreciating the new form-fitting black dress on her slim, petite figure. Between small, pert breasts, a V-neck opened to her navel. When she squeezed out a sponge, she exposed a back half covered in black lace, giving him a delectable sample of her flesh all the way down her spine to the valley between her naked buttocks.

Heat flushed up his neck and hit his ears. He snapped his gaze back to her face.

She definitely had not been wearing that dress before.

Probably a change to distract him from what had happened. It worked. He frowned at himself and tossed the sheets from his legs, intending to get out, only to realize he was completely naked. He covered himself before Peaches faced him again.

"What are you doing?" He cautiously eyed her dripping sponge.

The blush staining her cheeks deepened, and she refused to look him in the eyes, instead speaking directly to his chest. "They said... um... the disturbance was my fault, so it's my responsibility to clean up the mess."

He stopped her as she reached for him. That was bullshit, and they both knew it. Water dripped onto his abs, running rivulets down the grooves between muscles. "I'm many things, Sweetness, but I'm not a mess."

"I didn't mean it like that." She braved his eyes.

"It wasn't your fault."

"I panicked. I blew the powder at you. It kind of was."

"Was it your fault the soldiers attacked me?"

"I alerted them to your presence."

He scowled. "Was it your fault I attacked them back?"

"I suppose not."

"You didn't ask them to torture me." He paused. "Did you?"

"No! God, no."

"God?"

"Oh... um... I mean... Well, no?" She shook her head disparagingly. That was all the proof Haze needed that she was human and from the old world. There were gods and goddesses now, depending on what fae race you belonged to. The goblins worshipped a giant subterranean wyrm.

The wolf shifters had some kind of she-wolf honored during the Lupercalia rites. Vampires prayed to a moon goddess. But there was no singular god. The closest fae folk had to one deity was the Well.

Peaches squirmed under his scrutiny, and he found he enjoyed bringing out the flush in her skin. His cock stirred at the thought of what else he could do to elicit that flush, but she was a distraction wrapped in a pretty package, put there by the queen.

He tried to get a fix on Peaches' motivation. Yes, she'd blown the powder at him, but he'd put the original occurrence down to him surprising her in her room. She didn't seem corrupt. Why did she do it the second time? Did she refuse to go with him because of some kind of standing bargain with the queen? Or was she an Unseelie loyalist? Would he have to forcibly remove her from this palace?

He inwardly cringed at the idea, let go of her hand, and pushed her away.

"I just want to help," she said, biting her lip. Seeing him unconvinced, she circled her fist over her heart in the hand-sign for an apology.

His frown deepened, and he took the sponge from her hands. "I don't need help. I'll be fine in a minute. Then we can get out of here."

Peaches eyed him warily. "We?"

"Yes, Sweetness. You and I will go to the Order."

"The queen won't like that."

He stared at her. "She won't know until it's too late."

"I'm not sure that's a good idea." She took the sponge back and dabbed his torso. He sucked in a hiss at the pressure on his fragile skin. "And... maybe I don't want to leave here."

"Why in Crimson's name not?"

She shrugged and plunged the sponge in the bowl, washed it, and then wrung it out. "I suppose the queen looks after me. I'm fed and no one hurts me here."

"So long as she's interested in you."

Dark chocolate eyes met his and held. She knew he was right. That much was clear in her expression, but there was something else she kept from him. The sadness etched deep in Peaches' eyes went soul deep. It plucked at a place between Haze's ribs—like calling to like—and reminded him of what happened to the last female whose sadness he'd brushed off as none of his business.

He wouldn't leave this woman here. She needed him.

Decision made, he slung his legs over the bed and hissed in pain as the sheet he lay on stuck to his back wounds. A string of curses unfit for females burst out. Peaches stepped back, eyes wide. Before he could utter a word of apology, she rallied and placed a palm on an unwounded part of his chest.

"Let me," she said.

Her touch was a brand, scoring beneath his skin, right through to the organ beneath that lay disused and wrapped in thorns. The air thickened. He glanced at her. She stared at her hand.

She felt a connection, too. An unseen spark. It made his every sense heighten. Her sweet scent. Her nearness. Her bated breath. He itched to cover her small palm with his, to keep it pressed to his heart. But he couldn't move. *Coward*.

Peaches saved him from humiliation and inspected the sheet stuck to his back. She clicked her tongue. "If you'd left it any longer, it might have dried enough to rip off skin."

"Not like I had a choice."

She hummed in understanding, then searched around the bed. "I need scissors. Or a knife."

"Where is Justice?"

"Pardon?"

"My hammer." He swept the room with a glance. "Or my uniform and weapons?"

"I don't know."

A low, gravely grumble of discontent came out of him. She took it personally and frowned again. He'd only meant to claim his gear and use the dagger that had been strapped to his ankle.

"Guess I'll just have to go easy then," she said. "You ready?"

She spilled water down his back, dousing the wounds and sheet. He squirmed as she gently plucked the sheet from his flesh. The pain he could handle. Her feather light touch, not so much. It fluttered over him, moving like the kiss of a butterfly from his back to his front—positioning him and holding him for support. Her scent drove into his lungs, making his mouth water and his fangs ache in his gums.

Thirsty.

"Almost done," she murmured, tugging. "There."

He virtually flew off the bed with the sheet gathered at his crotch. Towering over her and acutely aware of his hunger, he wrapped the sheet around his waist and stormed about the room, searching for gear. There was nothing draped on the chaise. Nothing in the closet except courtier outfits made of feathers, wool, and embroidered black velvet. His nose crinkled in disgust.

"Where is my uniform?" He shoved the high boots out of the way.

"I don't know..."

He rounded on her, boots in hands. She flinched. He angled his head toward a black glass mirror and saw a demon staring back at him. His eyes were fever bright. His face was haggard and drawn. And he was twice her size. Exhaling slowly, he forced himself to calm down. She wasn't the enemy, no matter her mistakes leading to his current state.

She was a blood slave. A timid one.

After a long pause, he spoke. "You were mistreated by my kind."

Her pale throat bobbed as she swallowed. "Yes."

"You don't trust me."

Glossy lips flattened. "I want to."

He tossed the boots back into the closet. "You

shouldn't trust anyone. But know this, little human. It is my job to protect the Well. The oath I made extends to those who are Well-blessed, such as yourself."

She snorted. "I have no mana. I can't be Well-blessed."

His gaze slid sideways to her as he plucked out a pair of breeches with laces at the crotch. At least the pants were his size. "So you admit you're human."

She stilled. He resumed his search in the closet for a pair of boots his size. He wanted her to feel comfortable with him.

"The queen knows, and she keeps my secret."

In other words, if Haze told anyone, the queen would not be happy.

"Because she wanted you all for herself," he reminded her, dropping a second set of boots next to the breeches. "Don't think she's doing it from some kind of altruistic place."

"At least I'm safe."

"Like I said"—he turned, giving her his back and then dropped the sheet to put on the pants—"you're safe as long as you hold her interest."

The last thing he wanted to do was forcibly remove the woman. He refused to be the source of more fear for her. She was too vulnerable. Perhaps he would stay for this party and prove to her that it was safe to go with him. It would also give him a chance to refill his inner Well and heal.

He searched the closet for a suitable tunic.

"I have ointment," she blurted.

"What?" He turned to her, a tunic dangling in his hand.

Still standing next to the bed, and still with her eyes low—where his buttocks had been, and now his groin—she held a pot of salve. There went that flush again. His lip twitched, wanting to smile.

"It's for your back," she explained.

He strode over and sniffed the salve. It smelled like something Elven healers used. He supposed if he was going to wait until morning, it wouldn't hurt to put it on. He sat on the edge of the bed and braced himself for her touch. He warned his prickly heart to not get excited lest the thorns around it bite. By the time she was done, he was tense and irritable. She smelled delicious. Sweet. Juicy.

Time to find something to drink. He tugged the thin, almost sheer black tunic on, silently repulsed at the fabric choice. It would rip if he sneezed.

"I want my uniform," he grumbled.

"I can ask about it."

He glanced at her as she washed her hands in the bowl before picking it up and walking to the door.

"I'll be back to feed you," she said.

He stood. "What?"

She knocked on the door to signal her exit and paused as a guard opened it.

"I'm going to feed you," she said to Haze.

"But you're the queen's."

"She believes sharing me with you will be a show of her

regret over my mistake."

The crow shifter guard outside held the door open with a raised brow, unapologetically eavesdropping. Haze snarled at him. Unruffled, the guard stared back. Typical crow, sticking his beak where it wasn't wanted.

"I'm not feeding from you," Haze said to Peaches. "I'll drink at the party."

The blush drained from Peaches' cheeks. "But... she insisted."

"No."

She opened her mouth, but he took the bowl from her and pushed out of the room, barging through with his broad shoulders. "I'll tell her myself if I have to."

The queen's behavior had been out of character. He'd actually expected to be whipped if caught in her territory unannounced, but sharing her personal food source, knowing he'd figure out what Peaches was, and then to hold a party for him... It was a game and she'd made her move. Haze might be a big brute according to some, but he was as good as any when it came to subterfuge.

If he'd had any doubts about staying the night, they were now gone. The Order suspected the queen was up to something, and Demeter was going to tell him. A Winter Court party would give him an opportunity to spy in the open. It would also help him keep Peaches safe. No one volunteered their private food source to feed someone like Haze without a reason. Especially when that food source was as attractive, addictive, and valuable as Peaches.

TEN

Peaches chased after Haze as he strode down the palace hallways. The guard he'd pushed past rushed to catch up. Two palace guards at the top of the long, spiral staircase blocked his way with crossed spears.

Haze stopped short. Dirty bowl water sloshed onto the floor and hit his boots. Even though no sun existed at the top of that platform, it felt as though the light hid behind a cloud. Darkness pressed against Peaches. When she glanced at Haze, murder leaked from his dark-eyed gaze.

Panic thumped in her chest. She was supposed to keep him in the room until the party started. Haze's pointed ears flattened slightly at the guards, reminding her of an animal in defensive mode. His muscles solidified, pushing the subtle glow of his prismatic power enhancing tattoos against his thin tunic. Movement at her feet caught her attention. Haze's shadow slithered out from beneath his body.

Peaches froze, wide eyes darting to the guards to see if they noticed.

"Move." Haze's deep voice rolled like thunder, a potent warning of the coming storm.

So sure of their authority within the queen's territory, they didn't blink. But Peaches did. All she could think of was the sound of that woman's neck snapping in the queen's chambers. Of how the drapes and carpet had eaten the sound so it seemed to disappear as though it had never existed. Shuddering, Peaches placed a hesitant palm between Haze's shoulder blades. Strength and power rolled beneath her hand. He was hot and twitching for battle.

"Please," she whispered. "We should go back to the room until the party."

"Listen to your little pix," a staircase guard sneered. "Guardians aren't welcome here."

"Does it look like I give a shit?" Haze snarled.

The room guard stepped between those at the staircase and Haze, then puffed out his chest. He poked Haze in the chest. "We may have let you out of the dungeon, but you're still a coin-grubbing scumbag."

Haze glared at that finger like he wanted to eat it. His shadow circled the group, ready to pounce. The room guard's bravery turned shallow, and he paled under the reminder of Haze's power, of his status as one of the feared Twelve.

Peaches rubbed her temples. This was going to get messy if someone didn't give.

"Am I a prisoner?" Haze questioned, the promise of pain in his tone.

The guards shared a nervous glance.

"No," said one, swallowing. "But you're not free to roam the palace unchaperoned."

"Fine. Take this." Haze shoved the bowl at them. They panicked, and both scrambled to catch it with a grimace. Water spilled. Haze used the opportunity to barge past and step down the staircase. He glanced up at Peaches before continuing to walk down, tossing his next words over his shoulder. "Where's the kitchen?"

"Ground floor," she replied, hurrying after him.

"Five floors down. Fuck me," he mumbled as he descended. Haze's shadow moved a heartbeat behind her, almost as if it protected her rear.

Flushed and floundering, the room guard straightened his spine before following Haze, hurrying to get before him on the steps.

If Haze refused to drink from Peaches, then the queen would be angry, and that didn't bode well for her neck. Her only alternative was to trust Haze's promise to keep her safe. He seemed unaffected by the fact that she'd called the guards on him, or that she'd blown the sleeping powder—an event that resulted in his torture. But what if it was too late for trust? That portal stone was gone, along with his hammer and uniform.

What was a Guardian without his mana or weapons? Even if Haze had good intentions, he might not be such a safe bet.

God, she was such a coward. If she'd been brave enough to take his hand in the first place, she would have been out of there by now, possibly meeting other humans like her. Maybe. A bad feeling bloomed in her gut, but she kept pace with Haze and stayed close.

Meeting them at the kitchen door was the palace steward, Cyril—a portly fae with black feathers for hair and eyebrows. Peaches had always assumed he was a crow shifter from the look of him, but that had never been confirmed. When the world evolved during the nuclear winter, and DNA mutated with the magic of the Well, sometimes the result was neither human nor animal looking, but something in between. There were even humans who'd merged with plants. Peaches had heard of Oak Men who lived in the woods, part tree and part man.

Even though he was a lesser fae, Cyril didn't need mana to intimidate. His abrasive personality was enough. He'd been the royal steward for as long as Peaches had been there.

"Stop," Cyril chirped, looking up into Haze's determined face. "You cannot come in here. Turn back."

"I'm getting a little tired of being told what to do."

"The kitchen is off limits to guests."

"Perhaps you can feed me, then." Haze bared his fangs.

Cyril turned his judgement on Peaches. "Has she not offered a vein?"

Peaches wanted to shrink into the floor.

"I'm saving her for the party," he said.

"Then we will see you in the quartz ballroom in half an hour."

Haze spun around, almost bowling into Peaches. He steadied her. Their eyes met briefly, and then he plucked at his tunic with annoyance before glaring at the crow shifter. "Take me to my hammer and uniform."

The guard smiled. "No can do. We have a strict no weapons policy inside the castle. You'll get it when you leave."

"And when will that be?" Haze's eyes narrowed.

The guard shrugged. "Not my job."

A low, exasperated "fuck me" slipped out of Haze's mouth. He studied Peaches intently before motioning back to the staircase.

She didn't believe he would truly drink from her at the party, but there was no other way this would work. He needed to feed by the end of the night, or she would be in trouble. Neck-snapping trouble.

The moment Haze's back was turned, Cyril grabbed Peaches by the upper arm, his talons sticking into her skin. She knew better than to make a sound as he whispered in her ear, "You better get him to feed from you, pix... or else."

Cyril shoved her forward, enough to make her stumble.

Haze turned sharply, his profile a study in caution. Cyril walked away without a backward glance. Haze's eyes tracked him until he disappeared through the kitchen door.

"Your room," Haze clipped to Peaches.

The guard shrugged. "If you want to slum it in her room to feed, then be my guest."

"Wasn't asking permission." Haze shoved past him, this time taking Peaches' hand and keeping her by his side.

One of his long strides was two of hers. One of his thighs was the size of her waist. And his ass… she blushed again as she remembered him dressing. His ass was two globes of perfectly defined, smooth muscle. She couldn't get the picture out of her head and patted her forehead, already feeling sweat dappling there.

The entire walk down into the basement levels made her sweat even more. The guard's attention pressed in on her the entire journey. He tried to follow them into her room, but Haze blocked him, stating he wanted privacy for feeding.

The guard peered around Haze's shoulders and gave her room a once-over, checking the corners before backing out. "I'll be right out—"

Haze shut the door in his face.

Peaches raced to pick up the clothes she'd discarded during the day. After being summoned to see the queen, she'd caught little sleep. When she'd awoken, she'd had no time to tidy or make the bed.

"It's cold in here," Haze noted, looking around.

"There's no fireplace." Her apologetic smile seemed to anger him, and she felt even more inadequate.

His laser sharp attention cast about, picking up details. It was as though he touched everything with his gaze, turned it over and inspected it, casting a spotlight into the shadow. "You would get a fireplace at the Order. I would make sure of it."

She tugged on the neck of her dress, exposing the queen's favorite place to feed. While vampires had the ability to anesthetize with their saliva before biting, most didn't. Not when they thought her beneath them. Most of Peaches' scars had been erased by a healer upon arrival at the palace. Except the queen's favorite spot, and the glamor of pixie wing scars at her back.

Peaches tensed, preparing herself to count down the seconds. *It will only sting for a moment—hopefully—then he will lap at the skin for a few more. Don't think about his size, how he dwarves me, or how a small bite to him might be a gouge to me.*

"Which vein?" she asked.

"I'm not feeding from you," he sighed and rested his head in his hands. "Not now. Not ever."

She flinched. "Why? Because—"

"Shh." He glowered and walked about the room. He made strange hand-signs with his fingers. His tattoos flared, brightening the oil slick pattern. Energy hummed in the room, tingling her tongue as though she'd licked a battery. The rhythm and speed of his movements varied, reminding her of a sweeping dance or Tai-chi. Fascinated at his nimble fingers, she forgot to speak until he completed his walk about the small room and motioned to her. "Now you can talk."

"What was that?" Her eyes were still stuck on his hands, on how gracefully they'd moved, proving that they weren't just for killing, but perhaps something sweeter. She thought about the way he'd held her hand during the walk here. His touch had been gentle and warm.

"I created wards," he replied.

"Using your mana?"

He nodded.

"I've never seen it done before. Is it always so beautiful?"

A flicker of self-disparagement ghosted his expression. "Beautiful?"

"Yes. Beautiful."

His piercing gaze went straight to the epicenter of all that she was, trailing shivers down her spine. It was almost as though he stood behind her and ran his fingers down her back... or maybe his shadow did. She turned and cast her eye about, but found his shadow pooled at his feet like an obedient dog.

"Not all Guardians or Mages use this finger method of casting spells," Haze explained. "Someone taught it to me when I was younger. She had trouble weaving mentally."

"Weaving?"

"Moving currents of mana in the air to form a spell is called weaving. Some people can do this with only their mind. Depending on our affinities, we can direct the flow accordingly. You'll learn your affinities when you get to the Order."

"That's where you're wrong. I'm not like you." Longing ached in her chest, and she once again wished she wasn't human. She wished she was fae. Leaving with him wouldn't be so scary then, not if she could protect herself with magic. That reminded her of her duty.

"Please, will you feed? You're hungry."

"No."

"Why? Because you'll get drunk?"

He looked at her as if it was obvious. "I can handle a little inebriation. I won't feed from you because you've been abused, Peaches. I'm not going to add to the list."

That was not the answer she expected. No one had cared about her feelings in this time since Violet and Silver. Especially not a vampire. She didn't know what to do with his words. They were true. She had been abused in the most horrendous, nightmarish ways. Before coming to the queen, she'd been owned by a depraved and enterprising Autumn Court prince. But she also knew that it could have been worse. Much worse. Like, Sluagh kind of worse. Or the never-ending screams from the dungeons kind of worse.

"I don't mind," she said softly. "I've gotten used to it."

"To the abuse?"

"You know what I mean. It's not so bad now. The queen only feeds from me every other month. No one else touches me."

"Mm-hm," he added incredulously and arched a brow. "But she's forcing you to feed me. And how long were you her personal blood slave?"

"A couple of years." Unease crept up her spine as she realized where he was going with this.

"You're her property, Peaches. Her chattel. Like a cow or a pig, you're her thing to pass around at the dinner table."

Tears burned her eyes, and she hugged herself. So what if she was? The alternative had been worse. She wasn't strong enough to protect herself, not against high fae—those with abundant mana. He sighed at her hurt expression and looked away. She watched him scrub his shaved head and stare at the floor, thinking.

"Haze," she said. "About the sleeping powder, I'm..." She hand signed her apology.

"The steward said you had to feed me, or else. What did he mean by that?"

"You heard that?" Blood drained from her face.

"Of course I heard." His ears twitched as if to remind her he was a vampire. They were incredible hunters because they could hear so well, use echo-location, and smell prey from miles away on a dark windy night. "I'm not stupid. The queen wants my guard lowered at this party. Probably to work out my true reason for infiltrating her palace. The question I need answered is whether Demeter has turned on me, or whether he needs to be extracted too."

"I can't answer that. I don't know."

"Do you know what she's making in her basement? Do you know if she's perverting the Well? Do you know if she's trying to start a war?"

Peaches' mind cast back to all that she'd seen and done while being in this palace. The truth was that she witnessed very little out of the ordinary. There were screams in the dungeon. She'd always put them down to prisoners being tortured, but maybe they were something else. Haze took her silence as ignorance.

"I want to take you with me, but she can't know that, or she will double her efforts to stop me."

"Why are you so forthcoming with me? You don't even know me."

"Every Well-blessed human I've met has worked with us at the Order. You eventually will too."

Her eyes narrowed over his confidence... or was it arrogance?

Why did he keep insisting she was so relevant to the Well? Apart from ripping Peaches from her time, the Well had wanted nothing to do with her.

"You're right," she said. "You're not stupid. And you're definitely a lot smarter than they give you credit for."

"Sweetness, I'm a lot of everything." He flashed fangs in what she guessed was his version of a grin, but it was wilder... more feral. It hit the button on her desire, heating parts of her body that hadn't fired in years.

She dropped her gaze first. The tangible shift in the air made her squirm. Unable to stand the scrutiny, she went to her dresser and lined up her rock collection. He came up behind her, his big body crowding her in. Haze was in her every breath.

"Come to the Order, Peaches. I'll keep you safe. You have my word as a Guardian."

She wanted to believe him. She wanted to go with him. But that old devil on her shoulder kept screaming at her. *You've been safe enough here.* Prince Luthian couldn't get to her here. No one could. *Don't ruin it because a strong, sexy, fearsome warrior is offering protection.* She still didn't know a damned thing about him. The queen made threats all the time when it came to Peaches. She hadn't followed through with any because, unlike the human she'd killed in her chambers, there weren't many like Peaches around. She was Well-blessed, whatever that meant.

Her movements with the rocks became jerky, but they grounded her, so she kept rearranging them. Each rock represented a family member she'd lost. She lined them up according to age. Last week, it had been height. Halmi, her grandmother, was the eldest. Her rock was a yellow quartz, reminding her of Halmi's sunshine smile. Halbi, her grandfather, was already deceased before the nuclear winter had hit, but she had a rock for him too. A purple amethyst that reminded her of his ugly purple sweater he loved to wear so much.

"Say the word, Peaches, and we can leave right now."

"How?" she whispered.

"I'll find a way."

So cocky. It was harder to get out of this palace than he thought. Her fingers clenched, sharp rock cutting into her. "I can't."

"Because you're afraid of Maebh?"

She dropped the rock and faced him with sadness in her eyes. "You have no idea what it's like for me. After being ripped away from everything, I've finally found a place I feel safe. Everyone I knew and loved is gone. *Everyone.* My dad. My mom. My brother. Even my new friends from this time. I won't give this small haven up for someone I've just met. I don't even know why I'm telling you this."

Shadows crossed his expression. She could feel an acerbic retort waiting on his pointed vampire tongue, but he bit it back. Instead, he said, "The queen is up to something that will result in death for everyone in Elphyne. Our psychics have seen it. One of them is Clarke, a Well-blessed human from your time. She's a pain in my ass, but she's usually right. So, yeah, Sweetness. You should tell me everything you know."

He pressed forward, using his size to intimidate her, pushing her against the dresser. Her hands flew up to protect herself, but ended up resting on his hard stomach, feeling his heat seep into her skin through that damned thin tunic. God, she could see the outline of his abs, the lines of his tattoos, and the small dusting of hair trailing down into his pants.

Touching him was basking in the sun on a cool autumn day.

He slid fingers along her chin and guided her to look into his eyes. Perhaps he was going to say something, but he'd stilled, his gaze caught on her neck, on the vein pulsing there. His lids drooped lazily and she felt his hunger like flames against her skin.

"Drink," she urged, and tapped a finger on her vein. "And do it somewhere your bite can be seen."

He snapped. A breathy snarl ripped out of him. He lifted her like she weighed nothing to plant her on the dresser, displacing rocks and knickknacks. For some reason, she didn't care. All she wanted was to stare into his eyes. *Maybe he's mesmerizing me.* But mesmerization had never really worked on her, just as healers had trouble removing her scars. She'd always wondered if it was the old, plastic contraceptive implant in her arm, but dismissed it as being too small.

Besides, this want in her belly could not be forced. Her legs widened, her thigh exposed through the slit in her dress. A wildness came over his expression. Hunger. Need. Fever-eyed, he positioned her and dragged his nose along her neck, along the vein.

Her skin buzzed with awareness of him. He consumed

the air by her skin, running the tip of his nose along the erogenous zone behind her ear. A rush of heat pulsed between her legs and an embarrassing moan slipped from her lips. This was not good. She shouldn't be melting like this.

This was a transaction—her eyelids fluttered as she felt the press of his warm tongue on her flesh—the contrast of rasp and wet. Was he taking the time to numb her?

No. She was a quick meal for him. That was all. *Stay focused.*

But she couldn't. All she could think of was, what would it feel like to be cherished by him? To make love to him? All the strength she felt under her hands. How would that power flex? Would he move her as he wanted in a bed, or would he allow her to take the reins? Would they fit? She gasped as he splayed his hand on her lower back—his hand span almost reaching across the entire breadth of her body. He tugged her to the edge of the dresser, pressing their bodies together.

Then he stepped back, ghosts in his eyes. "We should go to this party."

"But..." Her hand went to her neck. The flesh remained unbroken. "Aren't you hungry?"

"I'll be fine until we get back to the Order later tonight." He moved to the door, placed his hand on the knob. "I told you, I won't feed from you."

ELEVEN

Haze arrived at the quartz ballroom filled with seductively posed half-naked fae and human thralls in the grip of Maebh's impenetrable mind. The latter were noticeable, not only because of their poorly dressed and malnourished figures, but because of the way their smiles stretched impossibly across their faces while their eyes silently screamed. Unlike the fae, they wore no masks, their humiliation on display for all to see.

These humans had most likely dared to steal and raid Unseelie land for resources. Maebh believed harsh and humbling punishment would stave off another war.

Haze knew the truth. She was a sadist. And curiously, since the Seelie High King had died a few turns of the moon back, she seemed to be getting worse. It almost made Haze think there had been a romantic relationship between the two. Or, on the flip side, some kind of hold the king had on her was now gone.

Whatever the case, this palace was no place for Peaches. It was twisted nightmares and cold stone. Peaches was none of those things. He had to convince her to see she was better off leaving with him by the end of the night, or he would remove her by force.

Her lingering scent still watered his tongue. She had been a temptation he'd almost claimed, despite knowing her blood would enslave him, just as Indigo had been after tasting Queen Ada. The vampire hadn't been able to fly straight without jonesing for another hit of the unique blood.

That Maebh could drink from Peaches and resist falling into a puddle of salacious need was a testament to her power. She was as old as the Prime of the Order of the Well, and rumor had it they'd existed since the dawn of Elphyne. At least since Crimson Jackson's discovery of the Well.

Unseelie gentry spilled into the ballroom under the lullaby of haunting flute music. Each wore a mask hiding their identity, freeing them for a night of promised debauchery and celebration. They gathered around performers entwined in ribbons dangling from enormous antlers on the ceiling. From the performers' glazed eyes and writhing bodies, they were already under the influence of divilixir—an Elvish aphrodisiac that worked not only to lower inhibitions but to increase sexual appetite... for hours. Servers prowled the room with trays balanced in clawed hands, handing out the blue liquor and animal themed masks.

Haze was a head taller than most. Peaches' height ended at his sternum. He glanced down at her delicate body wrapped in that enticing dress, her flesh on display for all to desire. He had the sudden urge to go back to her room and put her in the velvet dress she'd worn the first day they'd met. At least it had covered her body. *If any male touched her...*

"Stay close," he ordered. "And don't drink the blue stuff."

"This isn't my first rodeo."

"Rodeo?"

"Nothing..." she mumbled, and selected a white fox half-mask from a basket provided by a human thrall before holding it against her face. Her lips parted as though she wanted to say something, then shut them. Finally, she braved his eyes. "Are you trying to protect my dignity, Guardian?"

He almost snatched her mask, crumpled it, and forbade her to partake in the festivities, but kept his balled fists at his side.

"I'm trying to keep you—"

His mind stuttered. *Was* he trying to protect her dignity? He made a low grunt of frustration. Perhaps he was. He knew exactly what went on at this sort of wild party, and even though he'd just met Peaches, she was his to protect. At least until they made it back to the safety of the Order. The thought of her delicate fingers touching any of these disgusting perverts made his skin crawl.

At the insistence of the server, he shoved a mask over his face. After it settled across his forehead and nose, he tried to adjust it and realized it wouldn't budge.

"What the fuck?" He tugged it again. No luck.

"Don't worry about that," Peaches said, inspecting him. "It's spelled to stay on, but will come off at the end of the night. Privacy reasons. Plus... it looks good on you."

"What is it?" He hadn't paid attention before putting it on.

Her half-smile made him forget he'd asked a question. All he could think of was kissing those lips. He tugged at his collar and realized she'd just spoken. "What?"

"I said your mask is a bull's head. With horns. Ahem. Really... girthy horns." She smiled and brought his hands up to feel them—two smooth and fat conical lengths. "It suits you."

"A bull?"

"Yes, it's virile." She blushed and turned away.

Feeling his own cheeks heat—something he couldn't remember ever doing—he joined her in surveying the room. The ballroom seemed tame right now, but in an hour or so, masks and elixirs ensured all would throw inhibitions to the wind. In two hours, class and restraint would completely leave the building. It would become a free-for-all sex dungeon on steroids. Rough, sharp, bloody, and insatiable. Powerful elite would prey on those who'd ingested the elixir, or anyone considered weak. Morality would become a memory as they took as they pleased.

Unable to stop himself, and maybe because he liked it, he glanced down at Peaches' silken hair, her cream shoulders, and glimpsed that gap between her buttocks. He wanted to put his face right there. To trace his nose along that line and see if there was a vein nearby.

With a growl, he wrenched his eyes away and glowered at anyone looking at them, wondering again about the intensity of his feelings for her. These possessive thoughts weren't normal. He was thinking like a mated male, and vampires *rarely* mated. But he'd never fit the mold of a perfect vampire.

"This is female business. Go and let us do our job."

"I should be in there helping."

He shook the memory away and focused on his feelings in the present. Possessive mating feelings. All three wolf shifters in the Cadre of Twelve had recently mated, each with one of these Well-blessed females from the old world. Before then, it was unheard of for a Guardian to take a mate. But after Clarke joined their ranks, she'd foretold of many more like her to wake in this time.

Could that mean more were destined for each Guardian in the Twelve?

All he knew was that his impulses skewed around Peaches. Something like nerves started in Haze's stomach, but he smothered them with a cold dose of reality. If anyone in the cadre was going to mate, it wouldn't be the vampires. Indigo's parents were amongst the handful in the entire vampire community committed and in a monogamous relationship. The rest of their race was promiscuous by nature. The males fertilized. The females raised the pups.

"You did your job. Now it's our turn."

Haze snarled inwardly at the painful memory, trying to take root. Why now? Why was he dwelling on that time? It had no place in this ballroom. He occupied himself with scanning the room and assessing potential danger. If tonight went sour, he would need a quick escape.

Black clad guards were posted around the perimeter of the ballroom, manning exits between velvet curtains on quartz walls shimmering with veins of trapped manabeeze. The only other light came from candelabras on sporadically placed tall tables. No windows. The ceiling was closed and with sculptured antlers wrapped in thorns. Scattered about the room were leather settees. The performers' thick red ribbons spilled down like streams of fresh blood, a reminder of the dark and twisted possibilities for the night.

Revelers gave Haze and Peaches a wide berth as they walked further onto the floor. His mask covered his Guardian tattoo, but not his size. He looked even bigger next to Peaches' petite form.

Haze sought out the queen, wondering what her true intention was, because it sure as the Well wasn't to apologize for his mistreatment. Perhaps this party was because

Jasper recently humiliated her in front of her court, and she intended to do the same to him. Or maybe she truly tried to woo him because anything else—like the mild torture she claimed she had no hand in—would incur the wrath of the Order.

No. Maebh was hiding something. Something she didn't want them to know about, hence this party. A distraction.

That was the only logical thing he could think of.

Unseelie Lords and Ladies hid behind half-face masks of foxes, rats, and birds. Their fingers wrapped around crystal goblets twinkling with inner starlight. Their gazes glued to the ribbons entwining the performing fae, probably hoping to catch a glimpse of the erotic appetizer before the main event. But like breaking through cocoons, the writhing hosts only revealed a flash of naked flesh to tease, a moan, or a groan within. It was all designed to increase the tension. The tease of the butterfly.

The queen would say when.

She wasn't even here. The royal dais stood empty and barren. Only a ruby encrusted obsidian chair existed there, waiting for its occupant.

Servers glided about, holding trays laden with glass goblets and food. No blood. Since the queen herself was a blood-drinker, the absence of this liquid was sorely noted. Maebh definitely wanted him out of his wits or drinking without consent from a guest. His gut twinged with the sense of walking into a trap. The urge to leave surged through him.

He touched Peaches gently on the shoulder, about to reveal his intentions, but a well dressed and tanned elf with long copper hair blocked her. Freckles on his nose and diamonds on his arched ears. Blue eyes full of self-importance. A wreath of twisted branches with seven embroidered leaves covered the breast of his brown coat. One leaf was white instead of orange, signaling he was one of the seven children of the Autumn Court crown. Royalty, and D'arn Forrest's older brother. Their looks were where the similarities ended. Forrest was nothing like his family. They'd sacrificed him to the Well at the age of twelve, not caring if he'd survive, but only of the appearance of being loyal to the Well.

Being separated from that family was the best thing that had happened to Forrest. Or Aeron, for that matter. He'd followed Forrest into the ceremonial lake for reasons unknown to anyone but the two of them.

"Well, well," drawled the elf, his lecherous gaze on Peaches. He plucked a mask from a basket as a server walked by. "I wasn't going to partake in tonight's activities, but suddenly I'm finding myself frisky as a fox."

Peaches tensed. "Prince Luthian. I'm surprised to see you here."

He secured his mask—a red furred fox with yellow ears—and patted his chest with mock shock. "I'm surprised you remember me."

"You owned me for two years. You're a little hard to forget."

Haze's blood boiled. He might drink tonight, after all. Red foxes were particularly tasty.

Luthian glanced at Haze, but unlike the rest of the room, he wasn't ruffled. Royals had a habit of believing they were untouchable. There was nothing Haze enjoyed more than bringing them down a notch. He considered making his Guardian status known, but held back. The shock might come in handy later.

"Two years?" Luthian caught a lock of Peaches' hair. Her flinch made Haze clench his fists. Luthian smiled. "Seems shorter than that. A pity. We weren't done playing with you, *Peach*."

A tall, tawny-skinned female sidled up to Luthian and secured a rabbit mask over a severely cut black bob. Her sheer lace dress hid nothing. Nipples. Belly button. Pubic hair waxed into the shape of a heart. He saw it all.

She eyed Haze from top to bottom, her blood-red lips curving in approval.

"The name's Wisteria," she drawled, and then shifted judgmental eyes to Peaches. "You've certainly traded up. I can see why you left our court."

Peaches took a step backward, closer to Haze.

He lifted his nose and scented the air around the new female. Fresh blood on her breath. Vampire. Wisteria and Luthian had *owned* Peaches. And if so, Wisteria must have tasted enough to realize Peaches wasn't a pixie. Alarm bells triggered in Haze's mind.

Luthian leaned closer to Peaches and stage whispered, "Does he know how tasty you are, *Peach*? How much a single drop of you is worth?"

Wisteria's expression darkened. "You cost us a lot of coin when you left. I hope you know that."

Haze wanted to crush their throats. To feel tendons and muscle fold like paper. He wanted to feel the warmth of their blood flowing over his fingers. But before Haze could act out his fantasy, a murmur crossed the room like a chilling breeze. All heads swiveled toward the entrance. Those dangling from ribbon cocoons stopped twirling. Stopped writhing.

Around the room, frost manifested along hems and twinkled in hair. Icicles formed on the ceiling and pointed down like daggers. A hush. A collectively held cloudy breath. And then the Unseelie High Queen made her grand entrance.

Haze pulled Peaches to his front. She melted into him without a question, a fact that made his chest swell. Luthian and his lady companion gave him a curious look, and then all eyes were on Maebh as she glided across the floor toward her dais, her white voluminous skirt tinkling like broken shards of ice. She left a trail of snow in her wake.

A crown of ruby encrusted antlers and thorns rested on her long afro hair, plaited and twisted into lengths dangling down to her hips. A corset pushed her ample bosom up. A shimmering pearlescent substance coated her brown skin, giving a frost-touched look to her cheeks and purple lips. The ice queen had come out to play. A beautiful monster.

Maebh sat regally, and her *amados*, her harem, gathered around her with eyes forward and unflinching. Four, Haze counted, each wearing white leather pants with cutouts displaying plump and dimpled bare bottoms. Each wore masks, hiding their identities. The males had bulls, a fact that made Haze's temper flare. No others in the room wore bull masks. The queen must have had it given to him on purpose. Another step to unsettle him and throw him off guard.

Haze focused on the other fae on the dais—three serious guards in royal garb, black and red mantles flowing down from their shoulders, weapons at their belts. Among them, Demeter studiously avoided Haze's eyes. Finding a moment alone with him would be hard.

Peaches pressed into Haze's front as one last soldier stalked into the room, almost forgotten as the crowd had already begun to close ranks after the queen's walk.

Even though it was a futile act in a room of sharp-eared fae, Haze tried to keep his words quiet when he lowered his head to Peaches. "You know Gastnor?"

She gave an almost imperceptible nod, but didn't elaborate. Maebh's eyes tracked around the room, searching until they landed on him and crinkled with mirth. She lifted one black-stained fingertip and crooked it, calling him forward.

Fucking bull mask.

Gritting his teeth, Haze slid his hand from Peaches' sternum and placed it at the small of her back to guide her forward and away from the greedy eyes of a certain copper-haired fox. He wasn't sure the icy stare of the queen was much better. But he had no choice.

He stopped before the dais, but didn't bow. His lack of respect didn't go unnoticed. Interestingly, Demeter placed his palm on the pommel of his bone sword and stepped forward. When he met eyes with Haze, nothing but a blank expression came through. Nothing Haze could decipher. Not to be outdone, Gastnor took two steps. Except his scarred face glared at Peaches.

Haze's lips curved at the challenge.

Go on. Give me an excuse.

Maebh lifted her palm, staying the both of them. Her words were to Haze. "Your attitude tires me. We're here to put all that behind us. To celebrate."

"And what exactly are we celebrating?" he asked, still feeling the pinch of welts along his torso.

She smiled enigmatically and then narrowed her gaze on Peaches' untouched neck before sliding back to him. "Did my gift offend you?"

"You know why I refrain."

"Do I?" She leaned forward in her throne. "Because snubbing my gift means there is bad blood between us—

between the Order and the Unseelie."

He ground his teeth until his fangs cut the inside of his bottom lip, drawing copper, making his stomach lurch. The queen had kept Peaches' identity secret all these years. She wasn't about to let him shout it to the icicle antlers. But she did want to test him. To push him and make him uncomfortable.

If he snubbed her gift, he advertised there was an issue. He cast his gaze over the room. Guests openly watched their exchange from their stations around circular tables with candelabra centerpieces.

"She's your personal blood slave," he said. "I didn't think you the type to share."

Maebh sat back in her chair, her face blank, but Haze could feel her wrath in the chill in the air. Like termites emerging from the woodwork, hidden soldiers appeared in the corners of the room and between the crowd. Too many. The only way out of this tonight would be to play along with Maebh's game.

The hairs on the back of his neck lifted with Maebh's next words and the wave of her hand. "I don't like your answer. Your voice is hereby removed."

Shock barreled through him as he tried to reply, but couldn't. His words had no sound. She'd silenced him. He glared at her, silently sending her the most vitriolic thoughts and hoping she died from them. This was *not* okay.

She cocked her head. "You'll get it back, of course, *after* you accept my gift, because doing so is a sign of good faith. Don't you agree?"

He glared. So now she'd stripped him of identity, ensuring he could no longer get word out about his location to the Order. He doubted any of her soldiers or staff who'd recognized him would tell. This was her plan from the start.

"Nod your understanding." She waved her fingers up and down, her power forcing his chin to do the same. "Good. Now... do go and enjoy yourself. Dance. Drink. Be merry."

Although her words were directed at him, Maebh stared hard at Peaches.

This night was not going to end well.

TWELVE

For almost an hour, Peaches sat at the foot of the queen's dais, waiting to be called to serve her purpose—being Haze's meal. Just like the human thralls, sitting with their screaming eyes, Peaches was instructed to do nothing.

The queen was acting weird.

There had been a time she'd tried to wring Peaches for information about the current whereabouts of Violet and Silver, but after one of her Sluagh looked into Peaches' mind and found nothing—literally nothing beyond their original encounter—the queen's interest in Peaches became more gastronomical than anything else. But tonight, she hadn't once called Peaches to her throne for a feed.

Peaches had thought that her special blood would keep her protected, but now she wasn't so sure. It irked that

Haze had been right, that Maebh only protected Peaches while she felt like it. Soon her interest would run out.

A wave of self-loathing washed over Peaches, and her throat closed up. She bit her tongue to stop tears forming. Nothing much had changed since the moment she'd awoken in this time. From a prisoner held in a cage, to being fed on by multiple vampires, to being beaten when she talked out of turn, to being kept as a plaything by a rich, spoiled elvish prince and his vampire lover. Peaches shrunk into herself. She was too much of a coward to do anything but put up with it all.

A server walked past. With a scowl, she nabbed a glass of something that looked like a trapped galaxy. Purple and blue liquid swirled with little sparkling bubbles. She just wanted to forget about everything. If there was proper booze here, she would drown her misery. The galaxy drink couldn't be worse than divilixir, could it?

She tentatively lifted the glass to her lips, but as her eyes dipped to the liquid, a layer of ice formed, crusting over the surface, preventing the liquid from sloshing into her mouth. Frowning, she glanced up at the queen and startled to find dark eyes speared her way. Maebh turned back to the private performance in front of her. A nude male elf tumbled out of a ribbon along with other unfurling acrobats moving to the rhythm of a pan flute and drum. The tempo lifted and dropped artfully in time with the performers as they danced around each other, giving each other lingering looks and touches that would soon turn hot.

Peaches had seen this performance before. It wasn't so shocking the second or third time around. She placed the frozen glass on her lap and deflated. So she wasn't even allowed to use the substance to numb herself. Unease swirled in her stomach, making her feel ill. She wanted to leave.

Unwittingly, she sought out a tall shaved head and bull horns amongst the revelers. She found Haze by a table with a candelabra; the flames flickering high and painting his stern profile in golden hues. The tendons in his jaw popped as he nodded to two talking and masked elves, one female and one male. Was he getting propositioned? Was he the type to participate in tonight's events? All that power, muscle, and strength practically burst from his clothing. Of course, a male like that would have females—and males—tripping over to please him.

Why did she even care? He'd turned up in her room and had tried to kidnap her.

But had he really?

It wasn't as though he'd forced her. In fact, he might be the only fae who *hadn't* tried to force her into doing something she wasn't ready for. As if sensing her attention, he glanced at her, his eyes narrowing before returning to the elf. He'd been doing that a lot. Each time Peaches' stomach did a little flip thing.

To the left of the queen, a dance floor filled with fae,

and some kind of waltz began. Even though the Unseelie were often cruel and deceptive, they danced gloriously. Hands teased. Hips swayed. Lips lingered near ears. Longing pierced her numbness. To be included as one of their own, she'd glamored her hair and teeth. It was never enough. She would always be here on the floor, treated like a pet. Unless... she glanced at Haze again.

Biting her nails, she became lost in her thoughts as a server stopped before her with only a single glass filled with blue liquid. He held it out to her. She shook her head. "I'm good."

"Compliments of the queen," the server insisted.

"Oh?"

"She said, and I quote, 'I'd hate to see my special one miss out on the festivities tonight.'"

Shit.

That could mean only one thing.

The queen must have thought if Peaches sat with the other blood slaves and thralls, Haze would eventually return to her to drink. But he hadn't. Now the queen was tired of waiting. She wanted Peaches to go to Haze.

She smiled tightly and replaced the frozen glass in her lap with the new one. There would be no way out of this. Whatever game the queen was playing was being stepped up. Peaches was a pawn, the unwilling honey trap, and since mesmerization didn't work on Peaches, elixir and veiled threats were the next best thing.

Well—she stood up—wasn't she just saying she

wanted to drown her misery? A glass of this would make the night pass in a blink of an eye. There were worse to seduce than a chivalrous Guardian with buns of steel. At least this way she would please the queen. And at least she would have something to blame other than herself when regret kicked in the next morning. She tipped the liquid down her throat just as she noticed a particular old goblin minus his red cap waddle her way.

"You did *not* just drink what I saw you drink," Balos grumbled at her.

She licked the sweet liquor off her lips. It tasted pretty good, actually. It had gone down the hatch like warm honey, already spreading to her extremities and making her feel... tingly.

"I didn't have a choice," she said with a little shiver running through her body.

Dark, bushy gray brows lowered. "Stupid pix. You want to end up being fed to the wyrm?"

She burped, her head already spinning. "What?"

"I thought you had more sense than to lose your wits at one of these things. Haven't you ever noticed that some guests arrive but some never leave?"

"These parties are just rich people doing stupid things."

"Exactly." He gave her judgmental eyes. "You'll be tingling like a tinger in no time."

She bristled and lifted her chin. "I don't have to explain myself to you. You're not my father."

"No." He eyed her with disappointment. "If I was, you would certainly have more sense."

"And if I was your daughter, you'd certainly venture out of your cave more! And you'd remember to feed your-self." She narrowed her eyes. "Why *are* you here?"

A guilty look flashed over his wrinkled face. "None of your business."

"Ew. Gross. I don't want to know."

The broken capillaries in the goblin's cheeks grew brighter and he stuttered. "It's n-nothing like that."

"Sure. Sure it's not." She flexed her fingers. Her limbs felt loose.

"I'm here because the queen—" He clamped his lips closed so hard that spittle flew out.

Peaches sighed. "Say no more. I have one of those queenly things to do as well."

She thumped her chest as another tiny burp popped up. The thump set her spine tingling… all the way to that precious spot between her legs. *Jesus.* This worked fast. She searched the room for that perfect shaped head with bull horns, and then said to Balos, "Wish me luck."

"Luck is for the blind."

She blinked at him, then realized he waited for her to finish his proverb. "And prosperity is for the brave. Got it."

THIRTEEN

Haze had half the night to get through, and then if he couldn't catch Demeter on his own, he would find a way to leave this Well-forsaken place with Peaches in tow. While she'd been thankfully relegated to the queen's dais, he'd casually walked around the room and hunted for portal stones. His shadow looked in pockets while he nodded to ridiculous conversation as though he actually cared.

So far, no portal stones.

But all wasn't lost. His mana had refilled enough to shift his wings out and fly home. At this point, he was just collecting surplus. Trapped manabeeze in veins in the walls helped keep the connection to the Well ever present in the room, despite them being levels above ground. This kind of blended mana architecture gained its roots in the Unseelie kingdom, but it had spread throughout Elphyne.

He'd hoped for a quiet moment with Demeter, but the vampire studiously stood behind Maebh's right shoulder, eager eyes on his liege and the performance before them.

"Like I said—" A badger-masked elf leaned toward Haze, almost falling in his inebriation. "I 'spect the Well. I do."

Haze was only half listening. The other half was on Peaches, wondering why she had that forlorn look on her face.

"No." The elf laughed and then hiccuped. "Not s'pect. S'pect." A snort. "Y'know?"

There was no point letting the elf know the queen had taken his voice. If he hadn't caught it when it happened, then Haze wasn't going to enlighten him.

The elf nodded vehemently, his golden plaits shimmering as he continued to wax poetic about being an upstanding citizen and how these sorts of parties weren't usually his thing, but his friend had dragged him along. Haze hadn't caught his name. He was only here because this round table gave him a view of the queen's dais.

Haze was ravenous. His stomach gnawed at him. He figured if he bit the elf bastard, then he'd kill two ika fish with one mana stone. The elf would shut up *and* Haze would slake his thirst. His stomach rumbled loudly and he winced. He might not have until the end of the night before he had to feed.

Haze's gaze dropped to the elf's neck, half hidden by

lace ruffles. Vampire senses located the right vein, seeing it pulse under the soft candlelight.

Just a few more hours and he could get out of there.

He checked over his shoulder, expecting to see Peaches sitting quietly and safe. *Gone.* His heart jumped into his parched throat. His gaze darted to the queen and found her heavy-lidded eyes locked on the naked and nubile bodies before her, their performance taking on a more intimate turn. Haze searched the ballroom, seeing most of the revelers had shifted modes, too. The spectating portion of the night was almost over. Moans and groans and secret touches were louder and more obvious as divilixir took hold of greedy guests. Now empty of acrobats, the ribbons dangling from the ceiling were being draped strategically over lounges and chaises by bustling brownies. The red ribbons spread wide and overlapped to create private teepees for lovers inside.

Was Peaches inside one of them?

"You like the teepees?" the elf slurred, following Haze's attention.

Haze tipped his nose up and inhaled, something he'd avoided to help curb his craving, but he needed to locate Peaches. The air in this place was filled with a heady mix of musk, jasmine oil, elixir, and sweat. Isolating her sweet scent was nigh impossible.

Maybe she was on the parqueted dance floor.

He silently ordered his shadow to find Peaches. Darkness peeled away from him and flittered about the room, slinking between the shadows of others in the flickering candle and manabee light.

The elf blinked and glanced over his shoulder. "I mean, I like teepees too. I can ask my friend to join us... if that's what you're into."

A growl gathered and caught in Haze's throat. Frustrated, he shoved past the elf to conduct his own search. The elf knocked into the table, knocking the candelabra over. Flames jumped from the candle to the tablecloth. Haze relinquished a sliver of mana to snuff the kindling out and sent another scowl the elf's way.

Then he became a sword through water, cutting his path to the dance floor without hesitation. He yanked apart couples to see eyes and masks. He didn't give a spiked warada's tail if she was in the throes of passion or merely dancing. He would search the entire room, even the queen's dais—

The hairs on the back of his neck prickled. Slowly, he rounded and looked over the crowded room, past the red ribboned teepees, and through the sputtering candle flames. The queen's lazy eyes landed on Haze. He glared. She smiled and then tried to make it look like her smile was directed at the soldier standing next to her. Demeter.

Demeter also watched Haze, his vehemence tangible from across the room. And then the queen stole his attention by touching her skirt and pointing at the floor. She said something Haze caught above the revelry and music, "Kneel before your queen."

Demeter's eyes widened eagerly. His pointed tongue flicked out to run along his lips. He cast a worried glance Haze's way, but then Maebh tugged coyly at her lieutenant and pointed at the floor before her throne. Demeter sent one last look Haze's way, and then knelt before his queen, a greedy grin stretching his lips. As he kneeled, Maebh's gaze was on Haze. When the queen's skirts swallowed Demeter whole, and she lounged back in her throne, her eyes rolling in bliss, Haze knew he'd been dismissed, whether for the night or until she reached her climax. He couldn't be sure. But he'd gained a few moments of reprieve from expectations.

The queen had endorsed the party. Things were about to get debauched.

Haze shook his head. How could they have been so wrong about Indigo's brother? Clearly, he did not need an extraction. He'd smiled as though going down on his queen was the biggest reward. Still shocked that Haze's informant was not what he seemed, Haze almost missed his shadow coming back to him, vibrating with knowledge. It had found Peaches. Turning away from the queen and her public display of—whatever *that* was—he resolved to deal with it later.

"There you are!" Peaches giggled, flopping into him from the side.

She brought with her a mouthwatering scent of tongue

tingling sweetness. She embraced him, rubbed her face against his front like a feelion in a bed of mana-weed.

"Mm," she said. "You feel so good." She scrunched her fingers over his tunic. "So strong and muscly."

He pushed her away, but she'd latched onto him with two hands.

And those hands were doing things on his body, brazenly headed places he'd not let anyone touch in years.

Crimson. His stomach sucked in when she rubbed over the leather at his crotch—*fuck*—enticing what lied beneath to stir. He forcibly held her at arm's length and then surveyed her from head to toe. What had gotten into her?

Same lustrous peach locks. Same heart-shaped face and cupid's bow lips. Same—*no.* Through her mask, glazed eyes blinked at him. Flushed apple cheeks. Nipples like two pebbles pushing against her revealing black dress. Smooth satin skin erupted with goosebumps under his attention and she moaned, as if she felt the heat of his gaze like a lover's caress.

"I *need* you to touch me." She licked her lips, raking her heated gaze down his body, drinking him in.

I needed you not to drink the blue stuff, he thought.

She couldn't hear him and became enthralled with the laces on his breeches, looking at them as though they were her next battle in the Ring.

He scrubbed a hand down his face in frustration, but in doing so, he'd let go of her hand. She pounced on him. He stumbled back. They bumped into multiple masked fae. Beady eyes and bird beaks pecked at them.

"Get a teepee!" one barked.

Haze snapped at them. This wasn't the plan for the night. Damn it.

He eyed the dance floor. Maybe they could work off the elixir with physical exertion. He took her hand and made a beeline for the parquetry. Music increased in volume. The crowd thickened. The light over the dance floor dimmed. When they arrived, a dance was in full swing. He felt like an oaf next to her delicate beauty, but he'd be a *floater* if he allowed her dignity to be exploited by the queen.

This isn't my first rodeo. Her words came back to haunt him. He shook his head. Even if she'd participated in this sort of party before, so had he. Many moons ago. Each to their own. He wasn't her keeper, just her protector.

She pressed her soft front against him. He caught her intrepid hand on the way back down to his already hard cock and cursed himself for being a damned righteous prick about this. Never in his history at the Order had he been so tempted to forget about his job. With a heavy sigh, he redirected her hand to his neck and held the other to their side.

He looked down at Peaches. She looked up at him.

The world suddenly disappeared. Somewhere deep inside he knew the music still played and the people still danced, but right there, all he could see, feel, and hear was Peaches. Hunger and need slammed into him like a ferocious beast. Every cell in his body cried out to claim her. He *hurt* because of it.

Dance.

Haze swept Peaches around the dance floor. His steps were clumsy at first, and more than once he stepped on a foot. But never hers. She captured his heart and locked it in a cage made of peach colored hair and sweet smelling perfume. He was going to have her. Maybe not now, but someday soon. Eyes locked, they stumbled again, knocking into another couple.

This time, the fae he'd bumped misjudged their clumsiness and groped Peaches. Haze didn't realize what he'd done until the fae's nose spurt out blood, and Haze's knuckles stung. He'd punched him. Someone shouted in protest. He bared his fangs and sent daggers with his eyes, satisfied to see them retreat and use the hand-sign for an apology.

Peaches had no idea what had happened. All she'd seen was that they'd stopped and she could grasp the laces at his breeches. Perhaps a teepee was a better option. At least he could keep lecherous eyes off her while she was like this.

He pulled her after him and went for a teepee. They arrived just as others were doing the same, eager to snap up the private enclosure. Haze gnashed his teeth, successfully warning off the competition.

Haze had to duck to get in the small enclosure, but once in, he planted Peaches on the brocade sofa and then grabbed any gaps between drapes and shut them, sending a sliver of mana to stick them closed where he could.

Keep watch, he sent to his shadow.

Peaches vaulted from the sofa and landed on his back. *Good goddess in the moon.* He almost teetered from the sudden hit. Her legs wrapped around his torso, and her fingers went over his eyes.

"Guess who!" she giggled.

He tried to peel her off.

"Guess!"

He deadpanned and pointed to his lips.

"Mm, yes, your lips are fine. F-I-N-E, fine."

Peaches' mouth landed below his ear and sucked on the lobe. Pleasure shot straight down his spine, teasing him with what might happen if he allowed this to escalate.

And he couldn't.

He tried to unravel them without falling out of their tiny enclosure, but they ended up landing entangled on the sofa. Peaches was relentless. She scrambled on top of him, pushed him back, and kissed him everywhere. Little tiny sounds of pleasure left her lips and wrapped around his cock.

Well-dammit, maybe he liked this side of her because, for a moment, he didn't stop her. Her skin was too soft. Her smell, too good. His resolve, too weak. That dress of hers was designed to unravel him. Tantalizing glimpses of every illicit part of her body.

"Tell me how you like it." Her fingers relentlessly worked at the laces on his breeches.

No. The last person he'd trusted enough to tell had ended up in bloody tatters on the rocks out near the Rubrum City cliffs. After Holly's death, he'd promised himself he wouldn't give his heart over again like that. It hurt too much when it broke. After their baby's death, his soul had been crushed.

Peaches pushed against his weakening resistance. He almost called his shadow back in to pin her down, but with every passing minute, he found his reasons becoming thin. Hunger clouded his instincts. Want and need joined the storm. Instead of thinking of ways to get them out of this damned torture party, his mind stalled when she tossed her head to the side. The angle pushed her jugular out. The vein pulsed with blood. Her little heart pumped so hard in her excitement. One prick with his fangs and that sweet nectar would burst into his mouth like streaming moonlight, straight from the goddess herself.

With a silent sound caught between a groan and a growl, he threw his head back and stared at the red tunnel above him. He took a deep breath and tried to gather his resolve, but the scent of her arousal, her blood, her sweetness... it fucked with his mind, adding to the fog. Ribbon moved as fae bumped into the fabric outside. The party was amping up. Sounds of moans and flesh hitting wet flesh mixed with the increasing percussion of drums and confusion of a meandering flute. It was all designed to mess with heads.

Like his.

And Peaches.

Her fingers grazed over his abdomen, tickling his tattoos, resurrecting his desire... something that had been ash for years. He bared his fangs with a hiss as she succeeded in opening his laces, completely exposing his hard and aching cock.

"Fuck me," she murmured, awe in her tone. "That's..." She swallowed. "That's definitely proportionate."

Sense slammed into him.

He frowned and covered himself up. He couldn't focus. His training was better than this. She needed him to be strong.

Why was she doing this?

Her expression was a slave to her desire. Feverish eyes and flushed cheeks. With her dress hiked up, she rocked her hips, hitting the tip of his erection poking past his breeches. His eyes rolled at the pleasure. She was naked and soaked. His eyes fluttered at the blooming scent of his doom, for his resistance would last only a few more seconds if he couldn't get a hold of himself.

He gritted his teeth and held her by the shoulders, staring hard into her eyes.

Someone fell onto their teepee, shuddering the drapes. They burst through a gap, giggling. Since he couldn't roar with his voice, he roared with his power. Thinking only of her protection, wings ripped from his back. Night hurtled into the space to surround them in darkness. Air trembled, and he mentally called his shadow.

Curses and whimpers met his ears as he felt his shadow slide in and remove them. Then silence. They were alone.

Stand guard, he told his shadow. *Do your job properly.*

No more interruptions. Not while Peaches was vulnerable.

He couldn't explain it, couldn't rationalize it, but she was already more to him than a simple mission. She felt like that aching place in his chest finally had a friend. She was a manabee caught in his palm. A firefly in a jar. And she'd not noticed a single second of what had just transpired, intoxicated as she was.

"Haze." She nuzzled sweetly into his neck, licking along his throat. "You taste so good. Let's just forget about the why and enjoy this night." Her voice tightened. "We might not get another chance and you make me feel... you make me... ache. *Want.* It's been so long..." Her voice trailed off as she rubbed herself against him, embracing him and leaning against his chest. "Please," she whispered.

He opened his wings a little and let a small amount of ambient light in from beyond the teepee ribbon. It felt like unwrapping a gift. With her leaning against his front, he could glance down the length of her back. That one look was his undoing. Sheer lace covered back. Valley of her spine... curve of her pert rear. A glimpse further into her dress where shadow ran rampant with his imagination. His mouth watered again and the insufferable urge to bite that spot on her buttocks speared through him, coaxing his palm to her back, running it over her curves to dig beneath the hem of her dress.

He closed his eyes and hated himself, because he couldn't stop touching her. The soft to his hard. The fragile to his fortitude. His calloused fingers slid along her soft ass cheek, sliding over and under to that coveted place—he held his breath and curled between her thighs, stopping just before he hit the hot, intimate wet center of her body.

His breath came in ragged, shuddering gasps. *Stop. Stop now.*

"Haze," she moaned and took hold of his mask's horns. She undulated, gliding herself along his erection, bumping over the laces and leather placket he'd hastily thrown to cover himself. "Touch me more. I'm aching."

He dragged his middle finger through her wetness. The moan she emitted rattled the thorns around his heart.

We might not get another chance.

He parted her folds and traced along her sex, teasing her gently, rubbing erotically, inwardly dying as she begged for more and whimpered against his throat. Better him than one of those fae out there, right? This elixir was cruel if needs weren't satisfied. He should see to her. Better someone she could trust. Better...

His excuses died off as she took his rough jaw between her soft hands. He looked into her eyes and knew the only reason she wanted him was the divilixir. That she was too good for him, too precious. That he would ruin her like he'd ruined the last one. But then she kissed him, and he was gone in her taste, lost in her. For one small moment, he wanted to believe this was real.

We might not get another chance.

He pushed her face away by the jaw. And that was a mistake. The smell of her arousal on his fingers broke him. Unable to stop himself, his hunger took hold, and he licked along his knuckles, his tongue darting between, lapping up every last drop of her juices.

She tasted so... sweet.

"Oh god, that's so hot." She bit her bottom lip, watching him taste. She tried to pull him closer.

He wanted to lick her everywhere.

"Fuck me now. Feed from me," she begged.

He shook his head.

"Why not?"

The queen... Although they couldn't see through the red ribbon, he glanced in the direction of the dais.

"She's fucking someone now, too. They all are. Listen."

She was right. Sounds of sex were the symphony outside. Demeter had serviced the queen. Was she truly not watching Haze, a Guardian, in her midst? Were they safe for a moment? Could he—?

"She gave me the elixir, Haze. She told me to enjoy myself."

What? He sobered, blinking rapidly. The queen personally gave her the elixir?

Peaches tried to lick his lips. But it was enough of a revelation to throw cold water on his senses. This wasn't Peaches. This was Maebh.

When Peaches couldn't catch his lips, she returned to his neck.

We might not get another chance.

Her words took on a new meaning. What had the queen made Peaches do? What had she threatened? Anger speared through him, obliterating his desire. His wings vibrated with fury.

Enough.

His fangs dripped histamines, a byproduct of vampiric predatory behavior. The substance kept animals asleep as they fed. He refused to treat Peaches like an animal, but if he dipped his fangs into her vein, the histamines would inject too.

Just a dip. To ease the ache. On both accounts.

Haze flicked hair off her shoulder. She moaned and rocked into him, thinking she was getting more. He was a cruel bastard. He'd promised he wouldn't do this. But that was the thing about fae promises. They were easy to break as long as intention changed. The thorns around his heart clenched tight. His fangs pierced her flesh. Sank in. Sweet heaven burst on his tongue and he ripped himself straight off. Peaches' pupils contracted from pain. She gasped and looked at him in shock, in betrayal. It killed him. But her eyelids lowered sleepily and her shoulders slumped as the histamines started to work.

"What...?" she gasped.

Don't worry, love. Sleep.

"What?"

Her head lolled on her neck, drunk, and then she fell onto his chest. He stroked her silken hair, breathing calmly through his nose and then exhaling. This was all fucked up. The sooner he got back to the Order, the better. He could go back to his life. A life where his chest didn't feel like it was splitting in two. A life where her sweet taste didn't exist. A simple life. No drama. No feelings. Just nothing.

But as he cradled her, the scent of her blood filled the space, trapped by the cocoon of his wings. The taste of it teased him until every atom in his body cried out for more. *More.*

No. He glanced down at her still exposed neck, the trickle of dark blood oozing from his bite... all the way down her spine to that precious valley between her bottom.

Unholy craving ravaged him. His gums were on fire. As though his attention triggered the effects of that tiny drop of blood, bone tingling pleasure scorched down his spine. He wrenched away from her, but caught his wings clumsily against the couch. She fell onto his membranous wing and tried to curl into him like a blanket. He gasped for air, for restraint, but her sweetness was *there*. Both the remnants on his fingers and the lifeblood on his lips.

She would never forgive him.

He couldn't see straight. His mind whirled. He had to get out. But she was trying to wrap his wing around her, to burrow in deep. He instinctively shifted his wings away. Peaches tumbled from him and landed on the couch. He fumbled to keep her steady. His hands didn't belong to him. His mind was gone, trapped in her beauty and scent. Need so strong took hold of him. His vision turned red.

Have to get out.

Have to feed.

He sent his need to his shadow. His shadow understood without words. Outside the tent, the elf with golden braids waited for him. Had he been listening the whole time? Haze had been too wrapped up in Peaches that he'd failed to set privacy wards.

Haze split the ribbon and eased out of the teepee, his dark eyes landing on the elf in his mask. Pervert.

"I found her," the elf said eagerly. "Like you asked."

Haze's brow arched, hitting his mask. His gaze slid to the female at the elf's side. She, too, looked expectantly to him. Dark long hair. Rabbit mask. Black leather dress. A whip in her hand. She cracked it.

"Bulls want it rough, right?" She smirked.

Hunger took hold of Haze. He grabbed each elf by the neck and dragged them into the teepee. His shadow pinned the female while he drank deeply from the male's neck, trying to wash down the taste of Peaches' blood.

Trying to obliterate it before he caved to his raging desire and went for her instead.

He dropped the male to the floor. *Still hungry.* He took the female. She tried to resist, but he was so thirsty. So ravenous. No matter how much he drank, no matter how much his stomach filled with this second-rate blood, his thirst was not sated.

He'd tasted Peaches. Now everything else was dirt.

FOURTEEN

Peaches rubbed her eyes upon waking, her head full of cotton wool. Her body... her body was a mess of sleep, tender skin, and... horniness. She jackknifed up, the events of the previous night coming back to her. Previous night?

No.

Same night.

She was on the same couch, in the same red-draped teepee, still listening to the sounds of an orgiastic party in full swing. But strangely, two elves were asleep on the floor. Shadows flickered in the dark space, byproducts of the candles and lanterns outside. An alert and defensive looking wolpertinger sat at the arm of her couch, staring between a gap in the drapes. His antlers were luminescent in the dark, his chest was puffed out, and his chicken wings spread half out, either to make himself look bigger or to take flight. Haze was nowhere to be seen. The memory of her behavior around him creeped back in, along with shame and dread.

God, she felt like she was about to do the walk of shame.

She glanced down at her dress. The neckline gaped and showed everything. She'd offered herself up to Haze like candy on a glass platter. She rubbed her neck. The bite had already scabbed over. Haze had fed. Hadn't he?

Was she safe now? Would the queen keep her?

Somehow, she wasn't as relieved as she'd thought she'd be. A grimy, icky feeling swamped her stomach, dulling the last vestiges of divilixir still riding her system. She glanced at the elves on the floor and pressed her legs together, trying to feel out if she'd actually done something with them, or even with Haze. But her memory was good. Right up until the part where Haze had bitten her.

That grimy feeling in her gut evaporated when she thought of the big, surly vampire who'd been even sexier when he could only speak with his eyes and body language. Every touch had been magical.

The wolpertinger noticed she was awake, wagged its fluffy tail and then hopped and flapped onto her lap where it pawed her chest. She smiled and petted it. At least someone loved her.

"Hey, buddy," she murmured. "What are you doing here?"

Like a dog, it was too excited to do anything but sniff

and knock her face with its broken antlers. Petting soothed her nerves, so she stayed on the couch for a few moments, combing her fingers through its fur, trying to calm her hormones still tweaking with the after effects of divilixir. She wondered how long she'd been out for. Touching her neck, she remembered the exact moment Haze sank his fangs in.

God. She remembered him doing other things, too. Heat flushed between her legs, making her squirm at the thought of his fingers there. And he'd barely touched her. But he had. And she'd liked it. She squirmed again, unable to help the glaring need, to realize that satisfaction had eluded her.

Haze was gone. He'd taken what he'd wanted and left.

"I shouldn't be disappointed," she said to the wolpertinger. "I mean. He did what I told him to do."

The creature nuzzled into her lap, right at the intimate part.

"Ew, get off." She lifted it up. "You really do have a one-track mind."

Big, innocent liquid eyes stared back at her.

"I should give you a name," she mused. "Sniffer. What do you think?"

Its nose twitched.

"Okay. What about Heath?"

Its legs thumped.

"Thumper?"

A sneeze.

"Holmes?" He was a famous geologist. Plus, of course, the great detective. She could be Watson, and they'd investigate mysteries together. At least, they could in her dreams. In reality, she'd probably stay hidden, doing whatever she was told to do and avoiding confrontation. That was all she was good for. She sighed. "I don't need a fantasy detective. I need someone who'll make me brave in real life. Someone like..." Haze.

The wolpertinger made a growling sound, and she laughed. "You actually sound like him. Maybe I'll call *you* Haze."

She could keep one of them, at least.

Teepee fabric rustled. She startled, accidentally dropping the fluffball. He landed on his paws and flipped around to bare fangs at Haze as he ducked inside and then pulled the flap shut. Dark, concerned eyes landed on her.

"You shouldn't be awake yet," he said, taking in her appearance from head to toe.

"You can speak!"

Haze dropped his gaze to her neck. "I accepted the queen's gift. Enough to break the spell. You good?"

"I heal fast," she mumbled, suddenly feeling like detangling her hair, making sure she was presentable.

"That elixir could be in your system for hours."

"Oh, I still feel it." She pressed her thighs together.

The wolpertinger hissed at Haze and he pointed a meaty finger back with a snarl of his own. "I'm warning you, Tinger."

It binky hopped and flapped its wings aggressively.

Haze doubled his glare. "Shift forms and then say that to me. Show her what you *really* look like. I dare you."

"Don't hurt Haze," she said. "He was only trying to keep me safe."

She realized her slip too late. One dark, surly brow arched. Fists open and clenched. Haze spoke through clenched teeth. "You called it Haze?"

Peaches wilted a little. "I mean… he was trying to protect me. And you both snarl the same."

"We do not."

She snorted, a small smile curving her lips. "You kinda do. And his ears do this little twitching thing like yours." And then quietly, "He's also good at cuddling."

Haze looked at Peaches like she'd grown two heads. "Have you seen what it will shift into? What it does to unmated females?"

"It kidnaps them, I guess."

"There's a reason we have the saying, 'tingling like a tinger in heat.' If one starts mating with you, you'll be—"

"Okay, I get it!" She held up her hand, stopping him.

"I don't think you do." He stepped over the fallen elves and put a knee on the couch, crowding her space. His impact smothered all oxygen in the tent. "It will grow to my size," he said. "And even though it's bigger, it still has the mind of rabbit. It will pin you down and rut with you until it fills you with its spawn. The babe is born by eating its way out of your womb with those fangs."

She screwed up her face. It was hard to marry that explanation to the cute little fluffy thing at their feet. "I guess I'll find something else to call it."

"Don't call it anything at all," he grumbled and toed the wolpertinger, kicking it out of the teepee. It hissed and growled at him the entire way. "It's only here because it wants to take you home as its mate. Don't encourage it."

Peaches frowned at Haze. He frowned back. Her senses heightened, brought back to life by his presence. She squirmed and tried not to look at his fingers, tried not to remember how they'd felt.

"I didn't think you'd come back." The words tumbled from her mouth.

"I said I would take you with me. I meant it."

"But I want to stay."

"You are wrong."

Another stretch of silence where his attention was like a lick of flame against her face. Haze looked at her with such carnal intelligence, such male entitlement only someone used to getting his way could look. It was almost as if he'd decided he was taking her, having her, claiming her, regardless of what she wanted.

She blurted, "Did we, um... you know?"

"Sweetness. If we did"—his voice deepened—"you'd feel it."

She blushed crimson. Then noticed the elves on the floor. "And them?"

He studied her. "Would it bother you if you did?"

She hugged herself.

"That's what I thought." He pursed his lips. "Next time I tell you to do something, like not drink the blue stuff, do as you're told."

She startled, her eyes blinking rapidly. *Do as you're told?* That was exactly what she had been doing. For *years* she did as she was told. And now Haze was adding his voice to the chorus.

"I didn't have a choice," she whispered. "I never have a choice."

Her words must have annoyed him, because he tensed and looked away.

"But you fed from me?" she asked hopefully.

Again, her words annoyed him. His nostrils flared and his jaw clenched. He took a moment before answering with his own question. "Why did Prince Luthian and his female say you cost them coin?"

"I don't see how that's any of your business."

"I need to know the whole story if I'm to protect you."

Shame held her secrets down. The truth of the matter was, her blood had been used as some kind of drug for Luthian and Wisteria to peddle in the streets of Rubrum City. For two years, they'd drained her and bottled her blood. But if she told Haze that, then she relived the nightmare. It made her sick to think of even now. When the queen discovered her at an Autumn Court party, Peaches had been whisked away like a found treasure. From being treated like a product to being treated like... well, whatever she was now, it was better than the former.

"We're getting out of here," Haze declared.

Panic leaped into her throat. "What? Now?"

"It's time to go."

Images flashed in her mind. The queen. Her room of soldiers. All the strong, powerful fae surrounding them. Who cared if some were inebriated? Like she'd just proven, the effects didn't last long on some. Since she'd awoken in this time, she'd learned she healed fast. She suspected it had something to do with why her blood was so tasty and why she'd actually survived being frozen in the ground for two thousand years. But it didn't make her strong, and one puff of sleeping powder had taken this powerful Guardian down.

"I can't," she blurted, her fear taking hold of her.

The pitiful look he gave her brought tears to her eyes. "Yes, you can."

"You don't understand."

"This is a choice you can make." His voice softened. "Peaches, we need you."

Taken aback, she flinched. "For blood?"

"No! For your other gifts," he said. "And they will emerge, believe me. The Order needs special people like you to protect Elphyne. Our Seers have foretold of many battles, from within our borders, but most importantly outside them. The human who destroyed your world is alive in Crystal City. He probably already knows you're here."

Her stomach dropped. "You're right."

"I know—wait. What?"

"Six years ago, when I first woke in this time, there was another human who'd tracked me down. Her name was Molly or Maggie, or something. She was supposed to bring us back to Crystal City."

Haze crouched before her. "We need you. Even if you don't believe you're Well-blessed, you have knowledge that can help us. Nobody wants another war. Think of the innocent children, the weak, those who will be tortured. I've only known you for a short time, Sweetness, but I know you never wanted that for your world."

Her eyes burned. She shook her head.

"If the queen has her way, or if the human leader does, then that's what will happen again. Be brave. We need you."

Numb, Peaches allowed Haze to take her out of the teepee. A mass orgy assaulted her senses. Fae of all kinds went at it like, well, like wolpertingers in a mating frenzy. On couches, on the floor, some even wrapped artfully in ribbons dangling from the ceiling. The lights were dim, and masks were still on, hiding identities. Hot, thick air. Flesh and sweat. It smelled like a brothel's laundry hamper. The flute music had died, but someone still had the sense to beat the drums, low and lazily.

"Stay close," Haze said and took a few steps, but Peaches' feet were glued to the floor.

She wanted to hide under a table and stay there until the night was over. This paralyzing fear was immovable. Haze turned, saw she was frozen, and then tossed her over his shoulder so she dangled down his back. Her heart slammed into her throat so hard she thought she was going to vomit. Shit was happening. He was taking her out of here... and... she was letting him?

"Be brave, Sweetness." He squeezed her thighs reassuringly, then walked to the exit.

FIFTEEN

Haze had tried to do things the gentle way, but time was running out. He'd stayed hidden in the teepee for hours after drinking from the elves. Peaches' taste was still on his tongue, driving him to madness. He'd hoped to wait out the queen's plan, to let her reveal herself to him. There was a part of him that believed this waiting had been part of her game, that she was just wanting to see if he made a move. So he'd played it safe, stayed hidden, and kept to himself as the party became more wild and raucous around them.

Plus... he'd accidentally spent his mana when he'd shifted his wings out... and then back in. *Idiot*. He was acting like a horny teen vamp. A tingling tinger. *Him*. Silently disgusted with himself, he knew he had better sense than this. He was a good warrior. A good Guardian.

Unlike those who'd been offered as tribute to the Well, Haze was one of the few that had chosen this life.

After self-degradation had sobered him, he'd spent the time trying to remember the correct transference runes to scratch into his palm and call forth his hammer Justice. D'arn Thorne had only taught Haze the runes recently, and Haze struggled to recall the exact pattern. It frustrated him to no end, but all he'd ended up with was a bloody, scratched up palm.

Not long before Peaches awoke, the queen and Gastnor had left the party in a flurry of rage and hard looks. Something had happened that required her immediate attention. Curiously, Haze also noticed Demeter and Gastnor arguing. The lieutenant and the captain. Demeter drew the short straw and stayed to keep an eye on the event. But he seemed preoccupied with conversing with guards. It was the opportunity Haze had been waiting for.

He was going to carry Peaches out, perhaps pretend they would continue the party back at his guest chambers, and then use his shadow to hide their forms and slip out the palace the old-fashioned way. With her slung over his shoulder, hand on her rear, he looked like one of the many in the room. If anything, they were overdressed. Slinking out like this shouldn't go noticed.

But it did.

Demeter stepped before Haze as they made it to the exit. The tall vampire was unreadable in his expression.

Here we go. Finally, Haze would speak to the vampire directly. Time to work out his true motives.

"Leaving so soon?" Demeter's eyes took a pointed look at Peaches over Haze's shoulder.

Haze smiled flatly. "It's been hours, and as you can see, I've accepted the queen's gift."

"Cut the crap. Why are you here?"

Foe. Haze decided right there and then. If Demeter was truly on the Order's side, he already knew why Haze would come. He would also step aside and allow Haze to leave with Peaches. Once Haze settled on where he stood with the vampire, a change rolled through his body. He tensed, his senses on high alert.

He should have acted drunk on Peaches' blood. At least that way, Demeter would have underestimated Haze. Too late now.

"You sound unfulfilled, Demeter. Got blue balls?"

Danger danced in Demeter's eyes. He grabbed Haze's bull horns and yanked on them once. "Answer my question."

Haze considered sticking those bull horns through Demeter's dumb face, but then realized this was an opportunity for him to do his due diligence. He couldn't very well go back to Indigo without definitive proof of his brother's manipulations. So Haze checked over his shoulder, pretending to see if anyone listened, then lowered his head conspiringly. "You didn't turn up for our meeting, so I sought you out, in case Indigo's brother needed extraction."

Demeter's eyes narrowed on Haze. "Bullshit."

"You cut the crap, and so will I."

Fangs glinted in Demeter's mouth.

Haze went on. "Admit you never intended to tell me about the mana-warped corpses around Elphyne. Admit you're hiding something."

"What do you know?"

A lick of alarm zipped up Haze's spine, but he schooled his body language. His instincts screamed at him to leave. Now. Run and get Peaches somewhere safe.

Demeter's hand moved to the sword at his hip. "Put her down."

Peaches was a frozen lamb in Haze's arms. He considered making a run for it but eased her off his shoulder and placed her gently on the floor. He would need his hands to fight. She landed with a flushed face and took a step closer to him, not Demeter.

To him.

Peaches might say she wanted to stay here, that she couldn't leave because this was the safest place she'd know in years, but that step. That one step. That was all he needed to know.

Haze straightened his spine and looked down at the vampire with disdain. "I'm a Guardian. You cannot hold me against my will, or you will unleash the wrath of the

Order upon this city. Think carefully about what you say next."

They stared at each other until Demeter shifted his hate-filled eyes to Peaches.

"You fucked up, *pix*," Demeter snapped.

"I didn't." Her hand fluttered to her neck, to the small healing puncture marks.

"He's clearly not inebriated. So he must not have fed properly. If you can't do a simple job, then what use have we of you?"

"And what job was that?" Haze folded his arms. "Having her seduce and intoxicate me? Get me to spill my secrets?"

Distrust floated between them, staining the air with ill intent.

Demeter said, "Your request will be considered."

At first, Haze thought the comment was for him. But then realized it was meant for someone behind him. They all turned and found Prince Luthian's eyes on Peaches. His collar was untied and open to his tanned navel, his shirtsleeves rolled up to the elbow. A whip in his hand dripped blood. Mask still on. He gave Demeter a nod of respect—the promise of a bargain.

Whatever horrors Peaches had suffered under this princeling's hands had been too much for her to talk about. There was only one reason a female felt safer in an abusive relationship, like the one with the queen. To escape an even worse relationship.

Luthian's lips stretched wickedly as his gaze landed on Peaches, and then he pulled a small leather coin pouch from his vest's pocket and jingled it at her.

"We're leaving," Haze decreed to Demeter. "Get out of my way."

"I'm afraid that's not possible," he replied, and motioned to the soldiers behind him in the hall. They gathered along the doorway, blocking the exit. "The pix stays with us."

They both knew Peaches was no pixie, but Haze doubted they fully comprehended the prize she was. Being Well-blessed meant so much more than tasty blood. He had faith that Peaches would someday discover her innate power, just like Clarke, Laurel and Ada had. He wanted Peaches to achieve the same kind of inner strength. He would not leave her for the wolves.

"You seem tetchy, Demeter." Haze cocked his head. "I noticed Gastnor is still your boss. Is he also still the one Maebh fucks while you are good for nothing but your bended knee and pointed tongue?"

A twitch beneath Demeter's right eye. "Watch your words about our queen."

Haze's lips curved upward. "I'm right, aren't I? You're better looking. You're stronger. And yet, for some reason, she still holds onto that poor excuse for a captain. You're here while he's out there... doing what, I wonder. Clearly something important because you weren't invited."

Demeter drew his puny bone sword. It wouldn't stand a chance against Justice. If Haze had it.

"Fuck you," the lieutenant spat.

Good. Haze wanted him angry. Because then his attention wasn't on Peaches. Or Haze's shadow oozing beneath their feet, joining Demeter's, preparing to take him down.

Haze clicked his tongue. "Your mother would be so disappointed in you."

"My mother is a fucking pariah. So is my brother. I'm the only one in my family doing anything of worth." Demeter laughed. "I'm the lieutenant of the queen's fucking guard."

The soldiers in the hall didn't flinch. They stayed attentive and alert as if they dealt with this sort of occurrence on a daily basis. They were Unseelie. They probably did.

"This is how it's going to go," Haze said, a layer of warning in his tone. "We leave the palace unharmed, and you go about your lives. If you stop me, the moment the Order finds out about it, you will be declaring war. Do you understand?"

"They have to find out about it first," Demeter said, and thrust his sword toward Haze's middle.

SIXTEEN

Horrified, Peaches watched Demeter's sword come for Haze. She didn't want him to die. Her feet moved, rushing to Haze's side. She intended to shove him out of the way—so stupid considering their size differences—but she was too slow, too small, too worthless.

The sword tip went into Haze's side—well, she thought it did. He moved faster than anything she'd seen before. His hand windmilled out, smacked the sword away. He twirled like a dancer and drop-kicked Demeter's leg, toppling him backward through the exit and into the hallway, where he fell on top of the waiting soldiers.

Pandemonium broke loose. Peaches stepped back a few feet to hide near a marble column and tried to become invisible. But the fight filled the space before her.

Previously placid guards jumped into the fray. The

guests in the room stopped rutting and started panicking. Soldiers released their weapons—swords, knives, spears. Bodies went flying. Peaches thought she'd seen Haze's ability to fight near her room, but this was something else. He was both water to a rock and a hammer to a nail. He was everything. He pummeled and he danced. Brute force and flowing grace.

He smashed two heads together before dropping them. His fist darted out, crunched a throat, the body going limp. Blows glanced off him. Sharp blades deflected when his shadow solidified, taking the hit like a shield.

Demeter recovered from his spill, hardened his face, and then launched. But Haze's elbow went up, striking him in the face. Blood spurted on the hallway walls.

A guard shoved Peaches out of the way to get to Demeter, and she made an embarrassing squeak as she stumbled. Right into someone's awaiting arms.

"It was only a matter of time, *Peach*." Luthian's arms surrounded her, pulling her into his vice-like grip. She struggled, but he held firm. "No use fighting."

"On the floor in chains is where you belong," Wisteria said from the side. Her rabbit mask was gone, and she was fully clothed. The disturbance must have ended the party and broken the spell. Many masks were off, identities shockingly revealed Lords and Ladies humiliated to be caught in flagrante. Wisteria plucked the mask from Peaches' face. "Until you pay back every single coin you cost us, and then some."

Peaches wouldn't go back. Her soul couldn't take it. Maybe it was panic giving her strength. Or maybe it was seeing Haze fight. He never hesitated. He just moved, be damned with the consequences. *Be brave.* When Luthian leaned down again to whisper another retort, she slammed her head back. Her skull met his nose with a sickening crunch. Nauseating pain burst in her head, blurring her vision.

That wasn't as easy as she'd thought.

"Bitch!" Luthian clutched his bleeding nose.

Out of his arms, Peaches stumbled, her head still swimming. Someone yanked her hair. She tripped and fell. A thousand daggers spiked in her scalp. She screamed, seeing in her periphery the hand at her head belonged to Wisteria.

It was her enterprising idea to sell Peaches' blood. Defiance bubbled inside Peaches and she thrashed and jabbed to get to the vampire, but Wisteria held firm. Each time Peaches moved, her hair pulled. Wisteria laughed cruelly and dragged a taloned finger along Peaches' neck.

"You can't fight this—"

Strong fingers caught Wisteria around her throat, choking her words. She let go and Peaches dropped to her knees, free. She scrambled away and looked back. Haze was a demon wrapped in shadow, choking the female vampire to death. Rage billowed off him like smoke, his eyes the smoldering coals, his veins bulging with brimstone. With his mask still somehow attached, he looked like a demon from the fiery pits of hell itself.

His lip curled, flashing fang, and then he tore into Wisteria's neck, ripping into her jugular. Blood sprayed, and she dropped to the floor. She tried to staunch her wound. Haze yanked his mask off by the horns, moved between Wisteria and Peaches, and then spat Wisteria's blood out. Maybe a chunk of flesh. It landed on her face.

He glared at the prince. "Touch Peaches again, and I'll eat your heart."

Luthian, still cupping his nose, recovered from his shock. He used his mana to toss some kind of unseen force Haze's way. At the same time, someone did so from the other side. And another. They summoned a storm to take Haze down. Without his hammer to cut through the magic, Haze could do nothing but plant his feet and batten down the hatches. Soldiers converged with Demeter, surrounding Haze with a hurricane.

Clutching the marble column, Peaches saw it all happen in slow motion, and yet Haze still stood his ground —his fury directed at Wisteria and Luthian.

"Watch out!" she shouted.

Her voice did the unforgivable. It distracted Haze. The moment he glanced over his shoulder at her, Demeter called forth someone to his side.

Balos.

Hope surged. Balos was there to save them. But hope was a cruel bitch. Sometimes it felt like her whole purpose was simply to make despair worse. Balos ignored Peaches. He handed something to Demeter. A red rock—the fire opal. Demeter took it with a smile.

"This might sting a little." He shoved the opal onto Haze's chest. Lightning released. Haze roared in pain and convulsed as though hit with a Taser. The opal continued to release power into Haze, zapping him uncontrollably while the soldiers gathered around and laughed. Peaches could smell burning flesh. Unseelie guests who'd taken pause from their revelry now surrounded Haze and joined in the ridicule, like he was the court jester, not a victim.

"Go," Balos urged Peaches. "Now. Back to your room."

With a stolen glance her way, Haze finally lifted his palms in surrender and mimed the same word Balos had: "Go."

Peaches stumbled into her dark room, tears burning her eyes. Turmoil rolled through her, threatening to push the contents of her stomach out. She hated this. She hated herself! How could she just stand there while they'd hurt Haze?

But even as the thoughts formed, fear locked her arms and legs. She fell onto her bed in the darkness and rolled into herself, noticing how she no longer felt safe in this room. The walls were the same. The smell was the same. But she wasn't.

She wasn't okay with standing by idly.

But she didn't know how to be any other way. The simple fact was, she was weak. She was small. She had no mana. What could she do to help anyone, let alone save herself?

Peaches grabbed a handful of blanket and pulled it over, intending to smother her self-loathing until she fell asleep. Maybe she'd be lucky and not wake up. She grabbed something fluffy and froze. *Fluffy?*

With trembling fingers, she moved her hand about in the dark, testing the lump of fluff on her blanket. Warm. Little body. Feathers. Stickiness. *Blood?*

"Tinger?"

Peaches bolted up and rushed to light a candle. Light bloomed, chasing away the shadows. She couldn't handle any more hurt. She couldn't handle any more death. Forcing her body to move, she crept back to her bed and peered at the lump of wolpertinger in her bed. He was whole. Blood stuck to his matted fur and feathers in blotches. And his little chest rose and fell with fast, short breaths. Alive. Just.

Peaches last saw Tinger when Haze had forced him from the teepee. That was hours ago. Something had happened to him since and he'd come here seeking refuge. That's the only thing she could think of. No one would have put him there. He'd come to her for help.

"It's okay, Tinger." That was his name, she'd decided. Not Haze. "I'm going to take care of you."

She wasn't good at stopping a fight, or even protecting herself, but she could do this.

Compassion for the small creature overwhelmed her trepidation. She rinsed out a cloth in her wash bowl, then set to work cleaning the blood from the tiny, limp animal. Puncture wounds dotted his body, but she didn't think they were animal bites. Or from a vampire. No... this was weird. Like a needle. Maybe something was injected or taken out?

She took a closer look and noticed liquid metal—or mercury oozing out. Elemental metal. Deadly to humans, deadly to *any* living creature, but with fae, the metal would react to mana held within. Someone had tortured this small, weak being and stole its life force.

She needed help.

Without a thought for her safety, Peaches wrapped Tinger in her blanket and ran all the way to Balos' workshop. He might still be angry at her for getting in the way at the party, but he was always angry with her. He couldn't possibly know Haze was trying to help her. He might not even care.

Balos lived in his workshop room toward the back. She would plead for his help and not stop until he agreed, even if that meant promising to hunt the tunnels for whatever rocks he wanted.

Bursting through his door, she found him slumped on his little wooden stool, his head dipped and looking at his gnarled fingers. He glanced up when she entered.

"I need your help," she said, knowing full well she'd committed one of the greatest faux pas in the fae world. Asking for help could very well mean, like an apology or a thank you, that she would owe him something. But they'd sung this song many times together. She'd find a way around it. She shut the door. "Something bad has happened to Tinger."

Balos' bushy brows joined in the middle, and he slid away the tools and rocks on his workbench to make room for the wolpertinger.

"I think he's been poisoned with mercury," she said. "It's a liquid metal. Look."

Balos pulled on a head band with a monocle. He fitted it to his eye and peeled apart the fur on Tinger. His expression hardened.

"The Well will welcome him home soon enough. It is wise for you to let it."

"I can't." She choked up. "I can't do this anymore."

"Peaches," Balos said, defeat in his eyes.

He wasn't the same feisty goblin he used to be. She saw the same empty heartache reflected back at her and wondered if it was because she had his cap. It was still stuffed into the pocket of her dress in her room.

"You know things are wrong here," she said. "You've felt it in your heart for a long time."

The dip of his shoulders was a white flag, despite his words. "I'm Unseelie. This kind of behavior is normal."

She shook her head. "Not for you. You feel guilt. I see it

in your eyes every day. I see it in the way you hide out here. I see it in the way you teach and care for me. Help me, Balos. He's only a little creature."

"That shifts into a big, horny and raping son-of-a-witch."

"He's not once tried to hurt me." She stroked the length of Tinger's body, a sob caught in her chest.

Balos stared at her, long and hard. Nothing in his expression said there was hope.

"There has to be something we can do."

"It's metal," Balos said, shaking his head. "No mana will work around it."

"At all?"

He scratched his eyebrows. "Maybe if there was a skilled healer, but even then... it's metal. And it's been used to force mana out."

"Meaning?"

"Mana is the glue holding a fae's body together. Without it, we're mortal."

"So someone purposefully injected Tinger to steal his lifeforce. Who could be so cruel?"

The look Balos gave Peaches said he knew exactly who. And so did she. The queen. The reason behind the horrible screams in the dungeons. The reason behind the mana-warped corpses being dumped and hidden. The reason for Haze's visit.

She'd always known it deep down, but stuffed it in the same place where cold lived in her heart. She had never wanted to believe the safe haven she'd come to know was only a scream away from being compromised. She'd wanted to believe that her inaction was the safest bet.

"I have to do something," she said. Her mind whirled with solutions, grasping at memories from this world, and hers. Mercury was elemental metal. Mercury poisoning was usually from ingesting fish or something. But it still oozed from Tinger's punctures. It wasn't ingested. Maybe... maybe she could draw it out like venom from a snakebite. Maybe if enough was gone, Tinger would heal himself. She was different in this time. No colds, no flu, no viruses. Open wounds healed in a day or two. Tinger's immune system must surely be the same.

She had to try.

Peaches sealed her lips around a tiny wound and sucked until her mouth filled with a disgusting metallic taste. She spat into a bowl Balos provided and then went to work on the next puncture site. Balos watched curiously while she worked, sucking, spitting, sucking, spitting. When she was done, the old goblin hobbled over to a chest on his workbench and drew out a glowing clear quartz pebble.

"It stores and regulates mana," he explained, then added a turquoise crystal to the mix. "This one heals the mind, body, and soul. It also promotes good luck."

Emotion and gratitude flooded Peaches. She touched her lips and pushed her fingers down and out.

Balos nodded. "I've not seen mana forcibly removed

this way before, but these healing stones might help your pet now that the metal is mostly gone. If you can get him to shift into his bipedal form, even better. But with this kind of forced removal of mana, he might age and die, anyway."

"He's not my pet."

"After this, he won't leave your side."

Peaches would have to take that chance. Balos placed one crystal over Tinger's heart, the other on his head. He weaved his gnarled fingers about in a way that reminded Peaches of how Haze created his wards. Like moving currents of invisible water. It seemed so magical to her.

Slowly, the crystals lost their glow and Tinger's breathing smoothed out.

"I think it's working," she whispered in awe.

Balos studied Peaches for a moment as she petted the wolpertinger and cooed soft nothings to it. She could see Balos wanted to say something, but held his tongue as he went about his space tidying the tools and rocks swiped in his haste to make room earlier.

"Do you have family, Balos?" she asked after a while.

The goblin hunched and shoved masonry sandpaper into a box under his bench. He stayed down there as he replied, his voice traveling back up.

"I did. Had a son." The shuffling stopped. "He died."

Oh. Peaches focused on Tinger, on how helping him made her feel. It was the only thing that kept the sadness at bay. She wanted to tell Balos she was sorry, but knew it might only acerbate things. The only kindness Balos had responded to was action.

"I had family, too," she said. "Lots of them."

Balos straightened. "Dead?"

She nodded. "All of them."

They shared a moment of connection. A moment where two lonely people understood each other's pain, and then he said something she might never understand.

"My son died in the war against the humans." Balos' eyes defocused as his mind turned inward. "I was a general. A redcap. My son joined the army under my watch. He wanted to be like his da. He thought signing up for a frontline unit would prove he was as good as me. Humans slaughtered him."

Peaches' hand stopped on Tinger, resting over his little beating heart. Balos was talking about the first war between the humans of this time and the fae. The fight for rights to Elphyne.

This time, when Peaches met Balos' eyes, there was a new level of awareness to what they shared. Peaches was human. Balos knew that. Humans had killed his son, yet he'd helped her. This old Unseelie codger could have spent his life exacting revenge against human kind, but he'd chosen another path. He'd given his cap to her, given up the violence, and chose to make magic rocks in a basement and help save a creature everyone said wasn't worth it.

He wasn't the first Unseelie who'd belied his race's stereotype. There were also Seelie fae who weren't benevolent—King Mithras, for example. He'd slaughtered a village to get to his bastard son Jasper. The palace had been abuzz with the gossip for weeks. This new world was definitely as complicated as the old world, and Peaches was starting to see that some of these labels were made, not born. If this most vicious and murderous fae could change, then maybe there was a chance for Peaches.

"Why did you help take down the Guardian?" she asked.

Balos' eyebrow arched. "Getting involved with a Guardian will do you no favors. My advice to you, young pix, is to mind your own manabeeze-wax and stay in your room until this all blows over."

"But—"

"Unless you want your mana forced out too."

She clamped her lips shut. He knew she had none. Didn't she?

"He helped me."

"Fae don't do anything for nothing," Balos said. "And Guardians are the worst lot of us all. I'm surprised he hasn't demanded coin for helping you. Yet. Speaking of which..." Balos held out his palm expectantly. "I helped you with this hopping penis-on-paws. You owe me."

"I can give you your cap back."

"No," he clipped. "I don't want it back."

"I know where more fire opals are," she said. "I will find you some, if you like, but only if you promise to never use them on a friend again."

"A goblin never promises," Balos snapped, his beady eyes flashing with annoyance. "And I had no choice but to help the queen's guards. Better to have used the opal on D'arn Haze than what would have come if I hadn't."

"What would have come?" Peaches was almost too afraid to ask.

"Prince Luthian and Wisteria would have claimed like-minded payment for yours and D'arn Haze's affront."

"But he represents the Order."

"And the assault happened under the queen's watch." He pursed his lips. "The Unseelie Law of Eyes states that when a visiting Royal and his cohorts are grievously harmed, they have the right to claim like-minded payment."

"I didn't know that."

"The law ensures royals and diplomats have a certain amount of freedom here without concern for welfare. They know if something heinous happens to them, they can retaliate against an equal of their station, or anyone less. While the opal didn't rip open D'arn Haze's throat, it was excruciating. More so, I imagine, than what he caused Wisteria when he bit into her neck. Not exactly an eye for an eye, but more than enough to satisfy the law."

Peaches rubbed her temples, hating how every time she tried to help, she just dug the hole deeper. How was she going to get Haze out of this? Could she?

Balos cleared his throat and pretended he wasn't interested. "I suppose more opals will do."

She touched her fingers to her lips and pushed them down and out.

He gave a curt nod of acceptance.

"Now shoo." He waved her out. "You made a mess in here and I need to clean."

Peaches wrapped Tinger in the blanket and scooped him up. "I'll see you tomorrow," she said. "After I have lunch."

"I don't want your leftovers."

"Sure you don't."

"Take my advice, you ungrateful pix," Balos grumped. "Stay in your room until this all blows over. If you're lucky, they'll forget the hand you played."

The walk to her room involved passing through the screams of dungeon prisoners. Guilt slammed into her, wrapping around her heart, and she felt herself withdraw into that empty place with no feelings that had kept her alive for so long at the Autumn Court.

She put Tinger on her bed and checked on his breathing—growing stronger by the minute—and then went to her rock collection and rearranged them with trembling fingers until her heart rate slowed. Balos was right. She should remain hidden. This palace had a way of forgetting what was out of sight. But the guards might still come for her. And when the queen found out what had happened, no place would be safe. When her rocks were in order according to size, she started again with a different pattern. Igneous, sedimentary, or metamorphic.

Be brave, Haze had said. *We need you.*

Her fingers clenched around a jagged rock until pain bit into her. Holding her shaking, bleeding hand before her face, she realized something. Even the smallest stone had the power to hurt. It could kill a human or fae if thrown correctly. That was how David killed Goliath.

She had to stop thinking of herself as weak.

She could be a rock. She could take down a giant.

SEVENTEEN

Peaches spent the next day sleeping, wrapped up in her blanket with Tinger. When night came, and the wolpertinger stirred, she tucked him into a sling made from a scarf and hid him beneath her cape before going to find food. She did her best to stay out of anyone's way lest they remember she had been at the epicenter of trouble the previous night, but found her efforts were in vain because no one cared.

As two soldiers ran past her in the hall, without a care for her presence, it quickly became clear something had happened during the day. The palace was going into some kind of lockdown. Guards and soldiers were all in a tizzy as they tightened security. No one was getting in, and no one was getting out.

A short, fluffy-haired fae bumped into Peaches on her

way to the kitchen. It was a brownie wearing an apron and dragging a broom. Peaches grabbed her by the arm.

"What happened?" Peaches asked.

"Guardians," the brownie hissed. "They tried to enter the palace and have been turned away."

"What?"

"You heard me." She shook her head. "This ain't good. Publicly defying entry to Guardians? Not good indeed."

Peaches tried to get more out of her, but the brownie scurried off.

Stunned, Peaches slunk into the kitchen. No one seemed to notice her as she hid a loaf of bread, a couple of pieces of fruit, and chunks of cheese in her deep pocketed velvet skirt before heading back to her room. Her mind raced as she dropped Tinger little pieces of cheese. *Those screams from the dungeon. Tinger's injuries. Mana-warped bodies.* Could the Order have really come for Haze?

Hope surged, and then deflated when she realized Guardians would only come for Haze, not her. They didn't know her from a bar of soap. Even if they rescued Haze, she might be stuck here, anyway.

Well... did that change anything?

Be brave. We need you.

Haze was so certain that she had mana. What if he was right? She glanced down at her arm and rubbed the small, hard lump where her old contraceptive implant still existed. It was so tiny. Probably didn't even work after thousands of years of being frozen. She should really take it out. But what if it didn't make a difference?

If it didn't, she could still help. Maybe not in the fight with mana, but in other ways. It was her duty to try to fix the world her people had broken.

If the Guardians were here for Haze and she was left behind, she should still try to get to the Order. After the glimpse of her past at the party, and the contrast of how valued she'd felt with Haze, she wanted him to be in her life. She wanted a future where she had choices, and he was fast becoming one of them. Maybe her perfect life included a strong, sexy and loyal Guardian in it—if she was brave enough to ask him.

There was always that tiny kernel of doubt in her gut, telling her that Haze only wanted Peaches because it was his job. That he would turn around and ask for coin in return for keeping her safe, just like Balos had warned. But that was only a tiny kernel. It no longer ruled her emotions.

No longer did the walls feel like they closed in on her. No longer did the guards strike fear into her soul. Even the Sluagh kept walking by without sensing the hopelessness in her heart. She was a rock, albeit small. And she could hurt. She only needed to learn how.

With the palace tightening external security, Peaches was a low priority. No one came for her. No one cared if she walked the halls, but she rushed about getting food all the same. The thought of bumping into Luthian or Wisteria was bone trembling. Hopefully, they'd be up high on the guest floor, nursing their wounds.

She arrived at the basement staircase landing and paused before stepping down. Down the hall, guards at the door to the gardens were speaking animatedly. Her curiosity got the better of her, and she tried to listen in at the same time as juggle the increasingly ravenous fluffy and feathered creature in her hands. Tinger's antlers kept poking as he snuffled around in the sling for crumbs.

Part of her was so proud of herself for helping Tinger. He'd been on death's door, and now he lived. She'd done that. Well, her and Balos. They'd saved Tinger together.

Standing there on the staircase, listening, her mind wandered to what kind of plan she would need to get to Haze and get out of there.

If there was any time to start being a rock, a weapon, it was now. All day and night she'd thought about what kind of rock she could be, and how she could use her sharp edges to her advantage. The only answer that sprang to mind was her special blood.

The queen had figured it out. Luthian and Wisteria had figured it out. The only person afraid to use it to her advantage was Peaches herself. She'd been so caught up in her fear and being so different to these fae that she'd failed to see the benefit of having intoxicating blood.

She had also spent the past two years watching Balos turn rocks into weapons and objects of power. The next chance she got, she would sneak into Balos' workshop and pilfer mana stones to save for her great escape. Some stones might be helpful, some not, but at the very least, she could barter them for coin. She might even be lucky and find a portal stone.

With a solid plan formulating, she wasn't paying attention when the exit door burst open on a gust of snowy wind. The guards scrambled to close the doors. Tinger hopped out of her sling and bolted for the exit. Peaches ran after him, terrified that he'd be hurt. But the nimble little thing got past their legs and hopped straight into the eerie snow covered gardens.

"Tinger!" she shouted and ran after him. He was still too injured to be out there.

One of the guards, a shifter with fur-tipped and pointed ears, growled and grabbed Peaches roughly by the arm.

"What the fuck was that?" he snarled.

"Just my pet," she blurted, and tried to yank back her arm.

The second guard, a satyr with thick thighs and a flat nose, shoved her out into the snow. "Hurry up and get your creature in order. The last thing we need is for it causing havoc outside."

Peaches fell on her hands and knees into the snow, jarring her senses while the guards argued amongst themselves who was going to finish patrolling their zone while the other waited for her. Neither wanted to approach Tinger in case he shifted into his bipedal form. Cowards.

"Hurry, pix!"

She quickly got to her slippered, and now soaked feet. She chased Tinger down the path to a copse of trees. Giant evergreen canopies blocked the view of high curtain walls surrounding the palace ground. She hugged her cape and tried to ignore the way the wind bit her nose and cheeks, then trudged through the snow.

"Find that animal before I do," warned the satyr, his voice carrying through the mist.

Peaches followed paw prints through the snow and surveyed the garden with caution, silently grumbling that Tinger was not acting like a pet at all, despite what Balos had said.

Tall trees. Statues covered in snow. Frozen water features. Dark silhouettes of stone gargoyles perched on marble columns and wrapped in rose bushes and brambles. Wind teased her face, bringing with it the urge to hide.

"Tinger," she whispered loudly. "Come back here! It's not safe outside until you're healed."

She spotted him near the trunk of a tree as he cocked his leg to pee. When he was done, his antlered head swiveled and looked at her, two eyes staring hard.

And then it hit her. Maybe he wanted to escape as much as she did. While Peaches couldn't get over the high wall, especially not without trying to rescue Haze first, the same didn't go for the wolpertinger.

With a nervous glance over her shoulder to check on

the watching guards, she gave Tinger a little shooing motion with her hands. He hopped a few paces deeper into the trees, just like she'd hoped. But that was where her plan stopped. Because, in truth, there was no plan. Maybe Tinger wouldn't be able to get over the wall with those chicken wings. Maybe he'd freeze in the snow. Maybe this was a fool's errand.

She put her hand into her pocket and clutched the jagged edges of a rock for courage. She crunched over the snow a few steps, following Tinger. He hopped back to her and sniffed at her feet. She crouched and whispered, "I don't suppose you know how to actually fly, do you?"

Little brown dots of poop appeared behind the animal as he hopped about.

She deflated. "And I suppose it's too much to think you're one of those fae who can actually carry a message, maybe talk, maybe—I don't know." She palmed her face, feeling so stupid.

A gust of wind encircled her, prompting her to tug her cape closer and wince.

"Hurry up, pix!" shouted the guard.

She held up a placating hand and smiled tightly. "He's just taking a dump now! Won't be long."

The guard said something derogatory to his comrade.

"Oh well," she said to Tinger. "At least you didn't go potty in my room. And at least I get to smell fresh air for a while."

Caw.

Peaches startled and looked up. A crow perched on the web of spindly branches. Was it the steward? The crow cocked its head curiously, and hopped a branch closer and waited, almost as if it wanted to show her something. It tilted its head again. This time, she glimpsed a tiny blue glow near the bird's left eye.

Guardian.

A million words tried to come out of her mouth at once, but she held them in. A quick glance showed the guards still argued amongst themselves. One pointed in her direction. When she turned back, the crow was gone.

Moments later a horrendously loud boom rocked the ground and she almost lost her footing. Earthquake? No… something else. The guards went running through the snow, toward where the sound had come from—away from her. Up on the battlements, shouts rang out.

Tinger snarled at the hazy darkness behind her. Heart racing, Peaches strained to see beyond the misty shadowed recess within the grove. It was so quiet. Air curled around her body like a mini whirlwind, and then shoved her in the back, causing her to stumble forward. She clutched the rock in her pocket so hard, she cut herself. She closed her eyes and heard Haze's voice.

"Be brave, Sweetness."

When she opened her eyes, a sleek, muscular figure emerged from the mist. A man. A hot, naked man. She blinked rapidly. Tinger hopped in front of her and bared his fangs at the intruder.

Shoulder length, silken black hair fluttered around his face as though kissed by the wind. There was no wind. With narrowed eyes, he prowled around her like a panther deciding whether to devour her fast or slow.

"Pix." His voice was soft, seductive, and smooth. "Come closer."

It was the quiet ones you had to worry about.

The only reason her feet moved was that tiny blue teardrop tattoo beneath his eye. He was a Guardian, just like Haze. That meant she could trust him, right?

"Are you a Guardian?" she asked.

He inclined his head, eyes never leaving her. She shivered. Like Haze, a tangible element of danger whispered on the wind, urging her to use caution. Stories came to her, passed down through generations of fae and gossiped about in the palace. A beautiful bogey man made of flesh. He had no weapon, but she knew if he decided to silence her, she wouldn't stand a chance. She'd be dead before she could blink.

"I know why you're here," she said.

"Oh?" His brow arched.

"There's a prisoner you're looking for." She gulped in a breath.

His gaze raked down her body, assessing and judging. "Who are you to know the prisoners?"

"I'm a prisoner too."

Guards shouting came closer. *Hurry.*

"A big vampire?" the Guardian asked quickly. "Shaved head. Power enhancing tattoos?"

"Yes," she answered, swallowing hard. "That's him. Has bone studs in his ears."

Suspicion danced on the Guardian's expression. "Tell me more."

"He's probably shackled and beaten. But he's alive as far as I know."

"As far as you know?"

"Well, I know the queen won't risk killing him yet, especially not now that you're here trying to get in."

The Guardian stared hard at Peaches, as though he could see into her soul. "Tell him you spoke with Ash. Tell him we're working on it."

Another guard's boisterous shout grabbed her attention and when she looked back to the Guardian, a flurry of wind and black feathers was all she caught before he flew away in crow form. Peaches scooped up Tinger and dashed back inside the palace with only one thought running through her mind. Find Haze.

EIGHTEEN

Haze's body felt like it was being ripped in two. For two days he'd swung suspended in a cage somewhere near the Obsidian Palace. Or thereabouts. He wasn't sure. He'd been knocked unconscious when they'd dragged him in, but the moment he'd woken with the agonizing feeling of being cut from the Well, he knew this place had been designed specifically to torture winged fae. His shadow was intrinsically linked to his mana, so it had disappeared as well.

It was also colder than a witch's tit and he wore nothing but breeches and a torn tunic. His boots had been taken.

As far as he could tell, he dangled in the center of a tower made from obsidian and quartz. Steps jutting from the tower wall spiraled around him and descended further than he could see, even if he pressed his forehead to the cage bars. He'd clicked his tongue loudly and moved about the cage, testing out the drop distance with echolocation. Over a hundred feet. Deadly.

Through the cage bars above him, two curved openings in the tower filtered in light. Sometimes snow fell lazily on a breeze. Icicles forming beneath the cage were his only source of fluid. And it wasn't enough. It wasn't blood.

The sun had risen and fallen. Then the sun traveled again. Haze had drifted in and out of sleep, his body healing from wounds inflicted by soldiers on the night of the party. Occasionally, the pain of being cut from the Well lessened as his body acclimatized to the distance from ground level. They'd noted some Guardians could train themselves to draw from the Well at higher intervals than normal fae, just like they could train themselves to walk in the sun. But he was a long way from gaining his strength back.

No one came. Not even to feed him.

Daylight dragged his energy. He'd spent the time scratching transference runes into his palm, trying to get the right combination. He wondered why the queen hadn't come to gloat. He wondered why the soldiers hadn't come to hurt him more, especially Demeter. But most of all, he wondered about Peaches. Had Luthian taken her?

With hunger gnawing at his stomach, he mulled over the events from the party. Had a bargain actually been made for ownership of Peaches? What had Luthian said to Demeter? He couldn't pin-point anything for certain, only that Peaches had been terrified. That scared woman had tried to save him—a Guardian. Foolish. But endearing.

That ache around his heart squeezed again—he rubbed his chest. He'd failed her. He'd lost his temper when Luthian and Wisteria had goaded her. If he was a Guardian worth his salt, he would have ignored them. He would also have taken Peaches the moment he'd met her. He should have used the portal stone immediately and be damned with the consequences of activating within a tight space.

He rolled onto his side and stared at the black wall covered in lichen and ice beyond the five-foot cage. Some kind of substance coated the thick wooden cage, making it incredibly strong. They weren't fortified by magic. Couldn't be up here. Still, he'd tried but failed to make a dent. He'd also tried to swing the cage and reach for the wall, but his big arm was too thick to get between the bars. Without access to his mana, there was little he could do.

He couldn't give up. Peaches needed him. He had to find a way back to her. Licking his dry fangs, he told himself he wanted her so badly because of her blood. And he was hungry. But he knew that excuse was a lie. There was something about her that called to his instincts. He'd wanted her before he'd tasted her.

A sound below jolted him alert. He stilled and cocked his head, straining his ears. Footsteps. Small, hesitant.

Coming up the long staircase. He flexed his fists and readied himself for a fight. He didn't care who came. If it was the queen herself, he was getting out of there. But as the footsteps drew closer and louder, he became confused. He smelled Peaches.

So many emotions ran through him. Relief. Confusion. Trepidation. Guilt. Anger.

"What are you doing here?" he snapped as she came into sight. He rushed to each corner of the cage to peer down for danger, to see if anyone followed her. She moved slowly but steadily, her peach colored hair a beacon in the dark. No soldiers behind her. No other footsteps or scents.

She wore the same black velvet dress she'd worn when they'd first met, which was ridiculous. One slip and the skirt would trap her legs and she could fall straight down the middle of the tower. She clutched a bag slung over her shoulder and palmed the wall as she climbed.

Arriving at his cage, she smiled despite his gruff words earlier. Words she had ignored.

"Hello," she breathed, panting and flushed from the climb.

He shook his head, dumbfounded. "You shouldn't be here."

"But I am." Her grin widened, like she was proud of herself and, dammit, he should be too. But that feeling inside his gut wriggled away like a worm, allowing dread to creep in.

"You have to go," he said. "There's no way to help me."

She patted her satchel. "I brought some mana stones, and I brought a vial of my blood for you to feed."

"Peaches," he growled.

"I left Tinger in my bed because the moment I found out you were here, I knew he'd probably jump straight out of my arms and fall all the way down." She swayed a little as she glanced down, then pressed against the wall and closed her eyes. "I didn't call him Haze, by the way. He's definitely a Tinger. And—"

Tears gathered at the corners of her eyes.

"Sweetness," he breathed, crouching to her level. Concern pierced him. "What happened? Did Luthian—?"

"No. I've not seen him since the party. So much has happened." She took a trembling breath and opened her eyes. "I found Tinger in my bed. He was covered in puncture marks."

"Someone fed from him?"

"No. I think the queen injected him with some kind of liquid metal."

So it was true. The queen was conducting illegal experiments perverting mana. Months ago, Clarke and Rush had come across the leader of the human faction from Crystal City using a similar liquid to forcibly push mana from Rush's sister... and then drank it to de-age himself. Haze repeated what he knew to Peaches.

"And this Clarke," Peaches said. "She's another human like me?"

Haze nodded. "You'll like her."

She gave him a small smile. "Maybe."

He tried to reach for her, but his arm couldn't get through the bars beyond his thick forearm. *Four feet of air* between them felt like a chasm.

"How did you get up here?" He shook his head, bewildered. "The guards..."

"I used the only weapon I have. My blood." When her words came out, she almost sounded surprised at herself. "I sold it."

"You what?"

"I sold it to the guards in return for them letting me see you."

His brows lowered. "They've tasted your blood? They know you're human? Well-blessed? Dammit, Peaches. Do you know the kind of danger you're in?"

"It's fine. Luthian sold my blood in Rubrum City. Why shouldn't I do the same?"

"My bet is he didn't tell anyone where it came from, did he?"

She bit her lip.

"No," he continued. "He wouldn't have. Just like the queen kept your secret, they know what a valuable commodity you are."

Her expression shuttered at the word commodity. Fuck. "I don't think you're a commodity, Peaches. I just want to get you back to the Order safe. You believe me, don't you?"

But the words couldn't be taken back. *Shit.* He had to

get out of there. Clenching his jaw, he leveled his stare at the vial in her fingers. He reached. Without leaning too far, and fear flashing in her eyes, she stretched to meet him with the vial. His fingers brushed her knuckles. She made a sound of frustration and then slammed back against the wall, panting. "I'm not going to get it to you. And... I don't feel so good up here."

He looked closely at her face. Even in the low light, he could see the dark circles beneath her eyes and a light sheen of sweat on her upper lip. It was more than being out of breath from the climb.

"Are you ill?"

"I don't think I'm good with heights."

"Try tossing the vial."

"It's the only one I have," she said warily. "What if I miss?"

"We don't have a choice. I'm about to eat my arm off," he said. She gasped and he couldn't help grinning. "I have more control than that, Sweetness. I'm kidding."

"Good. I like your arms. Okay, fine. You ready?"

Peaches aimed and squinted at the bars. Then tossed. The vial arced through the air, turning slowly until it hit the bar, not the gap. On reflex his hand shot out, trying to catch the tiny glass thing. He brushed it, but failed. With a gut-wrenching feeling, he watched the darkness swallow his meal. Then a few seconds later, the wet crash of glass on stone.

He exhaled. It was worth a try.

"Haze," she said, an apology in her voice.

"It's okay. I'll get out of here somehow. You should go. The last thing you want is for the guards to change their minds."

"Oh," she blurted. "That reminds me. I met one of your friends."

"Friends?" Haze had no friends.

She whispered, "He said his name was Ash. He said to tell you they're working on it."

Haze stilled. "Ash?"

She nodded.

"What else did he say?"

"That was it. He just said they're working on it. But the palace staff were gossiping about a group of Guardians denied entry. The day after the party, guards were spooked and doing extra patrols. There were loud explosions outside. Something happened and now the palace is in lockdown."

"When? A day ago?"

She nodded.

"Anything since?"

She shook her head, deflated, but she'd given him hope. The Twelve knew he was missing. They knew he was here. It was only a matter of time before they forced their way in. If he could get proof out to them about the queen's experiments, then they'd have cause for a raid. Ash had probably come with a scouting party. After speaking with Peaches, they would most likely go back to the Order and get full support from the Prime. The next time they returned, it would be with the rest of the Twelve. He just had to wait it out.

If only he could feed.

NINETEEN

"I'm jumping."

Peaches' two words gave Haze a heart attack.

"What?"

"I'm going to jump over the gap and grab the cage." She nodded, as though silently convincing herself. "It's an easy gap."

"Are you mad?"

"It's fine. You can reach out to grab my hands and hold on to me. Then you can feed from me." She met his eyes. "I might not get another chance to come. You need to feed."

"They won't let me starve."

"You're starving now! I can see it in your eyes."

"Don't you dare," he said, but she was already looking up and around the cage, inspecting it.

"There's a rope pulley above. Maybe it's better if I get up to that and shimmy down to the cage."

He shut his eyes, unable to believe what he was hearing. She would fall.

His stomach bottomed out.

She would fall.

"Don't," he whispered. But his voice was so small, coming from a far distant place. He started to see blood and broken wings. He heard a baby wailing for her mother. Vomit rose in his gullet, but nothing came out. Haze forced himself to breathe through the memory. Not now. Don't lose it now.

But the hunger made him weak. It invited delirium to his side, like a thief stealing his sense. Sounds echoed. A part of him heard Peaches climbing higher. A part of him could see her slipping and falling to her death. And a part of him revolted. *No.* She would not die today.

He would protect her with his life.

He opened his eyes and located her. Two dainty slippered feet had climbed high enough that he'd lost sight of her face.

"Yeah," she muttered. "The rope up here goes straight down to the top of the cage. It's knotted securely. There's no way I can undo that and lower the cage. I'll climb down the rope. It's safer than me jumping. Easy."

"Crimson help me." The top of the cage was barred, just like the outside. He could see through. She was right. The staircase ended in a platform beneath the pulley. She touched the rope. The cage wobbled. He braced and balanced himself until the wobble eased. A trickle of hope splashed through him. Maybe she was right. Even though the next words hurt to say, he knew he had to trust her. To allow her this choice, even though his every instinct wanted to keep her safe. "You ease yourself down as slowly as you can."

"Got it."

"I swear to the Well, Peaches. If you slip, I will murder you."

A short laugh and then she lowered herself onto the rope and twisted her legs so she clung like a monkey. The pulley groaned and moaned, getting used to both their weights. He sent a silent prayer to the goddess that Peaches' arms would remain steady, that her grip would be strong. The cage rocked as she shimmied down. He held his breath and exhaled as she made it to the cage.

"See?" she said breathlessly. "Easy."

He shook his head. "You're insane."

"Brave," she corrected. Swallowed. "I've been doing as you said. They need me."

He stared. Blinked. Before he'd left the party, he'd told her to be brave. She'd listened. The desire to kiss her washed away any pain in his body, if only for an instant. "Yes, Peaches. You've been so brave."

"Now feed." She lowered a slender arm through the gap in the bars.

Suddenly, with everything he'd craved offered to him, inches from his face, he couldn't see straight. A surge of ravenous need coursed through him. His body turned to stone. He forced himself to move carefully to avoid his animal instincts tearing her apart. What he'd done to Wisteria was only a taste of what a vampire was capable of. Bloodlust was a real thing.

He scented the sweet skin at her wrist and licked along her vein. Tastebuds watered. With a groan of agonizing need, Haze's eyes fluttered closed, and he had to steady himself.

Breathe in. Breathe out. Don't rip her wrist into shreds.

Take the time to make it pleasant for her. Don't let it be like her other times. Respect her. He pricked his tongue on his fang, and then licked the vein, allowing his saliva and blood to coat a pink line, preparing it for an invasion of fangs.

"What are you doing?" she whispered.

"Preparing you properly."

"That's a thing? They usually just bite me. Or Luthian would cut me and drain me."

He squeezed his eyes shut. Fucking prick. He would rip his head off, be damned with the consequences. He would hunt the elf down and pick him off without anyone seeing. Then leave his rotting corpse for the tachi in Redvein Forest.

A fresh, juicy spot pumped with what he needed. He could resist his hunger no longer. His fangs sank in. Blood welled out. He laved, careful to run along her bite and force the drop of his own blood in. The effect was instant.

Peaches moaned and relaxed against the cage. Her

other arm fell through a gap and she rested her forehead against the wooden bars.

"Are you telling me I could feel like this every time?" Her eyes rolled in bliss.

But he'd already stopped hearing. All he could think of was how her blood tasted like some kind of precious jewel turned liquid. The sun. The moon. The Well itself trickled from her vein and he lapped it up like it was the air he breathed. Every time his tongue rasped over her flesh, she moaned again. With every drop of her blood entering his body, he too felt a change come over him.

He'd teased Indigo for how he'd behaved after feeding from Ada. But now Haze understood. This was the nectar of life. How on earth could Maebh resist this temptation every single day?

Because there was something she wanted more.

The more he licked and laved, the more his body turned to mush. His arms and legs tingled. His mind whirled. His pulse surged. His cock hardened.

Purer than a sip of divilixir.

He wanted her. He craved to be inside her. To taste her again. This time directly with his tongue on her slick sex, swiping up and down, driving into that tasty spot. His desire burned within him, pulsing as the heat of her blood warmed him from the center out. To find him, this precious female had fought against her crippling fear. To manipulate the guards. To climb a cage and feed him. There was something about her that called to every base instinct in his arsenal.

When he'd drunk enough to take the edge off his hunger, he forced himself to ease off. Too much, and his wits would take hours to return. It was the most painful thing he'd ever done, but he licked over her wound and lifted her wrist to her. She moaned and smiled dreamily down at him.

"Sweetness," he said, taking special care to enunciate his words when all he wanted to do was slur and fall into a puddle of sensation. "Hold your hand level with your body so you don't drip and bleed out." There were more explanations running through his mind about saliva and coagulants, but he couldn't catch them.

"More," she insisted and pushed her hand back down.

"I can't drink too much. Not while you're clinging to a cage suspended a hundred feet in the air."

"Mm," she murmured sleepily. "Makes sense."

"S-stay 'lert," he slurred. Fuck. Only a small amount of her blood made him feel like this. What would a full feed be like? He slotted his fingers through the cage and took hold of her waist.

"What are you doing?" she mumbled.

"Making sure you don't fall." His vision blurred and tipped, but he held her firm.

"You're the best." Her eyelids drooped and her head dropped again, squishing her face between the bars. With him looking up, they were an inch apart. He could kiss her.

A strangled groan caught in his throat. He couldn't stop staring at her lips.

"When we get out of here, when you're safe, I'm going to kiss those lips and then I'm going to ravage you." A different kind of hunger gripped him. "I'm going to feast between your legs, and then I'm going to fuck you until you can't walk and I need to carry you."

"I'd like that," she mumbled.

His bark of laughter burst his need. She made a satisfied humming sound. "I'm serious. I want that."

"Me too."

Her eyes fluttered.

"Don't sleep." He squeezed her waist, hating how all he wanted to do was lie down, too. Lie down on top of her and sink between her legs. Damn him, but he needed to do that.

"So kiss me," she said and licked her lips.

He lifted until their lips joined. He dragged his tongue across the seam before she opened to him. Once inside her mouth, their tongues dueled, rolling over each other with erotic heat and slick pressure. His knees weakened. They pulled apart, surprised at the intensity of their feelings, and stared at each other through the bars dividing them.

"When we're safe," she promised, nodding her head.

Her movement shifted her body, and the bag slung over her shoulder slipped. Out poured stones onto his head and shoulders. Peaches gasped and he moved involuntarily. The cage rocked and Peaches squeaked. He held her steady until the rocking stopped.

They both breathed a sigh of relief.

"Well-dammit," he cursed.

"My bad." She wrapped her fingers around the bars. "I got it. I'm good."

He nodded. His head swirled with a pleasant tingle. "I'm still not letting you go."

"Okay," she whispered. "Just until I feel focused."

Sounds below filtered up. Adrenaline jolted through him. Peaches tensed. Her knuckles turned white on the bars.

"Who knows you're up here?" he asked.

"Just the guard I sold the blood to." She bit her lip. "But we dropped the vial, remember? Maybe someone saw it."

"Or maybe someone is finally coming for me."

Haze glanced down at his feet. At the different kinds of stones spilled. He flared his eyes and tried to focus through the drugging pleasure, still trying to take hold of him.

"What are these?" he asked.

"I don't know. I grabbed a bunch of mana stones from Balos' workshop. I thought maybe if one of them was useful, we could use them to get out of here."

"Clever girl." He squeezed her. "I'm going to let go of you, just for a moment and take a look. Hold on tight."

She nodded. He crouched, using his hand to balance against the cage floor. The change in position hurt his still hard erection, and he had to adjust himself and take a moment to appreciate the zing barreling up his spine. *For fuck's sake*. Talk about the wrong place, wrong time. He was so hard, he could come with a few strokes. With her tongue even faster. Or to dip inside her tight, hot center… he would finish like a shooting star.

"Haze?"

"Yeah."

"You've been staring at the ground for a while."

He shook his head. Cleared his throat.

"When we're safe," he repeated to himself. He would have Peaches. He would claim her as his own. The idea felt right. Perfect. He didn't care if they weren't mated like the others in the cadre. He would have her anyway and fuck anyone who dared to say otherwise.

First, he had to sift through this mess. One by one, and hyper aware of the footsteps getting closer, he pushed all distractions away and focused. There were many mana stones. One for fire. One for warding wild animals away. One for warming water. One for summoning water.

"Any left in the bag?" he asked. "Any portal stones?"

"There's a few more in here, but…" She rolled a little to make room so she could dig into the bag. The cage tilted.

He jumped to hold her steady. Blood roared in his ears, pushing out his lazy addled brain fog. Footsteps grew louder. A few stones on the cage floor rolled and fell off the edge. *Shit*. He closed his eyes and held onto Peaches, dread sinking like a stone.

"What about this one?" she whispered hopefully. "It

doesn't look like the other portal stones Balos worked on. His safe was locked, but it feels kind of similar. Maybe it's just not filed down yet."

A jagged rock dangled in her fingers before his face.

He smelled ozone on it and recognized the runes.

"Fuck, Peaches." He grinned. "You found one."

"I did?"

"Yeah, you fucking did. Portal stones don't all look the same, depending on where they go. I've not seen this type before, but who cares. It will take us out of here." He kissed her again, and then the next problem came to mind.

They had to walk through a portal. Even if they could safely open one here, how would he get them both through? He was locked in a cage.

"What's the problem?" she asked.

He relayed his thoughts, their voices hushed and urgent.

"What about if you activate it beneath the cage?" she suggested.

Below? "How would we walk into it?"

"We don't walk. We fall."

Bloody limbs. Crushed wings. A baby's wail. The blood roaring in his ears grew louder, drowning out the climbing footsteps.

"Fall?" he repeated.

"I have a knife. Hold me again while I check my pocket."

He clutched her waist while she searched, flinched, and

screwed up her face. "Ew. Can't believe I forgot that was in there?"

"What?"

"Balos' red cap. Wait. Here it is." She pulled out a dagger and held it against the rope holding up the cage. "I can cut it. We can both drop through the portal."

A million reasons why not to whirred through his head. The stone might not work this high. He wasn't connected to the Well. They might kill themselves. They might fall through a portal into a hostile environment, or water. He turned the stone over in his palm, trying to see the location it was keyed to, and failed. But as someone shouted up, he knew they were out of time.

"You! What are you doing up there?" bellowed a male guard.

The look Peaches and Haze shared said it all. This was it. Their only chance out. The cadre might be coming for him, but it would be too late. Peaches had lied and manipulated to get in here. Haze could take the punishment, but he would never let her suffer on his behalf.

"We have to do it," she urged him.

"I know."

"I refuse to stay here any more."

She started sawing on the rope. He took the portal stone in his hand and pointed it at his feet, and then realized something. He wouldn't be able to activate it until he had access to his mana.

Peaches sawed against the rope.

What if his connection took too long to hit? What if he didn't have enough mana to activate the stone?

Behind the dark coated guard was another and a flash of white further down. When Haze zeroed in on it, his blood went cold. Maebh herself. She looked up, fury in her eyes. She hiked up her dress to increase her pace, pushing the first guard out of her way, heedless of him toppling and falling down the hole. The guard didn't even scream.

Maebh wouldn't be able to access her mana up here, either. If he timed it right. This could work.

"Stop him!" she shouted to the guard ahead of her. "He knows too much."

Frayed strings of rope plucked away as Peaches sawed. The cage dropped. Peaches screamed and clutched the bars. He held her waist. Together. They fell together.

The ground rushed up. Only after they passed the queen, her mouth agape, did he let go of Peaches. He shoved his hand outside the cage, pointed down, and when the rush of the Well greeted him like an old friend, he activated the port—

TWENTY

Peaches' scream died in her throat as she landed. Her bones jarred. Her head hit the cage, and she careened to the side as the impact threw and rolled her. They'd fallen down through the portal, but it had spit them out from the side. The horizon tumbled around and around as she rolled. She glimpsed gray sky, dirt. Sky. Dirt. Sky. Dirt.

And then she stopped.

Her mind thought they were still rolling. Groaning, she grabbed her head. Couldn't move. She laid down. The knife was still in her hand; her knuckles sore from grasping it. It was a wonder she hadn't stabbed herself.

"Peaches!" roared Haze.

He's okay.

Her heart lurched. She put the knife back in its sheath

in her pocket and sat slowly this time. She waved. "I'm here."

Where was here?

An empty, sand-filled courtyard littered with clumps of snow. Tall hedges with thorns and roses of all colors surrounded her in a square formation. Icicles on the thorns. Gaps in the hedges were at two intervals, like doorways. A large, high statue of a woman holding the moon was in the middle of the courtyard. *I know that statue.* She had seen the tip of it from windows high up in the palace. This was the labyrinth at the center of the Obsidian Palace.

"No." Tears formed in her eyes. "We're only here?"

She'd at least hoped the portal would take them into the Seelie realm.

Haze grunted. She whirled to look at him and gasped. He was still in the cage, and he was bloody all over, crouched and hunched, breathing hard. She'd never thought she'd be so happy to see a person's shadow, but his was there on the outside, trying to wrench open the cage. Haze's thin tunic was already in tatters and hung from him in strips. He grasped a chunk and ripped it off like he was too hot.

Too hot.

The sun was up.

She scrambled to her feet and rushed over to him. "Are you okay?"

He nodded. "Just need to get out of here."

"What can I do?"

"I need Justice."

"What's that?"

"My war hammer."

"Okay. Where do I find it?"

He hunched over his palms. "You don't. It finds me."

"You're not making sense."

His lashes lifted, and he met her eyes. The confident warrior was missing. He opened his mouth, then shut it, shaking his head.

"Haze," she said, reaching him through the bars. "What do you need?"

"You won't be able to help me," he said, holding up scratched and bloody palms. "I need to know the runes that are used in a transference spell. It will bring my weapon to me."

She frowned. "Can't help you? How do you know that? I mean, for all you know I've been studying runic spells for years."

He startled. "Have you?"

"Sort of!" She flared her eyes at him. "Maybe."

His jaw hardened. "Have you or haven't you?"

"Balos taught me some things. I know how to read Elven scripture. And I've been learning a little about how to infuse stone with mana. So, yeah. I guess I have." She lifted her chin. "What do you need?"

"Give me a stick." He gestured to the brambles and thorns. Peaches snapped a twig off and brought it back.

Haze bent and swiped a space in the dirt, then marked it with the stick. "The runes are something like this but I'm missing something."

He watched her as she studied the glyphs. With a swallow, she accessed the part of her brain that had been so good with studying in her time. She hadn't used it since college, and then in her daily job. Casting her eye over the marks Haze had made, she associated them with things Balos had taught her. Over and over she went, running through everything she could think of. Transference. No stones involved, so no need for associative marks that worked with particular rocks. Wait.

She glanced at him. "What are you calling to you? What substance is it?"

"My hammer?"

She nodded.

"It's iron and wood."

"That's it." She grinned, pointing at the final mark he'd created. "That symbol isn't linked to iron, but a generic metal. Make this change—" She swiped the dirt, clearing the symbol, intending to redraw, but a crunch of twigs snatched her attention, making every hair on her body stand on end. "What was that?"

Haze became deathly still. Clouds puffed out of her mouth as she peered around. Then something happened that made her rub her eyes. Thorny twigs topping the hedges moved, peeling away. Forming before her eyes were tall and spindly bipedal creatures made of wood and thorns. They had antlers on their heads, and sharp spikes running down their spines, thorns for teeth, eyes like black holes devoid of life. The face was a skull made of ropes of dead wood. Its rib cage was covered with skin-like bark that peeled and sloughed off.

Three of them. Four. *Five.* Peaches whirled around. Every time she turned, another made itself known, their branches creaking.

"Haze?"

"Finish the rune, Peaches." Haze's shadow stepped between Peaches and the twig-horned beings.

"What are they?"

"Dryads. Finish the rune. Don't look at them."

Oh god, oh god. This was why she'd stayed inside the palace. Elphyne was a scary and dangerous place.

"Hurry," he said. "My mana hasn't refilled enough to use defensively. I need my weapon!"

Right. Finish the rune. She bent down and dragged the stick through the sand, fumbling and trembling.

"Duck!" Haze barked.

She dropped as a branch swung over her head. Not a branch, an arm. She fell on top of the runes she'd been marking and had to start again. It didn't help that her heart was in her head, or her stomach was inside out. Panic paralyzed her. "I can't do it. I'm not—"

"Brave. Yes, you are. Ignore them. We need you." Haze's shadow tugged on a branchy arm, pulling while Haze cupped his mouth and shouted, "Come here, you over-grown plants. Pick on someone your own size."

Heads swiveled his way. The dryad closest to Peaches paused. She started writing in the sand again. But the dryad turned back to her, blocking the sun. Branches wrapped around her torso, slithered around her arms and neck, and squeezed. She went airborne, her feet dangling, breath strangling.

She dug at the branches wrapping around her throat, wincing through pain as her nails ripped. She plucked the vine-like spindles from her body. She kicked and thrashed.

She pulled every twig and root until she fell an inch closer to the ground. The dryad roared an inhuman sound, and it felt like every evil in the labyrinth turned her way. She glanced over at Haze. Dryads completely smothered his cage.

"Haze." He'd be a sitting duck in there. *"Haze."*

The knife! Into her pocket her hand went. She prayed it was still there, that it hadn't fallen out. Her fingers wrapped around the cold hilt with a cry of triumph. Cold, hard determination steeled her resolve. Her trembling stilled.

Peaches snapped.

She stabbed the knife into the dryad, over and over like a sewing machine needle. Bits of wood chipped off. Whole limbs severed. She didn't stop until she fell to the sand and snow. Then she jumped on top of the thing and stabbed its eyes and ribcage until manabeeze started drifting lazily from the dryad's corpse, signaling its death. Manabeeze. *Get back.* The last thing she needed was to be hit by one. She lurched back and raced to her scratched runes and finished.

She couldn't see Haze through the dryads attacking his cage.

Be brave.

She screamed and stabbed where she could, careful not to step on her runes. A dryad swung his big hand out defensively, hitting her on the jaw, sending her flying backward. She saw stars as she landed hard. But at least the dryads were distracted by her.

"It's done!" she shouted at Haze and pointed to the markings in the dirt.

His eyes met hers through the gaps, then dipped to the sand. He nodded and scratched into his palm, wincing as he drew blood.

Then he looked up and grinned. "Get back, Sweetness."

Peaches scrambled back as far as she could, ducking under more dryads as they reached for her. They were slow and cumbersome, she realized. Like dopey things with no brains. When her back hit the hedge, she looked at Haze. A shape materialized in his palm. Long bar. Bulky rectangle at one end. One side of the rectangle was pointed, like a pick-ax. When it completely formed in his palm, he swore with victory. Tendons bulged in his neck. Veins popped. Muscles flexed and hardened.

If Peaches didn't know him, she'd be more afraid of

him than the dryads. His fury seemed to suck the air away, even here, outdoors.

There wasn't much room in the cage, but he was a warrior with a mission. He spun and swung, using his might to smash the hammer into the thick wooden bars, splintering them. Haze obliterated it. He struck again and again until the gap was wide enough to fit through. When he emerged and straightened to his full height, the creatures around him hesitated.

The hammer was a tool for bludgeoning. Haze smashed wooden skeletons like they were pieces of straw. Peaches was filled with awe as she watched him. If she had to admit it, she was a little attracted to his power. It was almost like watching a lumberjack do his thing with an ax. A hot, half-naked lumberjack.

Roots and vines burst from the hedge behind her. They wrapped around her body like ribbons, pulling her against the sharp, thorny wall. She screamed, went for her knife, but couldn't move her arm. Darkness crowded her vision. The hedge. She was being dragged inside it. Something had her ankles. It yanked in the opposite direction until she screamed at the feeling of being pulled apart.

Fire exploded above her. The heat of the flames burned her face. She flinched, but then was dragged back out into the courtyard. Haze had her legs. His face was a beast to behold. Lightning in his eyes. Jaw clenched. Nostrils flared. Fury incarnate. Behind Peaches, flames still licked at the bush, crackling and spitting as the dead wood fueled it.

Haze yanked Peaches to her feet and held her against his chest. "You're okay."

It took her a moment to relax against his warm chest. And when it sank in that she was safe and he was out, she wrapped her arms around him and clung on for dear life. They hugged each other, trembling and tight. Hugged until she could breathe again. Finally, she pulled back and looked up at him.

With tender eyes, he brushed hair from her face, then cupped the back of her neck.

"We're going to get out of here," he promised. "We just need to wait a few hours until I refill, and then I'll fly us home."

Embarrassed at the depth of her emotion, she pressed her cheek against his hard, smooth chest. Haze's big hand held her head there. A deep rumble of satisfaction met her ear, and she squeezed him tighter. The sense of floating came over her. Neither of them noticed the sensation was sand at their feet until it was too late. It dragged them down, sucking their limbs.

"What's happening?" she gasped, stepping, failing. The muddy sand had her in its grip.

"Quicksand."

Her life flashed before her eyes as she gaped at him.

"It's fine," he said, both to her and his shadow who'd tried to tug him out.

"What?"

"Stop struggling."

She clung to him like a life raft.

"When it hits your chin," he said, "take a deep breath and hold it. We're going down."

How could he be so calm? "Where?"

"Goblin territory."

TWENTY-ONE

Haze held Peaches securely as they descended through the quicksand. When his feet touched the ground again, and air brushed his face, sand dripped onto their heads like globs of rain.

The hammer head was stuck in the sand ceiling, probably because of its metal properties. The quicksand acted as a secret door to this realm. He guessed the only reason the entire thing didn't fall on top of them was the mana holding it together. He checked on Peaches, but she still held her breath and squeezed her eyes shut against him. Unable to let go of his weapon in case it was sucked up, he threaded his free hand into her hair and grasped it in his fist. He tilted her head back.

"Peaches. Breathe."

She gasped. Two wide, gorgeous eyes locked onto him. Every cell in his body wanted to continue staring into those depths, as magnetic as the quicksand they'd just traveled through, but a yank on his arm forced his attention back to the ceiling. The surface rippled like waves that should be in a sea below them, not above their heads. The sand tried to take his hammer, sucking it away as though to spit it out in the courtyard they'd come from.

"No, you fucking don't." He put two hands on the handle and used his weight to battle the quicksand until the hammer fell. "Mine."

Cracking his neck, he exhaled and turned his attention back to Peaches, and where in the seven circles of the Well they were. He knew it was goblin territory, but Guardians rarely visited. Little glowing stones twinkled in the wall, providing a soft light for them to see. They were in a tunnel with bones embedded in the walls. When he looked closer, he found it was more than skeletons. Some had shapes around the bones. Some shapes looked like stone people.

"Fossils," Peaches said, running her hand over the stone people and then the glowing stones. "And... that glow looks like fluorescent sodalite. I've seen this type of rock around Lake Michigan." She ran her fingers over it. "Maybe not. I think natural light is needed to make them glow."

She dug her fingers into the sediment and tried to pull a glowing rock out. Haze remembered she had another of those in her collection. It wouldn't budge. She returned to the fossilized people, frowning.

"Fossils." He didn't know that word. Or the other ones. "Something from your time?"

She nodded. "It's when a body is encased in volcanic ash, or mud and silt, or something like that. The body decomposes, but their shape remains." She continued to inspect the bones in the walls. "These are people. Humans. Possibly from…"

Her breath hitched and she jerked back from the wall.

"What is it?"

"T-they're from my time. Look." She pointed at something stuck in the wall next to a bone. A thin line of some kind of degraded surface and a rusted metal buckle. "That's a watch band."

When she touched it, the parts of the band crumbled and fell apart. A few steps onward, Peaches touched a white, smooth, curved surface. She gasped as her fingers trailed over a faded, crumbled picture on the white surface.

"It's a styrofoam cup," she whispered, eyes glistening. "It's from a coffee shop in my city."

"Let's keep moving," he said. "Find a way out."

But Peaches' face had paled. She bent forward and started breathing slowly through her mouth as though she was about to be sick.

"Oh god," she mumbled, shaking her head, hands on her knees. "I might have known these people. Might have passed them in the street."

"Take a seat, Peaches." He helped her to the ground

and caught a drop of falling sand before it hit her head. "Just take a moment."

"I can't do it," she said, pointing to the white cup in the wall. "I tried. But I can't do it anymore. I've got nothing left in the tank."

He growled and smashed his hand onto the foam cup, crumbling it to pieces. "You have to."

"No."

"Peaches."

But she wasn't listening to him. Her body language was cold. She refused to look him in the eyes. He hadn't seen someone lose hope like this since... since Holly. His lover had come to him with pain in her eyes... no, worse than pain. He'd stared into her eyes and found emptiness. The sort of despair that was cold. He'd tried to break through, but he'd failed. The look in Peaches' eyes reminded him all too much of that coldness.

Holly had hated the trappings of motherhood. She wanted to be wild and free.

Haze fumbled with the handle of his hammer.

"Hey," he said, crouching to her level. "I know you've been through a lot, and we've got a long way to go, but I'm here with you. You're not alone."

Just like the quicksand that had sucked them down, her despair seemed to take her as well. He felt for her. The life she'd lived. She deserved happiness, and he wanted to give it to her. Not because of some deep-seated duty, but because she'd done so much for him already. He swiped a single tear running down her cheek with his thumb.

"Come on," he said gently. "Let's go. You don't get to quit, Peaches."

"You can't tell me what I can and can't feel."

"Now you're acting like a pup."

"You can't tell me how to feel." Great shuddering sobs wracked her body. "You don't even know me, Haze." She threw her hand at the skulls sticking out of the wall. "Those people knew me."

"You're right." He hand-signed his apology. "That was insensitive of me."

He didn't know what to do. This was where he failed. Feelings were for females, and Haze knew nothing about them. He hadn't known what to do when Holly had needed him. He didn't know now. He could see Peaches was hurting, and he had to try. Because one thing he'd said was right. No one was quitting. Not on his watch.

"I'm telling you not to quit because—" His words stuck in his throat. Peaches looked up at him expectantly. He couldn't lose her. "Because someone special quit on me once."

He stared at the ground, finally realizing what had driven him all this time. He hated Holly for what she did just as much as he hated himself for not being able to stop her. He blamed her and he blamed himself. She quit. She left him. And then their child had died. Holly was a free soul. He shouldn't hate her for an accident.

Staring hard at the floor, he rasped. "You have to be brave. You need to keep going."

"Because the Order needs me?" she mumbled.

"I need you too."

She shook her head. "I'm not the brave kind. I lied. I pretended. Back home, it wasn't me who was running track or competing in games. I was the non athletic type. At school I hid beneath the bleachers and played with rocks and built little stone houses for ants."

"Why did ants need houses in your time?"

She sniffed. "They didn't."

"So...?"

"Because it was fun. I don't know."

"It seems to me your kind had too much time on their hands." Haze eased himself down next to her and they sat side by side in the tunnel of bones, her people. It suddenly occurred to him that Peaches was the one left behind. While these people hadn't exactly quit on her, they were taken away, and she had no choice but to remain.

Like him.

He was the one left behind. The one mopping up the mess and trying to figure out how to survive and keep living when all he'd wanted to do was give up. Peaches sighed as he put his arm around her shoulders. When her hand snaked over his stomach and she rested against him, he squeezed her tighter. She felt good in the crook of his arm. She felt like a part of him. For a brief moment, he wanted to stay there in that tunnel forever.

"I'm…" She choked, took a deep breath, and then rubbed her fist over his heart instead of hers. A show of unity. Of recognition. "You lost someone special."

"Yeah." He took her smaller fist in his own.

No more words were needed. They both knew how much it hurt. How the pain never left. How sometimes it gnawed your insides until you couldn't sleep at night and yet other times all you wanted to do was sleep. Grief had made Haze do stupid things.

It made him jump into the ceremonial lake.

He'd always said it was because he wanted to protect, to avoid another Holly if he could, but a small part of him hadn't wanted to emerge from the lake. He was grateful the Well had looked into his soul and understood his truth. Because it had, he was here with Peaches helping her.

"You're probably right," she mumbled and wiped her nose.

"I'm right a lot, but you might have to be more specific."

"You said we had too much time on our hands back then. Too much money. Too much ego. You were right. We did. Do you know what my job was?"

"What, Sweetness?"

"I was a geologist. I hunted down rare rocks and studied them." A short laugh. "Can you believe it? I mean… what good is that now? I should have spent my time learning how to grow beans or—"

"Make houses for ants?"

She swatted him and laughed again. That tinkling sound warmed his insides. He wanted to tell a million jokes just so he could hear it again. He was tired of the grief. Of the hate for something that was no one's fault. That just happened. Perhaps he would act like the court jester or make a fool of himself for Peaches. But he would do it standing before her so he could watch her face light up.

"You know," he said, his fingers idly playing with her curls. "It seems to me your job was very important."

She scoffed. "Important enough to end the world. I helped locate uranium."

"No, I mean now. In this time."

She arched back to look him in the eye. "Wha-choo talking about, Willis?"

"Well... firstly. I don't know who that is, but I'm guessing you're having another 'your time' thing. Secondly..." He showed his scratched palm, wounds already crusted over. "You helped me work out this."

"I learned to read with Balos."

"And what else did you learn from Balos?"

"I guess... I guess I learned how to infuse mana into stones."

He nodded and lifted his brows as if it was obvious. "Stones?"

Dawning registered on her face. "Stones!"

His lips curved on one side. Seeing her fill with pride was like seeing the sun rise over the water.

"That's a very complicated profession," he said. "There aren't many in Elphyne who can do that because the theory behind knowing what stones work with mana is complicated. Do you think you can do this yourself?"

"As a geologist, I knew all about rocks and the earth." She patted his pec again as something else came to her. "I can make my own portal stones! Probably. I mean... I mean, I haven't actually done it, but I know the theory. I think I could. If I had mana."

"You can."

She rubbed a spot on her arm and looked wistfully at the fossils. "Yeah," she whispered. "I was a *good* geologist."

Her eyes slid to him and softened. He could see the word forming on her tongue, the thank you, so he swallowed it with a kiss. The moment they touched, every cell in his body cried out for more. She opened for him. Her tongue, her hands, the little sounds she made as he deepened the kiss.

He grasped the hair at her nape and held her firm, keeping her eyes on his while they breathed, their lips an inch apart. Everywhere he looked, he found beauty. Flawless skin. Lashes framing chestnut eyes. Pink tipped nose. Rosy, swollen lips. He dragged his nose along her jaw to her ear and inhaled deeply at that spot where females smelled so good. A deep, needy grumble fell out of him. Desire punched him hard, clouding his vision. All he wanted was to taste her again.

"When we're safe," he promised.

"Yeah," she breathed.

He cleared his throat, grabbed his war hammer, and stood. She joined him and dusted herself off. He needed to get her cleaned. Taken care of. She deserved to be pampered.

"So what now?" she asked.

He glanced up and down the tunnel. His mana refilled like a trickle of cool water down a parched throat. But he wasn't full yet. Even if he had enough to shift his wings out, they were trapped in a tunnel. "Can't fly home now, so I guess we find a way out of this underground labyrinth by foot."

"Haze?" she said, her voice going small. "How did you do it?"

"Do what?"

"How do you keep going? How do you continue to be brave?"

He cupped her jaw. "I admit, there were days I didn't want to get out of bed. I wanted to quit, too. But... I figured something out. Let me show you." He took her hand and stepped forward. "Like that."

She copied him. "I don't get it."

He grinned and squeezed her hand. "Do it again."

They stepped together.

"And again."

They kept going until they were walking side by side, down the dark tunnels. A few seconds in, she said, "I still don't get it."

He smiled and kissed her knuckles. "We keep walking. It starts with a single step."

"Okay…"

She sounded unconvinced.

"Life is hard, Peaches," he said. "And you're going to live for a very long time, so you need to get used to walking. And"—he squeezed her hand—"you're not alone."

"We walk together." She squeezed back with a smile. "Now I get it."

TWENTY-TWO

Peaches walked hand in hand with Haze through the dark tunnels, doing her best to ignore the hunger pangs in her stomach. Surely they would find a way out soon.

But with each twisted turn, it felt less likely they'd see another soul.

The fluorescent sodalite in the walls dimmed until even Haze couldn't see with his vampire eyes. He started clicking his tongue, using echolocation to help find their way through the underground maze. She trusted him and put one foot in front of the other.

It was the least she could do. His words had reminded her that, as painful as her history was, she was still here. She hadn't quit. And someone very precious to him had. She'd seen the pain in his eyes as he talked about loss, and it broke her heart.

They continued walking for hours. She was so hungry she could eat a horse.

They ended up near the glowing sodalite again. For a moment, she thought maybe they'd just come to another area like the first, but then she saw something. "Stop."

"What is it?"

"There." She pointed at the bones on the wall, more specifically to the watch band and white crumbling foam cup.

"Shit." Haze scrubbed his face. "We're going in circles."

"This is definitely a labyrinth."

He took a deep breath. "Okay, Plan B."

"There's a Plan B?"

He hefted his war hammer. "Start smashing things."

"Will that work?"

"Only one way to find out. Stand back." He waved her down the tunnel.

She stepped away and squinted at the rocky walls, pointing to a particular spot. "I think if you hit that porous spot between the granite, you might get through and prevent the walls from caving in."

Haze planted his feet and swung the hammer. The steel bludgeon hit bones, crunching and then thudding. Debris sprinkled down. Quicksand above them dripped. He swung again and again until a cloud of sand and dust bloomed in the air. Peaches coughed and covered her mouth. When the dust settled, they found Haze had poked a hole in the wall, but the look on his face was bleak. He caught her looking at him and quickly looked away, but she saw the disappointment in his eyes. The hole only led to a tunnel that looked the same as the one they'd already been down.

"It's fine," he said, turning stoic. "We'll find another way."

But her legs were aching. Her back was sore. And she was thirsty and starving.

"It's a magical labyrinth, right?" she said, licking her lips and inspecting the quicksand dripping from the ceiling. Mana held it together. It was safe to think mana was in the walls, moving things. "Maybe we need to start working with it. Do you think the walls shift to confuse us?"

"Maybe. Let's take another walk. There might be something we missed."

They went two feet around the next corner and stopped. Something had changed. In front of them, against a wall at the end of their tunnel, was a table laden with a feast fit for a queen. Peaches' mouth watered and she charged forward.

Juicy apples. Cheeseburgers. Grapes. Fries. Glasses of wine. Diet Coke! All her favorites! She plowed into the food and grabbed whatever she hit. Her stomach rejoiced as she brought food to her lips—a handful of fries in one hand, and a plum in the other. She didn't even care that it was weird to see items from her past. She was going to eat from both hands at the same time.

"Stop!" Haze boomed, arriving next to her at a jog.

"What?" she gaped, the salty fries making her mouth water. They were an inch from her lips.

He knocked the food from her hands. "It's not real."

"Smells pretty real to me."

"Take another look."

She glanced down. Air shimmered like a mirage at an oasis. Food turned to saw dust. Drink turned to sand. Critters and creepy crawlies skittered over her fingers. She squeaked and dropped everything, jumping back and wiping her hands down her velvet dress. The bugs scuttled away.

High pitched cackling taunted them from the darkness.

"Fucking hobgoblins," Haze cursed under his breath. He shouted, "Show yourselves!"

More evil giggles. Footsteps running.

Haze's jaw clenched. His shadow peeled from his body and went into the darkness, she presumed to find the giggling fiends.

"An army of goblins live under the labyrinth," Haze said. "All different kinds. Never been down here, though. Can't remember the last Guardian who had. They're unpleasant but usually follow the laws of the Well."

"Are they tricking us?"

"Or testing." He took her hand. "Come on. Keep going."

She couldn't help groaning in disappointment. "I so wanted real food."

"I know."

Her pace was slow. It must have been hours more,

perhaps another night gone by if they were outside. Surely! She hadn't eaten or slaked her thirst the entire time. She couldn't remember when she last drank. Probably in her room when she was—

"Oh no!" she gasped. "Tinger."

Haze squeezed her hand. "He'll be okay. Wolpertingers are survivors."

"I hope so because he was not one hundred percent. I tried to help him escape, but he stayed."

Haze shook his head in disbelief. "Can't believe you have a wolpertinger as a pet."

"He needed me."

"Yeah." Haze touched her face fondly.

They kept walking. This time, the glowing rocks and fossils eluded them. The shape of the tunnels changed. They narrowed. Walls became dirt entwined with roots glistening with trickling water. Veins of bioluminescence ran through the roots, bringing a soft, blue glow. At least they were making headway. The next corner they turned had another table set up against an adjacent wall. A single small statue sat on top. She squinted to see better through the dim blue glow.

Water dropped from the ceiling. When Peaches looked up, droplets pooled on the ceiling made of roots and thorns. The other ceiling had been made of quicksand.

"The water must mean we're under a lake or something," she suggested.

"You could be right."

Haze cupped his hand and held it out to catch a trickle. Once enough had pooled in his fingers, he sniffed it. "Smells okay."

"You can tell? Is it safe to drink?"

"There's a tang to it. And it feels... connected to the Well." He glanced up, squinting against the droplets as they fell across his face. He poked a finger into the roots and the trickle became a steady stream. A deep exhale swept out of him as the water sluiced over his face. His shoulders relaxed and he closed his eyes. Water created tracks down his dirty body. The tattoos started to glow in response, their oil slick colors brightened and swirled like a prism. He smiled at her, his lashes spiking under the stream. "It's a source of power."

He encouraged her to do the same, so she lifted her face to the ceiling and closed her eyes. As each drop of cool relief hit her, she relaxed. There was something about the water. Cool, but not freezing. A quick lick of the water told her it tasted fine. She opened her mouth and let the fluid replenish her. Her dress was soaked. Haze scrubbed a hand over his head like he was in a shower. When he started washing the dirt off his body, she couldn't stop watching.

Muscles bulged and flexed. Broad shoulders tapered to a narrow waist. Thick, powerful thighs. God, he was strong. Rivulets of water delineated all the right curves and valleys of smooth, olive skin. She couldn't look away. Now her mouth was open. Haze ran his hands down his face and smoothed his flat torso. When he lowered the waistband to clean it of trapped sand, he gifted her with an indecent glimpse of those glorious V muscles.

He gripped the roots in the ceiling and tensed, shaking his face under the water with an indulgent growl.

Every. Damned. Muscle. Flexed.

She must have made a sound because his gaze slid to hers. At first he frowned, as though he didn't like being watched, but then a slow, wicked grin spread on his lips. "You need help washing?"

No use hiding it. "I think I need help picking my ovaries up off the floor."

"Ovaries?"

She snort-laughed. "You all probably don't have an understanding of our internal organs. Ovaries are baby-makers for women."

The playful expression on his face dropped.

"Oh, I didn't mean it like—never mind." She'd only met the guy, and she was joking about ovaries. Jeeze. She quickly tried to change the subject and shifted her atten-tion to squeezing out her hair and inspecting the table that had originally stopped them.

On it sat a tiny statue, half cloaked in the shadows of the craggy rock wall behind it. Upon closer inspection, it looked familiar. She stepped closer. No... it couldn't be. She almost laughed, surprised it had lasted all this time.

Haze was suddenly there, splaying his hand on her chest, stopping her from moving forward. "Let me go first."

He gripped his almighty war hammer, readying it at his

side. Water dripped from his chin and landed on a gloriously wet pec. He could be carved from granite with that muscle. So strong. *Focus, Peaches.*

"Haze, it's just—"

"I've got this, Sweet."

He crouched like a tiger in the grass and stalked toward the table, cocking his head and twitching his pointed ears. She followed him all the way. When he got there, he straightened and rubbed his jaw scruff. She reached toward the toy. He caught her wrist.

"It's harmless," she said. "Trust me."

Haze let go, and she tapped the green head. It bobbled.

"It's a strange looking goblin," he mused. Then he took a turn at tapping it.

"It's a Baby Yoda bobble head," she laughed. "Completely plastic. I'm surprised it hasn't degraded, but I suppose—"

Haze brought down his hammer, smashing it to pieces with one mighty fell swoop. Peaches yelped and jumped back, sending him a look that asked if he was mad. The table had also split in two.

"It's forbidden," he grunted.

"It was just a toy."

He bared fangs. "Still made out of plastic."

"Okay." She sighed, rubbing her temples. "I get it. Let's keep walking. Maybe we should find a place to sleep for the night. I mean, I'm assuming it's night."

"What's that?" Haze flicked the shards of plastic and

found a folded piece of paper. He tried to unfold it with one hand, as he didn't want to relinquish his hammer.

"Let me." Peaches took it. Words were inscribed on the inside. "It's a riddle."

"Of course it is."

"You don't sound surprised."

"We're in the heart of goblin territory." He scoffed. "It's probably another test. Solve it and we won't travel in circles. Who knows what they want out of this ridiculous charade."

Peaches squinted at the words. "The instant my name is spoken, I am broken."

Flames engulfed her fingers. Peaches yelped. She dropped the paper as it burned to ash.

"That's what I think about riddles," Haze grumbled. "Waste of time."

"We can't go clobbering our way through life," she said, a little annoyed that he'd set the paper on fire while she was holding the damned thing. "And I knew the answer. You might have ruined it." Whatever *it* was.

He looked down at her, humor dancing in his eyes. "You're cute when you scold me."

She laughed. "Fine. Do whatever you want. You're the Guardian. But if you wanted to know, the answer was silence."

"That makes sense."

"Well, I said the answer. Do you think some secret door should open, or did I solve the riddle too late?"

"I wouldn't play their games," he said. "The answer has no relevance. Goblins like to play. That is all."

Haze's shadow came running back, just as ghostly giggling and cackling caused them both to startle. Well, Peaches startled. Haze stilled in the way only a predator could. He cocked his head as if listening to his shadow. Humor fled his expression. He stepped before her, blocking anything that might do her harm. Shadows darted across the tunnel and further down where the luminescence didn't reach.

"I've just about had enough with these games," Haze shouted, deep voice booming.

"I've just about had enough with these games," echoed a high-pitched, mocking voice.

"Fuck."

"Fuck."

"What?" Peaches whispered. "Is it something bad?"

"No, just fuck. I'm annoyed at the little shits."

"Oh."

Haze stalked forward, one hand holding the hammer, the other fashioned into a fist crackling with energy, ready to deploy some kind of offensive blast. Scampering little silhouettes multiplied until it wasn't just one darting about, but many. All the same size and form as Balos. The snickering turned sinister. Goblin sized shapes climbed the twisted roots until they swarmed the entire tunnel.

"Haze?" she said, her voice trembling. "Maybe we should turn back."

"Stay there," he replied. "We must be close to their dwellings. If we can speak to the right one, we can find a way out."

Peaches glanced back to the dripping tunnel with bioluminescent roots. It looked like a fairytale heaven compared to what was ahead of them. Darkness. Danger.

"One chance," Haze shouted at the goblins. "I'm warning you now. If you attack us, I won't hold back."

They pounced.

TWENTY-THREE

Showering from a power source had replenished Haze's internal Well. He wasn't surprised the queen had built her palace around a power source, or that it was in a labyrinth to keep it private and for her use only. But now that he was refilled, he had ample power to decimate the pests crawling over the tunnel walls.

Their spindly, little frog-like bodies dropped from the ceiling like spiders from webs. They leaped from the floor and scurried. Stupid to think they could beat him. Already gathering power in his fist, he slammed it into the dirt and pushed his energy out. A shock-wave rippled from the point of impact, blasting any creature within twenty feet, shaking the dirt from the roots so it showered on his head. Goblins flew backward. Some crashed into each other. Others knocked into the walls. Some rotated and landed on their feet like cats.

Haze paused. That was unexpected.

Those particular goblins moved with skill, as though trained for battle. And they were also the ones who'd stayed silent. No yips of intimidation. No taunting or insults. The ones mouthing off had gone down easily, like fodder, he realized.

This was an ambush, and a cleverly planned one. The most feared fighters must belong to the redcap goblin army. Although Haze saw no bloody caps on heads, it didn't mean they weren't there. They were clever and ruthless, just waiting to dip their first cap into his blood and claim a warrior's victory. Dread filled his bones. He faced Peaches and his stomach dropped. Behind her in the tunnel, dark silhouettes encroached. He sent his shadow to act as a shield.

"Come to me, Sweetness," he said. "Slowly. Don't look back."

Her eyes widened. "What's behind me?"

Fuck. "One step. And then another."

Horrified, she pointed over *his* shoulder. A presence creeped along his spine. He tightened his fingers around the hammer handle and drew enough mana to make the hairs on his arms lift. He kept his gaze steady on Peaches, telling her with his eyes that it was okay. And then he twisted and unleashed.

Brave goblins met the heavy end of Justice. Bodies went flying into the tunnel walls, buckling hard. Some of the beasties were proficient in spell casting. Useless, though. He had a metal weapon. He was sanctioned by the Well. Any time he sensed a strike using mana—fire or air or water, he sliced it in two with the metal at his disposal. The forbidden substance countered magic. Fire fizzled. Air calmed. Water fell.

Peaches cried out, warning him as a swarm of goblins came at him. Fear for her made his strikes sloppy. When he connected with flesh, another goblin jumped onto his hammer. Then another. They weighed Justice down until it hit the floor with a muffled thud. Haze roared his fury and started plucking the beasties out of the air, ripping into them with his fangs. Hot, putrid blood burst into his mouth. But he kept going.

Talons burst from his fingertips, helping him slice through goblin flesh like ribbon. Dark blood spurted everywhere until it rained down on him. Peaches made another sound. He turned to check on her. Hobgoblins had her arms. She thrashed and struggled as leering and beady eyes looked her over, whispering taunts into her ears. Haze stepped toward her, but something landed on his back.

Knobby hands wrapped around his throat. He grabbed the thing and tossed it. Sharp pain stung his side. He glanced down to see the tip of a dart wobbling in his torso. He plucked it with a snarl and then stabbed it into the next filthy creature.

Another sharp sting—his left arm, back, and then neck. His vision started to blur. Manabeeze started floating from goblin corpses, making it hard to focus. He moved underwater. *Poisoned.* He dropped to one knee and lifted his heavy head. All he could think about was that he needed to see her. A peach-colored blob slid into his blurred periphery and he locked onto it.

"Stop!" Peaches' wavering voice echoed in the tunnel.

A red blob joined the peach blur, but he couldn't comprehend what was happening. Did she have something in her hand?

Peaches ran to him. Her face came into focus. "Stop touching him!"

His vision crowded around the edges. Was he hallucinating, because one by one, each goblin got on its knees and bowed. To Peaches.

"Sweet?" His mouth felt like sand.

"It's okay."

"What's happening?"

"I have the cap."

He squinted at her hand. A red cap. Old, greasy and grimy and full of dried blood. Just like the most feared and murderous of all the goblins. He blinked, scanning the room. Where did she get it?

"We need to get out of the labyrinth," Peaches said as she put herself beneath Haze's arm and held him steady.

No one answered. Then a goblin wearing a similar red cap hobbled around the corner of the tunnel. He looked particularly murderous. Pointed, notched ears. Crooked and scarred nose. Patch across one eye. Tufts and clumps of white hair over wiry, muscled and damaged skin. A long, curved dagger dangled from his hand. He looked at Haze with disgust and then shifted his attention to Peaches.

"You have the cap of one of my kind."

"He gave it to me," she said.

The one-eyed goblin narrowed his eyes. "Stupid pix. A redcap *never* gives his cap away."

The bowing goblins snickered and tried to look up while still holding their heads down.

"Stupid pix," one of them said.

"Putrid pix," another added.

They laughed hysterically.

The redcap took another step. "How did you get it?"

"I bargained with him."

"You outwitted a redcap?"

She nodded. "Balos."

One-Eye snarled. A symphony of gasps dropped all around. The prostrate goblins sprung to their feet, excited, and started spitting out rhymes.

"She's clever."

"She's smart."

"She's going to break my heart."

Haze pulled Peaches closer to him.

One-Eye grumbled and stabbed his dagger into the ground. The frolicking goblins froze like startled stags. Then they snickered and started dancing again, this time, circling Peaches and Haze like they were performing some kind of offering to the goddess.

"A portal will get you out of the labyrinth," the redcap said.

"A portal stone," Haze repeated. "You have one?"

"We can get you a stone."

The goblins chanted, "Stone, stone, all for a bone."

"How long will it take you to procure one?" Haze growled. "And how will you get one if you can't get out of here without one?"

Tricky goblins. Haze spat on the ground. That's what he thought of their games.

One-Eye ignored him and looked at Peaches. "You must wear the cap if you're to make demands of us. You must prove you're worthy of being the only living creature alive to have bested Balos the Murderous."

"Gross," she mumbled under her breath and turned the cap over in her hands, but she slid it onto her head. *Brave woman.* "It's on. Now, please tell us how long it will take you to find a portal stone."

"How long is a piece of string?" said one goblin, dancing over the corpse of another, chasing manabeeze with his mouth. No wonder they were insane. The stench of fresh corpses burned the lining of Haze's sensitive nose.

"String, string, around we sing." Another joined the dance. Every time a manabee hit them from a corpse, the goblins slurred and swayed drunkenly.

Fucking floaters.

They whispered among themselves and then One-Eye answered. "A day. Maybe two."

"Or three," tittered another. "Or four."

"Or a door."

"Maybe a snore."

Crimson. Haze rubbed his eyes and tried to shake the poison. A shift would push the effects out of his system.

Peaches glanced at Haze, put her hand in her pocket and fumbled with something hidden. She lifted her chin and spoke to One-Eye. "I want food and drink and safe lodgings until then."

The Redcap gave a curt nod. "The owner of a red cap will receive anything they ask for."

Haze's inner alarm went off. This was all too convenient, and he was sure there was some kind of goblin etiquette that they needed to follow. A trick, or a twisted loop hole they had to know. Since he knew little about this underground culture, they would have to proceed with caution. He stood and shifted his wings out in an explosive blast, healing himself in the process, eradicating the poison. Bits of blood and dirt flaked off parts of him as his body changed. The great leathery span touched the tunnel sides, and then he shifted them away before they became a liability. There was no greater show of power than a fae who could double shift on command. He held his hand out to One-Eye and beckoned.

"My hammer."

The redcap looked at Peaches, waiting for her command. Haze bristled. He could simply transfer the hammer to his palm like last time, but that wasn't the point. His lip curled.

"My hammer," he said again. "Or perhaps I'll take *your* red cap."

His words had no effect on the goblin.

"His hammer," Peaches repeated.

Those hopping around them parted like the sea. Justice was still head down in the dirt, the same spot as before. Haze stalked over and slung it over his shoulder. Then he and Peaches followed the redcap further into their lair.

The further they went, the more their surroundings changed. Lanterns lit the way, brightening the path. Houses and dwellings were cut out of the tunnel walls, their facades delicately twisted and decorated with subterranean plant life. Female goblins and their children hurried out doors and into the tunnel to see a woman wearing a red cap.

It wasn't until the goblin showed them to a room with great arched wooden doors carved with twisted scenes that he remembered One-Eye hadn't answered his question. If it took a portal to get out of this underground labyrinth, then how was he going to procure a portal stone? Didn't that mean One-Eye must already have one?

TWENTY-FOUR

After they'd been shown to a set of guest chambers, Peaches spent the better part of an hour dealing with the infuriating and sycophantic hobgoblins. They'd been listening as she'd solved their riddle earlier. It only made them bow more at her feet.

She ordered supplies, food and drink in a direct enough way that she could be sure they weren't going to trick her. While she negotiated and demanded, like a true redcap leader, Haze checked every last corner of the stone, dirt, and wooden room for boogeymen. He lifted the red velvet duvet, tossed the tasseled cushions, and checked beneath the bed. He opened cupboards and tasted the supplied water for poison. He searched behind drapes flowing from the roots twisted into the stone ceiling. He even lifted the porcelain claw tub in the corner. Then he went about the room, setting wards with his mana, ensuring no one could listen to their conversations.

Not long after Peaches ordered food, a knock came at the door. Three hobgoblins shared the weight of a tray, peering up at her with lovelorn eyes.

"Tell us a riddle," one said. They waited with a smile, refusing to relinquish the tray.

"Um..." She glanced at Haze. He shrugged. "Okay. Let me think. What can't talk but will answer when spoken to?"

Three sets of eyes lit up. They whispered to each other. Then one answered. "An echo."

"An echo," said the other, and they broke out into fits of laughter.

"Okay, I'm taking this now." With effort, she pried it from their hands. "Now, the deal was for safety until the portal stone is found. Got it?"

They tried to fawn all over her like fans to a superstar. Other goblins waited around the hall corners, peering out eagerly as if waiting for their chance. She managed to kick them off and close the door before their touching became too rough.

"Ugh. That's too weird," she said as she took the tray over to a table wrought from twisted roots and roses. The food was surprisingly normal—chicken stew, plums, bread, and mouthwatering cider. "They're like little serial killers just waiting to pounce at the first sign of offense."

Since entering the chambers, Peaches had been

surprised. For a vile and tricky fae race, the decor was clean and almost regal. Nothing at all like the first tunnels they'd traversed. Definitely more civilized than they let on, but then again, Balos was nothing like the hobgoblins that rhymed and danced.

Peaches sniffed a piece of bread before taking a nibble. Definitely normal food. Haze stood by a wall of bioluminescent blue roots. He paid his filthy appearance no mind as he ran his hand up and down a root, tugging and testing its attachment at the stone ceiling.

"Air has to get in from somewhere," he mumbled, then prodded it. That and manabee lanterns gave the room a mixture of blue and glimmering white light, almost as though they were underwater, not underground. He scraped it with his finger, but no substance rubbed off. "I'd thought it was lichen, but it's not coming off."

Peaches wasn't paying attention. Her stomach rejoiced at the scent of stew and demanded she start stuffing her face. She was so taken with the delicious meal that she hardly noticed Haze turning the crystal faucet over the claw bath. Clean water poured out.

"What are you doing?" she mumbled through a mouthful.

"Running you a bath." He smirked as though it was obvious.

"Do you think we should really stay here? I mean, is it safe?"

"We don't have a choice." He glanced up from where he

knelt, testing the water temperature with the back of his hand. He grabbed a fist full of rose petals from the flowers twisted in the table roots, and then dropped them in the bath water. "We're safe for now. Your cap means something to these animals. If the redcap who promised us safe harbor betrayed that symbol, then he will be hurting his own status. They treat redcaps like royalty." He turned off the faucet and inspected where the ceramic pipe disappeared into the ground with suspicion. "For now, Sweetness, I want you to take a bath. And then I'll keep watch while you sleep. Once you're fed and rested, we can see about finding our way out of here."

She pulled the disgusting cap off and placed it on a bedside table, then she massaged her fingers through her hair, silently rejoicing in the feeling. The food and cider warmed her insides and, apart from her aching muscles, she felt pleasantly relaxed. She shouldn't be. She should be falling in a puddle of fear and despair.

The truth was, as long as she was with Haze, she felt safe. Even when goblins had been playing with her hair and jumping all over her.

She glanced up and found him watching her. He quickly looked away and went to stand by the door, where he braced a powerful arm over his head, careful to keep his eyes studiously on the wood carvings before him.

Silence stretched. Neither of them moved. Water steamed from the bath, enticing Peaches to walk to it. Haze had dropped in rose petals from the twisted table. She trailed her fingers through the water. It looked and smelled divine.

She reached around her back and unraveled the obnoxious ribbon. The rasp made Haze tense. Every muscle in that glorious back of his hardened.

Feeling acutely aware of herself undressing, she plucked buttons and then dropped the dress to the floor. It made a rustling sound. Haze exhaled and shifted his weight to the other foot. His fingers curled into a fist.

"Are we truly safe?" she whispered as she worked at undoing the laces of her undershirt.

"No one's getting in without breaking down this door," he promised, his deep voice coarse.

"And we're staying until we're rested?"

"They said it would take time to get the portal stone."

So they were forced to stay here for a day or two. And they were safe. Peaches sucked in a breath and summoned courage to speak her mind. "Then I believe there was something you said we'd do... once we're safe?"

Peaches bit her lip, waiting boldly for his response. Her skin buzzed as she completely undressed and submerged in the bath. Hot water engulfed her and a groan of bliss wrenched from her lungs. Haze locked onto her with heady bedroom eyes.

She sucked in a breath, butterflies in her stomach at the force of her attraction. *Be brave.* He was too staunch in his need to protect her. She wasn't the only one who'd been through tribulation. He needed to relax, too.

"Maybe you should get in here with me," she suggested, her voice surprisingly steady. "If you don't mind my water, that is."

"Sweetness," he said, his voice lowering as he pushed off the door and prowled closer. "If you bathed in it, I would drink the bathwater. That you've used it only turns me on."

Holy shit.

A bolt of heat zipped straight down between her thighs and pulsed. She pressed her legs together with a stifled moan. "You're playing your cards right, you know that?"

His smile liquified her bones. He kneeled by the tub, all masculine entitlement as he raked his gaze across her nakedness, and then retrieved the washcloth and squeezed with one fist. He twisted the cloth in deft fingers, squeezing again, wringing the last drop of her sanity along with the water. She'd never thought a cloth would be so erotic, but the sound of the water, the way he moved his strong fingers, the way he looked at her, all hot need and wicked intent...

"May I?" His voice rumbled down her spine.

Unable to form words, she nodded. Haze dragged the warm cloth over her jaw, smoothing it over her skin, dipping beneath her ears to clean. He grasped behind her neck, forced her to look into his eyes, and she gasped. Still holding her stare, he massaged gently, rapt at the change in her expression.

Her pulse slowed, her body let go of tension, and she

gave herself over to his care. Everywhere his hand went, his eyes did too. They soaked up his actions as though he'd been starved of a woman's touch.

She basked in his silent admiration, never feeling so beautiful. So cherished.

A dip into the water and he quietly scraped the washcloth over her breasts, still watching her face as he enticed her nipples to turn hard. She gasped as he swiped her again. She was so sensitized, it felt like sandpaper.

Haze kissed her neck and trailed the cloth down her stomach, deeper into the water. His tongue probed in circles behind her ear. He nibbled her lobe. Her breath came in panting hot waves and then the cloth slid between her legs and he pressed down with the heel of his palm. Pleasure burst. Her spine bowed with a whimper. God, she rocked her hips against his touch, sparking sensation at her core. Needing more. She wanted him to dispense with the cloth and drive into her, but he teased her. He washed her indecently around her folds before finally slipping his fingers inside her body.

She whimpered as he pulled out and shuffled to kneel behind her head. He slipped a strong hand under her jaw and tilted her head back to kiss her from behind. Only when she was breathless did he stop and drizzle water over her hair. He found a bar of soap and lathered her locks. Then he went to town with the massaging.

"Oh my god," she groaned, eyes rolling in bliss. She gripped the bath edges and held on as he found every pressure point. "For someone who shaves his head, you're incredibly good at washing hair."

The massaging stopped. She craned her neck and found emotion ghosting his face.

"Haze?"

He shook his head, shutting down his expression, and cleared his throat. "You should wash it out."

She frowned as he stood and dried his hand on a towel, then went back to standing sentry at the door. Had she said something wrong? She quickly dunked and washed the soap out of her hair, then dried off with the towel.

"Um," she said quietly, wrapping her body. "Will you use the water?"

He glanced at his state of disarray and frowned as though it annoyed him. Avoiding her eyes, he went to the tub and slid off his breeches. A long, thick, and hard erection sprung out, proving that he was as turned on as her. He wrapped his fingers around his length but didn't squeeze. A pained look crossed his face. He let go before stepping into the bath. Muscles rolled, biceps popped, and his jaw clenched as he lowered himself. Water surged, spilling over to accommodate his size. He put his arms on the length of the bath edge and leaned back with a sigh, closing his eyes and directing his brooding at the ceiling.

Whatever was going through his head had nothing to do with her. Not directly, anyway. She padded over and pried the washcloth from his fist. His eyes snapped open, and a line deepened between his brows.

"I can wash myself," he grumbled.

"I want to." She smoothed the cloth over his body, mesmerized at the strength rippling beneath her touch. "I've always wanted to," she confessed, with a stupid sigh of her own. "Since I first saw you asleep in my room."

His protests died. His frown eased, and he let her wash him, silently staring at her with a million thoughts running behind his deep brown eyes. When he was clean, she drained the bath and turned the faucet back on. Fresh warm water refilled the tub, and she continued to rinse him. He was clean, but she kept going, and he didn't say stop.

Maybe he liked the attention just as much as she had. She massaged his neck until he groaned in pleasure. Then she rubbed the cloth down his hard, washboard abs until she found the coarse hair between his legs. He sucked in a breath. She paused and checked his face. The frown was gone. His pupils were dilated, and an open vulnerability echoed back at her.

She had the sense she could ruin him if she did the wrong thing. This was Haze, the biggest, strongest, most feared warrior she'd ever met, and he couldn't bring himself to say no to her. But for some reason, he wanted to —she could see it in the way his lips parted, but he held his breath.

She studied him carefully as she lowered the cloth until his arousal jolted beneath her touch. Up and down the length she cleaned, stroked, rubbed. The fingers on one hand couldn't quite wrap around it, so she had to scrape beneath and above. Just like she'd pushed against him, so did he thrust into her touch. She used the friction of the cloth to wrap around him and tease gently until his breath turned ragged. But like he'd done with her, she eased off and smoothed the cloth back up his front.

His every muscle turned to stone.

Their eyes met. This was the moment. Forget the teasing touches, or succumb. She knew what she wanted. But did he?

TWENTY-FIVE

"Did I say something wrong before?" she asked, moving the cloth to his head and scraping it over the hair that had begun to grow.

"No."

"It just felt like something changed. One minute you were there, and the next you weren't."

The intensity of his stare was liquid fire down her face. When he didn't elaborate, she traced the cloth down the lines of his tattoo, marveling at the intricate patterns. He covered her hand with his, holding it right over his heart.

"It did change," he said.

Their eyes clashed. She slowly became aware of her rabbiting heart, the rapid fall and rise of his chest, the goosebumps breaking out on both their skins. A single drop of water ran from his thick neck, around his Adam's apple, and down his sculptured chest.

"The last female's hair I washed was the mother of my child," he revealed, voice almost a whisper. "They both died a long time ago."

"Oh, Haze..."

"There's more." He squeezed her hand almost painfully.

Her throat tightened, dreading his words, but knew she needed to hear them and that he needed to say them. A struggle began behind his eyes and ended in every cell of his body. His face hardened. Anguish. Heartache. Pain. She waited for him to speak, unmoving, her hand trapped beneath his, her knees hurting on the floor.

"Holly was a wild sort of vampire," he said. "She walked to the beat of her own drum. Unseelie to the core. Everyone wanted her because she was a beautiful, free spirit. But she fell for me. I couldn't believe it. We were smitten. In love, or so I'd thought. Then she fell pregnant." He paused, waiting to see Peaches' reaction, maybe waiting to see if she ran away. She stayed and so he continued, frowning at his memories. "She started to do and say strange things. Her behavior shifted. One minute, she teased me about flying as high as she could. The next she locked herself up for days and refused to feed, shouting that I did this to her, that I took her freedom. We fought a lot. I thought she was reckless and selfish. She said I didn't understand. And then she had the baby. A little girl." He smiled. "She was the cutest damned thing I'd ever seen, but I wasn't allowed to raise her. The females did all that in a separate roost to the males. It's how the vampire community works. I didn't like it, but it was okay because Holly was there. I stopped trying to force my way in because raising a pup isn't what males do." He let go of Peaches, but avoided her eyes. "Holly always boasted that she would fly to the moon one day, that the goddess and her were friends. I never believed she'd actually do it. I still don't know why she did it. To escape us. To have a moment of fun. To free herself. But of course, she flew too high. Her connection to the Well cut off, and... she never accounted for the pain of losing that connection. She was paralyzed with it. When she plummeted, she couldn't move her wings." His eyes fluttered closed. "I arrived too late."

Haze shook his head, washed his face, and stood suddenly—all arousal gone. Water streamed down his body. Peaches found a dry towel and handed it to him. Her heart broke as he climbed out of the tub with jerky movements.

"She was the special female who taught you to weave wards?" Peaches asked.

He nodded as he wrapped the towel around his waist.

"And... the baby?"

He met her eyes. "She died shortly after her mother. Malnutrition. There were no other lactating females in the colony at the time, and she wouldn't accept the milk of any other species. I didn't learn about it until too late."

Peaches threw her arms around him and squeezed tight. She wanted to give him all her feeling, her love, her compassion. He stood stiffly beneath her embrace, and then he melted. His big, warm, rose-petal smelling body enveloped her and held her as tightly as she did him.

"I didn't tell you for pity, Sweetness. I told you because —" He inhaled against her cheek. "I'm telling you because you were right. Something changed. I feel something for you I've not felt for anyone else, not even Holly. When I touched you in the bath, and washed you, I wished I could invade you with every inch of my soul, and I felt... I felt guilty."

Tears leaked from her eyes, and she smashed her face between his pecs, right beneath his heart. He crooked a finger under her chin and lifted her gaze to his.

"Don't cry for me."

"I can't help it. I made you relive that pain."

"No, Peaches, things changed for me because I realized if it had been you back then, the female who'd birthed my child, I would *never* have allowed you to live in a colony without me. You would *never* had made a stupid mistake like flying so high because I would *never* have left your side. I would have fought for you until the end." He gave her a sad smile. "And if you told me you needed freedom, I would have given it to you."

Fresh tears ran from her eyes.

"For a long time I hated Holly for quitting on me, for being the catalyst that ended our child's life... but... things changed now because I finally understood it was me who quit on her first. That's where my guilt comes from."

Peaches had no words to soothe him, so she did the only thing she could think of. She continued to hug him until the air cooled at their wet towels. She couldn't do anything else except... maybe...

"Are you hungry?" she asked, looking up at him. "You didn't have a full feed back at the palace."

Before he could hide it, his eyes flashed with need. His lip curled involuntarily, giving her a glimpse of sharp fang, but he shook his head and scooped her up, taking her to the bed. He carried her like she weighed nothing in his arms. This big, infallible warrior had cut open his chest and laid his heart out to her. When he rested her gently on the covers, she cupped his jaw. "Feed from me. Let me give you something you need."

"My sweet," he whispered. "I have everything I need already."

Their ravenous kiss burst stars behind her eyes and left her speechless. He allowed her a breath, and then he kissed her again. Haze was insatiable with his desire, with his tongue, his passion. Their mouths melded until her lips numbed and she pulled off him to unwind her towel, exposing her naked body. Heavy-lidded eyes raked from her top to her toe. He drank her in, as though the mere sight of her satisfied his thirst.

When he trailed a finger from her neck to her breast, she realized he was finding a vein. She started to pant, to want, to need. The memory of how he'd made it feel good last time was all she could think of. Her eyes dipped to the towel tenting between his legs and knew he felt the same.

"Here." She tapped her neck, almost eagerly. "Start here."

He shook his head and traced his touch from her neck to her collarbone, then inward to the valley between her breasts. She arched into him, silently begging for him to find her aching nipple, to squeeze it and alleviate her need. He rubbed his calloused palm over the bud. A zing of heat shot down her spine, but he moved south, continuing to explore around her belly button. He stopped at the top of her mound and lifted his eyes to hers, expression serious, dark and dangerously hungry.

"Move over," he demanded. She shuffled to the side. He dropped his towel and reclined next to her against the pillows. "Climb on top of me—no, the other way. Face my feet."

Unsure where this was heading, but completely trusting him, she did as she was told. He was naked. She was too. She was ready for anything.

"Put your hands on my stomach, knees on either side of my body. That's right. Spread your legs nice and wide like that. Now... rock back. That's right, Sweetness. All the way. I want your ass in my face." A gust of air—his breath —hit her wet core as she backed up. "*Crimson.*" He inhaled her scent. "This view has haunted my dreams at night."

He palmed her bottom, squeezing and kneading,

spreading her open with his thumbs. She was already moaning, her body ratcheting tight with desire before she backed into his greedy mouth, before she faced his hard and throbbing cock, sitting on his stomach, waiting for her. Hot breath tickled, teasing her intimately. And then her world exploded. His tongue speared into her core.

A long, shuddering groan came out of him as if he tasted heaven. To prove it, he licked her seam, front to back, and then did it again. That sound, that raw truth of his unraveling desire made her limbs weaken, and she slipped. But he caught her, repositioned her hips for his enjoyment, and then tongued her sex, licking and sucking, feasting, tasting, probing. Warm, confident hands massaged her rear, touching her everywhere while his mouth worked.

Definitely an ass-man, and she would never complain. *Ever*. She bit the inside of her cheek as relentless sensation drilled into her, curling her toes, blurring her vision.

His lips moved against her as he spoke. "I've wanted to do this since you wore that wicked dress."

She made some kind of agreeable sound, but then surrendered to his tongue again, to the onslaught of his passion. She was useless. Couldn't see. Couldn't move. Could hardly breathe. That he gave himself to her like this, after what he'd confessed, made it all the more precious. Her heart, her body, her mind all burst with feeling.

And then he slipped a finger into her tight entrance, testing.

"Well," he muttered, almost to himself. "Almost this."

"What?" she moaned, pushing back wantonly. "What do you mean, almost?"

Something sharp trailed up the back of her thigh, circled beneath her buttocks, and then nipped. She gasped as he nipped again and then licked where he'd teased as if to apologize for the sting. He held his breath and then said, "There is a vein right here, inside your thigh." He touched her there, but hesitated.

She looked at him over her shoulder and wiggled her rear. "Do it."

Dark heat flared in his eyes. He brought her right over his face and rubbed his nose intimately, seeking out the vein. Then she felt it. A prick. A sting on her inner thigh. It hurt for a second, but like last time, he made it feel good. The drop of his blood soared into her system, lighting a trail of bliss and ecstasy. He took his time with his meal, relishing while still sliding his fingers around her slick entrance. With her senses so heightened, she almost climaxed, but he wouldn't let her. He teased, torturing her to the edge and then pulling her back, sometimes dipping inside her, stretching her, sometimes trailing around the folds of her core, sometimes tickling with a puff of his breath.

A lion playing with the gazelle.

Her grip tightened on his waist and she worried she'd bruise him. She needed release so badly that she started making little begging sounds, to which he ignored and continued his lazy feast. So she refocused on what lay beneath her face. Long, hard, veined and magnificent. Indestructible, just like him. Needy, just like her.

She pulled away from him and wrapped her fingers around the broad width. He cursed and jerked into her hand. He stopped feeding, stopped toying, and stilled as she laved the broad crown of him, taking special care to tease beneath the tip. Peaches felt powerful. Strong. Invincible. One minute she'd been a mess of hormones and want, completely at his mercy. The next, he was a slave to her tongue, throwing his head back against the pillow and submitting to her onslaught, thrusting hard into her mouth and fisting the sheets.

The two of them were sweaty, hot messes. She grinned around him, scraping gently with her teeth. Her jaw ached from his girth, but she kept going, kept taking him. She couldn't stop if she tried. This was too good. Too right.

Haze slapped her rear, jolting her forward, and then he kneaded her again, muttering about the view. She stopped sucking and held on for dear life as he pulled her back and feasted again from behind. Like a man possessed, he brought her to whimpers, holding her prisoner against his mouth until she came with an explosion, sun bursting behind her eyes, heat ripping through her spine. She couldn't see. Couldn't hear. Her orgasm was that intense.

He pushed her hips down his sweaty torso, lifting his abdomen to drag through her slickness. She thought he said something about grabbing hold of his ankles. Maybe.

She managed to grab something. A touch at her swollen entrance had her moaning and panting as he inserted a finger.

"You're so tight, Sweet." He added another finger, stretching her internal walls. "You need to fit me."

He worked her, opening her, and then replaced his fingers with something better. With a hitched breath, she sank down onto his length. She paused when her body refused to accommodate him and tried again. She couldn't see him, but could hear his ragged breath, patiently waiting for her to adjust to his size.

He palmed her bottom. Squirmed beneath her. Struggled to hold still until she was ready to start rocking.

"I want to watch you move," he said and let go of her hips.

Feeling the sexiest she'd ever been, Peaches slid herself up and down his length, taking her pleasure from him. She glanced over her shoulder and caught his eyes on their joining, hot and lazy. He made little appreciative sounds, encouraging her, telling her how he wanted it, how she looked like a goddess to him. It was so damned sexy, but she was losing rhythm as her sensations grew. Her thighs ached. He sat up, scooped his arm around her waist and then drove into her from beneath. They continued like that —with her backed into his lap, with his mouth on her neck, his hand on her breast. He lifted her hips and then slammed her down hard. She couldn't keep up with his urgency, so gave herself over.

He sensed her submission and turned into a beast. He pushed her forward on all fours and took her from behind, grunting and kissing any piece of bare skin he could find. She gripped the bed covers and squeezed as the heat built again.

"Fuck," she blurted. "I'm going to—oh god. I'm going to—"

"Yes, Sweetness. Again." He reached around and pressed between her legs.

Bliss rolled through her, more intensely than the first time. Haze drove in, plunging to the hilt and stayed seated as he shuddered through his release. She could barely hold herself upright afterward. Her adrenaline must have blocked it during the sex, but now the histamines from his feeding rushed to the surface, making her drowsy. Her legs wobbled from all the walking.

"Haze," she slurred. "I'm going to..."

"It's okay, love. Sleep." His words were slurred too, but he pulled her back to his chest, positioning her for comfort. His next words came to her through the fuzzy darkness claiming her consciousness. "I'm not going anywhere."

TWENTY-SIX

Haze never meant to fall asleep. He'd intended to keep watch in case his wards failed, but Peaches' blood had done things to him. Things he'd wholeheartedly submit to if they were in a different place. He wasn't sure how much time had passed, but when he woke, and his beautiful and precious sweet thing slept peacefully in his arms, his pulse started racing.

The need to protect her hammered hard in his head.

The first thing he did was check with his shadow to find out what had transpired while they were asleep.

Nothing.

They'd been left alone the entire time they'd slept. This confused Haze even more than if the goblins had loitered outside their room. He must have moved because Peaches made a snuffling, sleepy sound and curled into his side. Her hand slid across his stomach and traced back and forth idly. That simple touch sent his hormones sky-rocketing. He hardened painfully with the need to claim her again.

Mating instincts.

They had to be the cause of his insatiable lust, his irrational possessive thoughts, and his all-consuming demand to be near her. Vampires rarely mated, but when they did, the initial coupling went for days. He sent his shadow to spy, instructing it to not come back until it found something interesting to tell. Peaches opened her eyes just as the shadow left his side. She lifted her head to watch it slide through the gaps in the door.

"Morning," he said.

"Is it morning?"

"Uh." His erection jerked at the sound of her throaty voice.

She smiled. "Maybe not. How long were we out?"

"I'm working on finding out."

"Oh. Your shadow. I saw it leave. So what's the deal with that anyway?" she asked. "Is it like a separate entity to you? Does he have feelings?"

He lost the battle with his will and touched her jaw. "It's just me."

"Okay, but... that doesn't really answer my question. How does it work?"

He shrugged. She adjusted herself comfortably, and a whiff of her natural perfume hit him. Every nerve in his body cried out to feel her tight, inner walls clamp around his cock. It was all he could think of. *Fucking mating hormones.* He toyed with her hair, hoping she didn't see his turmoil. "It's a part of me. It does what I would do if I can't be somewhere. A shadow of myself. I can tell it what to do, sometimes I can see through its eyes, and when it comes back, I share its memories."

"Cool." She walked her fingers over his abs. "That could be fun."

"Fun?" *I want to feast on you again.*

"Yeah, I mean. You know. Everyone could do with an extra set of hands or be able to spy and go where your physical body can't. You could even—" She rubbed her face on him. "Never mind."

He loved it when she pressed into him to hide her embarrassment. His mind started to descend into dark, lewd places. And then what she'd said hit.

"I could even what?" He arched back to look in her eyes.

She avoided his gaze.

"You know..." Her voice muffled. Words tumbled out. "Like use it during sexy times."

"Ah." He leaned back, smiling. "I never thought to do that before."

But I'm going to now.

"You haven't?" She sat up, pulling the covers with her. "I would have thought you did it all the time. I mean... wow."

"I don't fuck like this with anyone," he confessed and trailed a finger down her front to force her covers down. He focused on her nipple, rolling it between his thumb and forefinger.

Her breathing became shallow. "At all?"

"If I did, it was a quick release." He shuddered to think of his past sexual encounters. They were so empty compared to her. His eyes glazed over, thinking of why. "I wanted it to be over as fast as I could so I didn't have to feel."

"That sounds lonely." Her sad eyes turned impish, and she gave him a small, teasing smile. "If I wasn't sore right now, I'd jump on top of you again."

He grunted with satisfaction. "I said you'd feel me."

"That I do," she laughed.

"You'll get used to it."

"Because we'll be practicing?"

He shot her a grin, threaded fingers into her hair, and kissed her briefly before finally tossing the covers off and finding his breeches. They were stained and dirty, but dry. He shoved them on but left the laces untied. "I'll find you food."

He was losing this battle to claim her again and needed to stay alert. They had to figure out how to get out. True safety wouldn't arrive until she was back at the Order with him.

"There's leftover bread," she said.

His brow arched. "I'll find you fresh food."

She pulled the covers to her mouth, hiding her smile, but he could see it in her eyes. A rush of affection hit him between the ribs, and he was drawn back to her like a manabee to the sky. "Just so there's no confusion here, you need to know something."

He tugged the blanket down. The humor fled her eyes and worry bled in.

"You're mine," he declared.

She blinked at him, startled. Hurt and betrayal crossed her expression, dropping her gaze to the floor. His heart ached to see her unable to meet his eyes.

"Okay." Her voice was small.

His proclamation had come out wrong. She wasn't a vampire. She had no idea what he was doing.

"I don't mean you belong to me like you did to the queen, but you belong to my heart. Do you understand?"

Her eyes softened and she came to him on her knees while he stood at the end of the bed. She rested her head against his chest. "You're mine, too, baby."

"I don't care if there's no Well-blessed union here," he said. "And I don't care if you're human and I'm a vampire. I know how I feel."

"What are you saying?"

"That I want to be mated to you. Forever. Just you and me." He pressed her to him, holding her tight. "I want to wake up like this every morning. I want to feed from you exclusively. I want you to look to me to provide for you, to protect you, to pleasure you."

She said nothing, and for a moment he thought she'd reject him, but then she tightened her embrace and whispered to his heart, "Me too."

"Peaches, vampires rarely mate, but when we do, it's an obsession. I'll make you feel the effects of our lovemaking every single day. I'll kill anyone who tries to touch you. I'll —" He growled at himself, afraid he would frighten her away, but had to let her know. "You'll be my everything. There will be no lengths I won't go to keep you safe."

She wasn't afraid. She pulled him down on the bed and dug inside his pants, found his hard, aching cock and started stroking. A deep groan rattled in his chest. His restraint broke. He tugged his waistband just enough to free himself. She worked him tirelessly while he found her slick desire and circled her sensitive nub.

He never asked. She'd said she was sore. But she fitted herself over him and slid down, sheathing herself on his length. They made love, fast and then slow. He brought his female, his mate, to climax and then took his own release inside her. As mates should. Afterward, they collapsed on the bed, panting and gulping in air.

And yet still he craved more.

He should be home, locked in his room, where they could feed each other's obsession for days. But he needed to stay alert. They had to figure out how to get out. True safety wouldn't come until she was back at the Order, with or without him. With that thought spurring him on, he tried again to get himself in order.

He found her dress, shook it out, and then helped her put it on.

"Should I call one of them to the door and ask for an update?" she asked.

"Wait for my shadow to return," he said. "It might come back with insight."

"Okay," she said and nibbled at the left-over bread from yesterday.

"And then I'll find you fresh food," he promised.

Moments later, Haze sensed his shadow coming closer at a remarkably fast pace, and with it a sense of alarm.

"Peaches." He picked up his hammer. "Get behind me."

"What?" she mumbled through a mouthful, her eyes wide.

"Now."

Haze's shadow burst through the gap in the door and hit him squarely in the chest. Suddenly, Haze knew what had happened.

"The queen," he said.

"She's here?"

"That fucking redcap betrayed us."

The carved wooden door burst open, coming off the hinges and flying toward them. Haze brought Justice up, deflecting it. Wood splintered as pieces ricocheted away.

"Protect her," he said to his shadow.

To get out of this, to defeat the queen, he needed no distractions.

Queen Maebh walked forward, her legs snaking, her hips swaying. The obscene dress she wore was like oil on skin. Black fabric clung to her shape. Her hair was scraped back from her face and fashioned into a bun. Behind her stood two guards, Demeter on one side and Gastnor on the other.

"Only two guards?" he asked.

Not even one of the Sluagh. Haze's pulse raced. What did she know that gave her such confidence?

Maebh surveyed the room for any threats the one-eyed goblin may have failed to disclose. Ever distrustful, this queen was. Finally, her cold gaze landed on Haze.

"I don't need backup," she said. "They came because they wanted to gloat, plus..." She gestured at Demeter. He lifted something in his hands with a wince—iron shackles. "I needed someone to carry that."

Haze's blood ran cold. Those shackles looked different; a bolt ran straight through each cuff. For ten years Jasper was a prisoner at the Ring in Cornucopia and no one knew he was there. An iron mask had hidden his identity and cut him from accessing the Well by piercing bolts into his neck.

Once those shackles were on Haze—in his flesh—all hope of leaving this place would be gone. He'd be cut from the Well. He'd be in pain. And he'd be invisible to scrying Mages or Guardians. If his team couldn't find reason to raid the queen's palace soon, they might never find him.

"This is how it's going to go," Maebh said. "You're going to put down your weapon, submit, and allow us to shackle you."

"You're blatantly breaking laws of the Well," he said. "You expect me to roll over and die?"

"I'm not asking you to die, Guardian. I'm not stupid," she laughed. "I know killing you is signing my own death warrant. For now, anyway."

"So you plan on hiding me forever?" He shook his head. "It's the same thing. The Order won't stand for it."

"I only need a few more days, and then I don't give a shit what happens to you. You can ride off into the sunset with that sniveling human, for all I care."

He glared at her and completed an internal check of his body. He was healed, full of Peaches' nutritious blood, and had under half his mana stores left. It wouldn't be enough to kill her. He might not even maim her. If anyone else had come to claim him, he'd have no problem dispatching them and escaping. But then he'd have to contend with the goblins again. And find a way out.

Unease wormed its way into his gut, spreading doubt like a disease. A thousand scenarios ran through his mind, but they all ended with them trapped in this labyrinth, or dead.

He'd promised to keep Peaches safe, no matter the consequence. If he had to take this hit, but Peaches would live, he'd do it. He would do anything for her.

"What about Peaches?" he said, his heart breaking to hear the gasp behind him.

"She can stay with you or go."

"She can leave your service and return safely to the Order?"

Maebh inclined her head. "As you wish."

No. He didn't believe her. Maebh would find a way to keep Peaches. Her blood was too precious, as was her knowledge of the past.

Gastnor licked his fangs and leered at Haze's mate. He stepped to the side, blocking Gastnor's view with a snarl of warning. He knew then that he could never leave her like he left Holly. He had to be by Peaches' side. Even if that condemned her to imprisonment with him. His death would be the only thing that would ever separate them.

He glanced at his mate, ashamed at the train of his thoughts because weren't his feelings of possession exactly what she hated? Peaches frowned back at him. She had no idea he'd never be able to leave her. That reminded him of another problem.

"What about this one's promise to give her to Prince Luthian?" Haze jerked his chin at Demeter.

The queen hardened in a way that made Haze think she knew nothing about her lieutenant's arrangement with the Autumn Court prince.

"Peaches is yours to keep," she promised Haze.

Peaches was quiet behind Haze. She might not forgive him for this, but at least she'd be with him. He could protect her with his life and since Maebh had to keep him alive, he had a good chance of keeping Peaches that way, too.

Maebh wanting to separate him from his Guardian brethren meant Haze knew things he shouldn't. And the Order should. But his mind raced—he could think of no other way except to agree to her terms. It would keep Peaches safe, and it would give Haze time to come up with another plan. Demeter jangled the shackles and stepped forward.

Haze didn't stop him.

"Don't hurt him," Peaches said, her voice cold. She stepped out from behind him and lifted her chin. "I'll give you my blood."

Haze met Maebh's icy stare. In no world would he trade his comfort for Peaches' blood. "I want it written in mana. I agree to the shackles for a few days—"

"A week," Maebh said.

"Fine. We stay in your care for a week, and then you let us go."

"Haze," Peaches whispered. "We don't have to do this."

"I can't think of another way. Can you?"

She stared at him hard. "Wait a minute. Let's think about wording this right."

But Maebh walked forward and touched Haze's chest. Power rippled through their connection. She repeated his words, and the bargain snapped into place.

"It is done," she said. "You allow us to put the shackles on, and you come willingly. She stays with you."

Shame washed over him and he turned to Peaches. "It's better this way. We'll be together, and we'll be alive." His cadre would come for them.

"Well," Maebh drawled. "Alive is debatable." She

gestured for Demeter to come forward. "Put the shackles on him, and then send them to the pit."

TWENTY-SEVEN

The pit was a prison beneath the mountain the Obsidian Palace was cut into. The queen held up her end of the bargain, and after Demeter had pierced each of Haze's ankles with a metal rod, joining his feet together with painful shackles, the queen used a portal stone to take them straight into the hot, sweltering place without a second thought.

Haze landed on his hands and knees, biting his tongue to avoid a show of pain from his ankles. The smell of molten rock, piss and excrement burned his nose. Peaches was thrown in after him, also landing hard on the floor. She immediately gagged at the stench. There was nothing like human waste to curdle the gut, but when it was heated, it was nigh impossible to breathe.

The queen dusted off her hands and then left with her guards trailing behind her. They went through an iron door

—more contraband Haze would remember to make her pay for.

He forced himself to stand and almost passed out from the pain, but gritted his teeth and offered a hand to his mate. She took it, then realized what she'd done. A glance at his bleeding ankles and she let go with a frown.

"Can we get them off?" she asked. "They look so painful."

"I'm fine." He gathered her under his arm and glared at their surroundings. "We just need to last a few days in here." A week at most.

They stood on a rocky floor that extended far into the cavern and then dropped off in a cliff to a pit where heat and smoke billowed up. They walked far enough to see the pit was some kind of mine. Around the outskirts, from a spiraling platform, prisoners toiled with pick-axes against the wall. Haze wasn't even sure if they mined for anything at all.

Guards of all fae races used whips and maces to keep prisoners in line and productive. None of the guards had metal weapons. He might be able to over-power them, but he wouldn't be able to get out past the locked door.

Up here at their level, the rocky floor circled the pit and continued onward to where caves—cells—of all shapes and sizes were carved into walls. Soot covered prisoners emerged and eyed them warily.

Haze checked behind him at the door. A guard watched

warily, expecting retaliation, but as long as this debilitating metal pierced Haze, he was weakened.

No mana. No shifting. No healing at a rapid rate.

Haze tried to call Justice to him, just to see if it would work, but nothing happened. It was like shouting into an abyss, expecting an echo, only to have his voice swallowed. He checked and triple checked the runes carved into his palm, and still nothing happened.

Fuck.

Scanning the prison, the deep mine to the caves, he knew he and Peaches would be put to work soon. To survive the grueling conditions they had to find their own cave to hole up in and endure. But first, he had to find the biggest, ugliest, meanest prisoner. Then he had to kill him. Nobody would mess with Haze or Peaches after that.

SHACKLES CLINKED as Haze walked around the rocky floor overlooking the mine pit, refusing to acknowledge the pain in his ankles, refusing to limp. He held his chin high and kept his glare hard, making sure to funnel his aggression and audacity into his straight spine and broad shoulders. If he showed one sign of weakness, the prisoners would pounce. Let them see the metal in his ankles, and let them think because he was a Guardian, the rules of nature didn't apply to him. It was half right.

The first cave they passed belonged to a pack of

shifters. Glowing golden eyes stared at him from the darkness. Haze bared his fangs.

Too easy.

He kept moving. Peaches reached for his hand.

The next cavern belonged to a harem of pixies. Five males to one female. They looked hard and seasoned. Two males stepped out and folded their arms. One's blue dragon-fly wings were scarred and full of holes. Shaved blue hair down the sides of his head, long everywhere else. The shaved parts were jagged, as though cut with a blunt knife. Tribal patterns branded across his forehead. His companion was much the same, tattered and rough. Both were a head smaller than Haze, yet acted ten feet tall. He snorted and kept walking. *Also too easy.*

He could easily try to find a spare cave, but he needed to establish his dominance early—before his ankles gave out. His next step caused his right ankle to tweak against tendon and metal. He winced, limping involuntarily. The cave where he'd faltered held an orc. Tall, wide, and covered in pock marks. Food was stuck in his under-bite.

Curiously, this cave was stocked with supplies. And the orc had not moved an inch since spotting Haze.

The orc dismissed Haze and leaned over to whatever roasted on his tiny campfire. Haze let his gaze roam over the cell, taking in anything he could use as a weapon. Without the ability to shift, his own talons were stuck inside his fingers. All he had was strength and his fangs. But orcs bled the same as anyone else.

"Why are you looking at him like that?" Peaches whispered. "Let's keep walking and find our own cave."

"This one looks good to me."

The orc slid blood-shot eyes toward Haze and slowly unfolded himself, straightening to his full height. His obscenely bulky and muscled green body was covered only by a loin cloth made from shifter pelt. His bent cock and hairy testicles dangled at a fold in the front. Old and new scars criss-crossed his body. But it wasn't his appearance that disgusted Haze. It was the personal items collected in piles around the cell. Must have come from corpses.

"Listen to your little lady, fang-face," the orc snarled. "Move on."

Haze gently moved Peaches to the wall outside the cave so she was protected from what was about to happen, and then cracked his neck before glaring daggers at the orc. Pain was nothing, he told himself. Nothing compared to the loss if he couldn't protect Peaches in here.

"This cell is ours now," Haze warned. "Best you get out of here before things get bloody."

The orc boomed out laughing, spittle flying, drawing the attention of nearby prisoners. The orc's fingers curled around the handle of a pick-ax.

Haze needed the orc to come to him. The less he moved his feet, the better. The orc stepped forward, his feet untethered and free. He sidestepped his smoldering camp-fire and came to stand before Haze, eyes blazing with defiance.

Peaches made a little whimpering sound. She was afraid, but he had to be strong. Had to end this fast. Already leering eyes watched them from other caves, curious as to the exchange.

Hot, sour orc breath blasted Haze's face as he looked him up and down. He paused on the shackles.

"Damn, bro," the orc said. "You're one tough shit."

Err.

The orc waved them inside. "Come. Sit, sit. You want some grub? I got stew. I got mana-we-*eed*. I got some kind of foul smelling shit but it tastes *ree*-eal yum."

Haze's eyes widened. He glanced at Peaches and she shrugged. What the fuck was the deal with this orc?

"Ain't nobody ever wanted to share with me," the orc said and walked back to his spot by the fire. "The name's Roses." He barked a laugh. "Coz my shit smells like 'em."

"I don't share," Haze grumbled. "I said the cell is ours, so fuck off."

"Well, shoot," said Roses. "Then we got ourselves a problem, don't we?"

Peaches tugged on Haze's arm. "He's inviting us in. We should be nice."

"Nice gets you killed, Sweet."

"Or it gets you a friend."

Haze rubbed his jaw, irritated over the length of his scruff. Maybe Peaches was right, and this orc was a harmless dolt who just wanted a friend. But maybe Haze was right, and the moment they turned their back, they'd be the next meal on the campfire.

To prove his nerves right, the watching prisoners moved closer as Haze limped into the cave.

"Why are you here?" Haze asked Roses.

"Coz I ate sum-fin' I wasn't supposed to."

Haze arched a brow. "And that was?"

Roses grinned. "A bird."

That didn't seem so bad. But then he added, "Who was the queen's cook."

Peaches gasped. "So that's what happened to him."

"Yeah," Roses said with a sigh. "The shifter tried to cheat me out of coin when I sold him meat. Said I didn't know good meat if it hit me over the head. So I made him hit me, and then I ate him."

"That would do it." Haze glanced about. "So you don't like the queen?"

"She can kiss my hairy balls. We all hate her in here. Even more than Guardians, you feel me?" He pushed stacked piles of clothing, leather, and bones away to make way for them to sit. "You want something to drink, lady? Eat?"

He looked at Peaches and a snarl worthy of the animal kingdom ripped from Haze's lips. "She's mine."

"Easy there, tiger." Roses lifted his palms. "I'm not after her."

"Don't care. Fuck off out of here and you'll—"

"*Haze.*" Peaches frowned at him and gave him a look

that said, *get a grip.* But he couldn't. He couldn't breathe the same air as an unmated male around Peaches.

"I'm more interested in what's in your pants than hers," Roses said, waggling his thick brows. "If you know what I mean."

Peaches gratefully sat, tugged Haze down, and accepted a stone cup of some kind of liquid from Roses. Haze scented it for poison before allowing her to drink, and he made special care to keep himself between the orc and his mate. Just in case.

"Best be getting some rest." Roses leaned back against the wall. "Guards will come round soon and give you an ax. Once that happens, you'll barely get a moment's peace." He sighed and wiggled to get comfortable. "It's good to have a Guardian in my cave. Maybe I can finally catch some shut-eye."

Haze had expected to be met with more animosity than he got outside the prison. But he guessed everyone in here hated Maebh most. The enemy of my enemy is my friend. Within seconds, Roses started snoring, his face going lax.

Haze met Peaches' eyes, then shifted his stare out at the cave opening. He tucked Peaches into his side and kept watch, ignoring the pain flashing up his legs.

True to Roses' prediction, not long after they arrived, Haze and Peaches were brought a pick-ax and taken down the spiral to the mine below. With Roses at their side, they had surprisingly little push back from either other prisoners, or the guards. As long as they kept quiet, kept their heads down, and worked, they were left alone.

The days passed in the pit.

If it wasn't for his festering ankles, hurting more each time Haze woke, he'd have found a way for them to get out of there by now. But even though outwardly he looked calm and together, inwardly he was a mess. Peaches slowly stopped talking to him and retreated to that cold, distant place with sad eyes. He was sure it was for one reason: she was losing faith in him.

One night, after the exhaustion of working in the pit, he curled up on a layer of tattered clothes in the cave with Peaches at his side. Roses still worked in the pit. Peaches kept resisting when he tried to tug her close. She rolled to face away from him.

"Sweet," he said. "I know it's hard to stay hopeful, but my cadre will come for us."

She hunched in the shadows by the fire, her peach hair tarnished by the flickering light. He knew she was awake, but she refused to acknowledge him. He didn't think they'd said a word all day. She withdrew to some quiet place within herself, and it reminded him all too much of Holly.

"Please talk to me. Don't..." He rubbed his eyes. "Don't shut me out."

She rolled to face him, her eyes bleak. *Nothing*. It was as if the will to survive had left her soul.

"Sweetness." The word tugged at his heart. "What's going on?"

A storm swept over her face and she flared her eyes at him. "You never asked me."

"Asked you what?"

"When the queen came for us, you didn't even ask me if we should give up." She rolled to her back and stared at the soot covered rocky ceiling. "It's like my opinion didn't matter."

"You wanted to leave me?" His own irritation rose up to greet him. His ankles were killing him. He understood the risk coming into this pit, betting the fear of his Guardian status would be enough to avoid a fight, but they'd been backed into a corner with no other options.

She sat on her elbow and glared at him. "You claimed you wanted us to be mates. That I belonged to you, but not in the same way I was owned. Yet, you never even thought to check what I wanted. The same goes for when we got here and you wanted to fight the biggest threat to stake your claim as macho leader or something. Maybe I had ideas. Maybe—"

"There was no other way," he snapped, and rubbed the throbbing in his ankle. New blood had oozed from the bolts. "Believe me."

"And what about here?" she asked. "I don't think you've once asked me what I thought about anything. Like, do we try to escape, or do we try to get a message out?"

"I'm trying to keep you alive."

"But is this really being alive?" Hopelessness swamped her expression. She laid back down. "You'll have to forgive me if I'm losing faith. It seems nothing I do makes a difference. I should have stayed in my room at the palace. I should never have tried to rescue you from that cage. What's the point?"

"Don't say that." His voice softened. "Never think that. Please." His chest burned with his love for her. He took one of her feet and started rubbing the sole.

She made a little whimper. Tears glistened in her eyes as she struggled with her emotions. Anger, exhaustion... affection. She scowled at herself and tried to tug her foot away, but he held it tight.

"Rubbing my feet isn't going to help," she grumbled, but her eyes softened. "Although it feels good. But you still don't treat me as an equal."

He crawled over her body and kissed her gently on the neck. "I would rub anywhere you ask me to. Because I love you Peaches."

A sob caught in her throat and she dashed her eyes. "You what?"

"I love you."

For some inexplicable reason, this made her cry more. He froze, not knowing what to do as he watched water leak from her eyes. She started blubbering about his ankles being ruined and him massaging *her* feet and how she loved him too, but what was the use of love when it got them nowhere.

Haze lowered himself behind her, rolled her to face away and they spooned. She'd once hugged him so tightly that she'd stopped him from falling apart. He wrapped his arm around her and tucked his knees behind hers, brushing down the skirt of her dress.

"Peaches," he said into her hair. "You have my sincerest apology for making you feel like you have no say in this. You're right. I should have asked for your opinion. Many times." He paused, hoping the next thing he said wouldn't grow the rift between them. "Sometimes you have to trust that, as a Guardian, I'm the most experienced in these situations."

She tensed beneath him. He squeezed her thigh.

"I'm sorry I haven't respected your thoughts," he said again.

She craned her neck to face him. "You owe me." She poked him in the chest. "You said sorry and now you owe me."

He smiled. If it made her think about something else, he would apologize a thousand times. "What would you have of me?"

Anything. To see the sadness go from her eyes, he would storm the iron door and rip the neck out of every guard, even if it meant his doom. As long as she escaped, he would be okay.

She touched his jaw, now heavily covered by a beard. "Promise me not to treat me like the others did. Promise to be equals."

"The thought of caging you makes me feel ill. I want you to be free. I want you to live. Look into my eyes and tell me you believe that."

She searched his eyes in the dim flickering firelight. "That's not a promise."

His stomach churned, but he stuffed down the fear and just came out and said it. "You are not equal when it comes to me protecting you. Anything else, yes. But not that. If it comes to a choice between saving your life, or anyone else's, I choose your life. Always."

She blinked rapidly, her eyes glistening. He dropped his lips to hers and kissed her with all the passion leaking from the holes in his heart. He needed her to understand, so he showed her with his body. Growling from the depth of his emotion, his tongue dueled with hers. She responded with as much need as he felt, rolling and arching into him, taking his ears in her hands and kissing him back until she gasped for breath.

With a determined frown, she squeezed his ears.

"Ow," he said.

"Feed," she demanded. "You want me to survive? I want you to just as much. If you die, I won't live. So feed from me."

"I'm fed."

"My blood will help with the pain." Her lips flattened, ready to take him on with her request. "Show me that you meant what you said. Show me you respect me too."

"Promise to stop thinking about giving up." He gathered her skirt up her thigh and slid his hand beneath it. He found her wet center and dipped his finger in with a sigh. The only thing sweeter than her blood was the honey between her legs. He watched the change come over her face as he worked her, wishing he could toss her skirts and head down there. But he kept one eye on the cave entrance.

She let him work her with increasing urgency until she panted and tilted her hips against him.

"Sweet," he murmured into her hair, his heart thudding in his chest, his cock hard and aching.

She moaned. "Feed from me."

"I want you to promise me something else."

"Yes."

"Promise that no matter what happens to me, you survive. Do you understand?"

Her glassy eyes flew open and met his with shock. He worked her harder, teasing and pinching her where it counted. Her sounds became desperate.

"One foot in front of another. Remember."

"But—"

"Promise me," he demanded.

"Feed from me and I will."

He licked along the vein in her neck, numbing it. He pierced his tongue on a fang and smeared his blood. Then he bit down and lapped. All the while, his fingers kept circling on her nub, demanding her pleasure.

A keening wail caught in her throat. She tensed all around him. He gave her one last pinch, and she convulsed around his fingers, bowing her back with a gasp, arms reaching to clutch at his head, needing something to hold. When she came down from her climax, her bottom lip trembled, and she stared at the low smoldering fire for a long moment. Then she faced him and nodded. "I promise."

"Good." He withdrew his fingers from her heat. The taste of her blood triggered insatiable need. He rocked into her, his erection rubbing the valley between her bottom. She was right. Her blood turned pain into bliss.

"You promise too," she whispered and ground her rear against his front.

"Peaches," he gasped, his resolve undoing.

"*Haze.*"

He gathered her skirt, pushed aside her panties, and drove his cock into her tight core. He stayed like that, fully seated, and breathed through the sensations terrorizing his body. Bliss. Love. Need.

They both shuddered at the joining. He only needed to pump once, twice, and then his orgasm shot out of him in hot spurts.

"Fuck." He held her as aftershocks rode through him, his body pleasurably numb. That was too fast. He never wanted it to end. And he would do anything, *anything,* to keep her safe. "One foot in front of the other, Sweetness."

His words were enough for her. She sighed and rested her head, facing the front, greedily taking his arm and pulling it around her front. She was sated and relaxed, so he held her close and listened to her breathing until she fell asleep.

An ache pressed against his chest. He hoped she didn't realize he'd not made the same promise as he'd asked of her. If she died before him, he'd not survive.

TWENTY-EIGHT

Help arrived a few hours after Peaches fell asleep. From their spot in the cell, Haze could see the iron door. One minute the orc guard stared out at the pit with disinterested eyes, the next he glanced at the door and started walking over. Haze felt it in his bones. This was it. Their chance to get out. And not a moment too soon because the pain from the shackles was getting worse. The guard shift change wasn't due for another hour, so whoever was on the other side of that door right now wouldn't be the usual mob of twenty or so guards. It might be only one. They had to be ready.

"Peaches," he said, shaking her gently. "Wake up."

She grumbled at him with a frown. "Sleeping now."

"You still need to wake. Something's happening."

Her eyes popped open. "What?"

"Look." He pointed at the door.

The guard opened the slot and peered through. He startled at something the person said on the other side, then plucked keys from his pocket. *Fuck.* Haze hadn't even known the guard had keys. He'd never opened the door from this side. All this time, and all he'd needed to do was overpower that one guard.

"What do you think?" he asked quietly. "Should we go for it?"

She frowned. "You're asking me?"

He rubbed her arm. He'd been thinking while she was asleep, and she'd been right. While all he wanted to do was keep her safe, he had to respect she was her own person. Or he was no better than those who'd owned her. "Yes, I'm asking your opinion. Shall we risk it, or stay here and see if the queen will hold up her end of the bargain?"

She stared at the door. "Let's go."

The guard went through the door, but left it open a crack. Probably talking on the other side. Haze helped Peaches up and tugged her along as he limped toward the door. He couldn't hide his pain now. The effects of her blood were wearing off. Peaches gaped at his feet. He held his finger to his lips. *Not now.* On the way, he picked up a fist sized rock on the floor.

When they arrived at the door, Haze put Peaches behind him, then shifted their positions until they were out of sight. When the guard came back inside, the open door would hide them. Then he'd jump the orc from behind. He clenched the rock in his fist and waited with bated breath.

The door inched open. A little more. A dark-haired woman walked through and Haze swung, hitting her head and sending her to the ground.

"Stop, Haze!" Peaches grabbed his arm.

He paused, the rock in his fist hovering in the air.

"I know her."

What?

"Peaches?" muttered the fallen female, her hand testing the wound at her head. She hissed in pain and glared at Haze with so much animosity, he was a little nervous.

"Violet?" Peaches gasped.

Violet blinked rapidly at Peaches, her expression changing to something Haze could only imagine was affection. Peaches kneeled down beside her, tears in her eyes.

"It's you," Peaches said.

"I heard you were here," Violet grumbled.

Haze leaned down and squeezed Peaches' shoulder. Who was this female she seemed to trust? She wore leathers similar to a Guardian, but had no tattoo beneath her eye. Was she human? He didn't like it. And then he saw something that made his heart stop. Violet's hand had blue, glowing Well-blessed marks. She was mated... possibly to... one of his own? But he had to make sure. He needed to hear it from her lips first, to look into her eyes and see if she lied about who she was tied to.

With a quick glance over his shoulder to see if they'd been noticed, Haze let go of Peaches and limped closer to the interloper.

"I'm Violet," she said to him. "Indigo, Shade, Jasper and Ada are upstairs dining with Maebh. Others are waiting for us on the Aconite Sea shore, across from the palace. We need to leave now."

This was an extraction.

And they'd sent her?

Haze grabbed Violet's wrist and wrenched her up. He showed his distrust by tightening his grip. He lifted her blue marked arm and waited for an explanation.

"Indigo," she burst out. "He's my mate."

A gush of air expelled from Haze's mouth, and he relaxed. This was the woman Indigo had chased through Redvein Forest. Cheeky bastard. He guessed that worked out well for him.

Thank fuck. The cavalry had arrived. Haze might not get along with every cadre brother, but he knew they would always come for him. Of that, there had been no doubt. There was no time to waste. He straightened his spine and grunted, "Let's go."

Peaches and Violet shared a look that warmed Haze's heart. Suddenly he knew then that no matter what happened after they stepped out that door, Peaches had someone to look after her. To keep her walking forward if he could not.

Violet handed a dagger to Peaches, and Haze's opinion

of her went up. And when she withdrew a bone sword from behind her back, Haze liked her even more. Violet gestured at the two of them with exasperation. He assumed she was trying to cast some kind of magic weave, and failing.

"It won't work on you two," Violet gasped.

He nodded. "Don't worry about us."

"No cloaking spell."

"No spell," Haze confirmed.

"Shit. Do I even know how to get out?" Violet gaped, sweat dappling her upper lip. Haze had the sense she was new to this kind of work, but from the way she held her sword and her carriage, she was more than capable of looking after herself. Indi had done well to match with her. She would be a good balance to his often carefree attitude.

"I know the way," Peaches offered. "I've been out that way many times, and I always come back on my own. They don't think I'm strong enough to..."

Violet pulled a small cloth from her pocket and handed it to Peaches.

"I kept it," she said.

"You kept it," Peaches breathed.

"Hurry," Haze growled with another glance over his shoulder. Peaches handed him the cloth, and he pocketed it for her. "Now. They're coming."

Other prisoners had begun to notice. Haze felt a stab of guilt at leaving Roses behind, but knew this place was where he belonged. The orc had eaten another fae. He'd probably do it again if he felt like it.

"Should we leave the door open?" Violet asked.

"No, we fucking shouldn't," Haze snapped. "None of these floaters deserve to come out."

Peaches opened her mouth. "But what about—"

"None, Sweetness. *None.*" Haze's brows knitted and limped for the door, dragging Peaches behind him. This was one of those moments she had to trust him. He glanced at her, a void growing in his chest. *Trust me,* he implored with his eyes. Violet rushed to catch up. The keys had fallen next to the door. Haze took them and locked the door from the outside, just as something enormous hit the heavy metal door, shuddering it. He was sure it was Roses, but he had to remain firm in his resolve. Haze was a Guardian. He stood for what was right, and eating other fae because of a disagreement did not even fit in on the scale.

He dropped the keys, refusing to dwell on what he'd done. "Let's go."

Peaches took the lead and walked them down a dark tunnel, away from where Haze assumed the palace was. He winced and bit back a moan as he moved. Throbbing shot up his thighs, but he took Peaches' hand and followed her through the dim tunnels.

They walked for long minutes, never coming across a soul.

"Shouldn't you remove the manacles?" Violet whispered from behind him.

He grunted, "Can't."

"But if you shift, you'll heal, right?"

He glowered at her from over his shoulder. He didn't want to admit this in front of Peaches, but he had a sneaking suspicion the metal drained him of mana, as much as it blocked him from accessing it. "Before they put them on, I had little mana left. I have no idea if I have enough to shift. If I remove them, I might bleed out."

They continued to walk through the darkness, Peaches never wavering in her path. These must have been the tunnels she collected rocks from.

"Are these corridors deserted?" Violet suddenly asked.

Peaches looked over her shoulder and answered. "This used to be an old mine entrance, but now no one comes this way because a giant wyrm moved in. It still lives here somewhere. Don't worry. It's sleeping."

"How do you know?" Violet asked. "Your gift?"

Haze grumbled, "Let's talk about this when we get out."

They continued for a few more minutes before Peaches slowed and revealed to Violet, "I never got my gift. I'm immune to everything. How did you..."

When Violet stopped and caught her breath, Haze said a silent prayer. He wasn't sure how long his legs could take it. When he'd hit Violet with the rock, he'd swung poorly and twisted his ankles. Blood was oozing at a faster rate.

"I always had it, Peaches," Violet said. "The gift. It was there waiting for me. But I also had metal in my hands. Almost always, anyway. There's just something blocking you, like it did with me."

Haze leaned heavily against the wall and bent down to inspect the manacles. *Fucking bitch queen.* He would shove these through her legs next time he saw her. See how she liked them.

Violet stepped up to him. "Ada is here somewhere. If we can get to the rendezvous point, then she can heal you as soon as you get those off."

He nodded and rubbed his ankles. Peaches looked at him, compassion in her eyes, and in that moment, he had hope. They were almost out, home free. Everything he wanted was within his reach. Violet was right. Peaches had a gift. He was sure of it. They just had to figure out what blocked her. But he didn't see the same hope in his mate's eyes, which meant he had work to do when they got to the Order. He would spend all his time chasing away the sadness there.

Peaches shrugged at Violet, unconvinced. "I've not held metal in... Since I don't know how long. It's not like..."

Her voice trailed off and her eyes widened, snapping to Haze.

Haze frowned back. "What is it?"

"I've had this implant since the old world." She rubbed her arm, pointing to a small lump beneath the skin.

"The contraception implant," Violet said. "That's copper, right?"

"This one is plastic. I figured it wasn't hurting me. It would have run out of effectiveness, anyway. But I'm such a wimp. I couldn't take it out."

"Plastic," Haze rumbled, "is also forbidden."

Sounds behind them.

All three whirled around. Violet raised her sword—but it was only Haze's brothers-in-arms, Indigo and Shade. Both in their Guardian uniforms. But both looking at Violet with a strange stiff posture. Something was wrong.

"It's you," Violet said, lowering her weapon.

But they jerked toward her, like puppets on a string. Violet screamed.

"Move," she shouted, understanding just as Haze did. They were being controlled. Probably by the queen. "Get out," she said to him. "I'll hold them off."

A stab of guilt hit Haze through his alarm, but Peaches was his priority. She came first. Would always come first. She tried to protest, but he grabbed her by the collar and shoved her ahead of him. Then he stuffed his pain deep down and ran, the clinking of his manacles the only sound echoing in the tunnel. After a few ragged breaths and steps, blinding light burst behind them, bathing everything white.

And yet onward he pushed Peaches. One foot forward at a time.

TWENTY-NINE

They ran for too long through the tunnels beneath the Obsidian Palace. The maze was a mix of old mine shafts and wyrm paths. Haze couldn't tell the time or distance and he feared it was all part of the labyrinth, but Peaches insisted she knew the way.

His manacles were hot pokers searing up his legs. The pain engulfed him, but he trusted Peaches. She moved with dogged determination in one direction, pausing every so often to check the walls for markers only someone such as she would know. She recognized changes in sediment, in texture, in striations. He was only beginning to realize the depths of her cleverness, and he hoped he would see it all.

"I'm sure the tunnels lead outside," Peaches panted. "I glimpsed the exit once, but was too afraid to explore."

His heart went out to her. She'd been so indoctrinated into being a prisoner that she couldn't escape when the chance presented itself.

He repeated in his mind, *get Peaches out of here*. He refused to believe Indigo and Shade were the only Guardians at the palace. There would be others waiting. Surely. He only needed to hand her over to them. Then he could collapse.

At some point, his mate fit herself beneath his arm to hold him up. Their run turned to a jog. Their jog turned to a limp. Then they dragged.

"We're almost there, baby," she gasped, struggling under his weight.

Agony sliced through him. He dropped to a knee, taking her with him.

"Sweetness," he sighed. Crimson, forgive him, but he wasn't going to make it. "I'm sorry," he rumbled, staring at the ground, too ashamed to look up. "I'm so sorry."

"Stop it," she cried and cupped his face. "Stop it right now. I don't accept your apology. I won't. We're almost there. Just a little more. Look—" She pointed to a brightness at the end of the tunnel.

"I should have been stronger," Haze groaned, pain clouding his mind. "I can't..."

"Now you listen to me, you big brute," she snapped at him, her voice trembling. "If I can survive what they did to me, you can survive this. You're stronger than me."

Her fist glanced off his chest. He had no energy to

respond. How could she think him strong when he submitted to the suffering like this? He hated that metal. Hated what it did to him. Made him less than invincible. Two bolts through the flesh of his ankles... but not through his bone, he suddenly realized. If they were, he'd never be able to walk, let alone survive and work in the pit for days on end. Had Demeter done this on purpose? He could have just as easily shattered Haze's bones.

Haze had to try.

This was it. His final chance.

He gripped the chain dangling between the manacles, took a deep breath, and held it.

"What are you doing?" Peaches asked, trepidation lacing her tone.

"You were right," he gritted out. "I'm stronger than this."

His muscles bulged. His neck tendons popped. He pushed all his strength into his arms until veins wreathed like hissing snakes. And then he broke the chain.

"Don't..." Peaches shouted. "No more. It's not worth the pain."

"If I get them off, then I'll replenish from the Well. It might take some time before I have enough mana to shift, but a couple of flesh wounds won't kill me."

His words were braver than his thoughts.

There was no source of power nearby. No trickling water. No lake filled with mana. He would replenish at the usual snail's pace. It might be enough. That's what he told himself, anyway.

Haze glanced at Peaches, sucked in a breath and held it again as he pushed all his reserves into his hands. One chance. *Rip them out. Come on!* He grasped the bolts on either side of his ankles. He tried not to see tears spilling from his lover's eyes. And then he pulled. A broken roar of agony ripped out of his lungs. Pulsing pain threatened to consume him, blind him, but he pulled and pulled until the traitorous bolts slid clean out of his masticated flesh. Dizziness overwhelmed him. His lashes fluttered closed, and he hunched over, spent, too afraid to even look at the damage he'd done. It felt like he had no feet, like he'd chopped them off.

Peaches lifted the skirt of her dress, tugged her undershirt out and ripped a strip off the bottom. She should just go. They were losing time. Any minute, guards could be chasing them down the tunnels. The Sluagh only needed to sense the hopelessness in their hearts, and they would be able to locate them in an instant. But she wrapped his wounds and bound them tight.

"Go without me," he rasped, feverish heat flushing his face. "I'll catch up."

She stood back and shoved fingers into her long, messy hair. Determination plastered over her face and he could see she was done taking orders, even from him. The timid, fragile woman he'd met weeks ago was now like the poppy he always knew she was. Strong of spine. Beautiful. *His mate.*

She glanced at the dagger Violet had given her, and Haze's stomach dropped. What was she thinking? Before he could stop her, she pointed it at her forearm and dragged it through the flesh, deep. For a moment, all his fears came true. She was giving up. But then she gritted her teeth and dug her fingers into the wound, fishing around until she pulled out a tiny piece of plastic and held it bloody before her face.

"You." She glared at it. "You've caused me the most pain of all."

Then she flicked it, watched it flip and rotate in the air until it bounced off the ground. Was this the tiny thing that had been holding her back? What had Violet called it, an implant? What kind of fucked up shit were humans doing back in her time to voluntarily embed something forbidden by the Well into their flesh and blood? Peaches rushed back to him, put her hands on his knees.

"We made it, baby," Peaches said. "We're here. You did it, Haze. You kept me safe. These past few weeks have been —" She choked up. Liquid brown eyes met his. A tear leaked from her eye and dribbled down her face. He hated seeing her so.

"Sweetness." He rubbed the tear away. "You—"

She held her wounded arm out.

"Drink," she demanded. "My blood will dull your pain. It will make you stronger."

He couldn't give up now. Only a few more steps. He touched his tongue to his fang, deliberately showing that he drew his blood. That she would only feel pain for a moment. Then he latched onto her arm and covered her wound with his mouth, biting around her to make the blood flow again. More life-giving goodness rushed into his mouth, and he drank greedily.

Peaches held onto him to avoid falling down. It was he who should be holding onto her. The drugging properties of her blood filtered through him, dulling his pain. He started to feel recharged. Reinvigorated. And he couldn't stop drinking.

As though the goddess approved, as though the Well was on their side, he could have sworn blue light flashed. The ground shook. The walls crumbled, showering sand. But then Peaches jolted and convulsed. She seized. She lost her breath, and then finally, she gasped and broke away from Haze with a stumble. Horror filled him. What had his greed done to her?

Blinking through his blurred vision, he tried to force his eyes to focus. His head swam with the effects of her blood, but the blue light was still there. It glanced off the walls. Off his arm. Off... hers.

Well-blessed marks swirled and twined over their arms, pulsing with light, with approval from the Well. Lazy pride swelled through him and he almost cried. The only time in his life tears had welled in his eyes, and it was now. With her. Because everything was going to be okay.

"Violet was right," Peaches mumbled, mesmerized by her arm. "She was right. Look at us."

She laughed and then kissed him hard on the lips, pushing into him with passion.

The earth rumbled some more, showering more dust on them. But he didn't give a shit. She was his mate. His Well-blessed mate. Nothing would stop them now.

"I was right first," he reminded her stubbornly. "Not Violet. What did I tell you?"

She bit her lip, holding back a smile, and placed her hand over his heart. "That I'm yours."

Damned fucking right. A growl of approval rattled through him, and he levered himself up. "Let's go."

Together they hobbled to the exit, to the light. With any luck, if there were any guards this far out from the main palace, they would be distracted with Violet, Indigo, and Shade. A sliver of guilt flashed through Haze, but he clamped down on it. His brothers would be fine. Violet was strong.

Finally. They were free.

But no sooner had he thought the words, and only ten feet from the exit, Peaches doubled over, seizing in pain. Horrified, Haze tried to hold her up, but stumbled himself. Her palm hit the wall, and it shook with such ferocity that fissures appeared like jagged lightning, harbingers of doom. Dread filled Haze. The walls were coming down. Wooden support beams creaked above, cracking under duress. The earthquake worsened. More rumbling. More breaking walls and dust falling.

"Haze?" She met his bleak gaze, her voice helpless and pitched high. "What do we do?"

A loud crack sounded above. He shoved Peaches toward the exit just before a wooden beam crashed down. He caught it on his shoulder and staggered to the ground, holding the weight, preventing the tunnel from completely caving in and swallowing them whole. First, she needed to get out. Then it didn't matter what happened to him. Dust piled on top of his head and collected at his twitching ears.

"Hurry," he roared at her. "Run, Sweetness. Get out of here before it all comes down."

"No!" she cried, startling herself. But the rumbling wouldn't stop. More parts fell. Rocks. Bigger ones. One hit her shoulder and she flinched.

"Run, Peaches," he snarled, bending under the immense weight. "If you ever meant any of those things you said to me, run. Survive like you promised." She shook her head stubbornly, so he glared at her, making her remember what she'd said in the pit cell. "You promised."

Accusation and betrayal replaced the sadness in her eyes. She would never forgive him for this. Just as he'd never forgiven Holly.

"*Go!*" His roar rattled the air. "I'll catch up."

She *must* leave. She couldn't do this to him. All his life, he'd wanted to keep people safe. To protect them from their own worst enemy, themselves. Lately it had taken the form of being a Guardian, but now, with Peaches, he had found a true purpose. Her.

Thank the Well she listened, because she turned. And she ran as the walls came tumbling down and the darkness stole his light.

THIRTY

Peaches wasn't sure how long she wandered aimlessly outside the tunnel. Minutes. Hours. Days. At some point, she'd found a bush to hide behind and collapsed under the weight of her guilt. She imagined sensing Haze's heartache too, so went back to the collapsed tunnel and started digging with her fingers. The collapse was her fault. Her power. She'd felt it running through her veins, quaking with the force of her uncontrolled emotions.

No matter how hard she tried, the power didn't work again. She wasn't even sure what it was, except that it took the tunnel down. Electricity had lashed through her veins moments before the collapse. For a split second, she'd felt alive, powerful, *strong*. Now, emptiness. It ignored her. As if it too knew how wretched she'd been for walking away from Haze.

She wasn't even sure which Guardian found her, who plucked her from the tunnel, kicking and screaming, her fingers bloodied. Or who it was that flew her away from the evil Obsidian Palace. Haze was *gone*. The tunnel had swallowed him whole, and it was all her fault.

If she'd been stronger...

If she'd taken out that damned useless piece of plastic in her arm years ago, she would have had time to adjust to the raw power flooding her system.

If.

If.

Looking back at it now, from the safety of Haze's room at the Order, she was surprised one of the Sluagh hadn't found her and sucked her soul. She'd begged for it. It was through sheer luck that Violet's battle to save Indigo within the palace had taken most of the soldier's attention. She vaguely remembered an army of winged fae flying in formation over Aconite City.

As she laid in Haze's bed, scenting him on the pillow, replaying her cowardice in the tunnel, she remembered how strange it had been to think she could feel Haze's *need* for her to escape like a compulsion pumping through her blood. She'd thought she was brave. She'd thought she'd changed since waking up in this time. That loving Haze had made her strong. But she'd put one foot in front of another, and then left him behind like she'd promised.

Coward.

She was a coward.

Some time after the Guardian had placed her on Haze's bed, a blond woman named Ada came in and tried to see to Peaches' health briefly, but Peaches refused and Ada left. She was a healer, Peaches had gathered. Ada was also the Seelie High Queen, mated to High King Jasper Darkfoot.

Something in Peaches' cold memory triggered. Perhaps Haze had mentioned them. Peaches didn't really care. She couldn't make herself talk or move, or think. All she'd been able to do was scream Haze's name until her voice was raw. Over and over, as if that would bring him back to her.

To make matters worse, the marking on her arm pulsed and flooded her with a mix of distraught emotions she couldn't sift through, nor did she understand. It overwhelmed her. It smothered her.

A knock came at the door and she shut her eyes, curling into herself. It was Violet and her mate, Indigo. She ignored them, hoping they would go away. But then she heard the sounds of Ada coming back, and the three of them talking quietly amongst themselves.

A part of her wanted to be elated that her friend had rescued her lover, pried him from the bitch queen's hands. But all she could muster was a growing emptiness. That old friend protecting her from the worst pain. She used to count down the seconds, the minutes, the hours. But there was no passing of time that would erase this pain. It never ended.

Eventually, her friend's voice broke through.

"Peaches, Ada needs to check you over."

"I'm fine," she sniffed. "Go away."

A few moments of silence stretched.

"Peaches... the bond. Can you feel Haze? Is he alive?"

Something sparked in her empty soul. *Feel* Haze? No. Of course, she couldn't feel him. He was dead. And it was all because of her. She hadn't thought there were any more tears to cry, but they came.

"It's my fault," she confessed, self-loathing coating her insides. "I *made* the earthquake."

"Don't think like that."

"But it *was* me. My gift. I took the implant out and straight away it happened." Peaches opened her eyes, silently accusing her friend of not understanding.

Standing near the door, the three of them looked at Peaches like she was some kind of train wreck.

"Hey," Violet said. "I accidentally blinded Indigo the first time my light came out. I also just gave Indigo and Shade radiation poisoning. He's okay. He's forgiven me."

Indigo smiled at Violet the same way Haze used to smile at Peaches. She shut her eyes... then something Violet said clicked.

"You did what?" she asked. "Radiation?"

"Long story. But I turned my light into something that harmed the Sluagh hijacking their bodies. It worked. We got out."

Peaches stared. Violet used to be a nuclear physicist in their time. "You became... ultraviolet?"

They laughed. Just a little.

Violet huffed. "Don't ever call me that again."

Peaches rubbed her eyes, already feeling the emptiness creep back in.

"Anyway," Violet mumbled. "It was more like a gamma ray than UV, but—okay, shut up, Violet. I'm doing it again." She came to the bed and sat. She touched Peaches' blue markings and then her own. "Listen. This bond connects us to our mate. And I know this is going to be difficult, but you need to try to sense him."

Peaches frowned at her friend, wishing they'd never left each other, wondering if any of this heartache would have happened if they'd just stuck together. "What do you mean?"

"If you concentrate, you can feel your mate through your connected emotions," she said. "I can feel Indigo, even when he's not here with me."

Connected emotions.

The idea bounced around in Peaches' head. So she *had* felt Haze's need for her to escape. That wasn't her imagination. She'd felt it as though it had pressed down on her. Knowing it wasn't just her cowardice that had sent her running from him, but his desire adding to the commotion, she felt a little better, a little less soul crushed. She sat up and wiped her nose. "I didn't know that."

"Try it. Close your eyes and focus on the bond."

Violet took Peaches' hands in her own, bade her to close her eyes and concentrate. Peaches focused on the marks, on how her body felt different there. But it was all so new to her. She had no idea what she was doing.

"What do you feel?" Violet asked.

"I don't know what I'm looking for."

"You're looking for the other half of your heart."

Of course. A beat. An echo. She tried focusing again. This time, she sent her awareness down the bond and opened up. She felt her heartbeat. She listened. And then she realized what consumed her was heartache. It was the only thing she recognized right now, so she focused on that emotion and listened for an echo. If Haze was alive... he'd be heartbroken, too.

"I feel... I feel..."

The ache had a partner. Soft, ragged, devastated. Tears leaked from her eyes.

Haze?

A surge of hope smashed through the stones crushing her heart. She pushed that hope down the bond. It fizzled and faded with distance, but it was still there. Maybe Haze was too far away to receive it. Maybe it was stupid to think she could communicate.

But then she felt an answer. An echo of her hope, blooming like a poppy in the darkness. He knew she was okay.

"He's there, Violet. Oh my God. I can feel him."

Her eyes opened, tears blinding her. Her gaze darted between Ada and Indigo and Violet. All of them wore the same expression of relief. When Indigo slumped against the wall, his brow furrowing, Peaches realized these were Haze's friends too.

They'd missed him. They'd hurt for him. They would help her find him.

"Good, that's good." Violet patted Peaches' hip over the blanket. "If Haze is alive, we'll find him. We won't stop until he's back with us."

Peaches nodded, relieved.

"Peaches," Violet said gently, "you need to let Ada take a look at you. Haze would want you to look after yourself."

Survive. Keep walking. She could do that. One step. And then another. Until she found him. She nodded. "I promised."

"Good." Violet stood and waved Ada over. "I'm going to be just outside the door."

Violet and Indigo left, and then it was just Ada.

Peaches laid her head down on the pillow, then sat back up, suddenly aware of how dirty she was. And covered in blood.

"Let's take a look at those fingers first." Ada gently picked them up and turned them over, inspecting them in the candlelight. "Looks like you've gone two rounds with Freddie Kruger, am I right?"

Peaches laughed through the pain. She breathed deeply and slowly calmed. She watched as Ada adeptly worked on Peaches' body. Another human. *From their time.* Here, and a High Queen, no less. Ada was strong, smart, and compassionate.

As Peaches' aches and pains ebbed away, something occurred to her.

"Why do you suppose I couldn't access my gift, but magic could still work against me?" she asked. "They were able to erase many of my scars, and I could be glamored, but the Queen could never mesmerize me."

Ada bade her to lie back and hovered her hands over Peaches' body, much like a reiki healing. The corner of Ada's lip twitched as she considered Peaches' question.

"I'm not sure," she said. "I mean, I've only been awake a few months. I'm still learning this stuff. But if I had to take a stab, it would be that the tiny plastic in your arm was just enough of a block to stop some things like the Well-blessed union, but not enough to be consistent. Violet had used your little scrap of fabric to cast a location spell on you. That's how she found you in the pit. But she told me the spell's effectiveness dropped out some—" Ada gasped, her hands over Peaches' stomach.

"What is it?" Peaches jolted upright, panic in her heart. *No more bad news. Please.*

Ada met Peaches' eyes with wonder in her own. "You're pregnant."

"That can't be." Peaches snorted. "We've only... I mean... we've..."

"It's very new," Ada explained. "Days even, but it's there. I sense the change in your body."

"What?"

The walls closed in on Peaches. She'd never worried

about contraception. She'd always had the implant. After she'd woken in this time, it was just something that never occurred to her. And clearly not to Haze. A wave of nausea came over her, and it had nothing to do with the pregnancy.

What would Haze think after losing his own?

What if they couldn't find him?

What if she was going to raise this baby alone?

Ada smiled gently and took Peaches' hands in her own. "I'm a few months pregnant myself. Clarke and Rush have a mini half-shifter menace called Willow. You'll meet her soon, I'm sure. Peaches, you're with friends here. You're not alone. And Violet... she razed heaven and hell to find you. You've got an especially good friend in her."

Peaches didn't know what to say.

Ada patted her gently. "How about I run the bath for you? After you clean yourself up, you should get some rest. You're growing another life. But if you need help sleeping, I can help you nod off. I'll be right outside the door."

It wasn't just Peaches she had to fight for anymore. It was Haze. And a baby. She'd be dammed if she gave up now.

THIRTY-ONE

At dusk the following day, the Order wasted no time drilling Peaches for information on her time at the Winter Court. They summoned her to the temple as soon as she'd awoken. Having slept most of the day, and flying into the Order delirious with grief, the walk across campus was the first chance to view her new home.

Peaches walked beside Violet as they stepped out of the Twelve's two-story house and onto the empty training field of grass. Violet pointing to a dark house, similar to the Twelve's but covered in vines and cobwebs.

"That creepy house right there with the curtains drawn belongs to the Sluagh Guardians, The Six."

"There are Sluagh?" Peaches gasped, goosebumps lifting the hairs on her arms.

Violet frowned and visibly shuddered. "Remind me to tell you about their nonsense when we have time. For now, don't go there. Ever."

Peaches touched her stomach over the flowing dress she'd borrowed from Clarke. She'd met the freckled red-headed psychic briefly in the modest kitchen. Clarke had given Peaches a warm welcome, a hug, and promised they'd talk later before chasing after her child, Willow, who'd already begun to pester the house brownie as she was setting up for dinner.

"Those houses on the left are the Guardian barracks," Violet continued, then pointed at another, more regal house between lush gardens. "That's the Prime's house. Owl shifter. You'll meet her in a moment. And if we walked back that way, eventually we'd find the Mage academy, library, dorms, and mess hall. The forge and training yard are near the front gates."

Peaches hand-signed her thanks.

"Oh," Violet waved her down. "You don't have to worry about that custom with us old timers. We decided we can say thank you and sorry to each other if we wanted, bargains and debts be damned."

A warmth bloomed in Peaches' chest. That sounded so good. Fae customs were exhausting sometimes.

They stopped at the base of a long stone staircase leading up to the temple. Water trickled down culverts from the top down to where they either went into drains or continued along a meandering path into the campus. Even though the sun was setting, blue robed Mages and leather clad Guardians wandered the tracks. Dusk had always been the busiest time in Elphyne, a moment where the nocturnal and day dwellers crossed paths. Most of them gave Peaches a wary look. She dipped her fingers into her dress pocket, expecting to feel a familiar rock, but there was nothing. This was a new dress.

Violet asked, "Are you sure you're okay?"

She looked at her feet, at the borrowed sandals. "Yeah. I will be. I just need to find Haze."

"So... congratulations?" Violet made a pointed look at Peaches' stomach and smiled.

"Thanks, I guess."

"You guys work fast, huh?" Violet elbowed Peaches in jest. "I mean... you only met a few weeks ago."

Peaches raised her brow. "And you and Indi?"

A bashful look came over Violet. "Yeah. A couple of weeks, but at least I'm not knocked up already. That's all on you."

A quiet settled over Peaches. She knew her friend was just teasing, but it still hurt to think of all the unknowns. Violet must have understood the look on Peaches' face because she gave her an impromptu hug and whispered in her ear, "Don't worry. We're going to get him back. Once I set my mind to something, there's no stopping me." She pulled away and sent a glare at the onlookers. "And in case you're wondering, they're looking at me, too. I'm new here. They'll get used to us."

Peaches dashed burgeoning tears away and took a deep shuddering breath, nodding to herself as her resolve hardened. "I'm going to find Haze."

"I'll help you."

"You will?" She expected some push back, or at the very least, a flat-out dismissal of her desire. No one seemed to think Peaches was capable of anything. No one except Haze, that was.

"Abso-fucking-lutely."

It was good to see Violet smile. When they'd first met, she had been all hard lines and sorrow. She remembered Violet had felt so guilty about her role in the nuclear holocaust. But Peaches had sourced uranium. And Silver had worked in the factory that built the bombs. They all had a part to play, and for some reason, the Well thought they were perfect candidates to wake in today's world and... what? Give them incredible power? But not without torturing them first.

Bitterness oozed through her mind and she had to make a concerted effort to push it back. No more of that coldness. She had to find the love of her life.

Peaches wondered if it was all Indigo that had changed Violet, or if, like Peaches, there was more to their time apart.

"What have you been doing all this time?" she asked her friend, almost afraid of the answer.

Violet's good mood disappeared. She glared at a group of Mages shuffling past, gossiping. When they walked on by, she answered.

"I um... I was... ah..."

"An ax murderer?"

It was a joke, but the look on Violet's face turned serious. "I killed vampires."

Peaches blinked. Stared. "Like Buffy?"

They both burst out laughing. It cleared the tension.

Violet made a pattern in the dirt with her toe. "To be honest, you're not far off the mark. I moved around a lot. I found some metal weapons, and I used them to track and hunt vampires who tried to drink from me, or anyone else without consent."

"Oh, shit. You really did it?"

Violet nodded. "Some of them were assholes, yes, but some of them I may have been a little overzealous with my judgement. I'm not proud of it."

"Why not? I think that's incredibly brave. I wish I had been as brave as you."

"What have you been doing for the past six years?"

Peaches hugged herself. "I tried living on my own for a while. Found someone to glamor me to look like a pixie." She waved at her hair and teeth—except now she looked completely human. No piranha spiked teeth, no peach hair. Would Haze even recognize her? "I was doing all right, working at a silk farm, minding my own business, but then a vampire caught a whiff of my blood and fed from me." The sun went down behind the horizon, and a cold breeze trickled in. "I became a target, and then soon a prince found me and took me to the Autumn Court, where he bottled my blood and sold it on the streets. Word got to the queen, and I've been at the Winter Court for two years serving as her personal blood slave. She wanted me all to herself, so kept up my pixie glamor."

The blood had drained from Violet's face. "Oh, Peaches. I'm so sorry. We should never have split up. I should have stayed with you."

"We didn't know any better. We didn't know the Guardians. And, besides, it wasn't all bad. I met this crazy, grumpy, but surprisingly helpful old redcap goblin who taught me to read Elven runes and make mana stones. And the queen kept other vampires away from me." Her mind briefly traveled to Luthian and Wisteria. "Well, most of the time."

"That's not—" Violet stopped herself from saying anymore, instead nodding to herself, determination in her eyes. "We'll be different now. We're in the right place. It took me a while to see that too, but I'm going to start making things right."

"I like the sound of that."

They stared up the steps to the red-roofed temple at the top. The navy and purple sky filling with stars.

"I wonder what Silver's doing," Violet pondered.

"I wonder that all the time." Unease sank like a stone in

Peaches' stomach. If she'd had a terrible time, and so did Violet, then maybe Silver wasn't fairing too well either.

"I think we need to find her," Violet confessed.

"I agree."

"But first we find Haze." Violet slipped off her shoes and bade Peaches to do the same. She plonked them next to another row of shoes at the base of the steps. "Can't go in the temple with shoes on apparently," she murmured before taking Peaches' hand and leading her up the cool steps.

The temple overlooked the entire Order campus. Great columns held up a red roof dribbling water from rain chains, even though it wasn't raining. Must be run magically. *Incredible.* Awe filled her as she took in the grand courtyard with a tiny pool in each corner, a spike protruding from the water. A larger pool took up the center. This one had a big obelisk monument. It smelled like incense and jasmine.

"That's where they'll test your elemental affinities," Violet explained, pointing to the pools. "Knowing this will help you learn to manage your gift. Let's keep going. The council chamber is just through there."

They moved to another open room that overlooked the campus. A balcony without railings served as a landing pad for winged fae. Grand vases filled with blossoms were scattered about, their scent filling the air, mingling with jasmine in a pleasant, sweet bouquet. A number of fae were already present and talking animatedly amongst themselves. When Violet and Peaches walked into the room, they stopped.

Peaches forced herself to stand tall, to not shrink under the group's attention. But each had eyes that judged, that held secrets and power and history.

Only two Guardians were present. The tall, stately elf tossed his golden hair over a leather clad shoulder. The heavily tattooed crow shifter beside him flinched and scowled as the blond lock brushed his arm. His glistening, black feathered wings tightened. The scowl remained on his face as he turned to Peaches.

Three Mages in blue robes stood next to the Guardians. A pixie with prismatic dragonfly wings, pearlescent brown skin, and rainbow hair stood with her hands clasped together at the front, watching Peaches patiently. Next to her, a wizard-type brushed twigs out of his long white beard. They fell into the awaiting hands of the stocky female satyr next to him, as though she knew they'd fall.

And then there was the Prime, the only one completely still in the room. She wore a blue roman dress that flowed to the tips of her bare brown toes. White ringlets around her face. White lashes framed big brown eyes. Lustrous, white wings cascaded down her back like a queen's regal mantle. The Prime only had eyes for Peaches and Violet.

The only other fae Peaches had met with this aura of power bubbling around her was Queen Maebh herself.

A bat-winged angelic shadow suddenly descended from the night sky. *Vampire.* He landed hard, stumbled, and then straightened his spine. Without meeting anyone's eyes, he smoothed dark locks from his face. He looked familiar. *Where did she know him from?* Short, buzzed hair at the sides, longish on the top. Warm olive skin. A five o'clock shadow that gave him a sinful look. His muscular frame was more athletic than Haze's body-building type. It was made for endurance, where Haze's was for crushing.

The vampire's thick black lashes finally lifted. It wasn't Peaches he glared at, but Violet. Dark circles ran under his eyes, reminding Peaches of how ill Indi had looked last night. And then Peaches remembered. He was the other vampire who'd been hurt by Maebh. Violet had to force-feed him her blood, so he healed from radiation poisoning.

He was alive because of Violet, yet he glared at her as though he both hated and wanted her. *He's craving Well-blessed blood.* And there weren't too many of them around. They were all mated. Peaches didn't think sharing would be in Haze's or Indigo's vocabulary. Pity for Shade rolled through Peaches, but when he slid his hard gaze her way, she let go of it.

It was his choice to dwell on something he couldn't change. She'd done enough of that in her life.

"Now that we're all here," the Prime announced. "Let's get this council meeting started."

They all turned to Peaches expectantly, and the Prime continued. "Peaches, welcome to the Order. Like the others of your kind who have found their way here, and mated to a Guardian, we've made no demands—"

Violet made a disbelieving sound, and the Prime cut her a glare.

"But we do believe if you pledge yourself to our cause, to upholding the integrity of the Well and ensuring the long-term survival of Elphyne, that you will be a good fit here too."

In other words, join them or get tossed on her ass. Peaches sighed. Violet squeezed Peaches' hand reassuringly, and she remembered what Violet had said only moments ago.

We're in the right place. It took me a while to see that too, but I'm going to start making things right.

Peaches touched her lips. "I'm in the right place. And I want to find Haze."

The Prime stared, then nodded and gestured about the room, pointing to each councilor as she said their name. "Dawn is our Seer." The ram-horned female bowed. "Barrow is our alchemist." The wizard cleared his throat. "Colt oversees the Mages." The pixie's wings fluttered. "All are preceptors at the academy. I'm sure you'll cross paths with them as you learn to control your gift. Barrow even has a stone to help focus your power until you learn to harness it properly."

Dawn elbowed Barrow, who jolted as though he'd been asleep. Then he dug into his robe pocket and pulled out a smooth mana stone. He gave Peaches a tight smile as he showed it and then put the stone back.

She guessed she would get it later. If she wanted it.

"And the Guardians," the Prime continued, "you may have met already. D'arn Leaf is the team leader of the Cadre of Twelve." The sun-kissed elf nodded. Peaches couldn't help thinking he should be wearing board-shorts, not battle leathers. But the look in his eyes was anything but casual. She imagined he ran a tight ship. "That leaves D'arn Cloud and D'arn Shade, also members of the Twelve."

Peaches smiled and waved.

No one waved back.

"It's been a long few nights," the Prime said. "Please, if you will, we need to know exactly what you've seen at the Winter Court that breaks the laws of the Well."

"What about Haze?"

The Prime smiled patiently. "All in due time."

With all eyes on her, Peaches launched into a retelling of everything she knew. From the start of her time there to when Haze came along and after.

"But you didn't actually see the experiments," Cloud said.

"No... I was never in that room."

"But I was," Violet said. "As was Indi and Shade. Why does it matter if Peaches saw it too? We have enough evidence of misbehavior."

"Maebh also killed humans," Peaches said. "Right in

front of me. She hurt Haze. They beat him up and hung him in a cage, then tossed us in some kind of prison where we had to chip away at these damned rocks all day." With every word out of her mouth, tension drew her shoulders tight. "There was an iron door to this prison. They stabbed Haze with metal shackles through his legs. How will all this help us find him? Is he still trapped? What's—"

The Prime lifted a hand to appease Peaches. "We're just trying to establish grounds for action. With Maebh mobilizing her army, it won't be easy to get inside Aconite City, let alone the palace."

"Are you telling me no one has located Haze yet?" She gaped and looked around at the Guardians. Eyes turned hard. Jaws clenched.

"Don't presume to think you know what we do," the Prime clipped.

Indignation flowed over the room, and it was all directed at Peaches. Heat flared in her cheeks, but her time for keeping words to herself was over. She would never forgive herself for not doing anything and everything she could to save Haze.

"We have a process," the Prime continued. "And we must follow it, or we lose our standing in the community. The only reason fae fall in line is because deep down, they believe what we do is right. They believe the Well is the key to a long and prosperous existence. Do you disagree?"

Peaches couldn't. She felt like she was drowning. She

looked at her friend. Violet returned sad eyes but stood next to her in a show of solidarity.

"If we lose that standing," the Prime continued. "Then we lose the ability to police the realm above the might of crowns. Now, what else can you tell us? Were you involved with the contraband? What was your role at the palace?"

Peaches clutched her dress, knuckles whitening. Her breath quickened. She felt attacked.

"I must admit," Violet drawled, stepping forward. "If I'd known this was going to be an inquisition, I would have asked Indi to support us."

"He's not Council," Leaf said with a sigh, as though she was being childish for mentioning it.

"He won't care," Violet shot back.

"Enough." The Prime shifted her gaze to her councilors. "We know what comes next. We must give Maebh a chance to respond to these accusations herself. We must receive an official reason why she's attacking us instead of letting us in her palace. If we can avoid more bloodshed, and still uphold the law of the Well, then we must."

"So we do nothing?" Peaches' voice reached a fever pitch. "We just sit here and twiddle our thumbs while Haze could be trapped under rocks, or worse, being flayed alive by the bitch queen herself? She killed and murdered in front of us. She tortured one of your own. She used contraband like she didn't give a shit about what was right, or the prosperity of this world. All she wants is power. What more do you need?"

"She *is* power. She is the Unseelie *High* Queen," the Prime clipped. "While we want nothing more than to dispose of her, we cannot do so without starting a war. Thousands of fae will die. We barely stopped a war between the Seelie and Unseelie recently, and it had all been stoked by the humans in Crystal City. They want us to fight amongst ourselves so they can swoop in and take control of Elphyne. I *will not* give them the satisfaction. We must be better.

"All we have are eyewitness accounts. And while that is enough for us to believe she is doing wrong, it will not be enough to appease the Unseelie if we force her to abdicate, or if we execute her. There will be repercussions."

"But we did it to Mithras," Colt pointed out, her dragonfly wings vibrating.

"No," the Prime replied. "Jasper killed Mithras and took the crown by right of blood. The Seelie people are still warming to his rule. The only part we played was applying pressure through raiding the Summer Court, and we did that to extricate Jasper—who was still one of our own at the time. The Order cannot be seen as playing favorites. This leans to authoritarian rule, and if the people believe we approve of that, then it's not a far reach to wipe us out completely and put their own dictator in charge. We all know there are currently at least *two* vying for that role. None of them ideal."

Violet made a disgusted sound, mumbling something about red tape never changing.

The ringing in Peaches' ears wouldn't stop.

"Haze could be trapped," she whispered, her heart thudding.

Shade slid his honey-eyed gaze her way. It was the first show of compassion she'd seen in the male. "Haze can shift into a bat," he said. "He can crawl out of tight spaces."

"But he's still there." She held up her marked hand. "I can feel him. He's there somewhere. If he was okay, he'd be here. With me."

Her words rang out across the room. The only person who cared was Violet. She put a comforting arm around Peaches' shoulders and squeezed tight.

"He's a Guardian," the Prime pointed out. "And one of the Twelve. He knew what his job entailed when he joined our ranks." She pursed her lips. "And he's not dead, you said it yourself."

Cold fury burned in the pit of Peaches' stomach, and the temple floor and walls started to rumble. Each winged fae fluttered their wings, hovering just above the ground while everyone else crouched to balance. Her gift piggy-backed on high emotion. It wasn't until Violet cooed softly in her ear that Peaches realized the ground shaking came from her.

"Calm down, human," spat the crow-shifter, his blue eyes like burning sapphires. "Calm yourself before you take this whole place down."

She clenched her fists. "I've had enough of people treating me like nothing. I'm *not* nothing."

"I never said you were," he shot back.

Peaches forced her tear-blurred eyes to the landscape outside, making herself count the landmarks below. The barracks. The trees. The water fountains—there were a lot. Finally, her nerves eased, and the rumbling stopped. The Prime gave the Mages a pointed look. "Barrow, give Peaches the focus stone now. Colt, you will see to Peaches' tutelage immediately. Dawn, is there anything else you would like to add before we conclude this meeting?"

While Barrow handed Peaches the stone, Dawn looked on with pale eyes. Peaches tried not to shrink under the attention, to remain the strong poppy Haze believed her to be. She focused on the smooth stone in her palm. No inscriptions. A regular river pebble. Strangely comforting. Dawn's eyebrows rose briefly, as though she'd *Seen* something about Peaches. For a moment, fear skipped up Peaches' spine. She had the urge to make a run for it, but Dawn turned back to her leader and said, "Not at this point."

Peaches lifted her chin and straightened her shoulders. "So I'm to forget about my mate and, what, study?"

The look the Prime gave could have leveled the room, just as any earthquake. Peaches kept her cool and stared back.

Maybe this small act of defiance was what made the Prime say the next cruel words. "Your lack of control is what caused your mate to become trapped in the first place. Unlike other fae, you Well-blessed humans have a never ending supply of mana. Unlike us, you won't run out of power if you continue to use it. You could bring down mountains if you were so inclined. If you don't find a way to get a hold on yourself, then you are no good to anyone, least of all yourself or D'arn Haze. Heed our advice. Learn control. Or next time you see your mate, he might not survive."

THIRTY-TWO

"Look what we's found," hissed the hobgoblin into the darkness.

"Round and round," said another.

"A new clown."

"Maybe to drown."

"Look, he frowns. Tee hee."

Haze swam out of unconsciousness. His back bumped over dirt as he was dragged by the ankles. Sand in his nose. Beneath his fingernails. In his mouth.

"He's ours to play with."

"To keep."

"To make weep."

Giggling and cackling surrounded him, swirling and swirling. They dumped him in a deep hole. He landed with a bone-jarring thud, crunching on old bones and corpses. Dizzy, Haze rolled to his side and vomited Peaches' blood.

"He killed our brothers," whispered a hate-filled voice from above.

"Ours to play with."

"To keep."

"... to make weep."

A million hits landed on his body, blow after blow. They were rocks. Stones. The same spotted stones he'd seen in the tunnel walls with Peaches' brethren. He covered his head and curled inward. He tried to call on his mana, but it wouldn't rise to his touch. Perhaps he'd used too much shifting to crawl out of the tunnel collapse. Not much permeated his thoughts except to protect his head. Nothing existed here except the stench of rotting flesh and excrement.

"I'll fucking feed you to the Well Worms," Haze snarled up at them, throwing anything he could grab. The stones and bone projectiles barely made it to the top of the dark pit before falling back down.

A cackle and a gasp, as though a goblin had a great idea. "A gift!"

"To offer."

"To feed."

"Yesss. Our god will be pleased."

When the last of their impish voices faded away, Haze welded his lids shut and imagined his mate's pretty eyes. A blue glow seeped behind his eyelids. The Well-blessed mating mark flared, bringing light to the dingy corpse ridden hole.

He must be back in the underground labyrinth. *Fuck.* But at least he was alive. Peaches was alive. He'd managed to crawl out of the debris as a bat, but then had to shift immediately back into fae form. Exhausted, he'd passed out. That was when the goblins must have found him.

He went to scratch transference runes to bring Justice, but a cold snuffling met his palm. He startled. Something wet pressed in, and then something hard prodded his body. Haze glanced down.

"Tinger?"

THIRTY-THREE

"What are you doing?" Violet asked.

Peaches jolted at the intrusion, her fingers pausing on the mana stone she'd just shoved into a satchel slung over her shoulder.

"Busted," Peaches answered quietly. She opened another drawer in Preceptor Barrow's desk, hoping he kept the more special stones there.

It was late in the evening on the third day after the council meeting. They were in one of the classrooms in the academy. The lights were low and students and preceptors had left for the day. The night classes were about to start, but Peaches had snuck back inside to steal some stones and a jar of manabeeze.

For the past three days Peaches had done everything they'd told her to do. She'd had herself tested. She knew her elemental affinities. She'd started learning the theory behind her gift. She'd learned to move single grains of sand, but she could also do that if she opened her mouth and blew air. So she wasn't impressed.

There had been two more incidents where she'd made the ground rumble, and now she carried Barrow's calming stone in her pocket.

But she was impatient.

There had been no word about Haze. The Order was abuzz with the growing feud between the Order and the Unseelie realm. The Prime had already come and gone from a parlay with the queen, and while Maebh never denied Haze had been there, she denied knowing where Haze was now. It could very well be true. But Maebh also refused to acknowledge the crimes of abusing forbidden metals, and ignored accusations about experiments that perverted mana, instead claiming that the Order was on a power trip and had been since they tried to depose Mithras.

Maebh publicly accused the Order of trying to wrest control of Elphyne from its rightful leaders. She said the Prime favored the Seelie people. And then she threatened war if the Order tried to enter Aconite City again.

So here Peaches was, shoving mana stones into her satchel, and frantically coming up with a plan to go after Haze herself.

"You were supposed to meet me at the mess hall after class," Violet said, frowning.

Violet had also been instructed to do her time at the

academy. But while Peaches struggled to pick up simple concepts around practical mana use, Violet excelled. She was already at another level, in another class, and virtually teaching the teacher.

The only thing Violet couldn't do was explain how Peaches could control her mana. Apparently, accessing one's internal well was often instinctual. Most fae were born doing it, but some, like those who'd received the gift well into adulthood, couldn't. Clarke was the only person Peaches had met who'd had trouble connecting with hers. When Peaches pressed her for tips, Clarke had blushed bright red, mumbled something about libraries and Haze needing to teach her, and made an excuse about her daughter needing a bath.

To her credit, Violet had been the best friend a girl could have wanted. She had barely left Peaches' side. She ate with her, walked her to class, introduced her to people, and kept the grouchier Guardians at bay. The crow shifters were a little frightening and unpredictable. Shade had gone about the house at night, brooding or inviting multiple sexual partners over and loudly seeing to their pleasure.

It had been a bone of contention between Shade and Rush, Clarke's mate, because they had a child in the house. Shade had only answered that he was there first.

"Shouldn't you be with Indigo or something?" Peaches asked, trying to change the subject. "I remember him saying something about sparring with you earlier."

Violet folded her arms. The weight of her stare sat heavily on Peaches' shoulders. Her friend was only trying to look out for her. Peaches got that. But she couldn't sit there any longer trying to meditate on a gift that might never be in her control. Haze wouldn't sit still if she was out there, and neither would she.

Peaches sighed and met her friend's all too knowing stare. "I'm going after him."

"Okay. So what's the plan?"

Peaches raised her brow. "You're not going to stop me?"

"I told you on that first day, I'm going to help you."

"But... that was before the Prime said otherwise."

"Shh." Violet scowled at the door. "You never know who's listening. Saying her name is like saying Bloody Mary."

Peaches raised her brow. "She turns up behind you and hacks you to death?"

Violet rolled her eyes. "You know what I mean. You don't want her around. Trust me."

Peaches went to the window and looked out at the quad. Mages lounged and chatted around a tiered water feature. It reminded Peaches so much of her college days that an ache pressed between her ribs. If Haze wasn't missing, if she wasn't pregnant with his child, she might have enjoyed this place. She might have enjoyed sinking herself into learning about the theory behind building mana stones and alchemy. She touched her stomach. There were too many things to worry about now.

"Do you have a plan, Peaches?" Violet asked again. "Because going into that fortified palace now, even with my Sluagh obliterating skills, is mad. Not impossible. But a little insane."

Peaches focused on two Mages holding hands, smiling at each other under the rising moon. "I was going to portal my way in, and then follow where my bond leads me to find Haze."

"You know that's not a good plan. You can't fight. You can't use your gift."

"Are you trying to help me or insult me?"

Violet exhaled and tugged her long brown braid before flipping it over her shoulder. "If we had time, I could teach you to fight."

A sad smile flittered on Peaches' lips. "You know I'm not a fighter. Not like you and Silver."

"Then I need to tell Indi. We have to get a few of the Guardians in on it."

"They all had plenty of chances at the council meeting to make their opinions known. All they said was Haze could take care of himself. That he knew what he was getting into when he signed up for the job."

Violet scoffed. "That's what they say around the Prime. If there's one thing I know about this place, it's that they don't always do as they're told. They're probably working on a plan right now." She frowned, her eyes focusing inward. "In fact, Indi and Shade have been a little secretive lately."

"Will they tell you? Will they include me?" Because Peaches couldn't wait around any longer. "Or will they say I'm a knocked up female who should remain under lock and key?"

"They might, but…" The pitiful look in Violet's eyes said it all. No one thought Peaches was capable of anything. That meant she had to do this on her own.

She couldn't explain it but she felt sure. Like a rock. Solid. Steady. Capable. Peaches was going to rescue her mate, with or without their help.

"You'll go anyway, won't you?" Violet said.

Peaches nodded.

"So I'll go too." She squeezed Peaches' shoulder. "Indi will be pissed, but he'll understand. We just need to have a plan."

Peaches dug into the satchel and pulled out a handful of stones. "I've made some portal stones. And there are a few particular rocks inside the workshop of an old friend I think could be of use in a fight." She frowned. "I think I even had some local Unseelie rocks in my room that I can convert to portal stones in case we need them."

"Will your friend help us?"

Peaches' thoughts traveled to Balos. He didn't belong in that palace. He was as much a prisoner as she was. "Yeah, I think he will. I might even convince him to leave with us. I hope. And he'd be a wealth of knowledge against the queen. He'd be a great asset to the Order."

"Good. Good—oh shit. What are they doing?" Violet squinted outside the window to the quad.

The Mages had started scrambling in a single direction, looking back at the ground as though they'd seen a snake. No. Not a snake.

A fluffy, winged rabbit with antlers hopped along the grass by the fountain. It jumped up to the first tier and drank greedily from the water. Mages were pointing and freaking out, calling for someone to come and take the wolpertinger out of there before it stole one of their females.

Peaches dropped her satchel and ran outside.

"Stop, stop, stop!" she shouted, swooping in to scoop up the poor thing just wanting to quench his thirst.

An elf with a dark beard pointed at it, hiding behind a female with twitching deer ears. "That thing is evil. Get it out," he exclaimed.

"Yeah, you're real brave, Keldrin," intoned the doe-eyed female, shrugging out of Keldrin's hold. "They take females, not males. I think you're safe."

"He won't hurt anyone," Peaches promised.

Another Mage already had a ball of fire sparking in her palm. She looked at Peaches. "You have no idea, human. These things are deadly."

Peaches hugged the animal, just as Violet joined her

and sent a world class scowl at the Mages before shooing them. "Run along, nothing to see here—"

"Tinger?" Peaches' heart jumped into her throat as she took in the creature in her hands. Small, fluffy, a little ratty. His antlers were chipped. One tine was completely missing on the left, just like Tinger's had been. Peaches peeled apart the fur and checked his skin until she found what she was looking for—puncture scars. "It is you!"

She hugged him tight to her chest like a favorite teddy bear.

The Mages gave her a weird look and backed away quietly before rushing off. Probably going to tell one of the preceptors in charge. Or a Guardian.

"You know that thing?" Violet said, wariness in her voice.

"Tinger was with me at the palace."

"But don't they... I mean... has he—I mean, the baby is Haze's right?"

Peaches stared at her friend and tried to understand what on earth she meant. Then she got it and burst out laughing. Poor Tinger had no idea what was happening and trembled in her arms, but Peaches couldn't stop.

"No," she finally said, wiping tears from her eyes. "I've never seen Tinger change forms. He's always been like this to me. The baby is most definitely Haze's."

Violet's eyes widened, and she exhaled, slow and long. "Phew. I mean, for a second, I was like... worse things have happened. I mean, Ada and Jasper had to eat one once."

"They *what?*"

Tinger trembled.

"Never mind." Violet's eyes softened, and she stepped closer to look at the scared animal. "How can you be so sure he won't shift?"

"I don't know," she said, stroking Tinger's fur. "I think he had too much mana removed. I don't know if he can shift at all."

The thunder of flapping wings warned them moments before the vampires landed. First Indigo, rushing to Violet's side. Then Shade, less eager to rush anywhere. It seemed as though he'd been dragged unwillingly from bed. His usually slicked hair was disheveled. His tunic was open at the collar, the laces uneven. Peaches wasn't sure if he'd shaven in days. He gave Violet an empty stare and then raised his brows at Peaches and Tinger.

Indigo's leather battle uniform creaked as he checked his mate over. "You okay?"

"I'm fine, you dolt."

"I heard there was a wolpertinger on campus."

Violet rolled her eyes.

"Can't be too careful." Indigo eyed the tiny little fluff-ball with suspicion.

"No one is touching him," Peaches insisted. "He's coming home with me."

"You should probably not let that thing imprint on you, even if you're mated," Shade mentioned. "Especially without Haze here."

Too late for that. Tinger was hers, and she wouldn't abandon him, no matter what anyone else thought. Peaches calmed her breathing and petted Tinger until both of them stopped trembling.

"What do you suppose he's doing here?" Violet asked, also tentatively petting Tinger despite Indigo's scowl.

"He must have tracked me down. I left Aconite City so suddenly. After what he's been through, I'm surprised he made it all this way."

"What do you mean, all he's been through?" Violet asked.

"He was injected with mercury. The queen forced his mana out permanently. Balos and I tried to put some back, but I don't think he'll ever be the same."

Indigo and Shade went still. A slithering shadow snake oozed around Indigo's neck, its tongue flickering with agitation. Shade took a step closer. Peaches stepped back. Tinger bared his fangs.

"I just want to see," Shade said, holding his palms up. "Not going to hurt you."

"I'll do it." Peaches split Tinger's fur and pointed out one of the scars.

Indi and Shade both gave each other a knowing look, and then grunted in agreement, as if they both had the same silent idea.

"And that?" Indi pointed to some scratches on the antler.

Peaches squinted and frowned, trying to read them. "I haven't seen that before. They're Elven glyphs?"

"It means labyrinth," Shade said.

The ground tipped beneath Peaches' feet. Her heart stopped beating. She held Tinger up and looked into his eyes. Hope barely bloomed. Did Haze put those scratches there? Had they somehow bumped into each other? The animal's nose twitched.

"We should show Leaf," said Indi. "It's evidence against the queen."

"It has a name," Peaches said, handing him over. "His name is Tinger. Please keep him safe."

Indi and Shade raised their brows at her, but Violet elbowed her mate, and he acquiesced. "I promise, we'll keep him safe."

As the two vampires flew away with Tinger, Peaches turned to Violet. "I think that was a message from Haze."

"You think he's in the labyrinth?"

"Yes. And I know how to get back in." She started walking back into the academy and glanced at Violet over her shoulder. "Are you coming?"

Violet looked to where her mate had flown, seemed to consider doing the opposite, but nodded. "I'm coming."

THIRTY-FOUR

Peaches met Violet just after sunrise beneath a Weeping Willow in the sacred gardens behind the temple. Trees circled a lagoon with bioluminescent aquatic plant life. Morning birds twittered and hopped about finding worms and slugs. Limestone paving and retaining walls, along with a stone altar and abundant flora, made Peaches think this was some kind of ritual area. Maybe even a source of power. On the opposite side of the lagoon, a wild poisonous forest ran thick. Violet thought it would be safe for them to meet here.

She'd chosen early morning because most nocturnal fae were just going to bed, and the day dwellers were still asleep. Perfect time to escape. Peaches had her satchel filled with mana stones. Some she could use as weapons, and some for defense, and some to portal them in and out of the Obsidian Palace.

There were two options to get into the labyrinth. The first was to sink in via the quicksand, but then they'd have to deal with the dryads. The second was for Peaches to use a portal stone to get in. There were a few local stones in her old room collection. Once inside her room, she could turn one into a portal stone using the jar of pilfered manabeeze. She would find Balos if something went wrong.

If she could get to Haze, she had no doubt they would escape together.

Easy.

She just had to deal with some trickster and murderous goblins and not be caught by any of the queen's fae. But that was why she brought Violet. Violet had turned herself invisible once. She could do it again. Together, they would be okay. Surely.

Tension crept up her spine as the sun rose. Violet was late. Peaches squinted at rustling overhead. She whirled at a thud behind her. Three bodies emerged from the shadows beside the temple.

Violet, Indigo, and a Guardian she'd not met. He had long russet hair tied at his nape, elf ears, and a dash of freckles across his tanned nose. There was something about his face that gave her pause. And then it hit—he looked like Luthian, only his physique wasn't soft like a spoiled prince. He'd earned every muscle and callous from hard, back breaking work. And his eyes were warm.

Peaches swallowed and clutched the satchel. "Who is that?"

"Two Guardians are better than none," Indigo said, eyeing Peaches grimly and with disapproval.

Peaches glared at Violet. "You said it would just be you."

"We don't keep secrets." Indigo folded his arms.

"Don't worry, Peaches," Violet said, sending her partner a look that said to settle down. "They won't tell anyone. I promise."

"I'm Forrest," greeted the elf.

"You're Autumn Court royalty." She lifted her chin.

He held up calloused palms, abashed as he rubbed his neck. "Er... I was. Until my family shoved me in the ceremonial lake, expecting me to die. Violet told me about your time there. For your mistreatment, I owe you a boon. I hope you'll accept my help as a sufficient apology."

"What?" She twisted the satchel straps. Her heart slammed into her ribcage, hardly believing what she heard. This elf, this blood relative of the fae who'd tortured Peaches for years, wanted to help her? She didn't know what to believe.

"As do I." Another rustle in the bushes, and one more Guardian emerged from the shadows beneath the trees—a tall, brunette elf with long hair braided down his back. He checked the weapons attached to the bandoleer over his leather uniform and then rested his palm on the sword at his hip. He gave Peaches a nod of respect, introducing himself as D'arn Aeron.

How many were coming? This was all going to end

badly. She could sense it. "There's too many of you. This is supposed to be a stealth mission. The Prime will know so many of you are missing."

"Yeah," came another male voice from the shadows of the poisoned forest. "That's the thing about the Prime. We don't give a shit what she thinks."

The voice belonged to the crow-shifter on the council, Cloud. He arrived in his Guardian uniform, looking like a biker with an attitude. She half expected him to pull out a switch blade and start flipping it. Two more crow shifters prowled in beside him. The dark, enigmatic Ash, the one who'd flown Peaches home, and another with an impish smile and a blue tinge to his dark hair. He introduced himself as River.

"One of our own is missing," Indigo said, squinting at the sun, sweat dappling his brow. "We're not going to stop until we get him back." His gaze landed back on Peaches. "We only need a couple of us, but these warada-tails overheard and wanted to help." Indigo snarled at the crows. "They like to eavesdrop."

"Lucky we did," Cloud said, his scowl lethal enough to stop hearts. "You'll mess up somehow. There's no one better than us at getting in and out."

"That's because you're all thieves," Aeron pointed out.

Cloud and River flipped their middle finger up at the elf, who didn't even shrug, as though this sort of behavior happened every day.

Violet came to stand next to Peaches and squeezed her

arm. "We were talking about it all night, and we've got half a plan. Figured you had another half."

"Okay," she said. "Sort of. You go first."

"You were right. We can't all go in there. Only Ash and I can do a cloaking spell. Indi can hide behind shadow, but it won't cover everyone. But some of us can wait outside the palace and create a diversion if needed."

"How will they know if we need a diversion?"

"They have their ways," Violet replied. "And you? Is the plan still to get in and talk to Balos?"

"I thought about using the quicksand at the center of the labyrinth to get down, but dryads protect that entrance. And it's one way. Alternatively, if I can get to my room, nab that glowing stone and infuse it with mana, then it's a key to where the goblins dwell. No one even needs to know we were there. You see what I mean about needing to be stealthy?"

"I say go the quicksand way," River said, waggling his eyebrows. "I feel like cutting up some dryads."

The other Guardians considered it.

"It would be further from the palace," Cloud pointed out. "And less chance of being seen by guards."

Aeron shook his head. "Fighting dryads will be too noisy, even with a cloaking spell."

"Maybe we should wake up Shade," Violet suggested to Indigo. "He's got that shadow stepping ability, right?"

Indigo's eyes turned bleak, and he shook his head. "We'll have to do it without him."

Something passed unsaid between them.

"Are there any other Guardians who can create portals?" Peaches asked.

"Leaf, but he's got a stick up his ass," River said, rolling his eyes.

Indigo nodded, his jaw clenching. "He won't do this without Council approval, and they're too busy figuring out how to make a millennia-old queen pay for breaking the laws of the Well without an all-out war." He glanced at Cloud. "Jasper?"

"Fuck that furry-eared twat," Cloud said. "We gotta learn to do this shit without the Seelie High King swooping in to save the day. Nah—" he slid his eyes to Peaches and gave her a curt nod. "We got this."

Forrest raised his palm. "I vote palace."

"Palace." Aeron raised his palm too.

"Dryads." River quipped.

But he was the only one. The rest of them voted on the palace.

"So that's it?" Peaches asked.

Violet nodded. "Let's go back to the palace."

THIRTY-FIVE

Haze was being dragged again. This time, he was upside down and hogtied to a bar carried by goblins. But because they were short, the gap between the bar and the ground was less than his bulk. His back scraped along the dirt as they moved, shredding it to ribbons and leaving a trail of blood. At least his wings were shifted away. He couldn't move his arms or legs, and he couldn't access his mana. There was none to access. Glowing mana-leaching stones were tied in the ropes at regular intervals around his body. The stones had been dull at the start of the journey, but the further he was dragged through the labyrinth tunnels, the brighter the stones glowed.

They'd sapped his power.

He couldn't call Justice.

He tensed his arms and tried to snap the bonds, but the rope wouldn't budge. Those mischievous shits knew how to tie a good knot.

So if he couldn't shift, and couldn't draw power, then he was well and truly fucked. Thank the Well he'd been able to get Tinger out when some hobgoblins came to throw food at him. They'd been too engaged with seeing what would stick to his face, that they'd missed the small creature flapping out of the hole. The stupid goblins didn't even realize vampires don't eat food—or they didn't care.

He thanked the Well he'd drunk so deeply from Peaches before the tunnel had collapsed. That one feed, and all the micro feeds he'd had while in the prison, would sustain him for weeks. His chest constricted at the thought of his mate. The only thing getting him through was the knowledge that he could feel her life force through the bond. Occasionally, he received a small flitter of emotion. He latched onto that feeling and held it tight.

He fantasied about all the ways he'd use their new bond, how he would know exactly what she felt without asking. How he could provide for her. Keep her safe. Surprise her with gifts. How to pleasure her, where to put his tongue, or how hard or soft to make love. He dropped his head back, hit the dirt and winced. The sharp stab of pain brought him back to reality. He checked his surroundings. It was dark. The blue Well-blessed mark and the glowing stones were the only light. He could have sworn the tunnels were shaped differently. More round and ribbed. Less wooden beams above. Less sign of fae footprints.

"Where are we going?" he rasped.

Snickering. Hissing laughter. A yip or two.

"A gift."

"To feed."

"To dance."

"To bleed."

"To keep."

"Our homes."

"For your bones."

Haze thrashed and writhed. The goblins carrying him careened into the wall. A redcap came over and hit Haze in the face. Bone crunched. Pain burst at his nose. Tears blinded his eyes. Then they walked onward.

The further they went, the more dread dropped in Haze's gut. He knew where they were, he knew why the tunnels were changing.

To feed. To bleed.

To keep their homes?

Peaches had mentioned a wyrm used to frequent these tunnels. But she'd assumed it didn't live there anymore... no... she said it had been sleeping.

Fuck.

Haze had the sneaking suspicion the only reason the goblins had been able to live unscathed was because they fed it.

For your bones.

Haze would be their next sacrifice.

THIRTY-SIX

River, Aeron and Ash had taken a separate portal to the woods outside the palace and prepared to run interference if they needed to draw the queen's attention. That left Indigo, Violet, Cloud, Forrest, and Peaches. Still too many, she thought.

Their portal stone activated and opened into a tunnel not far from Peaches' room. Peaches had made the portal stone herself in Barrow's lab when he wasn't looking. It was from a stone she'd found inside her tattered black velvet dress.

This would have been the perfect location, except she'd forgotten to account for the small space. The charged atoms making up the portal sliced through walls, rock and dirt, kicking up dust and debris, alerting guards. Shouts came from somewhere. Footsteps came running. This lack of space was the entire reason Haze had been reluctant to use a portal stone when he'd first met her.

Whoops. Maybe they should have braved the dryads.

Violet cloaked everyone with a spell that reflected light particles. Seeing her friend master her gift made Peaches feel guilty for not taking the time to learn hers. She would probably get in trouble for rushing this rescue mission. She might even deserve it. But as long as Haze was found, she didn't care.

Since Tinger had turned up, a knot in her stomach wound tighter by the minute. The faint emotions she'd originally felt from Haze through their bond had changed. At first, hope had been there. Then it wasn't.

"Haze is in trouble," she whispered. "We need to hurry."

Next to her, knives appeared in Cloud's hands, and he silently stepped through the portal and dispatched the Unseelie guards by slicing their throats. He moved so casually, and it all happened so quickly that Peaches wasn't sure she'd seen it. Grace, skill, and a little luck. He was an expert at dealing death and the guards went down without a sound.

One invisible Guardian had dispatched four guards. The others hadn't moved. Cloud checked up and down the corridor, then waved the rest of them through the portal.

The trip nauseated Peaches, and she gasped until she caught her breath. She might never get used to the shift in equilibrium from portal travel. While she gathered her breath, the Guardians tossed the guard's corpses back through the portal, eradicating evidence before it closed.

"This way," she whispered and pointed in the direction of her room. She took two steps and then felt a sudden wooziness. She grabbed the wall to stop from falling.

"What is it?" Violet whispered.

"I don't know," she replied. "I feel dizzy, and my arm feels weird. Tingly."

"It's the bond." Violet frowned at Indigo. "Why is it doing that?"

Indigo stepped forward, concerned. "Is Haze in trouble?"

"I'm not sure." Another wave of feeling sucked on her arm. "Oh god, it feels like something is being drained from me."

Gray faces all round. Whatever the reason for the change in her bond, it wasn't good.

"Haze might be trying to borrow your mana," Violet suggested. "Well-blessed mates can do that to each other. When Indi borrows mine, I feel light headed, depending on how much he takes."

"That means he's probably in trouble, right?" Peaches' heart pounded in her throat. "We have to hurry."

They continued through the corridors, keeping quietly to the sides and praying they'd not drawn the attention of anymore guards. When they arrived at her red old door, it had been splintered and destroyed as though hacked by an ax.

"Well," she murmured, surveying the destruction. "That was unnecessary."

All they'd needed to do was open the door. Inside was worse. Bed tipped up. Her rock collection scattered over the floor. Clothes and pillows ripped apart. Feathers everywhere. Forrest and Cloud stood at the door, keeping watch while Peaches gestured at the mess to Violet and Indigo.

"The rock we're looking for is smooth. It kinda glows, and it's got spots."

Except for the Guardians keeping watch, they went down on hands and knees to search. Even Indigo's shadow-snake slithered around, hunting through the corners of the room and hard to get places. Once or twice Cloud and Forrest stepped inside the room, their weapons ready at their hands. Everyone froze and hushed. Then whomever was in the corridor walked past and the coast was clear. They breathed again.

"Found it!" Indigo said, holding up a rock. Hope deflated when Peaches saw it wasn't what they needed.

"That's not even spotted," Violet pointed out.

His face screwed up. He tossed it, then kept searching. Peaches found the glow-stone under an upturned bowl. She almost wept, but instead, removed the jar of buzzing manabeeze from her satchel and started working at scraping the right runes onto the stone with her fortified bone dagger. Once certain she'd copied the runes correctly, and with her own mana warming her hands, she opened the manabee jar, dropped the stone inside and put the corked lid back on. One by one, the runes sucked in manabeeze until there was nothing left but a stone inside an empty jar.

"It's done." She opened the lid and tipped the stone out. It felt hot in her palm. "This is it."

Portal stones were easier to make accurately if they came from their destination.

We're coming, Haze.

The sound of two bodies thudding to the ground was unmistakable. They whirled to the door, expecting the worst, but found Balos standing in the open doorway, his hand still out and dusty from blowing sleeping powder. Cloud and Forrest, fast asleep, slumped on the floor, snoring softly.

"Ungrateful pix," Balos snarled at her.

"Grumpy old bastard." She grinned.

For a split second, she half expected Balos to blow the powder at all of them, but he checked over his shoulder and darted inside. Without his red cap on, he looked completely different. Still big bat ears, nose, and bushy eyebrows. But somehow softer. Older. More frail.

"I thought you were dead," he said, eyes warily taking in Violet and Indigo. "Your blasted wolpertinger pet was whining after you for days, so I let him loose in the tunnels."

A rush of affection hit her squarely in the chest, and she gathered him into a hug. He squirmed and pushed her away, scowling deeply afterward.

"You need to get out of here, there was an explosion and someone has raised the alarm—wait—" Balos paused, his eyes darting from the empty jar, the new sizzling mana stone, and her Well-blessed arm marks. His eyes widened. "No. It can't be. You did that yourself?"

"I learned from the best." Her lips twitched.

Balos' chest puffed out in pride.

She held up her blue marked hand. "I'm also Well-blessed and mated to that Guardian Haze. He didn't make it out of the palace, and I think he's still in trouble. Have you seen him?"

Balos frowned, shaking his head. "No, the queen has been like a mad woman. You'd think she'd be seeing to her people after waging war on the Order, but she's been down in the basement, doing things to that despicable human she stole."

"Bones," Violet said quietly, her eyes shifting to Indigo, then back to Balos. "He's still alive?"

"Who?" Peaches asked.

"He's a human she's experimented on," Violet clarified. "I saw him in one of the rooms when I rescued Indigo and Shade. He didn't look good."

Peaches went back to Balos. "Haze is in trouble. I think he's somewhere in the underground labyrinth. We're here to rescue him. I came here to make a portal stone that will take us there. Please let us go."

Some kind of inner struggle went through Balos. She could have sworn she saw painful memories haunt his expression, and then he lifted his chin and tapped his belt where more pouches dangled.

"You'll need my help, then."

"Goblins?" she asked.

"Goblins," he confirmed.

"What about them?" Indigo pointed at his fallen brothers.

Balos wiped his nose, ran his finger over his pouches, and then opened a red one. He pulled out powder and blew it in Cloud's and Forrest's face. Cloud came out of his sleep, swearing and with murderous eyes, but as soon as he saw none of them were concerned, he settled for threatening Balos with a dagger if he ever tried that again. Forrest woke a little slower, but the moment he stood, he was alert and ready to leave.

Peaches surveyed her room one last time. The past two years weren't the best, but this was where she'd lived. She'd made it her home. Those rocks were her family. Just as Balos was. She smiled at him, even though she knew he'd hate it.

"Oh, you stupid goblin," came a droll male voice from the hallway. "It was only a matter of time until you led us to her."

Luthian and Wisteria wandered into view. Dressed in Autumn Court finery, Luthian's embroidered velvet brown coat stank of entitlement. Wisteria wiped her palms down her skin tight dress. It was more revealing than what she'd worn on the night of the party. The ragged pink scar on her neck was new.

Both vampire and elf gave Peaches a condescending look... and then their gazes slid to the occupants of the room. Their eyes widened. Their faces paled.

Peaches wasn't sure what they'd thought to find after following Balos, but it wasn't three deadly Guardians—and Violet—all dressed in battle leather and with savage glares. Forrest was the first to act. Upon seeing his brother, fury mottled his expression, and he became something else. Something entirely animalistic. He yanked on Luthian's collar, dragging him inside the room and started beating on him. Cloud pulled him off before too much damage was done.

Indigo went for Wisteria, but talons sprang from her fingertips and she slashed at his face. He ducked, almost casually, and then hard eyes locked onto Wisteria with purpose until she started gasping for breath. A shadow coiled around her neck and tightened until her vision blurred.

In a matter of seconds, the interlopers were removed of weapons and tied. For good measure, Forrest punched his brother squarely in the nose. There was a history between the Autumn Court royals, and from the anguish on Forrest's face, Peaches thought it might be worse than hers.

"You disgusting piece of piss," Luthian snarled through

a bloody face as his brother tied a gag around his head. "Father will be disappointed."

"Father can go float himself." Forrest tightened the gag, uncaring of how he caught Luthian's hair, ripping strands out at the root. Then he lowered himself and whispered in his brother's pointed and twitching ear, "Come for her again, and you won't just have Haze to deal with, understood?"

Before they left, Balos shoved his fingers into Wisteria's mouth and snapped her fangs off, then he gave them to Peaches. "I should have done that a long time ago."

Peaches couldn't breathe through her emotion. All these people had rallied to help. Even Balos, the grump. And Forrest, a fae she'd never met before. Her faith in justice restored. Her hope surged. But the sense of Haze down her bond was weakening.

She held up her marked hand, her worried eyes meeting Violet's. "We need to go."

THE NEW PORTAL stone took them to the tunnel Peaches and Haze had visited. The bones and fossils of her people were stuck in the walls, interspersed with glowing stones. The walls shook and dirt showered down with the water from the roof. Even when Peaches deactivated the stone and the portal closed, the walls continued to shake. Everyone looked at Peaches.

"It's not me," she said, throwing up her hands.

Balos scrutinized the ceiling. "These tunnels have had thousands of portals open into them. They've never collapsed yet."

"So what is it, an earthquake?" Violet asked, placing her palm on the walls to steady herself.

"I don't think so." No sooner had the words left his mouth, Balos' expression turned grim. "A wyrm," he whispered. "A god-sized one."

Peaches' blood ran cold. "I thought it slept."

Balos nodded. "It did. But occasionally it wakes hungry. Goblins feed it to keep it appeased and away from their dwellings."

Forrest gaped. "Are you telling me they're going to sacrifice Haze to one of those toothy giant slugs?"

"Fuck," Cloud swore and rubbed his face.

All three Guardians withdrew their weapons, determination hardening their posture.

"What does that mean?" Violet asked, eyes darting between them.

"It means we have to run." Peaches set off down the tunnel, following the sense of her mate down her bond. It intensified when she went in the right direction and softened when she went down the wrong path. Tears jolted from her eyes with every fallen step. Balos had to redirect her to help them take the right turns. The labyrinth messed with her head, sometimes telling her she went the right way when it was wrong. They rushed past the goblin dwellings. Some citizens ran out of their homes to watch as they ran by.

It was only because of Balos that they'd navigated the subterranean labyrinth without getting lost. She honestly didn't know what she would have done without him. They could have been circling for days. She made herself a promise, right there and then, to insist Balos leave the Obsidian Palace and to come to the Order with her. There was so much more he could teach her, and so much love she could give him.

After the dwellings, the tunnel started changing form. What was once squarish, supported by wooden beams, and dangling with roots became something more organic, round and ribbed, as though made by a giant drilling machine. Peaches had walked through some of these sorts of tunnels closer to the palace. They were where she'd found the fire opals. But never had she'd worried she'd bump into a wyrm.

How naïve she'd been.

More rumblings shook the walls. Dirt and sand fell onto their heads, but not a single one of Peaches' companions hesitated or wanted to turn back. And then suddenly it wasn't dirt dropping onto their heads. Spindly goblin sized shadows scampered and fell, brandishing weapons, unafraid to use them.

Must have been lying in wait.

Indigo's shadow snake snapped out and caught the first goblin in its jaws. A bright, blinding light flashed behind Peaches. She shut her eyes momentarily, but the worst hit were those dark dwelling creatures dangling from the ceiling. Blinded, goblins fell with a thud, then got to their feet, swerving drunkenly. Balos leaped into action, clawing into his brethren without a second thought, slicing them with his hooked knife. There was a look on his face—the whites of his eyes showed and he became a living, silver-bearded demon. For the first time since she'd met him, Peaches had a taste of the redcap General in the Queen's army. The one his son had wanted to be like.

She was sorry she lost his cap to One-Eye.

With every goblin dispatched, manabeeze floated from corpses, and more goblins emerged. Violet shouted at Peaches, "Go! Take Balos. We'll keep them occupied."

Peaches clutched her satchel and ran, ducking and weaving through the foray. When she neared Balos, she grabbed his collar and tugged. He was surprisingly resistant and sturdy. She almost fell over herself, but his sharp mind understood. He kicked off the hobgoblin he'd been stabbing. Then they ran together toward the end of the tunnel.

Around the corner, everything stopped. Heart pounding in her chest, Peaches was unable to believe her eyes. Strung across the spherical tunnel was Haze, hogtied and dangling from a bar. He was unconscious. The one-eyed redcap who'd betrayed them turned upon their entrance. Vile, furious hate leaked from his every pore. He spoke to the handful of goblins securing Haze's bar to the walls, preparing him as a sacrifice for the wyrm.

The rumbling walls and floor intensified.

The wyrm was almost here.

Haze was out of it, but the bond said he was alive. If she could get to him and wake him, maybe cut him out of his binds with her dagger, then all he needed to do was lean on her to get out. She'd given a few of the Guardians a portal stone back to the Order.

Balos stepped toward One-Eye, blood dripping from his dagger. "Release the Guardian, brother. Enough goblin blood has been spilled."

"You'd know all about that, wouldn't you, *brother*?"

Peaches gaped. They were family?

Balos clenched his jaw. "Release the Guardian. Even the queen herself was reluctant to kill one from the Order."

One-Eye gave Balos a scathing glare. "You never deserved that cap, anyway."

Peaches dug into the satchel and started plucking out mana stones. Which to use first? There was a fire bomb. A water summoner. Something that emitted smoke. She ended up retrieving two chunks of granite and tossed them at the goblins swinging from Haze's ropes.

The stones sparked and popped, then landed beneath. The goblins looked down, then at Peaches, and laughed. Two seconds later, hot lava spurted straight up, setting them on fire. They screamed and jumped off Haze to roll themselves in the dirt. She launched toward her mate, just as the wyrm oozed around the corner, his great spiked maw coming into sight. All mouth and sharp teeth, the giant wyrm's body took up the entire tunnel and would devour them all whole if they couldn't escape.

Rows and rows of teeth. Like a shark.

One-Eye tried to stop Peaches, but Balos cut him off, catching his arm and drawing him back. The two redcaps entered a fight so fast and lethal, it frightened Peaches. She'd seen Balos try to access his pouches more than once and fail. But this was her chance. She pulled out her dagger and ran to Haze.

"Haze," she said, sawing at the rope. "Baby, wake up. It's me."

He remained unresponsive until she removed at least half of the glowing stones on his body. His feet fell, his heels hitting the floor. With a groan, he woke up.

"Sweetness?"

She could have cried. "Yes, it's me."

He forced his eyes to focus. Then saw what was happening around them.

"Fuck," he grunted. He swiveled his head to the wyrm almost at their sides. "*Fuck*."

"It's fine," she blurted, cutting another rope. "We're going to be fine."

The walls were shaking so hard sand rained on their heads. Peaches tasted dirt with every breath.

An agonized groan of pain behind her sent her head into a tailspin. Glancing over was a mistake. One-Eye buried his knife deep in Balos' stomach. Blood gushed over his hand.

"No!" Peaches shouted. "Balos, no!"

Balos' pained eyes slid her way. "Get him out of here, ungrateful pix."

Something unleashed in her. Balos had been her only friend. And now he was dying. Haze was tangled in rope, leached of mana, and a fanged giant wyrm was upon them. She drew out stone after stone from her satchel, activated them and threw in all directions. Some at the wyrm, some at One-Eye. Fireworks went off in the tunnel, popping and sparking, causing chaos amongst the fighters. Water spurted somewhere. A stone hit One-Eye on the temple, bringing him down. Balos clutched the dagger at his middle, falling to one knee. Further back the way they'd come, Forrest pried goblins from his legs and waded through corpses, dodging manabeeze as they floated up.

Where was Violet? Indigo? Cloud?

Peaches fumbled with Haze's ropes, fear taking control of her dexterity. The dagger slipped. Dropped. The wyrm opened its mouth. Spittle dripped from its maw like wet, caustic slime. Peaches screamed and launched over Haze's torso to protect him. If they were going to die, it would be together. Her only sadness remaining was of the life growing in her womb, that she'd never get a chance to meet it, or even tell Haze.

The wyrm froze, inches from them. Spittle dropped

with a splash, inches from their feet. Haze took only a breath, then patted Peaches urgently.

"Quick," he said. "The knife."

"I can't hold it for long," Forrest grunted, strain evident on his face.

Two steps behind her, he had his arm extended, his hand reaching toward the wyrm. He'd halted the monster with some kind of mind connection or spell. Grunting, he fell to a knee. "Quick!"

Fuck, oh, shit. Peaches found the dagger, cut Haze's wrists free and then he took over. With every glowing stone removed, the color returned to his face. Dizziness swirled in Peaches' head as he unwittingly borrowed mana from her, but she refused to pass out. Finally Haze freed himself of restraints. He took Peaches' hand and ran back the way they'd come.

"Balos!" she shouted, skidding to her knees.

"I'm okay," he gasped, wincing as he stood, still clutching his stomach. "We need to go."

One-Eye crawled to his feet, his fingers digging into one of Balos' fallen pouches. "I don't think so."

"Leave it be, brother," Balos said, eyes sad. "We can't bring him back."

"It's your fault he died. You piece of filthy human-loving—"

Haze backhanded the redcap, knocking him onto his behind. Peaches' instinct took over. All she remembered was thinking she hoped the ground swallowed him whole, and then it did. One-Eye sank into the ground all the way to his waist. It was as though she'd turned Prime dirt into quicksand. One-Eye dropped the pouch and struggled to climb out, clawing the dirt.

"Help me brother!"

Forrest's hold on the wyrm broke, and it surged forward, its mouth widening. It crashed through the wooden bar and rope.

"Run!" Forrest bellowed.

"Help him," Peaches said, holding Balos up. Blood was everywhere. So much that she slipped and fell.

Haze hoisted the small fae into his arms and together they ran. In a blur of shouts, earth shaking rumbles and crackling ozone, one of the Guardians activated their portal stone. Peaches ran straight through the portal and stumbled out into the fresh air at the grassed training field in the mid afternoon sun. Nausea overwhelmed her. Vitriolic goblin curses cut off mid word as the wyrm slammed into One-Eye. The portal closed, rumbles and slushy crunches severed.

The rescue crew breathed haggardly as they checked themselves and each other for mortal wounds. They were all there. Cloud slipped his knife back into his belt. Forrest kneeled on the floor, rubbing his temples. Indigo and Violet hugged each other. Haze put his hand over Balos' stomach wound, staunching the blood.

Birds chirped, the breeze tickled, and the Prime landed with a flurry of white feathers, rage contorting her face.

THIRTY-SEVEN

Wincing under the heat of the sun, Haze handed over care of the goblin to a healer who'd arrived hot on the Prime's heels.

Ignoring the fuming owl shifter leader, he grabbed hold of his mate, and pulled her into a bone crushing embrace. He didn't care about the sun beating down on him. He didn't care about the reprimand the Prime gave to the others, or why she was furious in the first place. He didn't even pay attention to whether Peaches' friend was okay.

The smell of her sweet scent was everything he needed. For long, agonizing seconds, he inhaled his mate, basking in her relief and love as it poured through their bond. It was a tidal wave of emotion.

He lifted her clean off the ground. She wrapped her legs and arms around him and they kissed. It was everything.

They stayed joined together as he walked them into the shade under the porch of the cadre's house and he finally collapsed from exhaustion onto the bench seat. He sat back with his eyes closed, a frown on his face because the intensity of emotion was unlike anything he'd experienced before.

Peaches clung to him, quietly crying onto his filthy chest. He patted her head. "It's okay, Sweetness."

"I know," she sniffed. "I'm just so happy. She didn't even want us to come for you, but I did." Her expression sobered, and she looked out onto the field where Indigo, Cloud and Forrest were being shouted at by the Prime for their recklessness. Violet helped Balos with the healer. Behind them, from the main training field, Leaf walked with fast, furious strides.

Haze looked down at Peaches. Dirt tracks ran down her face. Like him, she was covered in dust and grime. "Are you telling me she was going to leave me there? As wyrm bait?"

He tried to stand and shift Peaches out of the way as rage burned every atom.

Peaches stopped him with two words. "I'm pregnant."

"What?" He sat with a thump.

She couldn't meet his eyes and shuffled to the other end of the two-seater like a naughty dog trembling in the corner.

Haze kneeled and took her hands in his. "Peaches."

"I'm pregnant." Two whiskey brown eyes met his.

"Why don't you look happy?"

"You've had such pain in your past," she said, her own eyes returning to that sad state he hated so much. "I didn't want to bring back any of those memories."

"Peaches." His voice was soft and gentle as he cupped her dirty face. "Yes, I will always be sad about what I lost. But this is new. This is a chance for a happy future for us. Do you understand?"

Her eyes brightened.

"What we have is precious," he said. "I'm going to be grateful every single day for it because I know how much it hurts to lose it." He lowered his palm to her stomach and smiled. "This is a gift."

He lowered his head into her lap and hugged her tightly. Moments ago he'd despaired his life was over and he'd never see his mate again. Now he was blessed with not only her, but more. The promise of a future filled with love. He vaguely heard someone come up quietly behind them, and whisper that Balos' condition was stable. When they left, he picked up Peaches and kicked down the front door.

He took her to his room, they bathed, he fed her, ensured she was healthy, and then he took his time making love to her—using the full advantage of their bond to know how to make her feel good. They fell asleep in each other's arms, knowing that life was about to change for the better.

And when a little antlered fluffball hopped onto the bed, he allowed it to stay.

THIRTY-EIGHT

Shade tripped over the two naked, sleeping females in his bed and stumbled onto the wooden floor. He vaguely remembered meeting them at the mess hall, more specifically at the tavern extension most Guardians and Mages frequented daily... or nightly.

What he'd had from Violet was supposed to sustain him for weeks, but it hadn't. He was just as hungry as if he'd fed from a normal fae donor, not Well-blessed human.

Probably burned through it to heal from the radiation poisoning.

His intention had been to feed all night. To keep feeding both his body and thirst. To drive the craving for Well-blessed blood out. He was a fae who lived and died by the rules he set for himself. Strict control, routine, black and white lines. The absence of rules and boundaries brought him to a dark place he swore he'd never go again, the same place that had kept him at the Obsidian Palace, serving in the queen's harem for decades. It was the same dark place that urged him into the ceremonial lake in a desperate bid for freedom. At any cost.

But his rules hadn't worked tonight. His bed partners had done everything he'd demanded and more. He'd fucked all night. Drank all night. And yet still, he felt the same crippling desire to rip into the vein of a mated woman in this very house. He could scent them everywhere.

Indigo had lasted months like this before finding Violet. Shade couldn't go a few days. It was humiliating. He went to the window and stared out as the sun bloomed on the horizon. Not long ago he'd heard Haze come back in, and what came after in their bedroom. He'd responded by throwing up privacy wards and drowning himself in his own hedonistic pastimes. The bedroom was a place he could control. A place he'd always controlled, even with Maebh. It was a constant place he'd had power and now... he was losing that edge. The hunger was taking over everything, driving him to insanity.

Looking at his rumpled and occupied bed with disgust, he slipped on pants and left his room. Maybe he could find some mana-weed in Jasper's old kitchen hiding spots. It might help him sleep without dreaming of things he shouldn't be.

Shirtless, he strolled into the kitchen and stopped. Clarke was waiting for him, sitting on a stool at the island.

She tracked him as he walked in. The look on her face said she was still furious about the guests he'd invited into the house, but they'd had this argument before. He'd almost come to blows with Rush over it. If they wanted a nice sweet family life, then this house was not the place. It was a warrior's house. A place males could wind down and relax away from the sniveling and groveling of the subordinate Guardians. They walked about half naked. They belched and drank. They fucked whoever they wanted without judgement.

He opened a cupboard and shifted aside a jar, found nothing, and then slammed the door shut.

"There's no more mana-weed," Clarke said.

He rounded on her. An insult was on the tip of his tongue, but then he caught a neck vein pulsing. Mesmerized, his mouth watered. He snarled and gripped the island, dipping his head to look at the floor.

"I didn't take it, if that's why you're so angry," Clarke said. "I think Jasper stole it last time he was here."

A frustrated growl rolled through Shade.

"But while you're here," she continued, completely oblivious or uncaring that she was in peril. "There's something I think you should know."

He lifted his gaze, his vision turning red, his hunger clawing at his stomach.

She stood and steadily met his eyes.

"Silver is your mate," she said, shattering Shade's

composure. "The sooner you find her, the sooner you'll have all that under control."

"Why didn't you tell me sooner?" he snarled, then ducked his head, ashamed. He was not this feral beast.

"Because I couldn't see where she is. I can barely see her in my visions. I'm... I'm not even sure she's one of us."

"What does that mean?"

"It means I'm not sure if she'll be so amenable to you or the fae." She pulled out a piece of paper from the island drawer and started writing on it. "This is all I know about where she might be. And this is where I think you should start looking for her. I've only figured it out because of the ripples she's caused, not because I've actually seen her."

She slid the paper toward Shade with a grim look. "You need to find her. We don't have a choice."

"Why?"

"I may not have seen her in my visions, but I have seen what will become of you if you don't find a solution to your cravings. Let's just say if I told Rush about it, you wouldn't be standing there." The pitiful look she gave him said it all. She tapped the paper. "I suggest you speak with Rush before you set off. Cloud too. They're the only two who've come out of that Well-forsaken place alive."

When he looked down at her words, his heart stuttered. *Crystal City.*

THIRTY-NINE

A few nights after Peaches rescued Haze, a point she liked to remind him about, they flew into a small Unseelie town west of the Autumn Court. It was where Haze had grown up, and although the house he'd lived in, and his daughter and her mother were long gone, Peaches encouraged him to visit one more time.

He'd told her in the goblin city that he hated himself for how he'd behaved. That his guilt twisted his soul. She didn't want to start a new chapter of their lives with any more negative thoughts still stirring.

The air was cold and frigid, but the snow was long gone as they walked across the grassy field before a cliff that ended in a valley filled with jagged rocks on the bottom. Wind gusted their faces as they stepped to the edge where a circle of stones had been placed. Haze touched them. One larger set of stones and a smaller circle within.

Peaches kneeled next to him and placed her palm on the dirt next to the grave, then she closed her eyes and concentrated on all the love she felt for him. The blooming beauty of life.

Soil turned beneath her fingertips, and sprouts of new life lifted out. Stems burst forth as thin green spikes. The tops grew to reveal buds. Bright vermillion crushed petals unfurled.

"Poppies," Haze whispered in awe.

"I've been practicing," she said, smiling and running her palm over her belly. "With everything going on before, I didn't even know what I was capable of. Now I do."

A slow, proud grin curved Haze's lips. "I always knew, Sweetness. I always knew."

Peaches put his hand on her stomach. "And we will raise this child together. That, I can promise you now. No one is going to stop you from being there every step of the way."

Haze kissed her gently on the lips and then rested his chin on her head. They looked out to the valley together as he said, "Every step."

The End.

THANK you for reading Haze's and Peaches' story. Next up is Shade and Silver in *A Symphony of Savage Hearts*. or read on for details on how to get to the **secret sealed section** where you'll get a bonus epilogue and nsfw artwork.

EPILOGUE

Maebh looked at her face in the handheld black glass mirror and touched the new wrinkles around her eyes. A small pang of regret hit her at the loss of her flawless beauty. After countless mana experiments, she now appeared middle-aged.

She knew her palace had been infiltrated again.

She knew the Guardian had been rescued.

She even knew her favorite mana stone maker was now gone.

None of it mattered.

Because she'd finally reached completion with her new creation. All that pain and sacrifice had been worth it. Bones, the Untouched human who'd woken from the old world, was now something else altogether. She'd sacrificed her own capacity to hold mana and pushed it into his birth. She'd taken that of every hated creature she could find, and she fused it with his bones.

Funny. She laughed, restored her youthful glamor, and then put the mirror down on her workshop table littered with broken glass. Bones' fate had been determined the moment he'd been given that name.

Maebh crouched low in her wet basement and watched with fascination as her new pet supped on the flesh and soul of a Sluagh.

Great vampiric wings, grotesquely muscled, bony and blistered body. A face disproportionate and deformed. Bones fed. And fed. And fed. And yet he was still hungry.

He reached for her, talons slashing the air, but she casually stepped back with a waggle of her black stained finger.

"No, my darling. Not me." She pulled a piece of cloth from her pocket that she'd kept for decades hidden away and preserved with mana to keep the scent fresh. Her favorite lover. The only one who'd ever made her feel anything other than dead inside after the loss of her daughter. She held the cloth before her creature and let him sniff the scent.

"That's right, darling Demogorgon." She'd named it after the most feared creature she could find in an ancient book. "Bring him to me alive, and I will give you what you need."

It was time for Maebh to take back what was rightfully hers.

Starting with D'arn Shade.

SECRET SEALED SECTION

EXTENDED EPILOGUE

Want more Haze? I got you, boo.

Because no one ever wants the story to end, I've created an extended smexy epilogue (just like I wrote for Pride) but this time I've added a bonus no-holds-barred illustration of our main male, Haze.

The epilogue is a super spicy bonus scene. There are no special Fae Guardians plot reveals in here, so if the spice isn't what you're here for, you won't miss out if you don't see this.

Proceed with caution.

Seriously.

Do not visit this unless you're ready for the full monty.

Still want some?

Be brave.

VISIT THIS LINK AND SIGN UP.
https://BookHip.com/LRQXQAF

NEED TO TALK TO OTHER READERS?

Join Lana's Angels Facebook Group for fun chats, giveaways, and exclusive content. https://www.facebook. com/groups/lanasangels

Also by Lana Pecherczyk

The Deadly Seven

(Paranormal/Sci-Fi Romance)

The Deadly Seven Box Set Books 1-3

Sinner

Envy

Greed

Wrath

Sloth

Gluttony

Lust

Pride

Despair

Fae Guardians

(Fantasy/Paranormal Romance)

Season of the Wolf Trilogy

The Longing of Lone Wolves

The Solace of Sharp Claws

Of Kisses & Wishes Novella (free for subscribers)

The Dreams of Broken Kings

Acknowledgments

Thank you to all the members of my ARC team, Lana's ARC Angels. Every book I release I thank my lucky stars to have you with me.

A few of you amazing readers helped me out when I was in a pickle naming Tinger. I put a few suggestions in there and ended up with doing something boring. Boo to me!

Thank you to my editor, Ann Harth, who always helps turn these books from black and white to full technicolor glory.

To the most awesome readers in the world… keep reading romance. It loves you too.

Be brave.

Love, Lana.

About the Author

OMG! How do you say my name?

Lana (straight forward enough - Lah-nah) **Pecherczyk** (this is where it gets tricky - Pe-her-chick).

I've been called Lana Price-Check, Lana Pera-Chick-ywack, Lana Pressed-Chicken, Lana Pech...*that girl!* You name it, they said it. So if it's so hard to spell, why on earth would I use this name instead of an easy pen name?

To put it simply, it belonged to my mother. And she was my dream champion.

For most of my life, I've been good at one thing – art. The world around me saw my work, and said I should do more of it, so I did.

But, when at the age of eight, I said I wanted to write stories, and even though we were poor, my mother came home with a blank notebook and a pencil saying I should follow my dreams, no matter where they take me for they will make me happy. I wasn't very good at it, but it didn't matter because I had her support and I liked it.

She died when I was thirteen, and left her four daughters orphaned. Suddenly, I had lost my dream champion, I was split from my youngest two sisters and had no one to talk to about the challenge of life.

So, I wrote in secret. I poured my heart out daily to a diary and sometimes imagined that she would listen. At the end of the day, even if she couldn't hear, writing kept that dream alive.

Eventually, after having my own children (two firecrackers in the guise of little boys) and ignoring my inner voice for too long, I decided to lead by example. How could I teach my children to follow their dreams if I wasn't? I became my own dream champion and the rest is history, here I am.

When I'm not writing the next great action-packed romantic novel, or wrangling the rug rats, or rescuing GI

Joe from the jaws of my Kelpie, I fight evil by moonlight, win love by daylight and never run from a real fight.

I live in Australia, but I'm up for a chat anytime online. Come and find me.

Subscribe & Follow
subscribe.lanapecherczyk.com
lp@lanapecherczyk.com

facebook.com/lanapecherczykauthor

twitter.com/lana_p_author

instagram.com/lana_p_author

amazon.com/-/e/B00V2TP0HG

bookbub.com/profile/lana-pecherczyk

www.ingramcontent.com/pod-product-compliance
Lightning Source LLC
Chambersburg PA
CBHW062012190726

48285CB00001BA/90